THE CITATION SERIES

BOOK 1

THE ANNEXATION WAR

THE CITATION SERIES

BOOK 1

THE ANNEXATION WAR

Mason Elliott

High Mark Publishing

High Mark Publishing
www.highmarkpublishing.com

Seattle & Portland, Chicago, London

THE CITATION SERIES

BOOK 1

THE ANNEXATION WAR

by
Mason Elliott
Kindle Edition
© 2014 by Mason Elliott. All rights reserved.
Published by High Mark Publishing
ISBN 978-1-930451-08-7
Watch for other titles by this author in the future.

Cover Art by
Frank Miller
frankmillerdesign.com

Author's Note

Please note that this book is the first volume in a new companion series to The Spacer Clans Adventures. That original series takes place throughout the pages of *Naero's Run, Naero's Gambit, Naero's Fury*, etc., and is primarily, straight-forward Science Fiction Adventure.

This new companion series, called The Citation Series, begins with Book One, *Naero's War: The Annexation War*, describing Naero's military service with the Alliance Navy as the intrepid strike fleet captain of Strike Fleet Six. In the existing timeline, The Annexation War took place during the course of several months, and is described briefly in the last chapters of *Naero's Run.* Therefore, chronologically, the events in this book take place between books one and two of the original series–before Naero's Cosmic powers began to return.

Please keep that in mind when you are reading *The Annexation War*. You could even read this book before you read *Naero's Gambit*, if you are inclined to do so. But this companion series was created both to stand on its own and to supplement the original series with further information and events that would not fit therein.

Many fans contacted the author, disappointed that they were not given a more detailed account of Naero's exciting naval service during those several missing months. Each November, many authors take the NaNoWriMo (National Novel Writing Month) challenge to draft a complete novel within the space of those 30 days. The author chose to take that challenge and wrote a 300-page first draft of this book, filling in the gaps of that missing account. The book was later accepted for publication, and presented in this format.

In a similar vein, Book Two in The Citation Series, *Naero's War: The High Crusade*, will detail Naero's military service attached with General Walker and the doughty Spacer Marines of Bravo Command, during the course of the Ejjai Invasion. As before, these events (which also covered several months) were touched upon briefly toward the end of *Naero's Gambit*. A more detailed account of the invasion, therefore, will be made in *The High Crusade*.

Enjoy!

1

Naero's flagship, *The Hippolyta*, was one of the latest, Dromon Class dreadnaughts. These warships were fashioned out of dense, iron-nickel planetoids, not less than half a kilometer in diameter. Incredibly tough and rugged on their own.

It took the most powerful mining plasma-borers–working in precise conjunction with construction fixers and an army of teks–months to hollow out armored crew quarters, lift and transport tubes, launching and loading bays. Next came space for power cores, sublight engines, jump drives, backups, gravitics, life support, sensor arrays, communications, navigation, weapons, main bridge, and backup bridge.

Set in the exact heart of *The Hippolyta* were its signature big guns. A quad of the largest production guns ever constructed on any ship of war: four, 16-meter, rapid-fire, particle beam cannons.

Cannons any larger than that exploded, melted, or otherwise were not feasible within the limits of current tek and materials. The warship also held thirty-six secondary batteries, assorted specialized weapons and gun emplacements, and forty-five advanced fighters.

The seven hundred and forty able crew included a full Rifle Company of two hundred and forty Spacer Marines and all of their equipment, vehicles, and gear for ship's security and rapid response deployment. Strike Fleet Six's Marines came from the 3rd Spacer Marine Division– known as *The Death Eyes*–because of their superb snipers and their overall, excellent marksmanship ratings. Marines made up a third of the warship's complement.

Their motto: *If We Can See It...We Can Kill It!*

The main bridge was a massive, armored dome constructed on top of the dreadnaught's big, metal, rough-hewn orb, protected by heavy blast doors, and the latest, most advanced shielding in the fleet. Within, the circular bridge was laid out in four levels under the huge dome, a dome sixty meters high.

Each bridge tier was separated by the height of a few steps from one to the next. The inner three levels could rotate in any direction, independent of the others.

The fleet captain's command nanochair and station occupied the highest tier. Each bridge station had its own secondary shielding, in case enemy fire penetrated the shields, the blast screens, and the hull.

In combat, bridges were routinely targeted, for obvious reasons.

From that primary vantage point, the strike fleet captain could direct battles in 360 degrees through an advanced battleholo display surrounding her, with full zoom data-feeds constantly updated by battle AIs. Naero could manipulate the displays by nanosensors programmed into the fingertips of her nanosuit gloves.

The battle display system also recognized her voice pattern, and would respond to voice commands, or commands punched in manually through pads on her command chair, or via other backups.

The next bridge level down from hers held the secondary bridge stations–Helm, Weapons, Communications, Navigation, and Scanning– spaced out equally along their ring.

The third ring held all of the twelve tertiary bridge stations, which monitored, controlled, and coordinated all of the ship's other important functions:

Engineering
Gravitics
Life Support
Power Supply
Security
Shields

Medical
Jump and Sub-light Drives
Damage Control
Alliance Fleet and Intel Communications
Main Computer
Launching Bays

The fourth ring went to the two powerlifts leading from the bridge to the other movers, decks, and levels of the ship. All lift and access points throughout the ship were constantly guarded by two battle-ready Marines stationed on either side.

If a warship was boarded by enemy assault craft during a battle, invaders could be cut off and eliminated between decks before they could reach a vital area.

Today, Strike Fleet Six had a mission–a simple one.

Captain Naero Maeris and her fifty warships proceeded to probe the next system on the outer, port arcwall of the Alliance advance at Beleron-4.

A routine run. Current intel assured them to expect little or no Triaxian presence or resistance.

By any stretch of the imagination, Beleron-4 was a nothing world, in the middle of nowhere, with zero, nacha–absolutely no strategic or tactical value whatsoever.

Checking it off the list of the pacified worlds of the Alliance system-hopping schedule was more or less just a formality.

But it still had to be done. And Naero and her lot drew the duty at random. So why did Naero's sense of warning go bonkers?

After they jumped in, in a simple Delta-India-3 stack formation, the reasons for alarm grew perfectly clear.

They came in right on top of twenty Triaxian fleets of the enemy's latest warships.

And a gigantic new flagship–as huge as *The Hippolyta*–the advanced design of which did not even register as existing.

It had never been seen before.

Naero shot to her feet, kicked her command nanochair back out the way and sent it down into the nanofloor of her top-tier bridge control station.

She instantly called her battle display holos up in spinning, horizontal glowing ribbons and rings all around her.

Data relays went wild. Her fingers flashed among the highlighted screen arcs, taking control of them and their parameters.

Multiple warnings sounded, and with excellent reason.

Nothing about this was good in any way.

Haisha! Twenty enemy fleets could chop them into confetti–well before any other Alliance forces could even jump in to help.

No strategy, no formation could possibly save them against superior numbers such as these.

"All ships, full withdraw. Emergency retreat on this vector, in Charlie-Romeo-7, cone-ring formation. Shields and all weapons full front and hot. Maximize all targeting profiles on the lead attacking enemy elements–they'll be on us in seconds. Whatever happens–we fight until our carriers and some of our ships can break free and jump out behind us. Get the carriers out first!"

For a split second, everyone braced for the sheets of flame that would quickly overtake and overwhelm them.

Yet those seconds passed. The enemy firestorm never came.

Leftenant Commander Nethan Donovan called out from his fleet communication station. "Sir, full status report and all initial data reads rushed to Intel and Alliance relays."

"Scanning–why aren't we under attack yet?"

Everyone looked on in stunned wonder. Nobody knew.

To their stunned surprise, all twenty enemy fleets broke off in all directions and jumped away...like ghosts vanishing.

Not a single shot fired by either side.

In a matter of seconds, Naero and her people were left all alone in the black, still retreating from Beleron-4.

The day hadn't started out so strangely. Strike Captain Naero Amashin Maeris went to PT–physical training–every morning as the Annexation War both continued and permitted.

Each day, she worked out, practiced, and sparred alongside her crews, among the fifty assorted warships of Strike Fleet Six.

Sometimes she remained on board her immense, planetoid flagship, *The Hippolyta.* On other mornings, she visited different ships, from enormous fleet carriers like *The Condor, The Bulldog,* and *The Starfall,* to heavy battleships such as *The Python, The Athena, The Choturri,* and *The Wombat.*

It could be one of her ten heavy cruisers such as *The Mohawk, The Jim Bowie,* or *The Michigan.* Perhaps one of her twenty destroyers, such as *The Jack of Spades, The Iron Clown, The Duelist,* or *The Beehive.* Missile frigates like *The Seraph* and *The Wizard, or* gunships like *The Ravager* and *The Hammerhead.*

Today, Naero needed to stay close to home, so she joined in with her primary bridge crew in one of the big, arena-like practice rooms on the 24th level. They warmed up and stretched under the watchful control of the current instructors–half of them tough, 3rd Division Spacer Marines.

After calisthenics, they ran nine laps around the outer track–three laps per klick. They ran each of the three klicks at a different speed: slow, fast as they could, and then fast. Then an extra slower lap at the very end to wind down.

Next, they padded up and took turns sparring together in pairs, or two, three, and four on one. Sometimes they sparred in zero-G.

Naero smiled, finally starting to work up a sweat.

She always loved this part, anyway–mixing it up.

Many of her people relished pitting themselves against the fearless daughter of *The Annihilator* and *The Invincible Cyclone*. Most Spacers enjoyed a challenge.

One of her four-person Marine bridge teams came at her with everything they had.

And from past experience, these 3rd Division people could really scrap.

Private First Class Khaeber Wilde got in close and tried to hit her with powerful elbow and knee strikes.

Naero blocked and dodged, grunted, taking hits.

Khaeber drove his knee painfully into her right thigh.

She whirled, backhanded him, then knocked him aside with an outward wheelkick, lightning-fast.

Lance Corporal Zhon Keller and Corporal Risa Lii tackled her high and low. The three of them tumbled and fought, grappling and striking, rolling and surging as Naero struggled to break free.

Staff Sergeant Jellien Patton and Khaeber jumped in, trying to stomp and kick her into submission.

A heel grazed her head.

Jellien punched her hard in the jaw.

Naero spun on the floor and kicked Zhon away. She rolled, punched, winded, and flipped Risa off to one side.

Jellien executed a perfect flying kick, thrusting her forward from behind. Khaeber jumped in toe-to-toe and exchanged rapid combinations of punches, palm strikes, and elbows.

Naero knocked Jellien down with double sidekicks, blocked and grappled with Khaeber, flipped him into Risa as she charged back in.

All four rose up and circled in once more.

Intense looks on their flaring faces.

Naero laughed and held up both hands.

"Hold, guys. Let's take a break. I need a slug of Jett."

She handed out icy-cold borbbles all around.

They drank freely, laughing and chatting while they watched the other matches unfold.

Like most Spacers, her bridge crew were accomplished athletes and martial artists. Some of them possessed serious skills.

But there wasn't any of them she couldn't take down one-on-one.

She had to fight them three and four at a time for them to give her trouble. Ensign Nesra Williams, Navigation, put her hands on her hips after she walked over.

"Let's be honest, N. Everyone here knows you outclass us, and why. You've trained with the best–with Galactic Fight Circuit Champion parents–since you could float. When we get together like this, we want *you* instructing us from now on. Most of us don't have half your moves–some of which we've never even seen."

Naero grinned and nodded. "I'd be honored."

As soon as they finished their Jett, Naero began drilling them.

Nesra she taught three new kicks.

Her new pilot, Enel Maeris, she helped correct slight flaws in his blocking arcs and techniques that left him open and vulnerable.

Draeden Khyber, Engineering, practiced several new grappling holds she showed them all.

Mirra Luna, Gravitics. She and Naero sparred for several minutes.

Surprisingly, Mirra was almost as fast as her, but not as strong by far. Naero gave her some further tips on hitting harder and building up her raw strength and power.

Mirra flashed her a bright smile, a pretty, slender thing with dark wavy hair, big blue eyes, and a face like a porcelain doll.

Brindil Lakota, Jump Drives. Naero nearly knocked her out, quite by accident. When Brin recovered, they went over several options on how to take hits better and reduce any damage.

Once the two hours were up, they had to clean up and report for duty that day. Workouts like this brought them all closer together.

Naero's people thanked her profusely, telling her how much they were looking forward to further lessons…especially with her.

These were good people. Good crew.

They worked hard, always striving to be the best.

If and when they got boarded by enemy sabotage and kill squads, better fighting skills might just save lives. And that was very important.

Later that day, they'd be back on the line.

6

2

At Beleron-4, Naero and Strike Fleet Six were still in the midst of their near-panicked withdrawal.

Ensign Varcus Adams, at his scanning station, blinked in confusion, just like the rest of them.

None of what they just witnessed firsthand made any logical sense.

"Sir…all twenty enemy fleets have…they've fled the field. Wait…now we're picking up two new enemy fleets jumping in. One close and about to engage, the other farther out and advancing rapidly to join the fight."

Two fleets–still better than twenty.

"Varcus, this still doesn't make any sense," Naero said.

She consider everything for a short moment.

"Were these two fleets part of the other batch?"

Varcus double-checked. "Negative, sir. Different—and apparently– completely unrelated. The closer fleet is the 7th Khaido, the other the 3rd

Khaido. The 3rd is firing at us from extreme range. The 7th will be on us in 12.4 minutes."

"Very well, then. All ships, come about. Let's deal with the fight at hand. Mysteries later. Sierra-Zulu-7, wolfspider assault formation. Defensive fighter screens, wheel in front and tight. Let's take down their heavies first. Accelerate to attack speed. Concentrate all batteries on these lead elements, in these optimized targeting profiles."

Her hands and fingers flashed on the battle displays, pweaking their attack vectors and firing profiles as her fleet roared into battle.

The 7th Khaido came at them in Bravo-Victor-4 block formation, with their big guns all blazing out in front.

A sound strategy. This Triaxian fleet captain knew his business well.

But Naero needed to shatter the 7th quickly, and put them down hard and fast, before the 3rd swept in to rip Strike Fleet Six's heads off.

"All fighter wings–in-and-out in rearward spin, punishing spirals. Continue to soften up their shields."

They closed and exchanged initial salvos at long range.

Only their battleships could hit each other like that.

The Hippolyta endured the brunt of the enemy strikes focused on her.

Let them do their worst. The amazon could take it.

Light damage on her other four bigs; slightly reduced shields.

"Helm, line up to rake all of their battleships with rapid disruption fire. Keep on them as they try to disperse. Weapons, coordinate firing profiles as we spin and weave. I want their shields down on all five battleships. Concentrate on their weak points and exploit them."

The Hippolyta's big guns punched across two or three warships with every shot, moving to keep them under heavy patterns of fire.

Strike Fleet Six's bigs moved and fought with them, adding their precise fire to the mix. Their sixteen, 12-meter batteries blasted the Triaxian battleships in rapid, consecutive order.

The rest of the strike fleet did their best to defend and go on the offense where they could.

"Scanning…report."

"Sir. Shields down on enemy flagship, *The Enfield, The Kentucky, The Brown Bess,* and *The Remington. The Springfield* is on fire and withdrawing, falling back."

They had them; Naero already knew it.

She called to her bigs, all of which still had shields at eighty percent or better.

Light to moderate damage on a few other ships.

"*Python, Athena, Choturri, Wombat*–take those bigs down. We'll soften up the rest. Get ready for their mates sweeping in."

Naero's four battleships closed with the enemy bigs and started to bust them up. *Kentucky* soon floated helpless. *Enfield* still fought. *Springfield* continued to evade and burn, apparently unable to jump. *Brown Bess* got swarmed on. After multiple explosions, she broke up. *Bess's* crew shot away in life pods where they could. *Remington* jumped out with heavy damage.

The enemy bigs that could still move pulled further back into their screen of smaller warships and fighters, to a more defensive mode.

They were trying to buy time for the 3rd Khaido to sweep in and turn the tide. All five enemy carriers jumped out with light to moderate damage.

They had already held back to the rear. Yet jumping away would strand many of their fighters–if the third couldn't collect them.

Her strategy remained ferociously efficient. Naero's adept hands flew over the battleholo displays as of she were a sorceress casting spells.

She continued raking the enemy lines with disruption fire, now focusing on the enemy cruisers. Then the enemy destroyers and lesser ships. *The Hippolyta* swept through the enemy lines or circled about, nailing several of the smaller enemy warships with each blast, continuing to line them up.

The capability to rapidly degrade or completely eliminate enemy shields proved decisive, time and time again.

Her people knew how to maximize and pinpoint attack damage. With Naero's help, they coordinated their fire on the enemy cruisers, ganging up on them three and four at a time.

Once the enemy battleships were all finally neutralized, Naero's four bigs added their cannons to the rapidly progressing gun battle as well.

Ten enemy cruisers: two destroyed, six burning and listing, two fled–in minutes.

Naero's fleet continued to chew through the remaining destroyers and lesser warships, just as the second enemy fleet swept in to attack.

In the resulting chaos, Naero first withdrew in several directions to cause confusion.

Some of the enemy held back, some attempted to pursue.

Naero pulled them in several directions, off balance and out of formation.

Her fingers jabbed at and punctuated the battle screens.

"Alpha-Charlie-2 cloud attack! Collapse back in on them. Take the bigs down first, then the others. Hit them ship-to-ship in close with all batteries. We'll continue to disrupt shields on their lines, and wear them down."

This became tougher, because the new enemy fleet was fresh and undamaged, providing the foe with a temporary advantage.

Naero quickly scanned her own roster of ships, checking the battle status of each one.

"*Wombat*, withdraw and jump if pursued. You're too beat up."

Wombat Captain Blue Ryan protested. "We can still fight, sir! Let's finish this."

"Negative, Blue. Your shields are at eight percent and two of your engines are on fire. Jump out while you still can. That's an order. Acknowledge."

"Yes, sir. On our way."

"These ships, I'm ordering you out of the mix as well. Jump back to the Alliance and report to the fixer clouds. We'll re-join you as able. *Panther, Vulturo, White Cat, Thunderbolt, Gray Typhoon, Duelist, Toparra, Lightning Bug, Star Witch, Hammerhead, Marauder*, and *Seraph*. I say again, withdraw at once. Stay together."

All dozen of them pulled out, withdrew further, and jumped–some of them quite heavily damaged.

Two of them had to be towed into jump by others.

Her ranks reduced significantly, Naero continued the fight.

Within seconds of the initial engagement, the five fresh enemy battleships gave her forces a very hard time of it.

Concentrated enemy fire quickly degraded her remaining bigs and the cruisers that formed up to support them.

The Hippolyta spun on her axis and charged in.

She quickly directed all four of her massive main batteries against each of the Triaxian battleships in turn.

The Hurricane, shields down, moderate damage.

The Tornado, shields down, re-positioning, still fighting.

Ensign Yon Cherokee called out from his shielding station on the bridge's third ring. "*Hippolyta* shields down to forty-three percent, sir."

All five enemy battleships suddenly pushed in close, concentrating all their fire from their primary and secondary batteries straight at *The Hippolyta*, pummeling her, beating her up.

Other lesser enemy ships joined in, trying hard to take her down.

Naero sneered and kept firing, right into their packed ranks.

"Bring your worst, scum! My girl can take it. Better than you have tried to take us down, and gone up in flames. All ships, cut them to pieces while they're focused on us!"

"Shields at twenty-six percent...fourteen..."

Hippolyta's next four gun salvo blasted the enemy flagship, *The Hurricane* completely to dust, damaging all ships close to it–whether friend or foe.

"Shields gone, sir," Cherokee reported. "Hull armor on bridge blast screens rapidly failing."

Combined main battery fire from three enemy battleships–*The Tornado, The Dark Typhoon,* and *The Maelstrom*–struck *The Hippolyta* bridge blast screens and finally punched through.

Enemy firepower enveloped the bridge and each of its shielded stations in a firestorm.

Naero felt her shields fizzle and fail. A powerful force smacked her down. Burning pain erupted across her upper left arm.

3

Automated damage and fire control protocols took over. Emergency shields sealed the breaches for now.

Naero scrambled to her feet, attempting to stabilize and control her flickering battle displays and holo readouts. All she could smell at first was ozone and smoke in the ionized air.

What shape were they in?

Could they still fight?

Enemy cannon beams had penetrated *The Hippolyta* bridge defenses and wreaked havoc. Multiple dead and wounded on the bridge and in other areas on board. Remaining crew moved efficiently to assess and control the damage and give assistance.

Weapons still online and firing. Surviving bridge crew continued to operate their stations.

Engineering had their shields back up at eight percent.

Hippolyta shuddered again as the enemy battleship *The Tornado* exploded. *The Dark Typhoon* burned out of control. All ships pulled away from it.

The Maelstrom attempted to withdraw, found itself trapped, and promptly surrendered.

The Vortex turned and fled in panic, along with the last few surviving enemy vessels.

Naero's fleet had indeed shredded the enemy while the enemy had focused all their firepower on *The Hippolyta*.

Once four of the five enemy battleships from the 3rd Khaido Fleet lay defeated, the battle was primarily won. The few remaining enemy warships that were able, broke off and attempted to flee.

"All ships, stay on them," Naero shouted. "Keep at them! Don't let them jump. Take them down as they run."

Naero opened a channel to the enemy vessels.

"Triaxian forces. This battle is over. Enemy warships, power down and surrender–or be destroyed. There is no need for further loss of life. Stop fighting, come about, and give up. All prisoners will be treated fairly and with honor."

The enemy ignored her and kept fighting and fleeing.

Naero and her fleet gunned them down on the run, leaving a trail of floating, burning wrecks behind them.

The rout became both desperate and deplorable.

Once enemy ships were clearly taken out of the fight, Naero's people stopped firing on them and simply pushed on to gang up on the next target.

The Hippolyta opened its battered blast screens slightly at the flick of one finger. Naero focused intently on the remaining elements of the fleeing Triaxian fleet directly in front of her forces.

By now, she wore a small, slap-on medpak adhered to the painfully scorched and formerly bleeding wound on her upper left arm.

The enemy fire that had penetrated the bridge killed two bridge crew outright–Ensign Draeden Khyber, engineering, and 2nd Leftenant Jisa Flynn, life support control stations–and one of her Marines guarding the lifts–Lance Corporal Zhon Keller.

Ten others endured various light to moderate wounds like her own.

Like their captain, they all still served defiantly at their posts.

Their comrades' corpses lay at hand within body bags, placed off to one side.

Naero had known them only for a few months, but they had already become her family.

They lived, worked, and fought side by side.

Each loss of one of her bridge crew felt like a dark knife stabbed through her already troubled heart. Naero still struggled not to cry when she lost people. For some reason, it was even harder in private.

Backup crew already came up to run their stations.

If any of them fell—including herself—others would step in to assume their duties.

Even if the main bridge was wiped out, her XO—Commander Jaylen Maeris—waited to take over command of the ship within the separate backup bridge, well below them, in the most heavily protected core of the ship. This remained Alliance SOP on all primary warships.

Naero's nostrils flared. Her battered strike fleet pursued the remnants of the Triaxian fleets they had broken around Beleron-4.

Most of the enemy forces they had engaged lay scattered and burning behind her.

In the wake of the relentless Alliance advance.

Holo readouts of each retreating vessel floated before her. Designation. Current status and heading, speed, damage reports. How close they were to jumping free of the battle to get away.

Her bridge crew fed her a continual stream of updated battle info.

One enemy fleet carrier, a pocket carrier, one G-Class battleship, two cruisers, three destroyers, thirty-one fighters and assorted transport, supply and support vessels.

After the mauling they had endured, half of the enemy ships were still on fire. And one way or another, half of those would never make it into jump.

Warnings flashed critical for a split instant

The enemy pocket carrier, *The Aspen,* suddenly went nova. Its shattered fusion drives, power core, and remaining ordnance detonated. The blast damaged the larger carrier, *The Cottonwood,* and the G-Class battleship nearby, *The Vortex,* even further.

Naero called out over the open channel.

"Enemy vessels. This is your last chance; I say again—there is no need for further loss of life. I repeat. Come about and lower your shields. Power down your weapon arrays and prepare to be boarded. Refuse, and we will resume our attack. Instantly."

Seconds passed. Some of the smaller enemy ships pulled ahead and jumped, if they were able.

Naero's fighter waves stood poised on the enemy's heels, ready to roar in and help finish them off.

Let alone Naero's white hot big guns on all of her main ships.

The limping enemy battleship came about.

But its captain's message to her roared defiance.

"Filthy, bloody, spacks. We'll die in flames before we let you enslave us. And we'll take you with us. For Triax! Death to the Alliance!"

The link broke off.

"All ships, dispersal formation Kilo-November-4!" Naero said.

Her sharp new pilot, Enel Maeris, broke in from the helm.

"Captain, enemy shields full front. Powering jump drives!"

Naero snapped in sudden anger. "I see it. Emergency wide dispersal, Kilo-Oscar-9. All weapons, fire at will. Cut that ship down!"

She rounded on her subordinate. "Ensign...interrupt me again when I am calling orders in a fight, and I will kindly shoot you in the goddam head."

Her new pilot paled and began to apologize.

Naero stopped him with one raised hand. "I can see what they're doing. Let me run things."

"Y-yes, sir. S-sorry, sir," Enel muttered.

Just before *The Vortex* activated its jump drives close in to commit suicide–and blast a path of destruction through them–an intense barrage of concentrated Alliance naval fire punched into it.

Direct hits tore the enemy ship apart and stopped it in mid-charge.

Then the gigantic quad guns of *The Hippolyta* finally cut loose.

All four 16-meter beams lit up the entire sector, blinding blue-white.

And blew the enemy battleship and its crew and captain straight to perdition.

Only two lesser enemy ships staggered away into jump.

All the rest came about and stood down, crying out in panic to surrender.

Naero glanced back over at the body bags on the bridge.

And they was just three KIA.

Naero clenched both her fists. It was all she could do to resist the urge to wipe out all of the enemy at their mercy.

Such was her contempt for Triax and the ways it conducted itself and its forces during the campaign.

Naero's people attempted to question the prisoners about the bizarre, twenty enemy fleets that had jumped out just before the other two fleets arrived.

The remaining officers of the 3rd and 7th Khaido fleets stared and blinked at them in confusion.

They obviously knew nothing about the phantom fleets, or what such large enemy forces had been doing in the middle of nowhere.

It would have been a different story completely if Naero and her fleet had lost the battle.

Unlike the Alliance, Triax took no prisoners.

They brutalized their own worlds and were not above sacrificing them and their populations, for little reason–*just like they had at Heaven-7.*

Anything to slow the Alliance advance.

To Naero's mind, after all that Triax had done to her people, their allies, and especially her family and her Clans, they did not deserve consideration. Let alone the crimes against their own people. Triax could not be crushed hard enough or fast enough for Naero's liking.

And she remained hell-bent and determined to see that mission through to its bloody conclusion, whatever the costs.

Triax, the first Gigacorporation, and by far the worst of its vile kind, desperately needed to be wiped out of all existence. That purpose never left her thoughts.

Yet she had to continually remind herself that many of Triax's long-suffering people were little more than pawns, dupes, and slaves themselves. Taught for generations to fear and hate "spacks."

That very term was an ultimate affront, a guttural, racial smear against Spacers from the days of the first, desperate Spacer War.

Most of the landers probably didn't know any better than the lies fed to them. Most landers never even met a Spacer. Yet they couldn't all be rabid fanatics like the captain of that battleship.

She wondered how his crew felt, being dragged into suicide with that lunatic, corporate zealot.

Damn it. All of those people could have lived.

Spacers upheld the laws of war, and took prisoners who surrendered.

That crew could have all survived the war and gone home to their families afterwards.

Hundreds. Such a waste. Poor people.

"Captain Maeris," Leftenant Surina Marshall called out from her com station.

Naero snapped her head around.

"What the hell is it now?"

Surina, a fine officer and *abani* or close mate by now, blinked in surprise.

Naero winced, lifting her fingertips to pinch the bridge between her eyebrows and above her slender nose.

"My apologies, Leftenant. I did not mean to sound cross. Please speak."

"It's all right, sir," Surina said quietly.

16

"No, it's not. Again, my apologies, Rina. Report."

Surina smiled slightly.

"Reinforcements will arrive shortly. Awaiting your orders to send our Marines out to board and pacify the enemy ships. And our recovery teams to collect and transport the enemy escape pods to the POW freighters. Thousands of them back there."

Naero nodded. "Orders given. All ships and crews, well done. Let the recovery proceed. You know the drill by now. Collect our people first. Elements not involved in the recovery, fan out and patrol the area in defensive sphere formation Delta-Zeta-15."

She watched her fleet go into action, tracking their coordinated movements on her holodisplays.

"Fixer cloud control, after you help put out those burning enemy ships, refit our own damaged vessels first."

They had only lost three ships during the battle, but that was bad enough. The light cruiser *The Longbow*, a heavy battleship, *The Python*, and *The Firehawk*, a missile frigate.

The Longbow had taken several direct hits and been vaporized. All hands lost. The latter two smaller vessels would be refitted by the fixer clouds and returned to service in a matter of hours.

Naero read the damage and casualty reports on her strike fleet.

The warships could be fixed.

323 dead Alliance forces could not–including her bridge people.

And this was just one small battle against enemy fleets that suffered far greater losses. More than seventy warships captured or destroyed outright–tens of thousands dead, wounded, or captured.

With its own bloated resources, as well as illegal mercenary fleets from the other Gigacorps, Triax would continue to hurl raw numbers at them. All done under their blood-drenched banner.

The enemy would continue to do so, in a vain attempt to wear the Alliance down or make the pull back.

Like Naero, the Alliance remained steadfast, committed to eliminating Triax as a threat–once and for all.

Despite the fact that the Alliance was still forced by treaty to fight with only volunteer and private fleets and forces.

Unless the Corps openly supported Triax, the elite Spacer Naval Fleets could not join in the direct battle.

But like the Corps, they could stand by and provide support in the rear areas, away from the hot war up front on the lines.

Naero felt her old sense of warning spike all at once again.

She smiled her half-smile.

Just like the old days.

"All ships. General recall. Posts and stations. Fire on these coordinates; prepare for battle!"

Fire from Strike Fleet Six tore into several enemy ships even as they jumped into the Beleron-4 system.

Leftenant Surina Marshall turned and stared up at Naero in awe.

"Five more enemy fleets jumping in and converging on our position, sir. It's a trap for certain. But how? How could you have possibly known the enemy would do this, sir?"

Naero directed her remaining forces, hands flashing among the holo arrays, optimizing formations and attack vectors.

She grinned like a shark.

"We took their bait, Leftenant. Now they've taken ours. They've wanted to catch us vulnerable in the recovery phase. Contact admirals Joshua and Maeris. Tell them the strategy has worked, and to send in even more reserve fleets as planned. Adjust to these vectors."

Without hesitation, Naero's entire strike fleet accelerated to attack speed and swept back into battle.

Five to one odds, but help would arrive at any second.

"All batteries. Open fire! Fire at will. Execute a parabolic sweep of the enemy fleets as they continue to deploy. Soften them up for our fleets en route. Put fire on them!"

4

The latest battle ended, and the remaining Triaxian forces fled. Afterwards, Naero flew her personal Ghost Dragon fighter over to confer with Alliance Fleet Admiral Sleak Maeris, her aunt, and Fleet Captain Zalvano. As well as several other strike fleet captains, Naero assumed.

Strike Fleet Six had performed brilliantly once again, and handed Triax yet another crushing defeat. Yet the strange incident had also raised even more questions.

Everyone worried about those phantom enemy fleets that had appeared like a mirage, and then just upped and vanished. No further sightings or any word on them. Such a large force could wreak havoc wherever it chose to strike. And now, nobody could find it.

This was a new enemy wild card that had to be taken into consideration.

From this point on, Alliance fleets would need to stick together more, and not get stretched out so far away from each other.

Naero kept walking and adjusted her high ponytail of long, blue-black, shining geisha hair with an ornate golden clip that had once been her famous mother's.

She strode quickly along the decks of the Fleet Carrier *The Pearl Harbor*, her aunt's flagship. The Nytex togs of her formfitting, plain captain's uniform hugged her tight and comfy. She had the nanomaterial programmed to include a short, black flight jacket, complete with the blazing gold stripe, star, and halo of her strike fleet captain's rank.

With her left gloved hand, she held her jeweled energy cutlass secured on that side. Otherwise, the weapon jostled and rattled when she walked this quickly. Her right arm swung easily, a Level-5 blaster strapped to her right hip.

An expert blade fighter, she carried numerous energized battle and throwing blades concealed in her rig, her high, programmed nanoboots, and her belts and jacket. All of this ordnance, along with several bandoliers of microgrenades, various bomblets, and other tricks. The flat tekpak on her back concealed a small but powerful gravwing, and two more vicious Spacer battle blades of Clan Maeris design, all developed for elite, Spacer Intel strike teams.

These were gifts from Intel Admiral Klyne, along with the shield generators on her belt and the neutron detonator device still in her wristcom.

Intel could still destroy her if she was ever captured.

They did happen to be at war with one of their worst enemies. And a very nasty, interstellar war at that.

Naero's philosophy had evolved to "always go everywhere heavily armed and ready for war at all times." After all that she'd been through, that was just the way she flew.

She couldn't help noticing that her presence and superbly trim figure turned heads among the crew as she swept by. Naero took some private pleasure in that, being the child of a celebrity.

She was as vain and as human as anyone.

Although she stood short and perfectly formed and proportioned, just as her champion mother had been, it did no harm to make use of everything in one's arsenal. That was how her hot-bodied Aunt Sleak liked to put it.

Yet, Naero's catwalk was always more military swagger than slinky. A mastery belonging to her mother and her aunt that she herself had little interest in achieving much further. Her performance skills and showmanship only went so far.

Some just looked on and enjoyed the view. A few junior officers and crew saluted.

Naero returned their salutes and kept moving, her slender, powerful, athletic legs flashing in skintight Nytex. Her aunt did not like to be kept waiting, as usual.

"*The Omaria!*" someone called out.

At that Naero stopped in her tracks and whirled about. Perforce.

They had called out a tribute to *The Omaria*, Naero's dead parents' ill-fated flagship of their lost exploration fleet. Triax and the Corps had had a direct hand in the destruction of that fleet, which, in turn, was just one of the events that had led to the current conflict.

Even after many months, the pain of their loss was still jagged glass in her heart.

Naero smiled sadly and lifted her fist toward the ceiling of the launch deck.

"Remember *The Omaria!*" she shouted aloud in response.

Every Spacer within the sound of her voice shot to their feet and lifted their fists and their voices in roaring answer.

"*Omaria! Omaria! Omaria!*"

"Huzzah! Huzzah! Huzzah!"

Naero drew her cutlass and favored them with a high salute to the honor they paid her dead. All hands present cheered even louder, simply eating it up. She swept low and bowed before them in appreciation of their high honor.

Then she sheathed her blade in one fluid motion, turned, and continued quickly on her way.

She stepped into an open mover and entered her clearance for the admiral's conference room, adjoining the main bridge.

When she walked in, Marine guards in full battle dress snapped to attention. One of them announced her arrival.

"Sir, Strike Fleet Captain Maeris is now present."

Her aunt and Zalvano waited for her, the only other officers in the chamber thus far.

"Alvon, Tem," her aunt said to the Marines. "Leave us. Take your posts outside."

The panel sealed behind her aunt's two Marine guards.

"Did I arrive too early?" Naero asked, looking around.

Zalvano spoke first. "We wanted you here, before the others, so that we could speak with you personally."

Naero started to wonder. Was she in trouble? Had she done something wrong? They had won the battle, quite decisively, in fact.

Her thoughts raced even more than usual.

Her Aunt Sleak smiled; not always reassuring, that. But at least her eyes didn't go all steely, nor did her battle face snap up.

"At ease, Naero. Let's sit. We're family right now. We just want to talk candidly–off the record."

Aunt Sleak being nice caught her even more off guard. Naero sat down with them at one end of the smart table. Programmed chairs melded up out of the floor for them to sit in.

She like the way Aunt Sleak made her meeting rooms smell. Floral and citrus without being sickening and cloying–pleasant, even. Whereas Naero's ships still smelled dull and aseptic. The contrast was stark. That needed to change.

Zalvano cleared his throat and spoke first. "You've done a good job with your command in the black, Naero. Superb, really, for one so young."

At the outset of the war, before the other Forty-Nine Spacer Clans sent volunteer fleets, the fledgling Alliance forces–few in number and lacking leadership–led to a number of compromises.

"Thank you, sir," Naero said. "Just trying to do my best for the war effort, sir."

She had been given a battlefield promotion, first to captain, and then finally to strike fleet captain–despite the fact that she was still only nineteen–still technically younger than the Spacer coming-of-age at twenty.

Zalvano waved one hand. "Relax, N. At ease. In fact, we think you're driving yourself and your people a little too hard. Ease up a bit."

Her savant-like gift for battle strategy and fleet tactics made her a natural born leader, at a time when the Alliance was desperate and outnumbered. Even with the war being only in its second month, Naero had already earned the respect of many whom she served with and among. And thus, her youth was normally overlooked.

Naero knitted her brows. "What are you two trying to tell me?"

Aunt Sleak sighed. "Don't get all defensive. You're doing very well, but you're still so young. You're not used to all of the various demands of a long, drawn-out command. It takes a toll on you and others, in many ways."

"I think I understand that. I think I'm doing my best and working through any issues."

Zalvano knitted his hands together. "We've had some reports that you've been...snapping at your crew above what is acceptable from a command officer, driving them too hard, expecting too much of them. Too much training and drilling. Not giving your officers and crews enough time to stand down and get R&R. They can get worn down, too, in a war zone. Everyone can, including yourself."

Naero paused for a moment. "I just want my people to be the best. To have the best chance to win, to defeat the enemy."

Aunt Sleak held her eye. "Admirable, and I would expect no less, but your focus is misguided and, frankly...unsustainable. Listen to us. Learn from our experience. In the long run, it will make you a better leader, and help your people perform better for you over the course of a long campaign."

Naero choked down her gall and kept herself from shouting back at them–like a defensive, spoiled brat. But she was in a war and needed to grow up fast.

Most likely...they were right.

She sighed.

"Thank you. I am willing to listen. I would be fortunate and glad to have your advice. You know I respect you both. Greatly."

Zalvano chuckled, even, breathing his own sigh of relief. "Glad to hear that–and here we thought this was going to turn into some kind of battle or shouting match. Ow! Why did the admiral kick me?"

"Keep playing the fool to disarm things, and I'll kick you harder next time," Sleak said. "We're past that point now, Zal. So let's cut through the crap. Very good, Naero. You're not acting and thinking like a headstrong kid anymore. And even though you're not technically of age yet, at least we can begin to talk to you like an adult, finally. Your tactical prowess is off the charts, as I knew it would be. You've grown up living and breathing fleet strategy and tactics all your life, but you are still inexperienced in many other ways."

Naero nodded.

"Just give it to me straight, sir."

"Very well, then. You've refused to take your strike fleet off the line on several occasions. You've kept advancing and attacking, even when given orders to pull back. There are several very good reasons that you cannot continue to do these things."

"In my defense, sir. On half of those occasions, my instincts proved both correct and decisive in achieving our goals and completing our missions. And on two precise occasions, my timely action prevented our forces from suffering heavy losses, and even brought us victories we might not have had."

Zalvano held his hands up and shook his head. "But you're acting like you and your people have to spearhead everything. They don't. What are you trying to prove? You can't win this war by yourself. We have many other units and commanders who are more than capable of–"

"I'm just doing all that I can to end this terrible war as soon as possible." She thought of her people, dead in those body bags. More every day.

"Again," Aunt Sleak said. "Admirable, but you aren't thinking clearly. Most of the Intel projections say that, barring any further surprises, we should be able to defeat Triax's forces within about three to four months. Sooner, if we can somehow convince the other Corps to pull their illegal fleets out of the mix."

"Well, that's great then," Naero said. "In a handful of months, Triax will be gone for good, their worlds will be set free, and we can all get back to our lives."

Her aunt looked straight at her. "But Naero, it is far from that simple. From the law of averages alone, by that time, you and your crews will all be dead–three times over."

Naero felt the blood drain from her face. "What?"

Aunt Sleak pulled up a holo screen in front of them and displayed reports and projections for Naero to see the facts.

"Just in the last few weeks, you've lost twelve ships out of fifty. A dozen warships, destroyed outright. That's more than twenty percent casualties alone. All of your vessels have been refitted three hundred percent more than the other strike fleets, and your KIA and wounded rates are also two hundred percent higher."

"The rotations are there for many good reasons, Naero," Zalvano told her. "One of them is so that all units get their chance to shine, and learn from their mistakes, and be an equal part of the war effort. Every unit deserves its share of time on the front line. And that way, we're always hitting the foe with fresh forces."

"And conversely," Aunt Sleak added. "All units also earn their time *off* the line. So that no one unit is constantly enduring all of the direct and indirect losses by itself. There are always going to be casualties in every action and engagement. We know that for a fact. But keeping one unit on point constantly will wear down and eventually destroy everyone in that unit. It simply isn't fair to anyone."

Naero took a moment and swallowed hard. A terrible realization came over her.

"So, you're saying that more of my people have been dying because I've been been reckless and stupid. I've been driving them forward too hard and too much. Taking too many risks. When other units like ours could do the same job more or less just as well, and spread around the random casualties that naturally occur more equitably."

"Yes," her aunt and Zalvano said in unison.

Naero stared for a moment and dealt with those facts and their searing ramifications.

Naero rose to her feet, ready to resign. "Perhaps I should not even be in command, if this is the case."

"Now, don't overreact the other way," Aunt Sleak warned. "Sit back down. It's a common mistake among young, driven commanders. They think they have to do it all. And if they can't–if they make mistakes–then they don't deserve to lead. You've been doing very well. You're a tactical genius in a dogfight. Don't lose sight of that major fact."

"Why do you think we met with you in private to explain all of this?" Zalvano said. "If the war drags on three or four months or longer, we all just have to pace ourselves. When it's your turn on the line, then you and your people can give it your all."

"And when it's your time off the line, get you and your people what you need," Sleak said. "Enough rest and relaxation to get back up to speed and maintain your edge, ready for the next mission."

Naero slowly sat down again. "I think, I'm beginning to understand," Naero said. "I'll strive to take a more balanced approach from here on out. Thanks for the kick in the head."

Aunt Sleak smiled. "Glad to give it, glad to hear you say it. Starting this moment, you and your people are off the line for one, perhaps two weeks. Use your time well–while you have it."

Naero hesitated.

Her aunt looked her right in the eye. "We've never really asked you if you are up for all of this, Naero. So I'm asking now. Are you? I know you're young. I know that you've been through a lot within the past year. The death of your parents. The loss of your best friend, Gallan. Your brother Jan's abduction by Triax. The Kexxian Data Matrix trapped inside you; your strange powers that came and went, your battle with your insane brother Danner–Janner's twin."

Even Aunt Sleak had to take a breath. "Now you're a *nud* again, devoid of all Cosmic or psyonic abilities. All of that insanity and loss, and then we throw you into a vicious war and make you command a strike fleet. We know that's a lot of pressure to place on one so young, however gifted you may be. The strain and the demands of fleet command alone are daunting.

"So I ask again. Are you up to these tasks? Can you do what is required of you? It is not going to get any easier from this point on, not until Triax is finally defeated."

Naero thought about it for a long few moments before taking in a deep breath, squaring her shoulders, and giving a full answer.

"Until this war is over, what is past in my life is past," she said. "I fully believe in our cause. For the duration, I am a strike fleet captain. Nothing else. This is my war as much as it is our war, the war of the entire Alliance, against evil and blood-soaked tyrants, completely devoid of all honor and decency. Even if we all perish in the deed–it will be worth it in the end–if Triax falls from power and is no more."

She held up her hands and conceded. "Yes, my strange powers are gone; I'm a *nud* again. I've come to accept that fact. Jan is still missing. I am tormented by that, and I will never stop searching for him until he is free again."

Naero clenched both fists. "Yet my duty at this moment in time is as clear as the clearest sky. My command and my crews are all that matter, and I am fully committed to them. I will see this mission through to the end, for my parents, for Gallan, for the sake of my Clans, whom I love more than my own life. For all of our family, friends, and allies, who deserve the right to peace and freedom."

Naero snapped to attention. "Triax must be completely and utterly destroyed. At the very least, I shall draw breath long enough to see it done."

Admiral Sleak nodded. "Very well, then, Strike Fleet Captain. Know that we fully share your commitment to these goals. You are hereby dismissed."

Naero still hesitated.

Zalvano asked her, "Something else troubling you, Captain?"

"You still have me questioning myself and my abilities, now. I wonder what my people really think of me. I wish there were a way that I could find out."

"Try this trick of your mother's, then," Aunt Sleak suggested. "Take some of your off-duty time and disguise yourself. I know with your Intel training that you're good at that. It won't take much. Then go around to your crews and work among them. You know very well how Spacers gab freely all the time among their mates. You'll hear all you want to hear, and then some. So, be careful of what you ask for, and don't be surprised at what you find."

Naero nodded. "My mom really used to do stuff like that?"

26

Aunt Sleak rolled her eyes. "All the time. You never knew? Your mom was a master of disguise, and a drama queen to boot. She'd make up whole personas and backgrounds for her aliases. Sometimes, even I couldn't even tell it was her. She loved tricking people…a lot like someone else I know."

Naero blinked. "All right then. Sounds workable. I'll give that a try."

Zalvano grinned from ear to ear and jerked his thumb at the door panel. "Then get the hell out of here, Captain Maeris. Don't you realize you're on leave?"

5

Strike Fleet Six held their wakes and funerals for their recent dead. These were always somber affairs.

Two days later, after a fleet-wide survey, Naero helped organize a gigantic shore leave party on Telandar-4, well behind the frontlines, in the rear areas of the conflict.

Huge troop drop-ships–on loan from the Marines–ferried her crews back and forth by the thousands.

They chose a large, temperate zone grassland and forested valley, set in an isolated region of a wide extent of foothills, leading to some spectacular silver-blue mountains capped with snow. The chosen area included some equally impressive waterfalls and river systems cutting through the valleys, vibrant and green in that continent's early summer.

The local Triaxian human population was for the most part grateful and sympathetic to their liberators.

But there was still a definite chance of revenge strikes and terrorism by small, fanatical Corps elements on that world, hence the isolation of the shore leave party. This also called for the deliberate absence of any native landers, despite the open willingness of many Telandarians to reward their liberators with…blatant fraternization.

Unfortunately, the overall risk of various problems and sabotage were just too great in the end.

Naero's trading and merchant suppliers purchased and shipped in all goods, tents, pop-up nanocabins, supplies, and equipment.

Spacer bands and entertainers arrived in droves to keep the troops happy.

Chefs and cooks from all the ships volunteered to prepare the food and get everyone drunk in rotating shifts, whenever Spacers were ready.

Those looking for a little romance snuck off with their partners as needed, or paired up on the fly.

Others chose quieter pursuits.

Some went camping, or hiking, or boating and fishing along the scenic waterways. Some merely slept in tents, read quietly, or got lazy on lakeshore beaches.

Many just want to be alone somewhere peaceful and quiet, with or away from their thoughts and troubles.

Naero made fleet counselors available to anyone who wanted or needed to talk to someone. She basically allowed her people to work out their issues however they chose to.

Only in certain instances did ship captains make therapy mandatory.

And a select few among them were at times deemed too troubled to continue serving at the front. Such individuals were quietly reassigned to serve out the rest of the war in the rear areas, while other replacements were moved up.

A weird situation.

Replacements who came to them, however, were trained hard, night and day, by veteran trainers. Every attempt was made to get them up to speed and keep them alive for when the fleet did go back to war.

In battle, the learning curve remained steep and unforgiving.

Nor had the replacements earned any shore leave yet.

Naero had to admit, Aunt Sleak and Zalvano were more than right about many things.

Time off the line had many advantages.

Namely, all the cold, frosty Jett she could suck down.

For the second day in a row, Naero had a seven–millimeter-thick, fresh steak of some local variety cattle, pink and medium rare, for brunch. These mouthwatering steaks were as big as the plate the chef served them on, rubbed with salt, and marinated to perfection.

She received a sudden call from her mysterious, outcast uncle–Baeven–without any warning, as usual. The man was steeped in intrigue, and moved through deep circles of espionage–the way normal people passed through the very air.

Although a pariah among her people, and wanted by Spacer Intel, Baeven and his unique skill sets made him the perfect choice to search for any signs of her missing brother, Jan, and his deranged twin, Dan.

Naero quickly scrambled back to her pop-up nanocabin to take that secret call in private.

Her outcast uncle came and went as he pleased, but he had promised her that he would continue a concerted search for Janner and Danner.

Perhaps this time, he finally had a lead.

"Hey, Baeven. Have you found Jan yet?"

"Good to hear the sound of your voice, too, Naero."

"Sorry. I'm glad you called me, but every time you do, I just keep hoping for good news."

"I'm afraid I must disappoint you once more, Naero. No valid leads currently on the location of either of your brothers. It is truly as if they have both completely vanished. I hear you are doing well with your command. Congratulations."

Naero fidgeted. "What about any invalid leads?"

Baeven sighed. "Mostly just stupid, routine traps that I don't tell you about. Triax keeps hoping you'll be dumb enough and desperate enough to fall for one of them. They still want the Kexxian Data Matrix that you carry on your DNA, very badly."

The KDM was another piece of the puzzle leading to the current war, but thus far, no one on either side had been able to decode any part of it. So it remained useless. Yet its data still promised the possibility of access to the tek secrets of an ancient, godlike alien race.

Naero persisted. "What if one of those traps could lead us to Jan?"

Baeven sighed. "Which of course is the exact reason why I don't tell you about them. Don't worry. I diligently follow up on each of them when I have the time, expose them for what they are, and then make certain that those involved do not set such stupid traps...ever again."

Naero paused. "You mean...you wipe them out."

"Yes, Naero. I kill every one of them. They are our enemies. You should know this fact by now. They will show no mercy or quarter to us. They murdered your parents, murdered your best friend. They tortured Danner for years and drove him insane. They could be doing the very same thing to Jan as we speak. When I find them, I make them all pay...severely."

Naero shuddered at the basic menace in her uncle's voice. She never forgot how deadly Baeven was. Perhaps one of the most dangerous champions she had ever met–a terrifying warrior, trained by their Mystics–with no equal that she knew of in battle.

They spoke briefly for a few moments longer. Then, as usual, he needed to go. Baeven always had things to do, somewhere else to be.

Naero left her nanocabin and returned to the grilling areas.

All the rest of that morning and part of the afternoon, Naero sat at her table with friends and other captains and officers who came and went. They talked and joked, exchanged stories and problems, offering suggestions and solutions as the day went on.

Her new pilot, Enel Maeris–a distant cousin from her own blood and Clan–stopped by and humbly attempted to apologize for his actions during the battle.

Enel was two years older than Naero herself. She instinctively liked him, and he came to her highly recommended.

At twenty-one, Enel was a stocky, muscular young man of medium height and build, with short curly black hair, piercing gray eyes, and a slight hawk nose. His hands and feet looked slightly larger than the rest of him in his basic black uniform.

Naero laughed and shook hands with him. She warned Enel how grumpy she could get, and told him not to give the matter any further thought. They were blood; they were family.

Naero watched her pilot walk away, hoping he felt better. She was glad to have him on her staff.

Lots of female crew members in Six already had their eye on Enel. Word traveled quickly, especially among Spacer women. Rumors abounded about the young ensign.

The Intel dossier on him said that Enel had been a big hit among the ladies, both at the Spacer Naval Academy and during his brief, sterling service with the Navy. He'd had his pick of several pretty, young Spacer gals who'd swooned and chased after him for his attention.

Naero could see why. Enel was the real deal. A young warrior-poet-lover. One of the brightest young pilots of his generation. He played the thiolin off duty. Enel was also an excellent fighter, and he had excelled on one of the naval WebBall teams.

And what's more, the few lovers he did choose to take claimed–and even bragged openly–that he sang to them privately. In fine voice, too, they said. Enel sang his lovers to sleep in his strong embrace with soft love songs. Most of his lovers sounded as if they would be glad to have him back.

Yet since joining Naero's bridge crew on Six's flagship, the only woman Enel seemed to even glance at was stunning Surina Marshall, Naero's communications officer.

But Surina was all career, battle, and business. She seemed generally unimpressed by most guys–including Enel.

Surina had strawberry-blond hair that she always wore in a long, efficient ponytail, and huge green eyes, like bright, verdant gems. A light spray of freckles made her pretty face just that much more stunning. She was tall, athletic, and high-breasted. Over half of her seemed to be all shapely legs.

Surina just turned twenty-one.

If she had a lover, she kept that fact a close secret.

Many had tried and failed to woo her. Surina repeatedly shot cute guys down in flames–including Enel.

At noon, Naero spotted her good friend, Wing Commander Saemar Maeris, in white shorts and an orange tank top and sandals, scooting by on the arm of a tall, darkly handsome Marine. An elite starfighter pilot, Saemar was a dish and then some–cute, short, and buxom, with curly auburn hair and dazzling sapphire-blue eyes.

After the tragic death of her fiancé at the hands of the enemy, something had snapped in Saemar. Since that time, she had led a decidedly polyamorous lifestyle.

Shortly after one, Saemar bounced back the other way, barefoot and voluptuous in a bloodred bikini and barefoot–with a stocky blond fighter pilot chasing her, trying to tickle her. Both of them laughed and ran, their eyes twinkling.

At two-thirty, Saemar came by again, slipping behind the table to the wooded vales toward the south. She wore a shirt too big for her and maybe the red bikini bottoms.

Maybe not.

A cute, lanky tek with long red hair in a braided ponytail held her hand in his.

At four o'clock. Saemar again.

Not one, but *two* handsome guys this time.

Naero recognized them: elite gunners from *The Highlander*.

All three of them in soft bathrobes, laughing like old friends.

Heading for the hot tub cabins.

Naero let out a heavy sigh.

Saemar sure wasn't wasting any time, as usual.

It turned into a very beautiful late afternoon.

After her second huge steak, and another short food-coma nap, Naero got up from her nanocot and mattress and went looking for her other fighter jock galpal, Wing Commander Chaela Maeris.

She found Chae, her Viking-like friend, snoring in her and Remy's popup nanocabin. Remy was Chae's long-term beau, who worked with fleet accounting. For once, Chae's long, golden hair was unbraided and undone. Her gold tresses starfished all around her tall, buff, alabaster body.

Remy wasn't around. Probably back on a duty shift somewhere.

Knowing how much Chae relished her sleep…and got incredibly angry with anyone who woke her prematurely, Naero did not disturb her tall friend's well-earned slumber.

She did notice that Chae had fresh paint-on vidscreens on her finger and toenails, images and vidshows flashing and panning on them.

Most likely the gift and handiwork of her fiancé. Remy loved doting on his beloved Chae–his precious Valkyrie.

Naero left Chae a note to join her that night at the WebBall matches. Chae was their resident WebBall fanatic.

She still had some time on her hands, so she followed the patter of gunfire over to the target ranges.

6

Naero stopped by the shooting ranges to locate their lander friend, Tarim Martan. He had ruddy Ramoran skin and dark hair and eyes, a lanky, athletic build. He wasn't a Spacer, but had lived and worked among them as a friend and equal ever since Naero had rescued and freed him from being a Triaxian mining slave.

He also served as Naero's Security officer, as well as her personal bodyguard when necessary. Since he'd become a phenomenal marksman, Tarim held various gun matches and shooting contests with other Spacers, snipers, shootists, and Marines.

3rd Division was famous for its sharpshooters.

Tarim's face brightened when he spotted her. "Good to see you, N!"

They shook hands, up to the elbow. "You seem at home here, Tarim."

He grinned. "I'm in my element. Will you challenge us with punching some targets? I've been bragging about what a shot you are."

"Gladly. You, bragging about me?"

Tarim laughed. "Here's one of our new friends from the Spacer Marines, Sergeant Jeremiah Hayden, one of their best pistol shots."

Naero smiled at the sergeant. Medium height and athletic. Short, sandy-blond hair. Soft, intelligent brown eyes; handsome, rugged features. Despite his young age, this was a man, not some untried boy.

This man was a proven warrior. She could tell by the precise, easy way he observed everything–his bearing–just the way he moved.

Hayden saluted her. "Captain Maeris. A high honor to meet you, sir."

She smiled and waved him off. "Stand down, Marine. No rank here. Just friends. Let's get some shootin' in, guys."

She competed with them for over an hour, using various rigs. Some of them new and experimental.

Tarim kept specialized fixers handy to modify and fine-tune various weapon systems. The little, advanced tek orbs were the only thing Naero had been able to pull out of the KDM. They had an infinite number of tek uses.

All of the shooters joked, laughed, and talked shooting tek, methods, and match grade equipment–ammunition types, optics, and targeting.

They used various robotic and holo targets, some in full combat mode.

They competed until the sun began to set.

The highest overall score went to Tarim, of course.

Tarim was like a savant or something when it came to marksmanship. Second place went to Sergeant Hayden, and a close third to Naero.

Naero looked at Hayden's 3rd Marine Division patch on his fatigues– narrowed green eyes on either side of a black number three, and their trademark lightning bolt.

"Death Eyes, huh?" she said.

The sergeant shook his head. "If we can see it…we can kill it. Ooh-rah."

"I've heard that. I have to admit, you're pretty good with pistols," she told Hayden. "I didn't think anyone could challenge Tarim the way you did. Or me. Let's have a rematch in the future. I'll beat you next time."

Hayden grinned and winked at her, "You'll try."

All of them laughed.

Naero shook hands and bade Tarim, Jeremiah, and the other shooters goodbye.

She went to catch up with two other childhood friends, Tyber the tek and Zhen the physician, before the games that evening.

A Marine on guard duty informed her that the inseparable couple had rented a pleasure boat, and were out on the placid lake, anchored offshore.

Naero thanked the guard and flew out with her gravwing.

As she drew near, she heard loud, unmistakable sounds of romance underway from within the pleasure boat's curtained cabin.

Let them enjoy each other. She had no need to interrupt their fun. Naero smiled and took a relaxing flight around the lake to give her friends their time together.

An expert pilot herself, Naero loved flying of any kind. She felt like a large dragonfly or hummingbird, flitting over the deep, crystal blue waters of the mountain lake. She zipped here and there as the spectacular colors in the sky caught fire and faded under the veil of night and stars.

Her poet-warrior father could have captured it all in a poem, but even his words would have still fallen short.

She returned to the happy little boat and found Z and Ty cuddling and drinking sweet, delicious, Spacer poteen on deck. Zhentisa, slender and pretty with her long brown hair and hazel eyes, and Ty, handsome with his dark mop and dark eyes. The couple talked and did some sky watching of their own, lying in each other's arms.

They spotted Naero's descent, and their glowing young faces lit up happily.

"Permission to come aboard?" Naero called down to them.

Her friends smiled, rose to their feet, and reached out to her.

"N, please join us," Z said.

Tyber held up an ice-cold Spacer poteen bottle from a cooler. "Have a drink with us."

Naero landed and embraced her good friends, and they her. Then she took the bottle from Ty.

"Don't mind if I do. Love poteen." She took a big, delicious swallow.

They brought the boat in to shore a half hour later. Then they flew over with their gravwings to meet the others at the WebBall arena, constructed in a deep, hollow vale.

Glittering and glowing above them in the night, the segmented contest globe and its zero-G field generated within pitted two teams of thirty-six against one another. All of the actual players wore short gravwings, specifically designed for the sport.

A circular web at the central, vertical diameter separated the two teams. Six open scoring goals appeared and vanished, fluctuating at random locations on the web, which tracked any scoring through them on the encircling score bands. Goals glowed for ten seconds before they changed position.

The WebBall itself was made of dark, glowing blue nanorubber, about the size of a human head, but perfectly spherical and firm, textured with fine stubble.

The basic rules of WebBall were simple. Once the server served the ball, no one on either side could catch, hold, or throw it until a score was made or a serve was broken. Then it could be handled to put it back into play, or given to the next server. Servers and goaltenders had to remain three meters from the web and goals at all times or face various penalties, dependent on the infraction.

To score, the ball had to be struck with any part of the body, and sent through any of the six randomly appearing goals to score a random number of one to six points.

If a team shot the ball back through the same goal within three hits, they could negate the other team's last goal and break their serve. There was a lot of strategy involved.

Naero, Z, and Ty watched one complete, twenty-minute match before Chaela joined them. Then Tarim. And finally, Saemar-the-love-goddess herself even took a break from her exertions, wearing some kind of floral sarong. But Saemar still seemed to be scanning the present crowd for future prospects, during the next two exciting matches between three Marine units.

Teams came and went, and more crew from their ships joined them in the stands. Fans reclined on huge folding chairs, staring up at the intense action. Or they got up in the air on their own gravwings, all around the outside of the playing globe, to follow what was going on within more directly.

Minor betting and wagers were permitted, but controlled. Nobody was allowed to bankrupt themselves or lose their togs.

Chaela kept bugging them all to form an amateur WebBall team of their own.

Finally, Naero relented and gave her permission–as long as practicing didn't take them away from any of their duties.

Chaela dove into the planning and coaching just as she always did, hitting up others and organizing everything.

Naero had to admit, everyone did need leaves like these–desperately. And truth be told, she had a grand time and forgot her own troubles for a few hours or days at a time, like at the current games.

She and her friends made sorties to the concession booths for Jett, snacks, and junk food as needed.

She stumbled back into her nanocabin well after midnight, tired, sated, and bloated with Jett. She burped like a volcanic eruption and collapsed face down in her nanocot and mattress.

Haisha. Any more days of taking it easy, and she'd have to get back to work, just to get a break from resting and relaxing.

37

Having fun was hard work.

7

Orders summoned Strike Fleet Six back to the front eight days later, cutting their shore leave short.

Triax Gigacorps remained a dangerous monster–a hydra with countless heads remaining and more sprouting anew–cornered and spiteful. A monster with plenty of venom and costly tricks left to play.

The enemy did everything they could do to punish and bleed the Alliance forces.

Casualties on both sides soared.

In all the systems blocking the way to Helapine-3, Alliance forces had to wade through nebulae of smartmines and attack drones, many of them cloaked. Such devices activated all around fleets without warning once they entered the kill zones.

Any planets and moons showered the attackers with a variety of ordnance from robotic mass-driver batteries.

Each engagement became a gauntlet of destruction that all the Alliance fleets had to grind and power their way through.

Triaxian strike fleets waited in the wings to swoop in and pounce on any units that got tangled up or ensnared in the defensive mire.

Alliance warships took a beating and routinely rotated through the fixer clouds.

Up against such dense defenses, the advance nearly ground to a halt. All reserves were called back in an attempt to discover a breakthrough.

The Matayan Fleet currently took point on the line. They were an important part of the Alliance, despite once being bitter enemies of the Spacer Clans.

Their objective today: continue clearing the Ogano-5 system in order to link up with the Alliance forces doing the same thing in the next system coreward, at Vettari-2.

Nevano Kinmal's Miner Consortium Fleet supported Prince Ellis in overwatch mode, both of them valued allies of Strike Fleet Six and Clan Maeris.

Then, as usual, everything went straight to hell–just as Naero and her strike fleet arrived on scene and got into position.

The point fleets proceeded past enemy defenses they had just spent hours eliminating, when another completely new, cloaked minefield popped up out of nowhere, cutting off the attackers and severely limiting their forward advance and maneuverability.

Triaxian shipkiller drones homed in and began pummeling the forward element deflector shields.

Mass-drivers on the nearby planet and moons cut loose against them, on cue.

Ten Triaxian fleets decided to seize the objective and lead an all-out counterattack–completely ignored by their own defenses, of course.

Let the slugfest begin.

Admiral Nathan Joshua hailed Naero as the fireworks erupted.

"Strike Captain Maeris. Can you help extract our friends? They won't last long in that hornet's nest. Our fleets are vectoring in to throw back the enemy counterattack. This is tight work. Lead us in."

"On it. Keep the bastards off of us for as long as you can. We'll bust our people out."

"Good luck, Captain. Give Triax hell."

"Will do."

Naero turned to her fleet.

"Delta-X-ray-3 attack formation. Heavy cruisers wing out, destroyers in. Battleships quad up behind *Hippolyta* and in front of the carriers. Gunships and frigates take the rear. All fighters out in front. Fixer clouds right behind them in low profiles. Don't block our big guns."

Tyber broke in from Tek Command.

"N, why are we sending the fixers into the mix? We're going to lose a bunch."

"I know, Ty. But we gotta get our people out. Use those new tek strategies we're developing with the fixers. Take down those mines and shipkiller drones. Make it work for us."

Instead of attacking Naero's strike fleet, the enemy concentrated all of their intense firepower on trying to take out both the trapped miners and the Matayans while they could.

Even as Naero rushed in with her forces, shields buckled and collapsed on numerous Matayan and mining vessels.

In a matter of seconds, she watched as over a dozen Alliance ships were destroyed outright.

A large patch of enemy defenses and ships suddenly lost power and listed in space around the miners.

Admiral Kinmal's daughter Shalaen made her move with her cosmic powers in a big way, even though such sweeping efforts taxed her greatly.

Mining ships burst out of the trap, rammed past the stricken defenders, and squirted away.

Naero's Strike Fleet Six sliced in like a butcher knife to cut the Matayans free.

"Good to see you, Naero!" Prince Ellis called out over his holo.

Naero smiled. The handsome, young Matayan bastard always looked good to her. It was still hard to believe that the Matayan Corsairs–longtime bitter Spacer enemies on the leash of Triax–were now fighting beside them within the Alliance.

"Why am I always saving your butt, Your Highness?"

Ellis laughed. "Because it needs saving; I've missed you, N."

Then a shipkiller drone smashed into the aft section of the Matayan flagship.

The resulting blast tore away two main engines and left the rear of the ship in wreckage and flames.

No more time for small talk. The Triaxians closed in for the kill.

Naero and her fleet interposed themselves between the enemy and the battered Matayans, who did their best to limp out or get towed away.

Naero slugged it out against all comers.

Her people took a pounding, and gave one back as well.

The Hippolyta held the center, rapid-fire massive cannons blazing.

Let the sixteens roar!

Her four battleships, *Phaeton, Athena, Choturri, and Wombat* backed her up, sweeping and raking the enemy line on either side with their own big 12-meter guns.

The Hippolyta rocked and shuddered, standing up against multiple enemy hits. Her dense, iron-nickel hide was tough.

The enemy poured fire at her, every chance they got.

But the amazon could take a beating and come back swinging.

Choturri endured several direct hits and was forced to withdraw in flames.

The Wombat's energy core suddenly detonated, swarmed on by mines uncloaking and slamming into it in devastating clusters.

Wombat vanished in fire.

Along with Captain Blue Ryan and 370 crew.

Just like that.

Seven of Naero's ten heavy cruisers war badly damaged within three standard minutes. Two were destroyed outright: The *Shenda* and *The Michigan.*

Four destroyers blown to atoms: *The Wolverton, The Iron Clown, The Trevia,* and *The Yokahama.* She lost the gunship *The Ravager* and the missile frigate, *The Wizard.* Hundreds more KIA, wounded, and helpless crew floated in life pods.

Naero and her people took a mauling.

Yon Cherokee called out from his shielding station.

"Captain, shields are failing. I repeat, they've taken our shields down."

Ensign Varcus Adams called out a warning from scanning.

"Three enemy missile frigates just fired full salvos directly at us, sir."

The enemy tried to take them out yet again.

"Evasive action and rotation; angle the bridge away," Naero ordered. "Concentrate all secondary batteries on taking out those missiles. Starfighters, don't let those missiles hit us. We're too vulnerable. Engineering, get even partial shielding back online!"

Naero watched the vast wave of missiles coming in at them.

Saemar led her fighters in a scattershot attack to cut across the missiles from above, taking out many.

Chaela led her fighter wing in to take out the stragglers one-on-one.

Still too many. Dozens of missiles penetrated the starfighter wave defensive screens.

Fixer clouds and other fighter waves from her carriers swept the enemy's forward defenses away.

They destroyed two of the three missile frigates that fired upon the flagship.

That left the Triaxians gutted and wide open to attack from the rest of the Alliance.

But Naero and her ship struggled to cut down the remaining incoming missiles with their secondary batteries and counter measures.

"Shields back up, at fourteen percent," Yon reported.

"Good work," Naero said. "Secure bridge. Activate all secondary personal shields around each bridge station. Backup bridge–get ready to take over–if we don't survive."

Globes of shielding energy shimmered around each bridge station, including her own. Her nanohelmet and clear visor pweaked up as her EVsuit sealed. Naero sat down in her command chair, feeling the nano material suck her in and strap her down secure.

Five smartmissiles slammed into *The Hippolyta*, throcking her like punches thrown at her from ginormous, flaming fists.

Two hits struck the bridge directly.

Even one of those shipkillers could have taken out a normal battleship with its shields down.

Main shields collapsed once more, but deflected and absorbed at least some of the damage.

Massive blast panels buckled.

A fireball swept through the bridge; Naero guessed a penetration missile with incendiary warheads.

Most of their station shields held off the fiery blast long enough to allow survival before winking out.

But everyone on the bridge still got burned. The heat was just too intense.

The AI-controlled blast screens that still functioned opened wide to suck out the flames and smoke, and helped put out the fires.

The screens snapped closed again. Emergency hull-sealing shields closed off the breaches.

Naero had vaguely heard the sudden screams of those who were immolated. Their personal shields collapsed too soon.

The sickening sweet smell grew acrid and intense.

She had first degree burns scorching her shins and her face through her melted nanohelmet screen. Second degree burns on her left arm and shoulder. Her smartsuit already struggled to counteract the damage.

Three stations held nothing but charred bones in their melted command chairs.

Mirra Luna, Gravitics.

Shim Steiner, Power Supply.

Brindil Lakota, Jump Drives.

At a quick glance, she saw others on the bridge who were even more badly burned that she was. She got up out of her chair and scrambled to pull out a medkit.

She coughed and tried to call out commands, but her voice croaked and her throat felt swollen and impossibly dry.

Seconds later, she could speak at last.

"Backup bridge…assume command, Jaylen. Keep us safe. Fight if we can. Medteams to the bridge…three dead, several wounded. Many burn victims. Bring–"

The Hippolyta kept maneuvering. Her big guns re-awoke and fired.

Naero smiled in pain from the scorching burns on her face and body. She raised her fist and shouted defiantly. "That's our girl. Show these fucks how tough you really are. You're one of the thirty valiant sisters, and you have never known defeat! Put fire on them!"

Similar shout-outs from her surviving crew.

Delen Taylor called out from her medical station, working calmly, quickly, and efficiently–despite her scorched hands, arms, and torso.

"Medteams arriving shortly, sir. I'm running triage and assessing all bridge personnel medical status to coordinate treatment. You're hurt, sir. Sit back down and wait for the medteams."

"To hell with that," Naero said.

First, she sprayed herself with the burn meds from her medkit.

She gasped. Her legs nearly buckled.

She hadn't suspected that anything could hurt worse than her burns and injuries.

But she was quickly proven wrong.

It felt as though white-hot insects ravaged her flesh.

Other crew who could still move around broke out medkits and began spraying the other wounded, who could not, with the same fast-acting, regenerative burn agents.

More screaming erupted.

Zhen had told her once that the pain came from the regeneratives that attempted to stabilize and reverse nerve and tissue damage.

It meant the agents were working, yet they were incredibly painful.

Several more people screamed as the burn meds hit them.

All four Marines posted at the lifts survived by ducking into them before the fiery blast. Marines wore full combat armor besides, with their own battle-level shields, designed to stand up under direct and indirect fire.

But the armored blast doors of the lifts had protected them the most, shielded inside and out.

The Marines stepped back onto the bridge and let the medteams pour up.

Two of the guards kept watching the lifts.

The other two took out medkits from the damaged nanowalls and helped spray the wounded with the burn-healing agents.

Once the medteams arrived in force, everything went like clockwork from there. No one else died, but it came very close.

While all around them, the shields came back up more and *The Hippolyta* kept fighting, led by the XO from the backup bridge.

Naero was proud of her people.

Many stayed at their stations while hurt, until their turns for treatment came, still feeding vital data to the backup bridge. Still trying to help the ship and fleet until the medteks dragged them away and put them on medbeds to transport them to the ship's hospital.

Naero was one of the last to be taken out, but she insisted on walking and riding to the infirmary, and took the lift with a few others.

Tyber came up the lifts with an army of teks to repair the main bridge systems quickly and set things right.

"Oh, N…" he exclaimed, when he spotted her. He instinctively moved to put his arms around her.

She pushed him away slightly. "It looks and hurts worse than it actually is, Ty. So please, don't touch me for now."

He nodded and swallowed hard. "Okay."

She stepped onto the lift with the others. "Get us back in business up here, Ty. I'll return shortly, after that quack of yours checks me out and patches me up."

Her ship was still in a fight. Naero didn't like not being a part of that.

But she trusted her XO and her people.

Other medteks dragged the gathered remains of the dead to the other lift sealed up in more body bags as the doors to her lift closed.

Then, while she was being treated, she could sense suddenly that the ship was no longer being hit by enemy weapons.

It slowed down from attack speed and came around.

The battle must have concluded in their favor.

Although Zhen told her to rest, Naero insisted on heading to the backup bridge.

Her XO let her take over instantly, as part of their agreement.

Protocol dictated that they could not be in the same place during a battle, so Jaylen went up to oversee the main bridge repairs.

Naero checked the displays and noted that the enemy losses amounted to almost two entire fleets–over eighty warships destroyed outright or captured. The combined power of the Alliance fleets closed in to hammer the rest of the enemy that broke and fled.

Naero analyzed their weakness and prepared to adjust her attacks to punish the Triaxians even further.

Then Admiral Kinmal cut in. "They're breaking and running, Captain Maeris. Let them go for now."

"Permission to pursue, sir."

"Negative. Pull back and regroup."

"But we can still crush them, sir!"

"Negative. We've defeated them, but we're too beat up. Regroup along the Beta line and put your reduced fixer clouds to work. Refits are going to take longer now because of your little stunt, but good work anyway. Those new fixer techniques worked well."

"I still want to make them pay," Naero said.

Admiral Kinmal sighed. "There have been enough losses on both sides today, N. I thought reports said you were severely injured?"

"Not badly at all, sir. Exaggerations."

"Then I strongly suggest that you go see to your own dead and wounded for once, Captain Maeris."

"But I–"

"Take this opportunity to do so. No excuses this time. Consider it an order."

In the aftermath of the latest intense battle, Naero did exactly as the admiral commanded.

8

Most of Strike Fleet Six's wounded were eventually transferred to their hospital ship, *The Columbia*, once the injured were fully stabilized.

Doctors and surgeons such as Zhen and other medical personnel also transferred over to assist–as needed and as able–with the sudden, heavy influx of casualties.

The aftermath of every battle like this one always meant more dead and more wounded.

Naero was always so busy that to her, they were just numbers and reports sent to her over more data feeds.

But standing in just one of the receiving bays of the hospital ship allowed her to put those numbers into a new perspective.

So many wounded, flooding in from the entire fleet.

Too many.

Naero noticed that as soon as she stepped on deck.

She instantly felt ashamed that she had not taken the time to do so during the first few weeks of the expanding conflict–until now.

On her direct, past orders, all busy medical personnel at times like this were exempted from the requirement to salute. Naero wanted them focused completely on their charges, without any needless distractions.

At least she had had the foresight to do that much in advance.

Naero knew very well, from past discussions with Zhen that if not killed outright, their injured had an excellent chance of survival, recuperation, and recovery. In most cases, it would simply take time.

Spacers healed rapidly, at least physically.

Brain and head injuries were usually involved in most KIAs. Then there were cases when bodies were almost completely obliterated, or reduced to ash or atoms.

But the fact remained, the brain was still too vulnerable and complex, and could not be routinely regenerated. Thankfully, almost every other part of the human body could be.

But the mental and emotional scars of surviving such terrible injuries often took longer to recover from, or affected people for the rest of their natural lives.

Naero went among the decks of the hospital ship cautiously at first, doing her best to stay out of the way. She offered encouragement where she could. The vast numbers of wounded from the fleet made her feel small and helpless. And this was just one hospital ship, with one fleet, from one battle.

Zhen had been her teacher about all things medical. Recovery was key to saving people. But being wounded or lying in a medbed for days, weeks, or months was incredibly boring, as well as depressing and intensely lonely.

Wounded often hungered for someone to talk to, to listen to them, or simply be with them. Someone holding their hand or staying nearby, just in case.

Naero had the fleet casualty report numbers in her head from her wristcomp. And this times the numbers were in fact very low.

Just 684 KIA. Most of those from the loss of *The Wombat*. A total of 1,205 wounded.

She witnessed the aftermath of every kind of injury imaginable, flowing around her in a steady, streaming sea of medbeds, like rafts on an open sea.

Part of her wished she hadn't seen so much all at once. It was quite overwhelming.

Burn injuries. Missing limbs.

Blast injuries. Shredding and penetration wounds. Bodies twisted and mangled in every way possible. Partial bodies. Partial faces. Partial torsos.

Bodies crushed and shattered, barely clinging the spark of life.

Naero volunteered to sit with a badly wounded fighter pilot from *The Cockatrice.*

The pilot was missing the lower half of her face; various tubes allowed her to breathe, hydrate, and feed when needed.

Naero did not know this Spacer fighter pilot personally, but she could tell that the wounded woman was smart.

The pilot had one sparkling green eye left, and half her nose. Nothing else down to her raw, exposed throat.

Everything. Gone.

She blinked at Naero with her remaining eye, until Naero figured out that she was using a basic Spacer battle code, made with short and long blinks.

It took a short while for Naero to figure it out.

By the time this pilot would fully regenerate and learn to re-use her reconstructed face and body, hopefully the Annexation War would be long over.

1st Leftenant Mariisha Elkins, of the 94th Alliance Starfighter Wave, 3rd Squadron, 10th Fighter Wing–*The Headhunters.*

That was her name and rank and unit from her holochart.

Only twenty-three years old.

Her 3D scan of her face and head, being used for reconstruction purposes, was heartbreaking.

Mariisha spoke in code with her one green eye until her pain meds wore off. The Spacer metabolism was fickle with pain meds, a running problem. The fighter pilots sole eye began to weep, and bulge in panic and terror.

Tell parents…family…I live…Please…do not…them see me…this way.

Naero touched her hair gently.

"Don't worry. I will inform them of your wishes, Mariisha. Personally. All you need to do, is focus on your reconstruction treatments. Our people are the best in the galaxy. They'll get you back."

Medteks arrived seconds later, at Naero's direct call, and doped the suffering pilot up again.

Spacers were immune or resistant to many poisons–as well as drugs– including most standard pain meds. That remained one drawback to their advanced, genetically engineered metabolism.

It took heavy doses of meds that were specifically attuned to their unique biology to put them under or relieve their pain.

Meds at levels that would kill normal humans.

Mariisha finally dozed off, her one green eye still half open.

Naero patted her hand and closed the young woman's eye gently with her own small fingertips.

Naero softly kissed the top of Mariisha's head.

Her brave people, like this beautiful young fighter pilot. What a price they paid. Damn Triax, damn the war, and damn...herself.

Naero moved on from medbed to medbed in that section.

Sometimes the wounded could interact. Some could not, or were still in shock or even anger, and didn't want to. A few just stared.

Some cried out repeatedly for their family, or perhaps for a lover or a cherished friend.

Their cries were the most heartrending Naero ever witnessed or endured.

It would take a heart made of pure steel not to be moved by such cries.

Many raved, or rambled, or sobbed.

Naero understood as best she could. None of this was about her.

If these poor wounded needed to yell or cry–let them–they could do so freely.

She never took any offense, even if a few noticed her rank.

Especially–when in their pain–some few of the wounded cursed or blamed her directly for what had happened to them.

Just one more price of wearing her gold halo and star.

She moved on if things got too abusive. Hanging around just provoked further outbursts. Such incidents were rare, but still painful and awkward to endure.

Yet thankfully, the vast majority of the wounded didn't give a damn either way what her rank was.

They simply wanted some human contact, comfort, or company.

They did not care who or where it came from.

Naero called to her ships and explained the overwhelming need for such comfort that the wounded had.

Once she fully explained that need, volunteers flooded over, to comfort or sit with other wounded Spacers, many whom they didn't even know.

Those who were off duty could give that much of themselves.

The next time, it could be them, or a family member or friend, in such dire need.

As she moved on, Naero discovered firsthand that burn wards could also be grim, tricky places.

First of all, the smell of the wards themselves was perhaps something Naero and many others would never forget.

Most Spacers, like Naero, had keen senses of smell.

Even with having been burned herself, the clinging, cloying smell of so many burned people, burned flesh, burned human hair, and the distinctive regenerative meds combined were quite overpowering. Especially when the victims were first tended to and brought in on the special medbeds designed for burn units.

The overall smell was an intense odor that would likely haunt Naero's nightmares for the rest of her days.

Yet she could choose to get away from it, in part at least, if it all became too much.

She could walk away and leave it behind, and duck out to another part of the hospital ship. Or leave the ship entirely to try to escape from it.

Then Naero thought about that and steeled herself.

What was it like for the victims themselves? They were stuck with the entire situation. They could not run away from it.

They could not get away from any part of their ordeal, let alone the intense smell. Not until they regenerated, which could again, take up to several months or more. Their long process was just starting.

These people were stranded with their condition each day until then. No escape. No way to walk away from anything.

The ones who could joke about it all called themselves "fryers," as in "the deep-fried." She had heard about this before and just thought it to be more dark, gallows humor among warriors.

But on a burn ward, that still seemed incredibly poignant to her–that some of the victims could actually be that flip about it, so soon.

Some of the wounded even took to calling each other "drumstick," or boasted about being "extra-crispy."

Of course, anyone who spent enough time around burn victims, realized very quickly that they were obviously still the same people trapped inside their outer shells, however damaged and horrific those outer forms became.

After several hours and repeated visits, Naero stopped seeing their burns, and interacted with them more or less normally.

But it did shake her to come across one of the burn victims from her own bridge, someone she knew personally. Knowing the person made the adjustment even more heartbreaking.

Kelment Walker, Launching Bay Station Control. Second and third degree burns over the front of his body, from his head down to his waist. He was missing his ears, nose, and three fingers.

He slept peacefully, as long as Naero kept her hand gently on the normal portion of his scorched left arm.

He started and woke up if she tried to slip away.

Naero stayed with him for two hours before another crew from *The Hippolyta* took her place, and Kelment's arm.

From what the other doctors said, the more people who could be around them to be supportive, the better and faster the healing process would go. Including the emotional component.

From the outset, these wounded wanted desperately to get back to being their former selves. To escape from their nightmare.

Many, like Mariisha and Kelment, elected not to allow family, friends, or loved ones to visit or see them, until they would be more or less completely restored and healed.

For them it was, in fact, better if strangers sat with them. It was better to be around someone who hadn't known them before.

They wanted to spare their family and friends the same pain and terror that they themselves were going through.

Naero still marveled at the modern, advanced medicine of their time.

How terrible it must have been before people had possessed advanced regeneration and restoration techniques. Their modern medical procedures that were now nearly taken for granted by those who did not need them.

Naero finally went back to her flagship after each visit–exhausted–but she slept fitfully, as usual.

She struggled not to blame herself. If she felt like crying for herself and her people, she did so and pushed on.

The war was at fault, not the people conducting and fighting it.

And their war still remained both just and necessary.

Each crew member took his or her own chances.

Any of them could die.

Any of them could be wounded.

At any moment, including Naero herself.

Naero ignored her own slight wounds and superficial burns. They were already healing. In a few days or weeks, they would be completely erased.

Nothing like what Mariisha and Kelment were going through.

But she or anyone fighting the war could still join them at any time–or join the dead, for that matter.

That was what everyone needed to understand. Not to dwell on or obsess about, but simply rationalize. Perhaps each person did so in their own way, and the path of denial simply worked best.

Naero returned to *The Columbia* each day for the majority of the next few days.

Sometimes, if the hospital ship was particularly overloaded, Zhen would hunt her down and put her to work.

"Get to it, N. You've had lots of medtek training. We need every pair of hands today."

In those situations, Naero pitched in directly, rank or no rank.

If she was off duty, she could do whatever she wanted to with her time, just like any one else.

Strangely enough, it was half-Yattai empath Shalaen who could not handle being around so many wounded all at once. She visited the hospital ship–only once. Then she balked and departed quickly, and never came there again.

Being around that many people in pain was extremely difficult for an empath.

The way Shalaen explained it to Naero–with haunted eyes–not being able to heal like her fully Yattai mother could frustrated and tormented Shalaen greatly. It left her helpless before the suffering and torment of so many others, gathered together in one place.

Shalaen could feel everything so many felt at once, and yet she could do nothing to help them, or ease their suffering.

For all of her empathic powers and Cosmic abilities, there were some things that remained beyond Shalaen's amazing abilities, and that lack served only to torment her beyond what she could bear.

After Naero's latest visit to *The Columbia* to help the wounded, she finally understood why Admiral Kinmal insisted that she should go among them at such length.

Casualty numbers would have a much greater and poignant meaning to her now.

And despite their heavy losses, at least the wounded still had a chance to recover and take up their lives again, whatever they endured.

Life remained sweet to all of them, and hope endured, as long as there was life and a chance at life.

But never for the dead.

The dead lost everything outright and up front. Death was unforgiving and offered no second chances.

She thought she understood that once, but war thundered and hammered that reality home every day.

9

Naero's first disguise that she used to walk and work among her crews was that of a starfighter pilot replacement.

With her youth, that was more than plausible. And she was already an excellent fighter pilot.

She wore a blond nanowig that fused itself to her own hair and could not readily be pulled off, even in a fight. The style was a sharp-cut bob with long, tapered sides that angled up to the back. Shorter in back, and much shorter than her own long hair, which was tucked up under the wig.

She found it rather fun and surprising to have a new look.

Nice to be a blond for a change, and it also felt liberating to also be someone else for a while—a clean break from the pressures of her responsibilities.

She called herself Amina—Amina Kurtz, from Clan Kurtz.

Amina-Naero was assigned for further training under one of Commander Chaela Maeris' starfighter squadrons. This allowed Amina-

Naero to come and go according to orders that she herself controlled, as the strike fleet captain.

Such transfer orders were not uncommon, especially among reserve personnel. They bopped around in many roles and situations on several vessels here and there.

Reserve personnel got shunted around as needed, and often came and went at a moment's notice.

Naero also decided to change her appearance by wearing a lot of programmable nanomakeup that was easy to apply and manipulate.

She normally didn't wear that much in the way of cosmetics, so she took a page from Saemar's playbook.

The results were startling.

Even she hardly recognized herself.

Amina-Naero joined The Fire Hornets, 147th Alliance Star Fighter Wave, 5th Squadron, 2nd Fighter Wing. Assignment: replacement reserve fighter pilot.

They flew a modified, souped-up version of the Joshua Tech F-100C Super Cobra, with its signature 50-mm heavy pulse cannons, mounted both fore and aft. Along with the added punch of three particle beam guns in each short wing.

All of that firepower made the Super Cobra a force to be reckoned with as a heavy tactical, space superiority fighter.

And since it had been updated and refitted with the latest avionics, power core, armor, and shields, the F-100C had one of the highest survivability ratings in the Alliance Fleets.

Pilots loved it because it kept them alive and brought them back. They made it their workhorse.

There was even an F-100T. The tango version was a two-seater training version, with the instructor sitting above and slightly behind the trainee, dual controls standard.

Amina-Naero checked out with 5th Squadron's training officer, Leftenant Commander Ortega, in one of the tangos. She officially got her wings and was cleared to be attached to the unit as a backup pilot.

Ortega was impressed with her performance on her training runs.

This, despite the fact that Amina-Naero was actually holding back, making several small mistakes that she wouldn't normally make—in order to further her cover.

She succeeded in making herself look promising, but still inexperienced.

"You still have a lot to learn, Ensign Kurtz. But whoever trained you did a superb job. I wish all of our reserve replacements came to us with as much talent and potential skill as you demonstrate. Good luck, ensign. Welcome to The Fire Hornets."

"Thank you, sir."

They exchanged salutes.

She learned that 5th Squadron usually formed up into two wings of ten starfighters each. When they fought, they took on the enemy in pairs, with a lead ship and a wingman. Wing commanders directed the two wings as needed.

When they did not have direct orders or targets, standard doctrine directed that they attack and defeat the nearest enemy available–until the foe was either destroyed, rendered ineffective, or chased off.

In war, there was often a lot of down time between battles, engagements, and major campaigns. Typical military experience: lots of boredom, and then a few minutes to hours, or days of sheer terror, chaos, and destruction all around.

Fighter pilots on duty had to stand ready to prep and launch in a matter of seconds or minutes at most, where every second counted.

Amina-Naero stored her gear and met with the other nineteen pilots in their barracks on board *The Bulldog*. Five others were new reserve replacements, just like her. She met the other backup pilot that she would be wingman to–another ensign named Laedon James. He had already survived his first battle.

His wingman had not. Hence the revolving need for another replacement.

To pass the time, Laedon and Amina-Naero played cards, stellar chess, or various vid games with the other nineteen pilots in her wing.

She'd been around Chaela and Saemar and other fighter pilots long enough to know how many of them behaved. She did most everything within the acceptable range, so as not to stand out or attract too much attention.

They gambled small wagers on cards, on stellar chess, on vids, dice, dominoes–anything with an element of chance to it.

"So, what am I getting myself into with this unit and your commanders?" Amina-Naero asked her new mates.

"Where'd you come from and who did you serve under?" came the standard response from one veteran pilot, answering her question with a question.

The woman did not even look up from her cards as she asked.

"I had my initial training under Admiral Sleak Maeris, with the 112th Alliance Star Fighter Wave, 4th Squadron, 6th Fighter Wing. I've bounced around a lot as a backup and reserve pilot since then. Haven't seen any action yet."

A very plausible answer. That sort of thing was commonplace, especially for young backups and reserves.

The veteran–already an ace many times over–at twenty-two years of age–grimaced briefly.

"Less chance to die. Count yourself lucky, kid."

Another vet chimed in. "Fleet Captain Maeris is a hard-nosed hellcat, much like her aunt, our glorious admiral. She does some crazy shit in battle–like some kind of a savant." This guy didn't bother looking at her when he spoke, either.

Amina-Naero put on her best worried face. "Like, what kind of crazy?"

"The best kind of crazy," the last guy added with a chuckle. "Crazy as in stuff the enemy doesn't expect. That drives them nutsoid and helps us beat their asses bloody. Don't worry, newb. If the fleet cap doesn't get you killed in the process, you'll learn to love her. You might shake your head a lot at first, but it'll be okay in the end."

The female vet got mad and threw her cards down, her face scarlet.

"Don't tell the kid that, Yuben! You can't know how it's gonna be for her or anyone. Not even you. How can you say things are going to be okay? Remind me when they have been okay?"

"Easy, Jem. Whatever happens, it's all gonna be okay. We can't control it anyway. So why worry about it?"

"Yeah, your pat, dumbass answer for everything. I'm just saying. The kid could go out and get blown to hell on her first mission–just like the last guy. That's the same thing you told him. So, you can't just say everything's automatically going to be okay. Because it isn't."

Naero let her eyes stare wide and swallowed hard.

Yuben frowned, squirming only slightly as Jem pressed her point.

"Like any of us can control any of that," Yuben said. "Don't let her rattle you, kid. Just do your best. That's all any of us can ever do. Then whatever else happens, it's all okay."

Jem shook her outstretched, trembling fingertips in the air like claws. "Idiot!"

Yuben ignored her frustration and focused on the card game at hand.

Amina-Naero quietly asked a few questions about several recent battles that she had heard about.

The squadron gave their opinions, based on their perspective and the information they had.

Aunt Sleak was right again.

It did help to get several opinions from different points of view. Naero gained valuable insights on those battles from listening to those fighter pilots debate stuff back and forth.

She even realized a few minor mistakes she had made here and there, and that she would strive not to make again in the future.

But it became increasingly clear that the life-and-death decisions she made always affected so many others. And although not everyone agreed with her every decision, at least they had an overall respect for her ability to fight, and her skill to lead them to victory.

Another problem presented itself.

Ensign Laedon kept watching her–a lot. Obviously enamored with her.

She knew she was still cute, even with her new look.

This sort of thing was bound to happen.

Fighter pilots were well-known for being a randy, romantic lot.

Saemar was one extreme, but there it was.

Laedon tried to talk with her, do little favors for her, get to know her better.

They guy wasn't smooth, but he wasn't a jerk, either. Just a normal, average guy, trying to make some time with someone new and cute.

Naero liked him all right as crew–but there wasn't any spark there. She just wasn't interested.

That wasn't her goal anyway–to fool around with some subordinates anonymously. Tempting, but that just wouldn't be fair to anyone. Naero had a strict policy about not playing games with people's hearts and emotions.

She was the polar opposite of Saemar when it came to casual relationships.

In fact, she often chided herself for almost continually going out of her way to avoid private and romantic relationships.

Hence her sustained and secret virgin status.

She was in fact extremely choosy, but that again was still just another excuse. She knew that as well.

Yet the more she evaded him, the harder Laedon pursued her. Go figure.

Predators always seemed drawn to prey that ran from them.

She finally let him down easy, explaining that she already had a steady guy somewhere else.

A lie, of course, but a convenient one.

Laedon took the hint, but he still flirted with her from time to time, just in case she changed her mind.

Naero spent time with The Fire Hornets here and there for about five more days while the fleet refitted in the rear areas, and then moved up toward the front lines again.

She learned most of what she wanted to know from that bunch during that time.

Many of her people seemed to see Captain Maeris as slightly nuts, but also skilled and gifted. That much was probably all true.

But at least they had great respect for her overall leadership, regardless of what they thought about her as a person. Most of them did not know her personally, so they just guessed.

Some even made up stuff.

Then several women and even a few of the guys started chatting excitedly, as a hot new rumor began to spread.

"Have you heard? Max Lii might be joining our strike fleet!"

"Max Lii? The throckstar?!"

"No, you derp–Max Lii, the dishwasher. Of course it's the throckstar. *Haisha!*"

The news and all the wild rumors along with it blazed throughout the ship, and then the fleet.

Secretly, Naero hoped those rumors were true. Max was pretty glacier. She and the fleet could use some good news, and a little excitement that didn't involve death and mayhem.

When the time finally came, Amina-Naero Kurtz took another transfer to another ship, in another fleet.

10

Just thinking about Max Lii made Naero go through her music feeds back in her private quarters.

She played several of his hits:

Fire in Her Eyes.
One Touch...One Kiss...One Night.
My One and Ever.
To the Stars.
Hearts Afire.
Throw Down.
Vortex.

As she listened to each song in turn, as she had done so many times, she finally noticed something.

Max Lii used the latest tek and throck music gimmicks and tricks.

Yet he also used traditional riffs, pipers, even the traditional Spacer tharp and thiolin–to heart-pounding or heart-rending effect.

Like her parents, Naero loved the sweet lilting strains and tunes of the traditional Spacer tharp and thiolin. Most Spacers grew up hearing them on the merchant ships of their Clans, playing the old songs, Spacer shanties and lullabies.

Just as Naero had. Like a soundtrack to the Spacer life itself.

Her parents had played stirring thiolin songs, solos, and concertos piped throughout all of their ships.

They called up holo images and performances of famous thiolinists– past and present–when they dined, had meetings, or they were just on their own, together or alone. And like Naero at their memory, the old tunes often brought her and her parents to reflection, and tears.

Yet they loved those tunes all the more, for they were laden with memory. Naero now understood why.

When she became a teen, naturally she had rebelled, and refused to listen to her parents' "old-fashioned-crap."

She made numerous complaints, but they simply ignored her.

But now with them lost to her, and her at war, those old songs and tunes seemed to have even deeper meaning and significance.

They were the memories, the history in songs, of a fierce and brave people. Their people. Their blood. Many of whom had given their lives for the sake of freedom.

As interstellar celebrities themselves from the Galactic Fight Circuit, her parents brushed shoulders with other famous figures, thinkers, and musicians. That included the greatest thiolinists of their age.

Mitsubishi Yuzuki, Grandon Kowalski, Rhiannon Fae, Seamus Flynn–and the Maestro, the old grandmaster himself–Ezekiel Luna Alexander.

The latter, the living legend and treasure of the Forty-Nine Clans. He insisted that everyone simply call him Zeke.

At 137 years, it was said that finally, the effects of old age had begun to slow him down.

And it was widely known that when he played now, he did so in great pain. Yet play he did, regardless, and vowed that he would do so, for as long as he drew breath.

Not many Spacers lived to such an age. Except for a few other elders, all of Zeke's friends and most of his close kin were long gone.

He had been a teen at the time of the Third Spacer War, and it was also said that the pain and sorrow of that great conflict, and those of the even mightier Fourth Spacer War after that were what gave his music the raw depth and subtle power.

He had lived and survived through almost one quarter of total Spacer History. When he did go out in public or to perform, he wore long elder robes of jet black, which set off his long white beard down to his knees, and his trademark, platinum white shock of hair that either cascaded down his back or was plaited into a simple Spacer braid.

In truth, to Naero he always looked like a fanciful character–some noble wizard of old, or a myth out of one of Ty's fantasy vid games.

Yet when the grandmaster lifted his exquisite thiolin and played…hearts broke, and many fell to their knees in high honor of the privilege–of experiencing his great art–perforce.

So great and mighty was his skill with a thiolin.

And Zeke played the most perfect, the most beautiful thiolins known to exist, touched and maintained by his expert hands alone.

In fact, Zeke had played at her parents' wedding–his priceless gift to them. He was said to be a huge fan of the galactic fights, and loved them and their grand love story very dearly.

All that night–the very night that Naero herself was conceived–the grandmaster serenaded her mother and father in high honor, until the bells of the late watches lengthened.

After her parents perished, she heard later that the grandmaster refused to play any music at all, for weeks on end.

Naero sighed, truly glad and excited that Max Lii might join them at some point. That would be thrilling.

But she gave the order for Zeke's traditional Spacer music to be piped throughout her fleet.

Let them feel what she felt.

What all Spacers felt when they heard an important part of their history.

Naero hoped that it would help guide and inspire her people, just as it did her.

*

They set up one of the smaller, boxlike nanopractice rooms for combat targeting and blade throwing.

Naero whirled and threw one of Tyber's latest charged throwing blades. She hit the next gravtarget dead center at fifteen paces when it popped up behind her.

A small, muffled blast burped, and the target dropped.

Another shot up right next to her at random.

If she didn't nail it, the damn thing would nail her with a painful shock charge.

Yet even as she cut at it with another charged blade…

One of Zhen's energy spikes pierced and disrupted it before it could zap her.

Naero grinned and nodded at her friend. "Thanks, Z. For a quack, you've always been a pretty good blade thrower."

Zhen grimaced. "Nothing like you, of course. Someone who just naturally excels at anything…destructive. But I stay in practice. I'm no brawler like the rest of our gang, but throwing blades has remained a hobby of mine since you and I could float. When Tyber told me you two had cooked up a way to pweak the energization in order to make our throwing weapons perform better, and in various modes, naturally, I had to tag along."

"That reminds me, Z. Tarim's most recent evaluation says your raw marksmanship scores are currently too low. Please schedule some combat training with him to bring them back up."

Zhen gave her the look. "Naero…I am busy with my patients and so many other issues. You of all people know what a terrible shot I am. I'm not a warrior."

"All Spacers are warriors; you've just never allowed yourself to fully embrace that, Z. But regs demand that I can't excuse you just because we're friends. Simply bring your scores up a little. I'm not asking you to outshoot Tarim. Regs are regs."

Zee smirked. "I'll remember that…the next time it's time for one of your checkups, and you put me off again. What good is combat training going to do me in my line of work?"

"Plenty–if the ship is boarded and infiltrators attack your sickbay."

Zhen rolled her eyes. "Maybe I'll take them all out with our new little throwing doodads."

"Just report to Tarim for training, Z. Bring your no-good boyfriend along with you, if you must."

Zhen giggled. "Ty, are you going to let her talk about you like that?"

"Uh…huh…" he mumbled absently.

"Ty…are you even listening to me?"

"Of course I am…hmm…almost got it here."

They glanced over at him.

Tyber shook his head, frowning, completely oblivious to them. He tinkered with the nanonodes on a low-profile throwing blade–like the one Naero had just thrown. He did so with the help of three of his specialized tinkering fixers, that hovered around him and his work.

He started humming absently again.

He manipulated the nanolevel circuitry for a few minutes longer.

"Watch this," Naero finally whispered to Zhen.

"Hey, Ty; how about the two of us strip doe-naked, and do you in tandem? Right here on the nanofloor?"

Zhen's jaw dropped. She slapped Naero's arm and whispered emphatically, "Are you crazy?"

Tyber kept humming and droned on. "Yeah...whatever...just stop buggin' me. Can you just give me a couple of minutes, here?"

Naero grinned, staring forward, waving her hand in front of her own slack face. "See?"

Zhen and Naero snickered together.

Ty stuck his tongue out the side of his mouth like he always did, when he was really focused on something.

"Nuts, we still don't have it right. That energized blade should have exploded with the same force as an HE microgrenade. Instead, it just popped and fizzled."

He and his fixers pweaked two more blades, two throwing stars, and two spikes.

Then he handed one of each to Naero and Zhen. "Okay. Try these. Let's see how they perform this time."

Ty stepped back; Naero and Z stepped up, back onto the grid, activating the combat program.

The throwing weapons energized.

Multiple gravtargets hurtled at them.

Naero struck all three of hers.

Zhen barely missed one of her targets and got zapped in the butt. "Ahhhgg!"

Naero swatted the straggler out of the air with a wheelkick.

"Damn it..." Ty fumed. "Why aren't they–"

All six devices went off at once.

The resulting detonation knocked the three of them off their feet, slamming them winded and breathless into the far wall. They were a bit scorched, too, but otherwise unhurt.

Naero laughed and gave a thumbs-up. "Perfect!"

"Hilarious," Ty said. "All right, give us a few more minutes to make further adjustments...and we'll try it yet again."

Naero and Zhen stretched to stay limber, and practiced with some normal throwing blades against stationary targets in the back, off the grid.

Within the course of another standard hour of tinkering, they finally perfected four modes: Explosive, shock-stun, flash, and shield negation.

64

Shield negation took the longest to get right.

"What about obscurement?" Naero asked.

Ty paused, wheels turning in his noggin'. "Hmmm, a smoke screen–interesting. Concentrated obscurement agents. There are a few to choose from that will create the right volume. Enough to fill a large room. To stand up to breezes. I'll have to think about that. Check back with me."

Zhen chimed in, "If you can do smoke, what about skin or eye irritants? Enemies can't fight if they are choking or blinded."

Tyber grinned and nodded. "Another good idea. Thanks, 'Tisa."

Naero looked at the small, concealable throwing blades. You could carry strips of them, layered down arms or legs or in bandoliers or arm and leg guards.

"What about a larger shield negation effect, T? Like a wave pulse or a negation grenade, or full a charge?"

Ty shook his head. "Not with these dinky throwers. Not enough mass to hold such a large energizing charge for heavy blasting or unit shield negation."

Naero instantly drew out two of her long, wicked-looking Spacer battle blades from behind her hips and upon her back.

Each of them was deadly and well-balanced for fighting or throwing. Some versions of them were even designed to fold up or collapse for greater concealability, and then snap back out with a flick.

Ty's eyes widened. He held out both hands.

"May I?"

She handed him one. "Of course."

He hefted it and especially focused on the handle. "Oh, yeah. Mama. We can install anything we want in these. We can make them do whatever we want–almost as much damage as we want. You'll be able to set the levels of shock, stun, explosion, and negation, within a wide range of effects. Just let me go to work."

Naero rested a hand on Ty's shoulder. "I'll leave it all up to you, Ty. I'll have the fixers send you crates of our favorite blades–all different sizes. You make them throck. Then we'll have some more practice sessions, before we make them available to our people."

Tyber rubbed his hands together in anticipation.

"These devices are going to be incredible hi-tek additions to our arsenals."

"Great," Naero said. "Once we have them perfected, we can share them with Intel and the Alliance."

Ty grinned from ear to ear. "Then you guys can strip, and we'll give that tandem sex thing a go."

Now Naero's jaw dropped. She caught it in both hands and covered her mouth.

Zhen turned red as roses and pounced on Ty.

"Ow! Kidding, I was kidding. Stop hitting me!"

Naero chuckled.

And here Z said she wasn't a brawler.

11

    Fighter squadron commanders Saemar and Chaela Maeris came to Naero formally, with strong, conflicting opinions on how Alliance starfighter doctrine could be standardized.

    Normally, Chaela and Saemar were the best of friends and got along very well. Like her other close friends, Naero had grown up with these two.

    Yet this matter had greatly strained the pair's personal and professional relationships. Zhen confided in Naero secretly that it had even nearly come to blows.

    Fortunately, Saemar was telepathic, so she read Chae's mind and cleverly avoided Chaela's frustrated swings directed at her. That allowed their Viking companion to finally calm down, and submit to their fleet captain's final authority to decide the matter.

    They sat grim on either side of the nanotable, with Naero on the end in between them.

Naero studied both of their rival proposals, and the training procedures and battle simulations they included with them.

At first, she resisted the urge to smile.

Her two friends were both so adamant and bullheaded that neither of them could see it: the obvious solution.

Chaela was so nervous that she fidgeted in her seat and couldn't remain silent any longer.

"So which is it, N? Just tell us straight on. Which one of us is right?"

Naero rose up and turned away from them both, folding her hands together behind her slender waist and pacing slightly.

"Commander Saemar, your methods are…how can I say this…mercurial. Your training methods and combat tactics are unorthodox, instinctive, adaptive, cunning, tricky, and unpredictable. Frankly, they defy logic and still manage to give Triax fits. You and your pilots routinely outfly and outfight the best that the enemy can throw against us. Your units have the highest survival rates in the Alliance. Congratulations. You are to be commended. I will forward your proposal to the Alliance Leadership, forthwith."

Chaela maintained her composure and looked down at the conference table, her lips forming a single, thin line. She was clearly disappointed.

"Commander Chaela. Your approach to starfighter training and tactics could not be more different. Your methods are highly disciplined, skilled, relentless, precise and accurate. You and your pilots regularly defeat enemy formations three and four times your size, and have the highest kill ratios in the Alliance. Congratulations. You are also to be commended. I will also forward your proposal to the Alliance Leadership, immediately."

Saemar and Chae blinked at each other.

Both of them looked confused.

Chaela curled her lip up. "You...you're sending them both on?"

Naero nodded.

Saemar shrugged. "Sounds good ta me."

"Can you do that?" Chae asked.

Naero turned away from her console.

"I just did, and why not? My parents always taught me that there was more than one way to fight, more than one way to learn how to do something. Different styles can work equally well for different people, of different mindsets. Both of you are very different people–different attitudes and styles. But both of you are also superb pilots, and excellent leaders. And I wouldn't just say that if it wasn't true, whether we were friends or not."

"So it doesn't have to be one way or the other," Chae said flatly, realizing it fully herself, perhaps for the first time.

Saemar most likely didn't even care, either way.

Naero grinned at them both. "No...it doesn't. Your two styles of accomplishing the same goals could not be more different. And that's why they both have equal value. Some pilots will respond better to one method. Others to just the opposite–two sides of one coin. I'm always for what works. Both of these methods work just fine. Each of you, and your pilots, have proven that. And all of you should take pride in that."

Her friends tried to salute her.

Naero hugged them both in turn.

"We are more than friends, more than comrades. As you have always been, you are my family, my blood. You are my sisters. And nothing can be closer or better than that. When I say how proud I am of you both and all of your valor and hard work–you know damn well that I mean it."

Saemar started crying and broke down. Even Chae choked up.

Naero called a meeting with her command officers on board *The Hippolyta*. Forty-two ship captains, minus the eight who had perished during the latest battles.

All of her captains were headstrong, young fire dragons, much like herself and most of their crews. Fearless, if not a bit reckless. They were excellent fighters, great pilots, and many of them fine young leaders. Their people followed them and served them well, into battle and whatever came their way.

If they and their crews drew the short lot and got vaporized…

Such were the fortunes of war.

Naero spoke once they were all seated. "I've called you all to this planning mission, because I think we're still suffering too many casualties."

As she expected, several of the young captains like herself blinked and tried to hide their obvious frustration with her sudden, increased concern. All of them clearly worried about where this was headed.

Cadey Patton of *The Gray Typhoon* tried to brush it off. "Our losses are no greater than those of the other fleets now."

Naero sighed. "That still isn't good enough for me," she told them.

She thought of their wounded on *The Columbia*. "Therefore, I want all ships to institute these new procedures, and protocols." She released the new regs.

Forty-two captain heads snapped down to study the new directives appearing on the data pads in front of them. After a few minutes, the same number groaned, almost in unison. And several began to voice protests.

Naero shot to her feet and silenced them, her face set. Most of them knew that look.

She had a rep among her fleet for decisiveness and an intense force of will. She had demonstrated that force of will often, in the face of the enemy, and before them, many times. They all knew that she could be harsh, when necessary.

"I expect all of you to get on board with this and assist me directly in these matters."

Some still persisted to object. Like Paulos Archer of *The Whiskey Jack*. "With due respect, Captain Maeris, doubling the number of lifepods on each vessel will be expensive and time consuming. It is also superfluous, extravagant, and not required by any current fleet regulations. Not to mention a complete waste of time and resources."

She focused her gaze on him. "We'll learn what works and what doesn't, Paul. But we're going to try these procedures out. All of you get used to that, and stop whining. The fixers can add the extra lifepods as we refit. Most of us have to refit heavily after each battle anyway.

"I'm having more fixers generated to handle the increased workload. And studies show that our crews are not having enough time to hit the lifepods during emergencies. This should improve their chances of abandoning ship and getting away once a vessel begins to cook off."

Imala Kalada of *The Warhorse*, Clan Apache, stood up herself. She was shorter than Naero even–which was hard to accomplish–but she too had a well-earned rep for being a ferocious knife-fighter. Much again like Naero herself.

"Are we at war or not? N, these regs will have us dumping our crews and our drive cores much sooner–if I'm reading this right. And possibly, right in the midst of heated battles. Last time I checked, Triax and their allies among the other Corps still do not take prisoners. They continually use our life pods for target practice. Better to die fighting to my mind."

"Imala, you and the other captains must still use your best judgment under the exact situation for you and your ships. I trust your judgment. But if there is a chance, I simply don't want to lose so many people during every battle. Our people are the best trained crews in the Alliance. We cannot waste them. The meat grinder is unforgiving enough."

Captain Imala sat down.

Dolph Kurtz of *The Hammerhead* put in his two bits. "Reduce casualties by prosecuting the war to its fullest extent. No let up. Drive the enemy into submission and crush them. Shorten the war that way. That will save lives more than anything."

Naero shook her head. "I used to think the same way. But the math does not support that view. This isn't going to be over in a few days, or a few weeks. We can't just push through and tough it out at all costs. Those costs will be too high, if we just charge ahead all the time."

She cleared her throat. "Now, answer me this. How many of you have spent some time with our wounded, after a battle, on *The Columbia*?"

None of them, from the way they stared back at her. Just as she suspected. Just like she had been–oblivious. That was also going to change.

"From now on, after each battle, there will be a rotation of able ship captains to visit our troops on board our hospital ship. I am not excluding myself from the rotation. Trust me on this. Expect an education."

They looked at her as if she were insane.

"Listen up, all of you. Trust our leaders who came before us. We can't just focus on combat alone. There's more to it all than that. We need to fight smarter and conserve our forces for a long term conflict. Our enemies are doing everything they can to bleed us and make us pay a very high price for each battle. We need to reduce those losses. This is going to take months, and wear us all down if we aren't disciplined, adaptive, and careful."

Moira Blooding of *The Starfall* asked a question. "Naero, will these new shielding procedures really protect our power cores better from direct hits? We've all seen other ships like *The Wombat* flare off in an instant and get vaporized. Not many can escape that. There just isn't time."

Naero nodded. "Intel and Admiral Klyne insist that these advanced shielding procedures should cut down on catastrophic explosion of power cores due to direct penetration and explosive strikes by thirty-one percent. By almost a third. And automatic core jettison protocols will help more ships survive as well."

Naero rose up and crossed her arms in front of her as she paced slowly, counterclockwise around the meeting table, narrowing her eyes at each of them the same exact way she'd seen Aunt Sleak do a jillion times.

"Now, we can continue to discuss all of your concerns. That is why I brought you all here and took this time for this planning session. I want to address these matters and debate them, one by one. But be advised. These programs are going to be put into effect and tried out to see what works and what doesn't. Results, people. Get it through your skulls. Results are what matters. If something doesn't work, we'll throw it out and try something else that will."

She turned her back to them and looked out through the viewport. She laced her hands behind the small of her back.

"You and your crews are all excellent, top-notch fighters. Difficult to replace. I want to save as many of you as I can to fight anew each day. And it's a selfish thing on my part, I admit. You can't kick ass for me if you are dead, or severely wounded."

Naero sighed and bowed her head slightly. "This is war. We've lost good ships and good crew. We all know we're going to lose more. That's a fact none of us can avoid. And we take our chances with the rest. But we can reduce those losses. We have months to go before all is done, and Triax is no more. And honestly…I'm already sick to death of wakes and funerals."

Not to mention what she witnessed on the hospital ships. She paused and bowed her head once more. The meeting chamber grew deathly quiet behind her.

"I know you all fight hard. Of that I have no doubt. But you need to listen to and understand this. Understand me. Every one of you is precious to me. You are…you are my brave lions. You are my swords of light. And I do very my best to wield you with all my skill and cunning. I don't want to lose any of you needlessly."

She signed heavily once more. "I want to do everything I can. Can't you see? I just want you all to fight smart. Let's do everything we can to give our ships and our people a chance to make it home from this war. By the Powers, we've already lost so many. I want some of us to to make it home at least."

Naero turned around and looked up.

Surprise dawned on her and she was very moved.

All forty-two of her captains stood at attention around the table.

All of them drew their cutlasses, and saluted her as one.

Michael Marshall of *The Condor*, her fleet Second, smiled proudly. "This is but one of many reasons why we follow you, Strike Fleet Captain Maeris. If you are a hellion, then you be our hellion. You have proven yourself both clever and fierce. We are your lions. And we shall roar into battle at your side, any time. Anywhere. You have but to command us."

Naero smiled and fought the urge to tear up. After fighting and bleeding beside them all for months, she knew their great worth and their valor extremely well. "Dammit, Mike," she said with a laugh. "If you make me cry here in front of everyone, I'm going to have to shoot your ass."

The meeting chamber erupted in booming laughter, slicing through the pent-up stress and tension. Their planning session could now continue.

Naero ordered a round of Spacer poteen or other libation for her thirsty lions. Regs or no. They had all earned their nip of grog.

Every damn one of them.

12

The new fragrances Naero instituted throughout her fleets made a huge difference, just like the music. A difference for the better, and she was glad for it. The air smelled less stale, less like machines and circuits, less unpleasant overall.

And Zeke's thiolin music wafted sweetly in the background of every warship.

Naero was pleasantly surprised when Tarim came to her in private, outside of their regular security briefings.

She rose from her comfy gelchair in her quarters and embraced her good friend. He looked slightly nervous for some reason. It had been a long time since she'd seen him act that way.

"What can I help you with, Tarim? You said it was a personal matter." She tried to guess.

Tarim and Shalaen had a long-distance relationship, and those were always problematic. Yet both of them seemed fine with it.

"Something with Shalaen?"

He shook his head.

She gave him a moment, and let him spit it out finally.

"I'm not…a Spacer, N."

Naero took that in and then blinked.

True. What did he want her to say?

"Everyone knows that, Tarim. But everyone still accepts you among us, as both a comrade and an equal. Don't they? You're not having any trouble with lander prejudice or anything of that kind, are you?"

He shook his head again. "No, not at all. God, no. There are just certain things I don't know…that I don't understand. And I wish I would. They…they make me feel stupid…and inadequate. Less than everyone else. Jeez, I know this is all in my head. It's just me. That's why it's bothering me so much."

He looked down, almost as if he were ashamed. He kept trying to find the right words.

"I wasn't…weaned on all this stuff like all of you Spacers were, N. I grew up a Triaxian slave in the mines–until you and your people uplifted me–at the age of twenty. Not like that wasn't embarrassing."

Naero was still at a loss. "I want to help, Tarim. But what exactly are we talking about? What kind of stuff don't you know?"

Tarim looked down again and sighed.

"I make a lousy Spacer, and yet I live among you guys 24/7. How can I describe how it is for me? You guys know so much, and I don't even understand you people or your way of life. Except for being good with guns, I'm a terrible pilot, an awful navigator, a weak fighter, a so-so leader. I keep trying, but I wasn't born to it all like you and your people were. Where do I even begin?"

"Okay, Tarim. I guess I can get some of that. I imagine it gets pretty discouraging."

"And I don't have smartblood. I don't heal overnight or in a few days like Spacers seem to. I break a bone–even just a finger or a toe, and it takes me one to two months to heal. I don't have increased speed or strength. After one sparring match, I'm so beat up and bruised, I can hardly get around for a week. But a lot of it is just day-to-day stuff. The way Spacers think, live, deal with everything. We're in the midst of a war that scares the living shit right out of me every day. And to you people, it's just a walk in the park."

"So, if I hear you right," Naero said, "you don't see or react to things the same way that we do, and that often leaves you feeling inadequate, confused, and afraid?"

Tarim nodded emphatically. "Damn straight. The war is just one big example. Look, I understand ground combat just fine. I get it. But I wasn't born in space, and never learned to understand the ins-and-outs of space combat. I don't even know the basics of interstellar naval battles. And yet I could die in one at any time. When it comes to that stuff, I'm a complete idiot."

Naero stared at him. Stumped again.

"Look at it from my perspective, N. We're in the midst of just such a complex war, and you and your people understand every aspect, from history, to vessels, and strategy and tactics–all in great detail. A huge amount of information. While I feel utterly ignorant and stupid. Because I am. Other than failing at several vid games, I don't have the foggiest notion about how space combat works, any more than I have a clue to Spacer culture, and the workings of your society."

Naero tried to speak, but Tarim cut her off.

"I feel really isolated and alone a lot of the time. And quite frankly– that frustrates and scares the living hell right of out me, every time we go hurtling headlong into the next terrifying battle. However I look at it, I'm still an outsider, a stranger living among you paragons."

Naero finally nodded. "Okay. Let's look at it rationally. You're not a Spacer, but you are a smart person, Tarim. You've been able to learn more things in a shorter length of time than anyone I've ever known. Okay, so you have big gaps in your knowledge base. We could pick a few things. I could have instructors and trainers tutor you."

Tarim shook his head and waved his hands violently. "No. I don't want anyone else to know, N. I couldn't handle that. It's bad enough that I'm telling you, but I don't know what else to do. At least I know you care about me."

"I do, Tarim. What do you want?"

"Could…you teach me, N? Even just the basics–about space combat, about understanding your people and your ways. Just enough, so that I feel more at home among you guys. I just…feel humiliated enough by it all." The poor guy hung his head down.

It hurt Naero to see Tarim like that.

She grinned and placed both hands on his shoulders. "Sure, Tarim. I can explain things to you; whatever you want to know."

Her friend perked up and smiled sadly. At least he had some hope now.

Naero continued. "Let's take, say, ten to twenty minutes out of our weekly security meetings. We can speed those briefings up a bit, and we'll be in the conference room anyway, with access to the training systems. We can talk, and I can try to answer any questions you may have."

"Sounds good, N. I can't thank you enough."

"Once or twice a week, if I have time, you can also join me here for dinner or some other meal. It's not like I don't take most of my meals here already–most of them alone."

Naero thought about that. How pathetic was she?

"Thanks, N." He looked around and checked the time on his wristcom. "I've got some time right now. What can you tell me about space combat to start with?"

Naero chuckled. "I'm afraid I don't have much more time today, but you can get with gameboy Tyber about vid games. Don't worry. Tyber's a geek, so he won't suspect a thing. Just don't let him turn you into a vidgame junkie like him. But seriously–you can learn a lot of the basic concepts of naval battles, strategy, and tactics from vidgames. Some of them are quite realistic, and they can even demonstrate what past wars were like through historic simulation. You can see how interstellar naval strategy, tactics, and warships, and weapons have evolved–up to the present."

He looked uncertain. "Uh...I already said I tried vid games, N. I kept losing. Badly. They just make me feel worse."

"Ahhh...but you didn't have Tyber–the mighty gamemaster himself–guiding you along the path to true enlightenment, grasshopper."

Tarim just stared at her, his face blank. "Say what?"

Naero waved her hand, laughing. "Ty's a good teacher–if you are willing to play various dumb games with him. Trust me. Try him first for about a week, and then I'll start training you. As for your other questions, we have a briefing two days from now, and we can have dinner the day after that. We can talk then."

13

The very next day, on the bridge of *The Hippolyta*, Naero received a direct and open communication from the enemy. From the High Command of Triax itself.

That in itself was both rare and unusual.

Triax–and the Hevangian High Council–had a direct message for her and Strike Fleet Six–specifically.

Surina Marshall, her com officer, put the link on hold and notified Naero of the situation. Both of them found it extremely odd.

"Is this some kind of joke or trick, Rina? Where is this link actually coming from?" Naero asked.

Surina studied the com tracings on her displays again. "Sir, it's being bounced around the relays, but it does seem to originate from deep within the Hevangian Systems. And it does match their codings. Do you want to take it, ignore it, or shunt it to Intel?"

"Let's hear what the Hevangians have to say to us, Rina, on my command. No doubt, some kind of threat, or some such. Keep the link tight, so they can't scan our bridge or any of our systems. And make sure Intel is getting all of this, by a direct relay."

"Done, and ready, sir. Give the word."

Naero spread her stance, put her hands behind the small of her back, and lifted her head high.

Her battle face snapped up automatically.

"Open the link, Rina–main screen."

The tall figure of a powerful man appeared over the holoscreen. Imposing. Black hair shot with dark-gray steel, pale blue eyes–so pale that they gleamed like twin ghosts. A hard-angled, jagged face that might have been handsome once, without the Hevangian penchant for battle scars.

Several such badges of Hevangian honor ripped ragged across the high officer's looming visage. He wore a red and black Hevangian dress uniform and high boots, and a carried golden baton of command in his gloved hands.

This man was a killer–a killer of many–he seemed to reek and ooze of death, even over a transmission. That was the impression Naero had of him.

When he moved, Naero could see that his uniform and his hands were stained and splattered with blood.

He announce himself.

"I am High General Garrok Shul Dreth of Hevangian Intelligence, Lord Assassin of the Triaxian Imperium, and a ruling board member of the Triax Gigacorporation, Military Defense Council."

"I am Fleet Captain Naero–"

Garrok Shul Dreth cut her off abruptly, his face twitching with suppressed rage. "I know very well who you are, Captain Maeris. I knew your parents–after a fashion. In fact, you could say that our two families have had many dealings with one another over the years–ever since the Third Spacer War."

Both of them knew very well that the Hevangians and Spacers had been bitter enemies for nearly three centuries.

"Say what you have to say, general. I'm busy. I do not have time for social calls…to rehash old times and old disputes."

He laughed. "Such a pity, youngling. The old hatreds are the best, the most enduring. It was too bad my strike force did not kill both of your brothers that bloody day, so very long ago. Yet we did cripple the one brat. How we tortured that little spack runt–for years–and drove him mad in the labs. And now we have the other one as well."

Naero wasn't going to let him bait her with Jan.

"General–" Naero tried to interrupt, but he kept raving.

"And I was also present when death finally caught up to your illustrious parents as well. How very satisfying that was–them betrayed by their own insane whelp. Let me tell you about your heroic parents, Captain. How they perished in their own blood–squealing and begging for their lives, like cowardly pigs–like the wretched, filthy swine all of you spacks are."

Naero sighed briefly. "A lie to any who knew them. I will ask you once again, general. Is there a purpose to this communication, other than to heap further insult upon me and my family?"

"Did you ever wonder what happened to your parent's dead bodies, Captain? I can assure you–they were prized very highly. Considered priceless trophies, really. I have seen them…on display."

"Go away, general. You are a brutal thug, without honor, like most of your foul kind. I'm ending this little rant of yours."

Garrok Shul Dreth laughed. "Welcome to the Hevangian Sectors when and if you reach them, Captain Maeris. My people, and my extensive family, remember Clan Maeris very…very well. Whatever the outcome of the war, we shall be looking for you, at every opportunity–*with many surprises laid in store for both you–and the Alliance.* With the greatest anticipation. You have no idea what you fools have set forth in motion."

"So be it, general. And we shall respond in kind, as ever, to your many evils. Until we meet, then, upon the field of battle."

"We earnestly look forward to that, spack filth."

Naero broke off the link from her own console.

14

Nothing was ever simple. Especially too much of anything new.

Many of the new practices and protocols Naero instituted across Strike Fleet Six proved fruitful and actually cut and prevented losses. They worked just fine, and integrated into the daily routine seamlessly, with a modicum of adjustment.

Yet, unfortunately, some of the new regs that sounded good in theory did not work very well at all in practice, and only led to confusion and disarray.

There was always a trade-off, it seemed, a learning curve, a price to pay for everything. Several ships dumped their power cores too soon.

Some of them right in the midst of battle.

They either got the auto protocols wrong, or their onboard AIs reacted prematurely, dumping the cores as soon as the ship's shields went down or the core areas sustained a near hit.

That proved both embarrassing and, in one case, even deadly.

The destroyer *The Wellington* was set upon and obliterated by the enemy.

Yet doubling the number of escape pods on the fleet did manage to save more than two thirds of her crew. Still, a very costly mistake, and a very high price to pay.

Naero and her captains agreed to readjust the core jettison protocols back closer to the prior combat levels. They coupled that with pweaking the responsiveness of the fleet AIs. She had Tyber and his teks and fixers kept working on the problem.

The new core shielding, however, did work better and saved many lives.

But the casualty estimation flows were a complete and total bust.

In the heat of battle, there were just too many variables at work. Potential casualties simply could not be predicted in any rational way.

Studies showed that the test groups using the calculators performed much more poorly during a fight. They were a constant distraction to their captains and officers. In some cases, it caused them to pause or hesitate too much.

A battle might even sweep in another direction and pass them by in a matter of minutes, while they attempted to study predictors and variables. They became paralyzed by what *might* happen to them.

Or, even worse, the enemy might see their holding back as weakness or inexperience, and pounce on them even more quickly, in order to exploit and crack through a weak link.

That experiment was promptly dropped. Testing proved that it was better for the captains to rely upon their experience and instincts. Battle computers and AIs could only evaluate so much.

They possessed no power to predict the future completely in any rational way.

Naero reported all of their findings to the fleet. The bad ideas were studied and dropped. Many of the good ones were implemented throughout the Alliance, but only if they proved effective.

The Alliance continued to strive to adapt and improve against the many tricks and strategies and tactics that the enemy threw at them. Sometimes these changed from day to day.

Naero adjusted her own patterns and practices.

She struggled to remain cunning and hardnosed, but neither reckless nor bloodthirsty—nor heedless of the damage and casualties her ships and crews endured.

Balance, where everything was chaos and out of balance.

*

A week or so later, Naero and Tarim had dinner in her quarters. A hearty seafood stew, bread, and cold meat and cheese sandwiches on sweetbread. And of course, lots of Jett.

Naero waved her hand at the frozen holoships above them, and the two vessels started fighting again.

"The standard goal in naval combat is usually to close with another vessel or vessels and duke it out with them. You wear down their deflector shields first, and then degrade their armor. Then you start doing actual physical damage to the ship and its vulnerable systems that keep it functioning and able to fight back."

"Like the power core," Tarim said. "I've watched your warships target enemy power cores time and time again, with great success."

Naero smiled. "So, at least you have paid some attention. Power cores are great targets, because they more or less control the entire ship. Take out a ship's power core, and the ship ceases to function. It's no longer a threat and is more or less dead in space. And if you damage a power core badly enough, the entire ship can explode and be destroyed, although lately, Alliance battle doctrine now seeks to avoid destroying enemy ships entirely."

Tarim jumped in on that point. "So that we can capture even severely damaged enemy ships and convert them with our fixer clouds to Alliance use."

Naero nodded. "You can't convert something very well that has been blown to smithereens. I see the strategic wisdom in that policy, but given the choice between completely taking out a ship from a fight, or letting it still shoot at and possibly destroy me…I'm going to take it out and be sure it can't fight back. Every damn time."

"Sounds reasonable, N."

"So, that's why each warship does its best to protect its power core as best it can. Other vulnerable systems to target directly on starships include the bridge, of course; take out the ship's command and control. That is why all primary Alliance warships have a secondary, or backup bridge ready to take over if the main bridge should be taken out."

"I think I get this part. Take out a ship's systems, and it can't function. Knock out its scanners and communication, and it becomes blind and deaf. Take out its weapons, and it can't fight back. Destroy its sublight drives and jump drives, and it can't move or get away."

Naero continued. "Take out its gravitics and life support, and it can't operate very well, and the crew won't last long. Plus, damaging starships in general usually sets them on fire and forces them to void the battle and flee–if they want to survive and fight another day. If a ship is in danger of cooking-off and exploding, the crew will normally abandon ship in lifepods as a last resort, in order to get a safe distance away."

"I've seen a lot of the enemy warships simply give up and surrender after they've been licked. But Triax does not take prisoners."

"No, they never have. Throughout all four of the Spacer Wars with the Gigacorps, Triax and the others have not taken prisoners, and show no mercy to our helpless crews. We tried to negotiate that into the last treaty as well, but the Corps usually ignore it. When we capture their people, they are put on huge POW. ships, and sent to wait out the end of the war far to the rear."

"But first," Tarim noted, "enemy vessels that surrender must be boarded and pacified. That's part of the process of their crews becoming prisoners of war. Usually our Marines are put in charge of that. I've seen that firsthand. I've gone along with some of the Marine boarding parties during pacification operations."

"Yes," Naero said. "That's why each Alliance warship has full detachments of Marines stationed on board. Marines train constantly to be experts at pacification, security, and boarding operations. This also includes all ops on the ground on liberated enemy systems, worlds, and bases."

Tarim looked up at the two battling holoships once more. Both of them sustained minor damage and a few fires on board.

"So, negate the enemy warship's deflector shields, punch through their armor, and damage their systems sufficiently enough to eliminate them as a threat. Destroy them, leave them floating helpless for later capture, or force them to turn and flee."

Naero crossed her arms in front of herself and began to pace slightly.

"Most naval space battles are not static, Tarim. They're very dynamic and complex, with many variables and strategies at work. Fleets of fifty ships fight in all three dimensions and are usually constantly moving and maneuvering at attack speed, in various complex formations. They do this in order to gain advantageous attack vectors and gunnery profiles to concentrate the effectiveness of their massed weapons."

"I've noticed that most warships primarily rely on one to four main guns, usually in a spinal mount configuration."

"Yes, Naero said. "That is based on the limits of current tek. The standard primary weapon remains the particle beam cannon–usually the bigger, the better–and it has been that way since the Third Spacer War. But size has been limited by tek and available materials. Main guns require large quantities of energy from the well-protected central power core in order to fire. But the basic tek has changed little overall. Most of the recent advances have been in power supply and rate of fire. A ship with a smaller main gun that can fire rapidly can–in theory–do more damage in a shorter period of time than a huge main gun that fires slowly. But it also has to get in closer to do so."

Naero popped up another fourpak of Jett and tossed Tarim one.

He caught it, took a slug, and asked her, "So, is it the size of its cannons that determines a ship's class and function?"

Naero winced slightly. "Perhaps in part, but that's putting the cart before the horse. Size, mass, construction materials, displacement tonnage, power supply, and other parameters determine what a warship is configured to be, its primary role, and what size armaments it can effectively support. You could put bigger guns on a smaller ship, but it wouldn't produce enough power to be able to utilize those weapons effectively.

"And that would also take away from the ship's allocations for shields, armor, and other vital capabilities. Ship design must take all of these factors into consideration and come up with a balanced, workable approach."

Naero pulled up holos of standard ships and designs in front of them.

"Larger warships usually have bigger guns, with the exception of carriers. Carriers are primarily used to deploy fighter waves. Carriers usually do not have spinal guns or primary batteries. They focus on heavy secondary batteries for defensive purposes.

"At the opposite end of the spectrum, destroyers normally have multiple main guns, ranging from 0.5 meters to 2.5 meters in diameter. Cruisers can be one, two, or three times again the size of destroyers, and support fewer, but larger, main guns anywhere between 3 and 6 meters. Battleships are at least twice the size of cruisers, and are armed with the largest production particle beam cannons possible–7 meters to 12 meters normally. But now, new cannons can be up to 16 meters in diameter– usually on dreadnaughts, or what we call 'super-battleships.'"

Now it was Tarim who grinned. "That is why *The Hippolyta* and all of the other Dromon Class dreadnaughts are so formidable. They wield the largest main guns ever produced–16 meters–enormous. And their rate of fire is staggering. If there's one thing I can appreciate, it's big guns and heavy firepower."

"Indeed. The Amazons are true shipkillers, but they are also difficult and time consuming to manufacture. You could produce five or six conventional battleships with greater firepower overall, in the same time frame that each dreadnaught is completed. Yet the trade-off is survivability. The Dromon Class is simply that much tougher. They've suffered severe damage, but not a single one has ever been destroyed outright."

"The admirals should just have the dreadnaughts focus on destroying ship after ship."

Naero grinned and shook her head. "You might think that. But actually, the Dromon Class dreadnaughts have proven themselves to serve an even better purpose–one that even the designers did not foresee."

"And what is that?"

"The Amazons and their huge cannons are unmatched in taking down enemy shielding. No other warship can negate enemy shields as quickly. Sometimes even multiple ships at a time with each blast, if the firing profiles can be lined up correctly. That leaves multiple enemy vessels almost instantly vulnerable to the other strike fleet ships roaring up behind. Even shield negation missile frigates cannot get in close enough and take out the enemy shields as fast as the Dromon can–and almost at any range."

"What, then, is a mass-driver?"

"More or less a glorified, high velocity rock-chucker. A railgun, shooting a projectile at hyper-velocities. The same basic principle as your gauss sniper rifle. Mass-drivers were a primary weapon during the first two Spacer wars, even more effective than the long-obsolete pulse and beam lasers. Mass-drivers are still effective as planetary or system defenses, as we've seen Triax use them against us within various worlds, moons, and asteroid fields. But mass-drivers still need ammunition. Particle beam batteries do not, plus they do more damage, and have a higher rate of fire overall."

"Does a larger cannon have a greater effective range?"

"Yes, just like a rifle can usually shoot farther than a pistol. Dreadnaughts and battleships can engage targets at extreme ranges that other ships cannot. They have the biggest guns and the most power. Cruisers, destroyers, and frigates have smaller guns and specialized weapons such as shield negation missiles, but can usually rely on their greater speed and maneuverability to get them in closer to do damage faster and get back out. And it is far easier to have smaller weapons fire at higher rates of speed. So, if they do get in close in the mix, they can do a lot of damage very quickly, especially if they fight in formation and optimize their concentrated fire."

"Then why doesn't the Alliance simply build all dreadnaughts, if they are the best? Why have all of these different ships? Different sizes. Different types. Fleet carriers, strike carriers, pocket carriers. Dreadnaughts, battleships. Heavy cruisers, strike cruisers, light cruisers. Destroyers, missile frigates. Gunships and drone ships. Minelayers. What good are all the various starfighters? Why not have just one all-purpose fighter that's the best of them all?"

Naero laughed, and popped up some more comfortable nano lounge chairs for them to recline in after their meal.

She sighed. Tarim had so many questions. This was going to take some time. More than she thought.

Above them, the blue battleship finally blew up the red one. Naero swiped that simplified holo simulation away with a wave of one hand.

She proceeded to explain why modern interstellar navies used different types of warships–even highly specialized ones–for different purposes and missions.

"Tarim. Look at all of these designs. Different types of warships serve different functions and are better at performing certain functions and tasks than others. A standard fleet is normally fifty main warships:

"Five Assorted Carriers, three main types. Usually launching their fighters in coordinated sorties from the rear, or behind the protective screens of the rest of the fleet. Carriers could also be used as flagships.

"Five Battleships, sometimes led by a Dreadnaught Class ship, or super-battleship as the flagship.

"Ten Cruisers, three main types.

"Twenty Destroyers, three main types.

"Five Specialized Missile Frigates

"Five Specialized Gunships

"Plus assorted minelayers, couriers, transport, supply, and lesser support ships. Lesser craft aren't considered primary warships, or ships of the line. And don't forget, a ship may serve for decades, until it becomes too obsolete, or it costs too much to refit it."

Naero went on explaining the capabilities and uses of each type of warship, and their roles in the fleet.

Carriers both protected the fleet from other enemy starfighter waves, and sent fighters on the attack themselves. Truth be told, all warships of destroyer class or larger carried their own complement of starfighters, however small, for ship defense. Carriers could simply carry and deploy large numbers of starfighters at a time in waves. Once they launched their contingents, carriers were such big targets that they normally defended themselves to the rear, or in the center of battles, behind the main formations of the other warships.

Starfighter waves were often wild cards that could turn battles either way. They could slip in quickly and cause lots of damage, and then rip back out just a fast to go somewhere else.

Dreadnaughts and battleships had the firepower, heavy defenses, and moxie to go right at the enemy and take the fighting straight to them, ship-to-ship. Cruisers and destroyers normally protected the flanks and rear of the fleet. With their high speed, high rate of fire, and exceptional maneuverability, they could do many things and pull tricks that the larger ships could not.

Other specialized ships served their specialized functions as needed.

They broke off their conversation not long after dinner.

Naero had other duties she needed to attend to.

Tarim thanked her profusely, insisting that between Tyber's vidgames and her training, he was finally beginning to understand.

Naero promised to continue working with him. He still had a lot of questions about Spacer society in general and their form of self-governing.

She hadn't even begun to discuss those matters, or firing profiles and attack vectors, or jump drives–let alone all of the various standard and specialized fleet formations, that all warship captains and officers were expected to know, understand, and execute.

But Tarim was right. He wasn't a Spacer.

Spacers like her understood and studied all of this kind of complex naval warfare data from an early age.

The survival of the Spacer Clans had often been determined by such mastery, time and time again, many times over.

15

They cycled through the rear areas to refit and resupply for a few days.

Naero accepted a challenge for a knife-sparring session with Captain Imala Kalada of *The Warhorse*. She looked forward to a good workout in one of the special knife rooms she was developing.

And Imala promised to give her one.

Captain Kalada was seven millimeters shorter than Naero; a tiny, wiry young woman with brown eyes and straight, shoulder-length, jet-black hair. When she smiled the right way, one could easily mistake her for a cute young girl, or perhaps even a child.

Naero knew better than that.

For sparring practices, they obviously could not use real blades.

Any ship captains who would allow themselves to be wounded in sparring matches, and thus rendered unable to command, could be brought up on lapse of judgment, negligence, and dereliction of duty charges by their superiors. And rightfully reprimanded or disciplined.

Instead, for knife sparring purposes, Naero and Imala used various energized shock blades, made out of semi-flexible conducting filaments. These practice blades were specifically designed to have a similar weight, heft, and balance as real blades, and could even be thrown with great accuracy.

When the blades struck properly, they gave the opponent a painful shock, and left behind a bright, programmable, fluorescent stain to mark a jab, stab, slice, or cut. Such markers could be reset after each match.

Quite ingenious, really, and invaluable for training purposes.

Naero moved quickly and deftly on her feet, not letting Imala tangle her up or trip her. Footwork and positioning in any up-close fight situation were crucial.

Imala knew that well, too.

For once, Naero thought she might have an advantage against someone shorter than her. In truth, not many Spacers were.

Yet Imala remained tricky, fearless, and quicker than a box of snakes.

After several initial passes and a few grappling sessions, all of their clashes ended in mutual kills. A deadly tie.

Neither one of them could claim any victory over the other.

Imala was equal to her in speed, raw skill, and ferocity.

Naero had a slight advantage in size and strength, but strength in a knife fight did not always count for much.

Slower opponents thrice Imala's size would do well not to get into a knife fight with the little Apache woman, whatever their strength.

She would cut them to pieces and lay them open in seconds.

After half an hour, their stalemate endured.

Each time Naero thought she found an opening in her opponent's defense, Imala would also manage to slip through hers.

Both of them were sweating after such an intense workout.

Sweating but happy. Each of them kept probing and trying various tricks.

Naero tended to smile when she fought.

Imala's face usually remained impassive.

But every now and then, Imala would voice a fierce war cry and launch an attempt at another overwhelming assault.

Naero had her own war cries that she used to inspire and drive herself on.

They clashed repeatedly. Sometimes they stood close in together, cutting, jabbing, feinting, parrying, and blocking each other for several intense minutes.

They finally took a breather.

Imala burst out laughing once they sat down to replace some fluids.

"This is hilarious. It's like fighting my whole family in my Clan. My mother and father, my brothers and sisters. We have the same problem. We've all gotten so good with knives–that we're more or less equals. We can get lucky here or there, but none of us can ever really defeat the other."

Naero handed Imala a frosty borbble of Jett.

Imala eyed it suspiciously. "I've seen this stuff around before. What the heck is it? I usually don't enjoy soft drinks."

Naero grinned.

"Boy, do you have a treat in store for you. Jett is a citrus-based beverage, based on the black night orange. You'll love it. It's my favorite."

Naero sucked one down and reached for another.

Imala took a sip, and then shrugged–as if it were nothing–and slowly drank hers.

It was Jett. Naero couldn't believe it.

"You don't like it?"

How could people not like it?

Imala shrugged again. "It's okay. At least it's cold and quenches your thirst." She even made a little bit of a face. "A little too sour for me." She finished hers, and then reached for another box of the standard, fruit punch nutrient lix, which most practice rooms stocked as a default.

How could anyone in their right mind pass up Jett for that regular junk? Oh…well. More for her.

They went back to talking blades and knife tricks.

Each of them had their own strong opinions and ideas.

Imala suddenly shook hands with her, right up to the elbows in the warrior's embrace. Naero returned the favor.

She smiled for the first time. "Thanks, N. We'll have to do this again. It's just what I needed."

"Anytime, Imala."

"My friends and family call me Ima. I wish you would, too. We fight side-by-side and protect each other. I'd be proud to call you my sister."

Now it was Naero's turn to smile. "We are sisters, Ima. I'd like that. Some of us are closer than others, but anyone who fights beside me, I consider my Clan, my blood."

Ima grinned again. "As it should be."

They embraced briefly.

Ima offered Naero one of her special Clan Apache fighting knives.

Naero in turn gave her one of the new battle blades that Tyber had developed. She showed her all of the different modes.

Ima lifted her eyebrows. "Impressive. We've tried to do something similar, but our teks couldn't get them to function properly."

Naero nodded. "We had a lot of trouble with it, too. I'll send Ty over to have a little training session with your teks and knife fighters. He'll teach them what to do."

Ima stood up. Their time was up. Both of them had other duties to attend to. "Next time, N. Let's try sparring in zero-G. That'll be fun. Bring some of your best blade fighters, and I'll bring a few of mine."

"You bet. Let's plan on it."

"Oh, that reminds me. We're also having a little problem with our shield buffering on our power core on board *The Warhorse*. My people are stumped, and engineering was never one of my strong points. Do you think your guy can check it out and give us some tips?"

"Sure. In fact, he actually helped develop the new shielding profiles and adaptive parameters for the Alliance. I'm sure he can sort out what your bug is."

"Thanks. Later, N."

She waved after Ima as she ducked out. Then Naero gathered up her own gear.

"See ya!"

16

Naero spent another evening with Tarim, in her quarters, having a fine dinner. They enjoyed a pasta and cheese dish with a sweet red veggie sauce and really excellent garlic-cheese bread. They sipped a nice red wine.

Dessert was a yummy citrus cake. This evening, they chose to engage in an in-depth discussion concerning basic Spacer politics and governing philosophy. Naero had two different holoscreens pulled up with highlights of Spacer political history.

"Since I'm living among Spacers," Tarim said, "I always want to understand your people more, and how they function, both as a culture and a society. All of you take every part of your culture and your ways so much for granted. I look at Spacers and their ways, and all I have are more questions."

Naero scooped another bite of cake into her mouth, chewed slowly to savor it, and then swallowed happily.

"Tarim, I'd be happy to answer and discuss any philosophical questions that you might have. Spacers as a people are pretty practical and straight forward. We don't want to waste a lot of our time, or our lives on duplicity, or what my dad always called it–bullshit."

Both of them laughed. "But you don't even seem to have an active political system," Tarim said. "You have a Council of Elders, who serve at the pleasure of the Forty-Nine Spacer Clans–apparently only when they need to. You rarely have elections of any kind."

"The Elders and the Clans only pass new laws when there is a need for them. The legal system we have now is simple, flexible, and fair, and has served us well for over two centuries with occasional modification. Because we have specifically designed it that way, and agree to keep it that way."

"Adorable, N. Why haven't the rest of us thought of that?"

Naero flung up her hands. "That's what we don't understand," she said. "You probably would have by now, if it wasn't for the Corps."

"But I've always been curious, though. Corps or not, all other humans seem to be constantly going at each other. Why do Spacers work together so much better than landers? That's a fact, and it's a huge difference."

Naero grinned, drinking Jett in addition to dessert. She tossed Tarim one. "There's a great deal of variety of experience, attitude, and lifestyle among the Forty-Nine Clans. Somewhere among all of that diversity, people can eventually find a good fit for themselves. And Spacers are very open and understanding about that need for individual freedom, and yet also the overall baseline of stability, which makes such freedom actually possible."

Tarim crossed his arms. "And it also doesn't hurt that you seem to have non-existent crime and very little infighting among yourselves. I admire that, too."

They were suddenly interrupted by a call on Naero's comstation. A minor matter which she dealt with, and then turned back to Tarim.

She put her feet up on her table after the fine meal, leaned back in her flexible gelchair, and stretched her arms and legs in opposite directions, groaning happily. "Tarim, this is how it is with Spacers. From the very beginning of Spacer society, Spacers could not afford to betray one another. They had so many enemies–the odds were so heavily stacked against them as it was–that honor and adherence to one's word became paramount. If you look at our basic history–"

Tarim nodded, pulling back from both of her holoscreens. "I have. To save us some time, I think I have a good idea of the basics. The Forty-Nine Spacers Clans evolved from Spacer families or cultural groups, who all scattered out into space to find freedom. There were many other groups and families at first. Most of them died, but there were survivors. Each of those groups that survived out of the crucible of the past six centuries make up the Forty-Nine Clans."

Tarim stretched and yawned. "Uh, I think I ate too much pasta; fighting a food coma. So, as the foundation of their society, all Spacers agreed to strictly follow a basic code of conduct and laws based upon honor. Honor is paramount to Spacers. I get that."

"Correct," Naero said, "but you have no idea how much that code of honor, and the belief in honor, guides and binds Spacers together in a common cause, fellowship, and a system of conduct and belief. They are required to respect each other–demanded to, really."

"So…what if a Spacer does break this code?"

"In the old days–back on Old Terra among landers–betrayal, crime, and breaches of honor were all too commonplace, and had to be dealt with harshly in space by Spacers–either by ostracization or even execution. Being part of the Clans quickly became the difference in Space between life and death–and life was already harsh and unforgiving. In many ways, ostracization was a far worse fate than a quick death."

Tarim chuckled. "That's why people say that Spacers can be assholes at times, but never criminals?"

"Yes. Exactly. It's quite true. Spacers can still be jerks–it's not illegal to be a jerk–but the criminal element and the criminal impetus was very quickly weeded out among Spacers. The Clans strove to create and sustain a self-governing society, where Spacers worked together for the mutual benefit of the individual, the family, the Clan, and the society as a whole. They all needed each other very badly, and they could not even begin to survive or accomplish anything if their people were constantly trying to screw each other over. The freedom to behave irresponsibly could not be tolerated–if Spacers were to even have a chance to survive."

Tarim shook his head and held up his hands. "You make it sound so simple, and yet no one else ever has been able to do it."

Naero slugged down some more Jett. "In order to establish and maintain these basic concepts of Mutual Benefits and Sustained Existence, everyone—as Clans, and as individuals—had to sit down, discuss, and agree to uphold a certain basic philosophy and a specific code of conduct and honor. It had to be something that everyone could agree to live with…and live by."

Tarim finished chewing his last mouthful of cake. "And those who could not adhere to that code and accept that general philosophy were eventually removed from the general population, in one way or another?"

"Yes. That was vital, Tarim."

"N, I still don't see how Spacers maintain their system. Your people just do it. You trust each individual Spacer to a very high degree. No one else can do so with their people."

"Then answer me this. Is it really so hard to be a decent, honorable person, Tarim? You are a lander, and yet you do the same thing we do–every day. You may feel out of place among us, but I don't see any desire on your part to rob, or rape, or kill, or exploit, or commit crimes. You uphold your own code of honor, just like we do. Maybe we're not all so different; we don't have to be. Joshua Tech. The Miners–by the Powers–even the bloody Matayan Corsairs are seeing the wisdom of our ways. Any lander or sentient of any species can freely choose to do what we do–and it is really not that hard. Honor earned and deserved is honor given–or withheld, when the need is there."

Tarim knitted his fingers together, carefully following her train of thought. "So…the individual has a right to be free within the limits of a reasonably free society, which all people discuss and agree upon. Neither the individual, nor the society, nor the state exist in a vacuum. Personal freedom does not grant any entity license to exploit, enslave, or destroy others for anyone's sole benefit."

Naero clapped. "See? Was that so hard? You're more of a Spacer than you know."

A call came in on Tarim's comunit this time. He stood up quickly. His eyes brightened.

"It's Shalaen. If you'll excuse me, I think I'll take this back in my quarters, N. She sends her warmest greetings."

Naero smiled. "Give her mine, Tarim."

He grinned. "Thanks for dinner, and the continuing education, N. Very interesting."

Naero nodded. "Like I said, Spacers don't have a perfect system by far. But it functions overall, and you are now part of it. Have a great night, my friend."

Tarim left her quarters. Naero turned back to some of her fleet work to attend to. She also pulled up a selection of top, random dumptunes off the galactic net and listened to some hot, new music.

She reminded herself that she had another sword practice with some of her captains, coming up very soon.

17

Naero had another vital epiphany one day, after a certain incident.

The Alliance proceeded along its chains of stepping stones. They jumped on three Triaxian fleets in what appeared to be a lackluster enemy defense of Vaelos-1.

Vaelos-1 was just a minor Triaxian system. Definitely not a big cog in the Triaxian wheel.

Naero was even surprised that they found three fleets there. No attack drones to speak of, and very few cloakedmines.

As soon as they commenced their sudden, surprise attack, something strange happened.

These Triaxians either jumped out of system immediately–in complete and utter panic–or they broke in confusion, tried to surrender, or even fought briefly among themselves.

Naero and the other Alliance captains were stunned.

They brought some of the Triaxian officers and captains together to question them, for intelligence purposes, after the landers had all formally surrendered to the Alliance.

Yet some of these landers were so distraught, they were besides themselves.

One admiral and several captains got on their knees and begged her.

"Please, spare our families down on Vaelos-1!"

"Shoot us, cut our throats, push us out of airlocks like we've heard you spacks do to your captives. But please, for the love of humanity, don't eradicate our populations on our world, the way you did at Heaven-7 and all the others!"

"We hoped that if we surrendered quickly, that you would at least show some of our civilians mercy. Please, please spare them."

Naero and her officers blinked.

For an instant, they did not know what to say.

These terrified men and women were in total earnest. Naero could tell that they actually believed what they were saying, sobbing and blubbering in abject fear. Not for themselves—but for their people.

For what they thought the spacks were going to do to them all.

Naero licked her lips before she spoke.

How could she begin to undo generations of propaganda and brainwashing?

"Admiral, I want you and your officers to hear this and really take it to heart. The Alliance forces are warriors–not murderers. Our mission is to take down Triax Gigacorps and free your worlds, not ravage them. We are liberators. Not conquerors. You got that?"

The admiral and the others stared back at them in shock and disbelief.

Naero went on. "We know that your worlds are deep in the core of Triax, and all that you hear about Spacers and the Alliance is the propaganda and fear mongering that the Corps spin on INS, the Interstellar News Service. But you've been lied to. For centuries."

Shalaen joined them in the conference room at that moment, at Naero's direct request. She had just arrived To visit her father, Admiral Kinmal. She had not even seen Tarim yet. Now she slipped past them all. glowing as she always did with a pale blue light. Her child-like face was beautiful and serene.

And all of them–Spacer and lander, parted for the angel who walked among them.

She placed her small, gentle hands on each of them as she passed, and stirred and calmed them with but a touch.

"Captain Maeris speaks the truth. For generations, the tyrants who have oppressed you and your peoples have taught you to fear and hate without just cause or reason. To fear and hate those who mean you no harm or ill will. Those who would trade and share with you as friends, as your brothers and sisters, if you would only choose to live with them in peace and harmony."

One of the Triaxian officers broke down and wept, visibly shaken.

"It…it can't be true. You've invaded and crushed our fleets, destroyed dozens, hundreds of our worlds. Killed trillions of our helpless people with atomics, poison gas, gene plagues, and bio-weapons. Waves of death drones–just like what you did to Heaven-7!"

Naero caught her breath.

"No matter what you think, or what you have heard, that wasn't us. What happened on Heaven-7? That wasn't the Alliance. That was all Triax's doing, every bit of it." Naero stood side by side with Shalaen.

"And it is Triax who refuses to take Alliance prisoners, and executes our captives, without right, cause, or honor," Naero continued. "Vile practices that we have never shared or followed. Once this war is over, any captives on our side shall be released and sent home, safe and free. While Triax continues to murder our people unjustly each day."

Shalaen attempted to speak once more, over their murmuring and denials.

"And as far as the death and destruction on Triax worlds…" she began.

One enemy officer shook with suppressed rage and fury. "I have seen the vids. How can you stand here and lie, and deny your many atrocities against us? Helpless people. Women and little children. Slaughtered in the streets! Cut down by gleeful spack invaders. Gassed to death. The flesh melted off their bones by spack bioweapons! I have seen the evidence. We all have! Many times over."

Shalaen calmly folded her hands in front of herself.

"You have been grossly deceived and misled by Triaxian propaganda. All of you and your worlds. Such terrible things have indeed been done– but again, not by us. Only by the bloodstained hands of your own rulers. They turn around and blame it all on us, on spacks and the Alliance, as they have always done. It is a plot to smear and demonize us."

The man winced in shock. "But why? Why would they do these things to their own worlds, to their own people?"

Shalaen shook her head. "Captain Maeris, speak true. Does the Alliance use such weapons and tactics against civilian populations?"

Naero stiffened at the mere suggestion.

"Never. They are not even in our arsenal–though we have put a stop to their use, whenever and wherever possible. And we have captured and confiscated *many* such weapons of mass destruction on numerous, liberated Triaxian worlds, where they were set to go off and scorch those worlds with senseless death and destruction in the wake of Triax's cowardly retreat."

The poor, shattered man shook his head in denial. "No. It cannot be true. It must not be true. These things come from you, our enemies. I can't believe it."

Naero pulled up holos in the very air around them and on the conference room viewscreens. She displayed numerous lethal and deadly weapons and devices.

"Look at all of those production markings. Look closely; Triax does not even bother to hide the evidence. It is easier for them to merely deny the truth, or silence anyone on their own worlds who in any way discover the real truth. These production marking and the materials they are constructed out of are clearly Triaxian. They do not come from the Alliance, because we do not make or use such weapons against civilians, especially against worlds that we seek to liberate. We are not destroyers and killers. How would that serve us?"

Another haughty Triaxian officer stepped up beside his fellow captain.

Naero bristled. She did not like the slightly crazed look in this man's eye.

"Filthy, lying spacks. Kill us and have done with it. And you bring that stinking mindwitch from the miners to try to twist our brains? We know the truth." He waved a trembling finger at the evidence all around them.

What was this guy so nervous about?

"Those vids mean nothing. All of that can be faked. Every bit of it."

"If so," Shalaen said calmly, "then they can also be faked by Triax, by your leaders as well. Let us show you vids that we have tried to broadcast among your worlds. To warn them about Triax. We can show you how Triax Intel twists these vids around, edits them, and uses them as propaganda and lies to demonize us, making us and our forces appear to be murderers and aggressors. Let us show you the proof."

The man continued to shake his head and look jittery. "No. You're lying. All lies, just as they said you would."

Shalaen held out her hands to them. "We are not the liars. Take my hands. Let me prove it to you."

"No. Get away from me. Stinking mindwitch!"

The man drew a hidden plasteel dagger, razor sharp, and plunged it straight down at Shalaen's breast.

Even the Triaxians moved to stop him. Too late.

Shalaen did not blink.

The dagger point halted a breath from her heart.

Buried in Naero's iron-hard left forearm, defending her friend faster than eye could follow.

An instant later, Tarim had a pistol nudged into the man's temple.

They all froze in place.

Tarim's icy voice commanded. "Drop. The knife."

Naero's small, powerful right hand crossed over like a clamp of steel. She kept her eyes locked with the attacker's as she stepped the man back and calmly stripped his fingers away from the hilt of the dagger.

The lander stared and swallowed hard at her fierce, enhanced strength.

Tarim kept his weapon trained while Naero's Marines stepped forward and put the assailant in flexrestraints.

They had every right to shoot the attacker right then and there, to execute him. Nobody would have questioned it.

Naero winced only slightly as she pulled the blade free of her arm and snapped off the blade.

Zhen stepped forward to examine the wound, but there was little bleeding. Spacer smartblood already sealed the injury. Z applied an accelerator to speed up the healing process.

The Triaxian Admiral snarled at the man, "You stupid fool. They were negotiating with us. You've murdered us all!"

Naero smiled, rubbing her arm with a twinge. "As we told you before, we do not kill captives. I will see fit to forgive such an outburst once. *Only once.* All of you have been mislead and deceived by your leaders. You do not know or understand us at all. We are not the bloodthirsty killers you take us for."

She paused and paced slightly with her hands clasped behind her back in her normal fashion.

"How about this. What if I ask you all to accompany us down onto the surface of your world, to search for and neutralize any genocide devices Triax has left behind to delay and trouble us all? Will you then believe?"

The admiral shook his head.

"No, our people have been told to expect the worst. If you invade our world, millions will die–by their own hands."

Naero was curious. "How so?"

"They told us the Alliance forces would ravage our world, raping and pillaging–torturing and killing us. Our population is in a frenzy. The government distributed poisons and suicide devices to every household, to take or blow themselves up with. If your ships begin to land, our people will panic and start using them. Many will die before you can stop them."

Naero rubbed her face. This was an all-new low...even for Triax.

"I see," she said. "Then will you go speak to them in our place?"

The enemy admiral did not understand her.

"What?"

"Go back on board your ships, go down to you world, and land in your starports. Explain to your people that we have no wish to harm them. Simply tell them and your planetary government to stand down and offer no resistance."

"You...you would do this...for us?"

Naero nodded. "Yet be warned. Any who so resist will still be put down, swiftly and without mercy. Triax has many zealots and fanatics on every world who will try to sow confusion and discord, even as terrorists. And we have already scanned and located several Triaxian mass-destruction devices. Some we have eliminated from orbit. Others through various means. Still others might present themselves. Will you help us save as many of your people as we can?"

The admiral looked to his captains.

Each of them nodded their assent.

The enemy admiral turned back to Naero and held out his hand.

"Agreed. My name, is Henry. Henry Sandusky."

"Thank you, Henry." She held out her hand. "Naero Maeris."

He started slightly. "The daughter of the two Galactic Champions?"

"I am." Naero shook his hand and smiled as she released it. "Thank you. Return to your ships with our good will, and go down to your people. Send for us when you are ready, and we shall land to meet with your leaders and arrange terms. Your world shall remain free and your own, just no longer a part of Triax. It is that simple. Send for us if you need our assistance in any way."

True to their word, the defenders landed in various starports and cities all over Vaelos-1.

It took a few hours for the word to spread, but at last the arrangements were made for the annexation meeting.

Admiral Sandusky reported that some scattered resistance still remained, as expected. Yet thankfully, there had been very few incidents of panic and suicide among the civilians, and such devices were being collected by many local officials.

The admiral's own people had discovered and neutralized a couple of genocide devices in two locations. One proved to be atomic, the other biological.

All of the devices were clearly Triaxian. There was no doubt now in anyone's mind.

They were suddenly interrupted by a call on the conference room comstation. Naero took the link right away. She recognized the voice.

"Sir, this is Captain Kono Decker of *The Silver Devil.* We're on patrol, and we're detecting some very strange energy signatures and multiple shielding echoes at our extreme sensor range. It's possible we've finally detected those twenty missing enemy fleets."

"Great job, Kono. Alert Intel–"

"Already done, sir. But we're the only ones this far out this way, and the signatures are fading rapidly. Do we pursue, or let them slip away again?"

"I'll leave that up to you, Kono. I don't want you and your people out there all alone, chasing twenty enemy fleets."

"Sir, I think we can shadow and track them at extreme range for an hour or three, until the other fleets converge. My people and I would like to stay on them and give it a shot."

"Very well. Permission granted. Keep us informed. And if any enemy forces head your way, I want you guys jumping out, pronto."

"Copy that, sir. We'll be careful. Hey, I've got a new move I wanna show you at our next sparring match. I learned it off the fight circuit."

"I wanna see it, Kono."

"You will, sir. Kono out."

The very next moment, fresh reports poured in from Vaelos-1 about poison gas bombs going off in one city, and civilians dropping and convulsing in another.

A blinding explosion down on the planet surface–visible from orbit– erased yet another population center, in a radius of six kilometers.

Now the panic-stricken leaders of Vaelos-1 desperately requested assistance.

Naero gave it without hesitation.

She turned to Shalaen. "Will you come down and help us?"

Shalaen nodded. "Of course. I'll do whatever I can."

"All ships. Rescue, detection, and security teams down to the planet surface. I want deep, detailed scans of the entire planet, and every remaining city, to locate weapons and genocide devices. Coordinate with Intel. Do everything we can to neutralize any enemy agents or Corps terrorists at work."

A priority message came in from Aunt Sleak.

"Naero, bypass Vaelos-1 and return to the line. We're going to need you and Strike Fleet Six back at the front."

"Sorry, Admiral. Say again? I'm in the middle of an important situation here."

"It will have to wait. And don't–"

Naero used the secret comtek Baeven gave her to cut and block the link.

"Say again, sir. Transmission garbled. You're breaking up…"

It was in fact splitting hairs, but technically, Naero did not have to obey orders she never fully received.

18

On the surface of Vaelos-1, Naero, Shalaen, Tarim, Zhen, Tyber, and their rescue teams and Marine unit guards left their ship, entered the starport, and then arrived at the outskirts of the capital city.

They meant to link up with Admiral Sandusky there and coordinate rescue and search and defense efforts with the local authorities.

Naero partially recognized the good-looking Marine leftenant with the brown eyes leading their security detail.

He told them to hold up suddenly. Naero remembered his face; she just couldn't recall his name. What was it?

"We're supposed to meet up with a detail from the admiral a short distance from here," Naero told him.

They both checked the coordinates on their scanners.

"Affirmative, sir," the leftenant said. "Unfortunately, my recon patrol found the admiral's people dead, blasted with grenades and shot to death in the head."

"Terrorists? Triaxian zealots?"

"Most likely, sir."

"That's not good. I'm sorry. Leftenant...?"

"Hayden. Jeremiah Hayden, Captain Maeris."

"My apologies. I meet so many people. Congrats on your promotions?" She remembered now. From the shore leave shooting matches with Tarim.

"Thank you. I understand, sir. Don't worry. My Marines and I are prepared to keep you and your teams safe. We've already eliminated several enemy agents and threats. Intel forces on the ground are helping us coordinate."

Naero grinned. This man was a pro, she could tell by his bearing, the way he moved and spoke–like a true warlord. One with the authority and surety of a martial king.

"I'm sure you will. What's our plan now?"

Naero received a com from Admiral Sandusky. She took it.

Then she announced. "Admiral Sandusky is sending an armored transport to these coordinates, on a private landing field, less than a klick from here."

She shunted the data to Hayden's comp.

He took a moment to study several possible approaches.

"We can reach it in minutes by a short jump with gravwings," she said.

"Il-advised," Hayden said. "We've neutralized several hi-tek Triaxian snipers. Hevangian professional sharpshooters–assassins with cloakedguns."

"Cloakedguns?" That was something new.

"A very recent threat. The enemy snipers are cloaked. Even their weapons are. They fire cloaked ammunition. No trace signatures, no sound, even after they take a shot. Almost impossible to detect and track. The rounds uncloak just before they hit, and there's no way to trace them back to the shooter. We've encountered poisoned, explosive, armor piercing, and shield negation rounds."

"Sounds formidable. How do we defend against them and their tactics?"

Hayden smiled. "I said they were *almost* untraceable. Intel found a way. They've developed another new technique using Intel microfixers. They can overlay a scanning net across an area, and pick up trace shadows of cloaking fields, ghosts, and reflections. But patterns emerge over time. And all that cloaking sucks up a lot of power."

"The agents have to recharge occasionally," Naero guessed.

Hayden nodded and pulled back slightly from studying their position. "Yes, that's how they found them at first and noticed the patterns. Their presence would flare for a few seconds and then disappear again. You're as smart as you are attractive, Captain Maeris, just as everyone said you are. I continue to be impressed."

Naero grinned and winked. "Aww...I bet you say that to all the pretty girls. Now let's stop flirting, before I blush, and get our people to that landing field."

Hayden nodded. "Copy that. Our best chance is to stay out of the open. We'll take a path through several buildings that will provide us good cover for eighty-one percent of our approach. We'll keep shields down to help avoid being tracked, and use gravwings only as a last resort. Intel and my teams have the area under surveillance and will respond swiftly to any threats."

"Looks good," Naero said. "I see you have several potential escape routes for us. Good spread and positioning of your various fire and support teams. My compliments."

"Good tactical eyes, Captain. You'd make a great Marine. Let's move out. You're with me...you and yours."

They spread out and moved forward, quietly and quickly. They passed through two buildings. A few frightened locals turned pale and scattered and ran whenever the Spacers moved through.

"You know," Naero said, "I trained tactical with the 9th Division when I was fifteen and sixteen, and had to do my two year's service, but I love starships too much. No offense."

All Spacer youths at that age had to complete two years basic military training and service.

"None taken," Hayden said. "Our loss is the Navy's gain. So, you actually trained with the Bloody Niners, huh? That's a hard-ass unit."

Naero smirked. "You ought to try serving under my Aunt Sleak."

Both of them chuckled. "No thanks," Hayden said. "I've heard a few stories about Admiral Maeris."

"I'm sure everyone has. And I can warn you, most of them are true."

"I'll take that under advisement. I didn't read your dossier deep enough to know your were an honorary jarhead, though. Welcome to the club, Captain. Once you're one of us, we don't let you out."

"What's your story, Leftenant?"

Hayden shrugged, "Not much. My family's all Marine. Pretty much anyone old enough to serve."

He made tactical adjustments as they kept moving forward, calling adjustments quietly into his comlink in his helmet.

"Chang, pull on your pants and keep up; your unit's falling behind too much. Sergeant Borelli, move you fire support team and set up on these coordinates. Mark." He punched them in on his arm pad.

They moved through what appeared to be a hovercar parking garage toward a multilevel dwelling center connected to it. Low-cred apartments, with the laundry facilities and rundown gym showing through the glass windows, the lights cut off.

Scans showed the locals hiding still in their cubicle-like dwellings, cowering in the dark.

Naero stopped them from proceeding forward, her warning sense spiking.

"What is it?" Hayden asked.

"Everyone get down!" Naero said.

A hovercar behind them exploded.

Small arms fire erupted from four separate directions.

Shalaen deflected the attacks away from them in an instant.

The vehicle Naero just passed got shredded by automatic fire.

Marines swept in, expertly isolating the four attackers and cutting them down hard and fast in a hail of precise, interlocking fire.

"Sir, Hevangian assassins," Sergeant Archer called out.

Naero drew her auto-blasters and prepared to fire at any target that presented itself.

Another hovercar detonated, this time on their right.

The explosion shattered windows in the apartments nearby. Sirens went off. Landers started screaming.

The Marines kept everyone moving from cover to cover.

Brief firefights all around alerted them that this was a coordinated attack by a significantly sized force.

Naero slipped around a hovercar, crouched low.

She suddenly worried they were being herded in a certain direction.

Hayden grabbed her arm and pulled her off to the right. "This way; they want us to go that way."

He sent a fire team to check it out.

Heavy weapons launched up ahead.

"Rockets. Grenades!" Marines warned, diving for cover.

"This way," Hayden said, leading them into the apartments.

Explosions rocked the parking facility, spinning flaming hovercars in several directions.

"Don't worry," Hayden said, scanning his readouts on his battle monitor in his face shield. "My people will deal with those goons."

They moved through the darkened laundromat for the dwellings. Loads of wash were spinning and drying in a few of the units.

As they moved toward a multi-door hallway, a panel slid open.

All weapons lifted and trained.

A startled lander woman with two little kids and a laundry basket emerged. All of their mouths dropped open, and they turned pale.

The kids froze. The mother gasped and shielded them with her body. She started talking fast.

"Please, please don't shoot us. Take me if you have to, but don't kill my kids!"

The looks on their trembling, shuddering faces. The way they shook. The way those little kids looked at her.

Naero would never forget it.

She sheathed her blasters and held up her hands. "Relax. We mean you no harm. Terrorists are after us. We just want to pass through."

Leftenant Hayden merely lowered his pistols. "We don't shoot kids, ma'am. Personally, I've never shot a kid. None of us have."

The woman clutched her two little ones and closed her eyes, still shaking beyond control.

"You're spacks. The vids say you've come here to murder us all. That we should kill ourselves and our kids before we fall into your hands. They gave us poison pills for the adults to use. Poisoned candy for the little ones. We didn't think you'd be here this soon."

Naero held her tongue.

Triax. So very evil that the depths of their depravity sickened her to her core.

Shalaen came forward, cloaked in deep midnight blue, face veiled, hands gloved. She took down her veil and removed her gloves, placing her hands on the mother and her kids to calm and reassure them with her empathic abilities.

"Don't listen to any of those lies," Naero said. "Tell your people not to hurt themselves or their kids. You should be hearing some new broadcasts from your officials very soon."

The poor woman shook her head. "I could never do it anyway. But some people have. They killed themselves in their rooms…out of fear."

Hayden checked his scans and suddenly spoke with grave urgency. "Captain, we have serious unfriendlies. Inbound."

To the mother, he said, "Ma'am. Is there another way out of this complex, to the north?"

The woman looked confused. "Which way is north?"

Naero and Hayden pointed directly behind her.

"On the third floor, there's a hallway that leads to the sweatshops in the building next to us. But with the war, they're all closed. You won't be able to get through the locked doors."

Naero smiled. "Can you take us there, please?"

"We brought keys," Hayden said, also grinning.

On the way, the little girl, about six, stared up at Naero as they walked quickly, her eyes as big as viewports. The mother carried the little boy of perhaps four in her arms; he looked sleepy.

"We ran out of food yesterday," the girl said plainly. "My brother and I are hungry."

Naero yanked out two thick meal bars in foil wrappers from a pouch. The girl's eyes went even bigger. She ran up and handed her brother one that she peeled open for him. The little boy came alive and lunged for it over his mother's shoulder.

After two chomps, his mouth cheeks were stuffed full as he chewed.

He broke off another chunk and popped it into his mom's mouth. "Here momma, it's yummy."

The little girl tore hers open with her teeth and wolfed it down.

When they reached the sweatshop doors, Naero sped forward and drew one of her glowing blue, energized battle blades.

She sliced off the metal chains and thrust the doors open with a swingkick.

Hayden came up with a supply bag full of various ration bars, hurriedly gleaned from the Marines and Naero's people.

"Thank you, ma'am. Share this food with your neighbors. I've thrown in a few Corps credbands. Not much, but enough to buy your people some food on the black markets over the next few weeks. Thanks again, and good luck."

The woman took the bag and her mouth fell open. Her kids waved, still eating.

"Get back to your home and stay there with your kids," Naero warned her. "If the fighting gets bad, get down to the basement or shelter if you have one."

She caught up to Hayden and they led their group through the darkened sweatshop. All the machinery would help conceal them from scans.

Then explosions rocked the city square. Hover vehicles landed, and fighters battled it out in the skies above.

Naero and Hayden took a peek out of one of the filthy sweatshop windows.

Five heavy Triaxian gravtanks with clear Hevangian markings brazenly filled the square, cannons and weapons pointed all around them.

Four hovering gunships marked just like them covered the gravtanks from above.

Each of the tanks had a genocide device mounted on it.

Hayden scanned them before Naero could.

"This is bad. Two biological, one nerve gas, and two atomics. Everyone seal up!"

Everyone sealed their smartsuits or various battle armors.

"They can level this city with just one of those devices," Naero said. "Kill everyone in it."

"That includes us," Hayden noted. "Intel is sending microfixers in to attempt to neutralize those devices. We need to buy them some time. About five, ten minutes."

Naero frowned. "That's a lot of time in a fight."

"Let's see what they want. I think we're going to see some kind of demands. Someone's coming out."

One of the gravtanks opened up. A female Hevangian Field Marshal emerged, in black and scarlet tanker armor. Short golden hair and a badly scarred porcelain face that might have been beautiful once.

Hevangians were extremely militaristic, and wore their worst scars like badges of status, honor, and virility.

A loudspeaker broadcasted her message.

"I am Field Marshall Constance Dreth. No on has to die here today. We want the invading spacks to surrender. In particular, we insist that Strike Captain Naero Amashin Maeris surrender herself instantly, along with the mindwitch, Shalaen. Come forward, hands up, no weapons–or we shall commence our attack to level this city."

Half a standard minute passed.

"Very well then. All units, commence attack! The slaughter will cease when the Alliance fools surrender, or join the dead."

Marine sniper fire impacted the enemy's dense shields.

Field Marshal Dreth ignored the attacks.

The two atomic genocide devices lit up and hummed ominously.

The other tanks began moving, spraying the nerve and bio-agents into the neighboring buildings to the far side, blasting death through the windows and vents.

Stricken civilians poured into the streets, trying in vain to get away. They flung themselves out of the windows and off rooftops.

The Hevangians leveled the nozzle jets right at the fleeing masses, engulfing as many as they could.

Those stricken by the nerve agents gasped and collapsed, convulsing on the ground and clawing at their faces and heads.

The bio-agents were even more horrible. Victims bled out of their pores and every orifice, until their very flesh dissolved off their bones.

Shalaen stepped forward, lifting her hands, her eyes blazing. "I must stop to this madness."

The nerve agent and bio-agent genocide devices imploded on the backs of the tanks and then blazed with fire, consuming them entirely.

Shalaen placed a containment field around the two infected areas.

All within those areas except the enemy were already dead, so Shalaen immolated everything within them, including the two advancing tanks and their crews. They vanished in a vortex of fire.

Leftenant Hayden gave one command. "All units. Take 'em!"

"Gladly!" Naero snarled.

She drew her biggest bombs and crashed through the third floor window, spiraling down at the enemy with her gravwing.

19

Concentrated Spacer Marine fire from heavy weapons units chewed through the shielding on the enemy gravtanks and gunships. The Hevangians battled back with heavy fire of their own, devastating the civilian buildings, with no concern for civilian casualties.

The nerve gas and bio-weapon tanks within Shalaen's containment zones continued to cook off, their roasting crews dead.

Field Marshal Dreth stood by calmly, maneuvering and firing back in her gravtank, still shielded.

Marine fire had not still not penetrated her stubborn defenses.

No one used explosives or heavy weapons, for fear of setting off the atomics.

The enemy commander's face remained placid as she pressed detonators to do just that.

She looked both concerned and angered when nothing happened.

One atomic device shut down and lost all power completely.

The other seemed activated, but frozen somehow.

Naero spotted Shalaen floating in the air, both hands extended toward the device. Her other field collapsed. She looked like she was straining.

"Get the bomb away from here," she shouted. "I can only hold back the blast from activating for so long!"

Two enemy gunships focused their guns right at them.

Shalaen shielded them from that as well, heavy fire impacting her protective fields.

Marine pilots and a Spacer Ghost Dragon slipped in fast to cut the enemy gunships down out of the air, sending them crashing and burning onto the streets below.

Naero attacked the other gravtank with the active atomic device that Shalaen had frozen.

Hayden joined her, along with a full squad.

They penetrated the shields. Hayden and the Marines placed plasma-cutting charges to rip the tank turret open like a can of Spum.

When the turret burst open, Naero jumped in to cut the tank crew down.

They tried to draw blaster pistols, but she was too fast.

Hayden flung the dead tank commander out of the way and jumped in at the controls.

He set them to carry the genocide device straight up, and then leaped out.

Shalaen, Tarim, and several others went after it with their gravwings as it rose, trying to get it as far away from the city as possible.

Field Marshal Dreth dumped her inert atomic device, spun about, and shot it twice with her tank cannons, trying to set it off.

Nothing. Intel's microfixers had done their work well.

Dreth turned at bay as Naero, Hayden, and his Marines closed in on her for the kill.

Enemy agents in full battle dress charged out of the buildings behind the last gravtank and shot forward.

Naero and Hayden's Marines intercepted them halfway, and the firefight was on.

Hi-tek weapons from both sides barked and punched at close range. Warriors dropped or were flung back, dead and torn apart.

Captain Hayden drew both of his microgrenade pistols and fired a sheet of exploding fire into the enemy's surging ranks.

The microfusion blasts vaporized the foes right in their armor. Their armored legs were all that remained, and flopped over to either side.

Two Marines in gravwings tried to set more plasma charges on the final gravtank.

114

Dreth came at them and beheaded one with an energized short sword.

She sprayed the other Marine with what appeared to be some kind of gellied flame gun mounted on her forearm.

Naero saw her opening and charged in, two battle blades arcing and crackling.

Dreth smiled, drawing a long energy dagger to go with her short sword.

On top of the gravtank, they dueled.

Foes still inside the tank shot up at Naero with blaster pistols.

These shots barely deflected off her shields.

But shields could not stop blades.

Naero popped in a few microgrenades behind her, and pulled the knife battle down onto the back of the gravtank.

The enemy crew inside popped out of hatches to escape and fire at her again.

Hayden and his Marines shot their heads off.

A second later, Naero's microbombs cooked off.

Field Marshal Dreth fought well, her speed and strength enhanced somehow for a lander–speed drugs, most likely.

Skilled blades flashed and sparked when they clashed.

Dreth cut Naero down one arm, slashed her shoulder, and jabbed her in the right hip.

But Naero ignored her minor wounds and gauged her opponent's skill and fighting style within a moment.

She dazed the field marshall with a wavekick, then slipped under Dreth's defenses.

Naero's iron-hard hand rammed a long, blazing blue battle blade up through Dreth's upper breast, neck, and out the top of her helmet.

Dreth's eyes and mouth gulped and froze wide open in startled shock.

Naero's glowing blue energy blade lit up and sizzled the flesh in her enemy's mouth and skull.

She withdrew her blade and stepped away. Field Marshal Dreth crumpled down dead, rolling off the back of the shattered tank, to bleed in a widening dark pool on the dirty street.

Former Triaxian warships surrounded the city square, secondary batteries in ground assault mode, cutting any remaining terrorists down. They were clearly working in full support of the Marines.

Admiral Sandusky blared down to them over their link and via loud speakers.

"Are you all right, Captain Maeris? When you didn't reach the transport, we heard fighting with terrorists erupted and came to help."

Naero smiled. Better late than never.

"We're fine, Admiral," she called back.

Things could have gone much worse.

Just then, the atomic genocide device went off in a blinding flash, high up in the atmosphere.

20

Admiral Sleak Maeris was more furious than usual after the events leading up to and after the various incidents concerning Vaelos-1.

When Naero returned to *The Hippolyta*, Mike Marshall, the captain of *The Condor* and her fleet Second, promptly placed her under arrest and in restraints, backed up by a full squad of Marines.

Mike's face was grim. "Sorry, N. Admiral Maeris's strict orders." That's all he would say.

All of this was just temporary, Naero hoped.

Leftenant Hayden and his Marines were ordered to help escort her immediately to the conference room on board *The Pearl Harbor*.

An informal tribunal of Aunt Sleak, Nathan Joshua, and Nevano Kinmal, also with grim faces, awaited her there on a panel set high above Naero and her escorts.

At least Naero hoped this was an informal tribunal–with three Alliance admirals.

The trio conferred with each other, apparently on the rapidly evolving situation on Vaelos-1.

Admiral Nathan Joshua, of Joshua Tech spoke to her first. "Captain Maeris. We are pleased that you could take time out of your busy schedule to join us."

Okay, start with a joke, maybe; perhaps things weren't so bad.

Naero gestured with her flex cuffs. "Me too, sir."

All three heads snapped up. Faces harsh and set.

Very well. No jokes, then. Haisha…tough crowd.

Shalaen's father spoke next. He knitted his fingers slowly in front of himself and smiled, speaking calmly. But his eyes looked right through her.

"Captain, we realize that there is a maturity gap at work here, what with you still being under your coming of age and all. Perhaps you were given a fleet command too soon, despite your clear strategic and tactical gifts. We want to take this moment to impress upon you the seriousness of these matters and our concerns."

Naero opened her mouth to speak in her defense.

Aunt Sleak shot to her feet, and splintered the nanotable with one fist where she struck it. The other two admirals couldn't help flinching.

"What in the bloody, flaming hell were you thinking, Naero? Here we were, driving hard on Helapine-3, major battles on fire across the entire front. And like some idiot, you disappear off the grid and run away to nearly get yourself and Admiral Kinmal's daughter killed–or captured–by enemy terrorists, on some nameless rock?"

Don't scream, don't yell back. Keep your temper. Breathe.

Naero lowered her chin on to her chest and focused on the floor.

"Admirals Maeris, Joshua, and Kinmal. My deepest apologies. There were vital reasons that I acted as I did. Not excuses–but there were good reasons. I'm sorry–"

Admiral Sleak shattered another section of the table, causing the other two admirals to jump yet again.

"You're damn right you're sorry! We need every fleet. Every ship. Not only are we hamstrung by dealing with all of the defectors and smugglers–riddled with terrorists and enemy agents–just itching to cause havoc in our rear areas. But every time we even try to approach Helapine-3, we get heavily ambushed by major enemy support from Kysarra-5, just waiting to crawl up our backsides and shoot the hell out of us!"

Leftenant Hayden tried to speak up in Naero's defense.

"Admirals–forgive me, but you may not have been informed yet–Captain Maeris and Commander Kinmal have worked out an important new sweeping agreement with the defectors that they think will–"

Aunt Sleak shot Hayden a withering glance that shut him up in his jump boots.

"Enough, Marine. You do not have permission to speak here. Captain Maeris doesn't require your help in these matters. We are well aware of the proposed agreement and its future...possibilities and ramifications."

"Nevertheless," Nathan Joshua said, calmly folding his arms in front of himself. "Direct orders and the chain-of-command must be upheld and respected–by all. No exceptions. Do you fully understand the gravity of that, Captain Maeris?"

Naero bowed her head again, as contritely as she could manage. "I do, sir."

Shut up. Very important not to say anything more.

No explanations.

No excuses.

"By rights and fleet regs," Admiral Kinmal added, "You should be stripped of your command and face a full court martial."

Naero nodded. She squared her stance and lifted her head high. "I take full and sole responsibility for my egregious actions. I respectfully request that none of this should reflect upon or impact any of my junior officers, or the other ship captains under my command, in any way. I accept the decisions of my superiors, and will comply with any punishments."

Aunt Sleak studied her intently.

Tense seconds passed.

"You're still not as good an actress as you mother, but I suppose your little act is sufficient. Naero, the worst punishment we can devise is to keep you fighting for us on the front lines. Stuffing you in a cell somewhere to sulk out this war would only help our enemies."

Admiral Joshua smiled slightly. "Even at your age, you have few equals in battle, Captain. But you still have much to learn about obeying orders and being a true leader. Everything isn't fighting. That's the key. We want you to fully grasp and understand that."

"Fight the enemy, not us," Admiral Kinmal advised.

Naero bowed her head again. "Again, my apologies, admirals. I will strive to do better in the future."

Her aunt struck the splintered nanotable a third and final time.

Sleak's compatriots still flinched.

"You're damn right you will. Sparring match. Mandatory. Just you and me. Tomorrow morning, five bells!"

Naero knew what that meant.

Good. She might endure a beating, but she was getting better on her own, too, from constant practice with all the new fighters in her fleet.

She had a few tricks planned for her aunt.

Shalaen and many of Naero's other friends and officers from her fleet suddenly burst into the conference room, with Zalvano trying to hold them back.

"Father!" Shalaen insisted. "Before you and the other admirals pass judgment on Captain Maeris, you must hear us out!"

Kinmal held up his hands. "You are too late, my daughter. You are all too late. Sentence has been passed. Captain Maeris has been severely reprimanded and punished. But your show of loyalty is…still moving. Fortunately, for all of us, Captain Maeris will be serving her punishment while she is still on duty, and still acting as your fleet captain."

Admiral Maeris spoke plainly. "She fully understands now that any further acts of insubordination will be dealt with…swiftly, and severely."

"Permission to speak," Naero said.

Aunt Sleak nodded. "Granted."

Naero held her arms out wide. "Admirals, as long as we have everyone gathered together here already, can we please discuss the secret agreement that we now have with Admiral Sandusky? This is an urgent matter that I think can help us greatly in the future."

All of three admirals leaned forward eagerly, having read the initial reports.

"Very well. Proceed," Nathan Joshua said.

"Sandusky claims—with evidence—to be in direct contact, through back channels, with a secret network of thousands of Triaxian ship captains and officers, who see the inevitable outcome. Triax will fall. And they see no reason why they and their crews should perish, simply to delay that outcome for a few bloody weeks or months."

Even Aunt Sleak nodded. "Sounds reasonable. More defections mean fewer ships for us to chew through. Initial responses from Admiral Klyne and Spacer Intel say that they would be willing to discuss these matters further and assist in any way that we can."

"Good," Naero said. "Because that's exactly what they and we are going to need. Help with making sure the Triaxian defectors aren't blown up when they make their defection runs. Coordination with their homeworlds, so that we infiltrate, capture, and pacify those worlds beforehand, and help make sure that the zealots don't punish and murder their populations with genocide devices and mass destruction."

Nevano Kinmal shook his head.

"After Heaven-7, we all know what Triax is capable of," he said. "But we still cannot guarantee that any of that will not repeat itself in the future. Triax is controlling these genocide devices and their use, not us."

Naero jumped in. "But we can still do all that is possible to prevent as much death and destruction that can be avoided, for the good of all."

"One major problem with that. It can't work," Aunt Sleak said, looking down at her data pad and shaking her head.

Everyone stared at her.

Sleak looked up at them. "Look at the raw math–the logistics. We'd need so many ships, crews, Intel agents, boots on the ground. Hundreds of liberated worlds to pacify and cleanse already. Hundreds more coming online. Billions, trillions to protect. To accomplish all that would bring the war to a whimpering halt, and that cannot be. Above all else, Triax must fall."

Shalaen glanced at Naero.

They held hands for a moment, looked into each other's eyes, and then nodded to one another.

"There is still another way," Naero said.

"Impossible," Admiral Joshua said. "Admiral Sleak is correct. You would need another force–almost the size of the Alliance itself. There is no such force in existence."

Naero placed her hands on her hips.

"Wrong. There is such a force. We already control hundreds of billions–trillions of Triaxian prisoners and populations. And tens of thousands of captured Corps fleet ships, military and private. Even among the Alliance, we can't train crews fast enough to refit and re-launch those ships in time to be used for the war effort. So why not let the defection teams use them as is? They'll work just fine for that."

"What are you saying?" Nevano Kinmal asked.

"Recruit the Triaxian naval prisoners. Put Admiral Sandusky and his network in charge of the defection process, on a scale we could never hope to organize. Let the peoples of these liberated worlds pursue the zealots and terrorists directly harming them–as only truly free people can."

Aunt Sleak nodded, staring down at her shifting calculations again, adding the new parameters. "That...could work. But there will be infiltrators, turncoats."

Naero held up her hands. "Then they will be put down, with extreme prejudice. What do we have to lose? No system or effort is going to be perfect during wartime. Yet this will still save many more lives than if we do nothing, and simply prosecute the war to its end. And this way, the liberated worlds will taste their own freedom and responsibility for the first time, and join the Alliance in these ways, protecting their own worlds and populations against what they see now as their true enemies."

The three admirals conferred and came to a quick agreement.

"We will need to discuss these matters in great detail with Admiral Sandusky and Spacer Intel," Aunt Sleak noted.

Very grudgingly, her aunt added briefly, "Good work, Captain. This has the potential to be a major breakthrough that we weren't even looking for.

Naero smiled and let out a great sigh.

"Of course," she said. "Thank you, sir." Naero saluted.

And she meant it.

21

Once she regained her command, Naero learned that *The Silver Devil* had somehow gone missing during its pursuit of the enemy phantom fleets.

It happened, unfortunately, during the events on the surface of Vaelos-1 and thereafter.

Naero and Strike Fleet Six went immediately to join the wide search to help track and locate the lost vessel, scanning near its last reported positions.

The Silver Devil was a three-thousand-ton light missile frigate, with a crew of 130, led by Captain Kono Decker. Their crew also included a Spacer Marine rifle platoon of forty-eight Marines from the 3rd Division Death Eyes, commanded by Second Leftenant Mickey Flynn, and Staff Sergeant Kaely Chang. Naero knew them all well.

The longer the search went on, the more Naero grew worried about what they would find, if anything.

In any interstellar naval war, the distances were so vast. A small ship on extended patrol could get separated, ambushed, and destroyed by larger enemy elements before any help could reach them. It could happen by nothing but unhappy chance.

Yet it continued to be strange that no distress calls reporting any initial trouble had come from *The Silver Devil*. Just her last auto-reported position…and then, nothing.

In most cases like this, there was at least something to go on.

Enemy jamming during such an attack was possible, but warships did not normally vanish without a trace. Even if they were blasted to pieces, there would be wreckage or debris left behind that would show up on scans.

On the second day of the search, they finally located her.

The Silver Devil floated lifeless and without power in an asteroid field. That was why they couldn't find the ship until they got close enough.

Naero guessed the ship had been attacked and then dumped there to hide it.

Towships ventured into the asteroid field and brought the lost ship out.

Everyone understood at this point that nobody on that ship was left alive. Scans showed many bodies, but no survivors. This was a recovery.

Naero insisted on joining one of the investigation teams, once it was determined that there were no enemy booby-traps or demolitions awaiting the investigators–ready to detonate.

Tarim insisted on accompanying Naero, her regular guards, and her recovery team.

Leftenant Hayden had led the initial boarding and inspection team, after several full scans of the wreck. On closer inspection, *The Silver Devil* was found to be riddled with holes that could be clearly seen on visuals, more than twenty in all, at key breach points around the hull.

Yet the scans also revealed that none of these breaches in the hull were from enemy cannon fire. There had been no naval battle.

All these holes were clearly from boarding tubes and boarding insertion craft.

Even on the largest warships, most boarding attempts by the enemy occurred during the heat of battle, when crews were naturally kept busy by their duties and actions during a fight. But even then, the boarding access points were no more than ten or twelve at a time.

Each enemy boarding party could be from twelve to two dozen heavily armed attackers. Even if they couldn't take over a ship, they would obviously do whatever they could to damage and disable it as much as possible–before the intruders were cut down or captured.

Several times, Naero's ships had suffered heavy damage from such enemy boarding and sabotage teams, right in the midst of important battles. It continued to be a major concern.

"What do we have here, Jeremiah?" she asked over their link, on the way over with her people. "What happened to Kono and her crew?"

"Captain, the on board vid feeds have been destroyed, but it looks like they put up one hell of a fight. They were boarded–apparently by surprise–and eventually overwhelmed."

"How many attackers?"

"I'm estimating nearly four hundred. Join me on the bridge for the walk-through. That's where the attack started. Be prepared, Cap. This isn't pretty; not at all."

Naero pursed her lips and gritted her teeth. Poor Kono and her brave crew. None of their family and friends knew that they were all gone yet.

More Marines stood by, preparing pods of body bags for the recovery once the investigation was complete. Teks and their fixers already scurried about, under close guard, trying to get the vessel up and operating again. They'd tow it if they had to.

Hayden and the rest saluted Naero as she joined them on the bridge.

She saw Spacer dead everywhere, in bunches and ones or twos.

She saluted in return. "Leftenant, proceed with the walk-through. I trust your expertise in these matters. Tell me how you think it went down."

"The attack began here on the bridge. Captain Decker and seven of her crew were completely surprised and quickly dispatched. They were killed right at their stations. It's hard to tell that now, because the bodies have been floating around."

She spotted the eight bodies–one of them Kono. More Spacer dead floated just inside the bulkhead blast doors leading into the bridge, and even more bodies down the corridor leading away.

"How were the captain and the bridge personnel killed so quickly, Leftenant?"

Hayden held up a clear evidence pouch.

Naero recognized the bloody contents–the infamous shape of a long, broken, metal battle blade. She knew that pattern very well.

"We took this out of the captain's back. She was stabbed repeatedly, and the blade broke off at the hilt most likely. Do you recognize this style of–"

Naero cut him off. "I know my signature blades, Jeremiah. It is a ritual *shokkog*–the infamous calling card of the Hevangian Imperial Assassins of Triax Gigacorps. I'm guessing these blades were highly poisoned, too?"

"Indeed," he said. "A cocktail of lethal, synthetic poisons–powerful enough to kill a whale. Even our Spacer metabolism couldn't handle anything this toxic. The other seven bridge crew were knifed or cut down by them as well. All it had to do was enter their system. Even just a cut."

"I get it. Continue," Naero said.

Hayden led her out the bulkhead. "The rest of the bridge crew raised the alarm and fought their way off the bridge. Now it turned into more of a gun battle, and people fell on both sides. There was still gravity working on board, so you can still make out the bloodstains on the nanofloors and walls. Scans reveal which bloodstains were from Spacer crew–by name– and which were from the enemy invaders."

Hayden sighed briefly and went on. "More combatants on both sides perished at the bridge entrance, and made a brief stand in the corridor, waiting for help to arrive. Even more fell here during the course of the intense fight that progressed."

Leftenant Hayden led them back through the vessel, explaining how the battle progressed throughout the ship. "I can only think that the enemy must have jammed the ship, keeping anyone from getting off a distress call. But all ship's logs and coms have been destroyed. From what we can tell, the crew rallied and armed themselves, and made their way toward the forward areas of the ship to deal with the attackers. From the numerous blast impacts, the enemy held them off with grenades and explosives."

He pointed to the first access points of the enemy boarding teams. "Once the crew surged forward, the enemy gained further access to the ship from these many, undefended rear areas, in multiple locations, at well-chosen points. The foe had excellent timing. They then flooded the ship with more attackers–killed personnel wherever they were found, captured key areas, and then surrounded the remaining crew on the remaining decks, and swarmed on them to cut them down with heavy weapons and grenades."

Naero studied the schematics of the ship, and where they found the largest piles of bodies. It looked like Hayden had it about right.

She saw where Marine Second Leftenant Mickey Flynn had gone down with one of the crew's last stands, defending the access points to decks three, four, and five.

Jeremiah pointed out a failed push by Staff Sergeant Kaely Chang– and about forty Marines and crew–who nearly reached the power core with fusion charges, in a last-ditch attempt to blow up the ship.

"For what it's worth," Hayden added, "the enemy took their dead and wounded with them–and there were a lot of them, by all of the blood spots left behind on the nanofloors. Bioscans tabulated–like I estimated–nearly 400 enemy KIA or seriously wounded."

Naero sighed deeply. "Kono and her crew took the enemy down more than two to one. But in the end, all of our people still died–cut off and without help. This cannot be allowed to happen. Whatever we need to do to prevent and avoid this, we need to do it. All long range patrols will be in pairs from now on, and they must keep a few fighters deployed around them at all times."

"Captain," Tarim protested, "that will spread the fleet too thin, and pull our long range patrols further back. More Alliance ships will be required to patrol the same areas. You're talking a logistics nightmare. The admirals will never buy it."

Naero snarled and looked around her. "Then I'll sell it to them, as hard as I have to. I'm not losing any more ships like this. *Haisha!* Damn it all."

She leaned against the hull and took a few deep breaths.

"I'm sorry, sir," Leftenant Hayden said, his voice low. "Do we have your permission to begin the recovery phase?"

Naero shook her head. "Yeah. Go ahead. Have the teams collect our people, and prepare them for wakes and burial. Have the teks keep working on refitting the ship enough for us to bring her in."

She stopped for moment.

"Jeremiah," she said. "One thing still bothers me."

"What's that, sir?"

"I believe, just as you said, that the attack began on the bridge, and then from the other boarding points, once the crew charged forward to retake the bridge. But that still doesn't make any sense. How did they penetrate the bridge to begin with? None of those twenty access points were anywhere near the bridge."

Hayden shook his head, too. "That's the mystery part, sir. I can't figure it out either but that's how it went down."

"Kono and her people were dead before they knew it," Naero said. "How in the hell did the initial, enemy assault forces get on the bridge, and surprise Kono and her people so completely? It's as if they came through the blast doors and the hull–and fell upon the crew like ghosts or something. It doesn't make any sense."

"It does not. The enemy doesn't have teams of psionic users who can phaze through walls."

Naero snorted. "I've met a few Spacers who can phaze through solid objects. It takes a lot of concentration, and usually they have to be naked.

They can only do so slowly, and it's very risky and even potentially lethal–especially if the user gets stuck in a solid object."

"Perhaps more information will come out, sir."

"I hope so, Jeremiah. We don't need any more mysteries like this one."

22

Naero held another sword practice days later, designed especially for the ship captains of Strike Fleet Six–this time focused on the use of the energy cutlass.

They met in one of the sword rooms: specially designed practice areas established on board *The Hippolyta* and other vessels, filled with various types of swords, from thousands of worlds, cultures, and historical periods. Naero even had Ty pweak special fixers that could manufacture any type of custom sword or practice weapon.

By now, she and Ima had also helped modify their special practice rooms for knife fighting along similar lines. So many Spacers prided themselves on their skills with various blades that the captains expanded the program throughout the entire fleet.

With some bladefighters such as Naero and Ima, blade skills bordered on being an obsession. They had been raised by their families to master such weapons, on the level of an art form.

But the energy cutlass was widely recognized as one of the badges of a Spacer ship captain.

It was not merely a gilded accessory, but a deadly weapon in its own right. And it took long years of practice and training to achieve and maintain one's skill level with it.

At least thrice each week, when possible, Naero made time for her people to train with the energy cutlass—and other swords—if they were so inclined.

Her ship captains saw it as a chance to blow off some steam with her on a personal basis.

And several of them—being as competitive as Spacers naturally were—strove to best her, at something at least.

A few had come close, thus far—but Naero had not lost a sword match yet.

Naero set that bar high and defended it, as usual, with all of her exceptional ability and skill. If she lost a match one day, she lost. But she would make the victor earn such a victory.

Yet today, all the chatter was about the new ship captain arriving with one of the replacement ships. A new advanced battleship, *The Strongheart*.

But it was the new captain of *The Strongheart* that had everyone talking, whispering, and buzzing.

And these weren't just rumors any longer. He was actually here.

Max Lii—the famous Spacer throckstar was in fact joining Naero's strike fleet that very day—the vibrant young hunk whose dreamy, powerful music and catchy lyrics pounded the music streams as many ships shot into battle.

He was especially popular with young female fighter pilots, who all but swooned for him.

Max had a thing for female fighter jocks, and openly dated several top starfighter pilot aces, who also happened to be incredibly hot themselves.

Other than her parents in years past, Naero had never spent much time around a real celebrity before.

This could prove to be interesting.

Captain Max had already promised that he and his various bands would help entertain the crew on shore leaves. Like many others, Naero enjoyed several of his hit songs and had many in her personal mixes. They were heady, romantic, even wild and heart pounding. Max was clearly a superb entertainer. But he was also a Spacer.

He had insisted on being assigned to Naero's strike fleet.

Aunt Sleak insisted that despite his fame as an entertainer, Max was an excellent leader and pilot, and a fine warrior.

He'd better be–if he was going to command one of Naero's newest heavy battleships, *The Strongheart.* That ship was the permanent replacement for the loss of *The Wombat.*

Max could show up at any time for his first sword practice.

Naero dueled with captains as they came and went, but everyone seemed to be hanging around that day, hoping to meet their new fleet celeb.

She crossed swords with rugged Mike Marshall, her fleet Second in command of their lead carrier, *The Condor.*

Mike was tall, lanky, strong and quick–one of the seven who kept coming close. But everything with him was overpowering full-on, frontal assaults with nothing held back. Daunting and formidable, but Naero still used several clever tricks to slip around his predictable attacks and defeat him.

As with knife-fighting practice, of course they did not use real energy cutlasses. In routine practice and for technique training, they used flex swords that simply bent.

Yet for actual sparring matches, they used holo sword blades with flex filament shock markers.

A holo blade could appear to penetrate a body if enough force went behind a hit. And the shocking filaments would hit a person with an appropriate, painful shock charge, and leave behind a bright, programmable fluorescent stain, showing exactly where a hit occurred.

Match AIs tracked hits and would call out serious wounds or outright kills. All of this resulted in a realistic but non-lethal form of sword fighting that was as real as sword practice could get.

Naero spun to the side and ran Mike Marshall through from armpit to armpit. He gnashed his teeth as the shock charge hit him.

"Instant kill," the match AI announced.

Naero patted him on the should. "Better luck next time, Mikey."

Peni Kim, of *The Black Mosquito*, jumped at the chance to get her licks in next.

"Get ready for a fight today, N. I'm in top form and I'm coming straight at you."

"Then bring it, gal. Let's see what you've got!"

Peni leaped in and the fight heated up, intense and flashing from the very outset.

Another of the seven, Peni was small and fast, like Naero. Her skin was light brown chocolate, her long, shining black hair divided to either side of her like dark ropes in hair clasps.

Her hair glittered like her large black eyes. Her wide, expressive mouth snarled like that of a lioness. She was a skinny little fireball, built like a teen girl, but with a ferocity ten times her size–unlike anyone Naero had ever fought.

They clashed and spun, and whirled and kicked.

Today might just be the day.

No one was on top forever.

Then a commotion erupted behind their match.

People began to shout and scream.

"He's here. Max Lii is here!"

"There he is!"

"Haisha, he's gorgeous!"

Music erupted, loud and throbbing.

Peni Kim couldn't help sneaking a glance that way.

Right as Naero cut her down.

"Instant kill," the AI announced.

They said Max made music everywhere he went.

He hammered out one of his hottest tunes on his holo-spolymered kitar–the one shimmering with blue holo flames. His expert hands and fingers blasted out notes from the heavy triple strings, in a flaring rendition of "To the Stars!"

He was in fact a hot, dreamy mug. Naero had to give him that much. She could see what all the excitement was about; pictures and vids didn't do Max justice. His perfect, wild plume of black hair, dark looks, and killer, cobalt-blue eyes. A tall, lanky, athletic form. That low, sultry voice of his that could roar, croon, or whisper–like hot velvet.

It was instantly clear that Max Lii would never spend a night alone–if he didn't want to.

Everybody swarmed around him like a bunch of teens.

The women, and even a few guys, stared at him like they wanted to eat him for breakfast, lunch, and dinner–right then and there.

Max's aura and his personal magnetism were that potent.

"Hey, everybody. I'm Captain Max Lii. Happy to be here. I told them to send me and my ship to the top unit they had. My people and I are ready to join you, and give our enemy hell, and we can have some fun along the way, too. I'm very proud to be here with you all."

Everyone clapped and cheered, and then made way to introduce him to Naero, their fleet captain.

Naero grinned and decided to take the direct approach.

Even though he was much taller than her...

Haisha! Almost everyone was taller than her, but she never let that slow her down.

Naero stalked right up to Max.

She grabbed him by the front of his pistol and sword belt, and yanked him in right up against her.

Max actually paled slightly and dropped his kitar.

Someone caught it.

Naero flashed her own big, violet search lights right up into his eyes. "Welcome aboard...Captain Lii."

She could feel him tremble against her with excitement, every bit of him iron muscle.

She snaked herself around him, curling one arm and hand up behind his neck and his thick mane of hair, bending his handsome face down to her as she tipped her steamy lips up at him.

Everyone present held their breath.

No one expected anything like this. Ever.

Naero's other hand felt around his slender hips, until she grasped the hilt of his energy cutlass, sheathed and inverted in custom rig, behind his hips and up his broad back.

Naero could feel his heart and breath quicken–right along with her own, as both of them stood there and smouldered.

She thrust herself against him, and smiled up at him wickedly.

He jumped as if she sent a heavy shock charge through his entire body.

She whispered to him tenderly.

"I'm your sweet little fleet captain, Max. But you've gone and interrupted my sword practice. Now I must know...can you use this thing...on your hips?"

Max Lii swallowed hard at that.

She shoved him away, sprang back, and held her own blade out and at the ready in a flash.

She grinned her half-smile once again.

"...or are you all just for show?"

Max's lips parted slightly in eager wonder.

Then he smiled, too–instantly digging their little drama. He kept his eyes on her and slowly circled around, looking her up and down, licking his lips. He obviously liked what he saw, up close and personal.

"I am sure going to enjoy...serving under you, sir."

Naero laughed. "Let's dispense with rank in the practice room, Max. Here we're all just friends and Spacers. Now grab something hot and hard to thrust with...and try to surprise me."

"Oh, I'm just full of surprises, Naero, honey."

He drew his energy cutlass slowly from behind his back.

Max apparently preferred a wide blade, one that blazed white-hot like lightning.

Naero laughed. Impressive.

She turned to the crowd and rolled her eyes, speaking aside to them behind one hand.

"But...like all guys...he still only has just one."

Everyone oohed and ahhed at that, and then burst out laughing and cheering again.

Naero went on, extending both arms. "And as always, the question remains. What can he do with it?"

More jeering and cheering.

Max didn't give an inch of ground.

"Give me a chance here, honey...wait for it." He smiled and reached up with his other hand, and used the same slow, fluid motion.

Max drew out another matching cutlass, a twin to the other, and held them crackling in both hands.

The crowd went crazy, laughing and roaring. They couldn't believe it.

Max tossed his pretty head of dark hair. "As a matter of fact, I do have two. Surprise!"

He snapped into a fighting stance.

"And surprise again, I even know what to do with them." He grinned and then glared at her once more.

Naero clapped her hands and laughed with eager delight. "Oh, I need to see this play out. Somebody take those hangers and give him a matching set of practice blades. We are so doing this."

Once the switch was made, Naero charged in.

Only the best swordmasters fought with two blades. She kept that in mind.

Within seconds, Naero could tell that Max knew his way around swords.

He defended against her almost effortlessly, using the advantages that his two weapons gave him.

Then he pressed his own attack and drove her back.

The fight was on.

Then, to her surprise, he kept taking the fighting in close.

And when they were close–he sang to her.

Even as they fought fiercely.

Max sang to her. And it was one of her favorite love songs of his–"Hearts Afire."

Max's words and his sultry voice pierced her heart and distracted her–more than his blades ever could.

The biggest threat wasn't his blades or his skill with them.

Max was clearly a consummate seducer. He made his living at it. That was the real danger.

Raw seduction and magnetism were clearly among his best weapons.

He leaned in quickly at one point and brushed his lips against hers.

Naero felt herself shudder and gasp.

She lifted her parting lips back up toward him for but an instant.

No one had ever seduced her like this.

Max smiled and stepped back.

Everyone gasped and grew silent once more.

The point of Max's right sword poised above her heaving left breast.

The blade of his left sword was horizontal before her uplifted, alabaster chin and throat.

Naero gulped in air, still feeling overheated with an incredible surge of desire.

Max shook his head slightly, and smiled sadly.

"Love conquers all, honey. Just like the song says. Do you yield?"

Naero glared at him without blinking. She let her practice swords fall.

They clattered to the ground beside her.

"Never."

"I've beaten you."

She grinned back at him with her own wicked smile.

Time for her to go after him on his terms.

"You've won a single pass. If you know anything about me, you would know that you will never defeat me. I say let's go again–another pass–all out this time."

He leaned in. "What's in it for me?" he whispered playfully.

"A prize..." she whispered back, eyes askance.

He snorted slightly. "What prize could you offer me to continue?"

Naero giggled and spoke softly for his ears along. "To be yours. Tonight. All yours. In every way, Max. And here's my secret. Forget anything else you've heard–I've never been with another. You...would be my first."

She felt him shudder again, right up against her. And he whispered back.

"I can't believe this, honey. Sure, I'll fight for you, with everything I have. To tell you true–you're all I've been dreaming about, honey. Just you."

She kissed his ear. "Then it's a deal."

135

She pulled away.

Max nodded to her. "Choose your weapons, N. I already have mine. I've never been more ready."

He saluted her. "And I've trained cutlass since they could place them in my hands as a young boy."

Naero smiled playfully this time. "Well then, if you use two swords, then it's only fair that I use two as well."

Max grinned eagerly. "Use whatever you like. I don't care."

Naero went over to the practice wall and picked out her favorite pair of holoflex practice katanas. She stroked them with affection.

"Let me tell you a story, Max. My father and my grandfather both practiced with twin katanas. My father was so huge, he had to use specially forged tachis and nodachis for a warrior of his size. They both passed the swordarts on to me. Both of them used swordart as deep forms of meditation. Yet several times, they were each challenged to sword duels. Sometimes…to the death."

She paused for dramatic effect, eyeing him intently without blinking as she moved like a young female panther–all liquid muscle in tight black Nytex.

Max couldn't take his eyes off her.

"Neither of them ever knew defeat by another wielding swords. And though I never knew him very long, on the day I was born, my grandfather Amashin placed two small swords in my tiny hands to grasp. And growing up, each year thereafter–even after he was gone–I received a gift of a pair of twin swords of the finest craftsmanship.

"Each set was a work of art, perfectly measured and balanced for my size, weight, and strength. You speak of being raised with swords? I, too, have grown up with the surety of live blades in my hands–since before I could float."

She gripped her favorite set of twin practice katanas, held up her proud face, and saluted.

"This is the blood I come from."

She sighed and strode back into the fighting ring–utterly fearless. Her face was set, her violet eyes fierce and merry.

Naero undid her dark ponytail and let her waves of black, shimmering geisha hair flow free.

She loved doing battle with everything on the line.

She loved it more than she craved the breath of life.

And she would keep her word.

If Max beat her fairly, she would do everything in her power to please him–all night long.

She almost giggled.

Losing wouldn't be so bad, either.

They fought together for more than an hour, while all the other captains looked on in stunned silence at the amazing match unfolding before them.

Until at last, Naero held both points of her blades hovering over Max Lii's heaving heart.

He looked at her with heartbreak and very real sorrow in his eyes.

He took a step forward.

Naero inched back quickly, to spare him the intense pain of the shock charges.

"I've won," she spoke softly, her breast heaving heavily also.

"Have you?" Max caught his breath and swallowed hard again. "To me, honey…it seems…as if we've both lost."

Naero looked down and nodded slightly. "Perhaps you are right. But for now, this is the way things stand between us. I'm sorry, Max."

He nodded sadly and dropped his swords. "Day will come, Naero– even if it is not me–that a man of honor shall win past all of your defenses, and love you, and pierce your heart, the way it should be taken."

Max thrust himself forward onto her practice blades, ignoring the pain, and pulled her close to him.

"…as you have pierced mine."

He held her close to him for a moment.

Naero gasped.

Haisha, how could anyone smell that good?

Then he kissed her brow, caressed her porcelain face once, and pulled back away, acknowledging her victory.

Their comrades applauded and cheered their amazing contest.

And that was how Naero Amashin Maeris met and exchanged defeats with throckstar Max Lii.

23

On her next little disguise run, Naero uncovered quite a little secret of her own.

She went on board the heavy destroyer *The Jack of Spades*, posing as Jooli Logan, a replacement gunner sent there for secondary battery training.

She played the role of a spunky, carefree redhead this time, with multiple hair tassels and braids, and again, lots of teen makeup.

In a day's time she was getting along famously with her new mates–a little too much, actually–and had to turn down ready offers of high-octane sex with five different males on board, and two females.

One of the guys was, in fact, completely gorgeous, a dreamy fighter jock one deck above them. Saemar would have been so jealous.

Naero was sorely tempted, but held fast to her plan. If she could resist the charms of a super-hot throckstar, she could hold out against this guy.

Then some of the crew absently showed her the black market, digital porn sites that sprang up as fast as they were shut down on the galaxy webnets.

Vid stars, galactic athletes, famous people–Spacers, landers...even aliens. She scanned her parent's names on some of those lists as well.

They had been famous too so that made them fair game on the black market porn sites.

The various porn systems could generate any type of sexual paring that could be conceived, between any public person or entity that was ever scanned into the system.

And then use those lifelike 3D skins to produce porn romps and fantasies for any taste, or lack thereof. Instant erotic fantasies that looked incredibly lifelike. Embarrassingly so.

The detail was so real, it was scary.

She found them silly and humorous at first, if not sordid and outright weird. Naero had seen porn before and knew what it was.

Then she saw the list of current Alliance officers and personnel.

For example, there was a long-running, highly rated vid of a threesome between Admiral Sleak Maeris, Admiral Nathan Joshua, and Fleet Captain Zalvano.

She had to cover her eyes and look away when someone pulled a preview up.

Strangely enough, there wasn't one for Wing Commander Saemar Maeris. She wasn't on any of the lists.

Saemar–the one person who would have been perfect for this kind of thing.

She probably would have felt flattered.

Then the atomic bomb hit.

They flashed over the special "Captain Naero Amashin Maeris," porn generation page.

One of the most popular pages on all of the galaxy porn sites.

Right up there with Max Lii and other top celebs.

There was even a new porn vid of her and Max fencing, cutting each other's clothes off–and then getting busy in zero-G. Complete with holographic fireworks going off all around them.

Haisha!

News apparently traveled quickly in every circle of the webnets.

She resisted the urge to check out that particular vid for herself.

But the eye-popping fact still staggered her.

Without even realizing such things existed, she had been transformed into a top-flight—digital porn star.

She read some of the onsite reviews and just could not believe them.

Captain Maeris is soooo...hot!

I want to show her how it's done...all night long...

Please tell me they have a sexbot based on her. I'll pay anything!

I love the one where she's directing the battle completely naked!

Haisha! All this, and here she was still technically a virgin in real life. Damn it!

It just wasn't fair at all.

Even her digital avatars were getting more action than she was.

Haisha; how pitiful. She still slept alone each night, by conscious choice!

How utterly embarrassing. Anyone could buy and watch these damn vids.

That fact made her blood turn to icy slag and puddle down in her boots.

There had to be a way to put a stop to this madness.

But she knew very well that the various black market sites were insidious, and extremely difficult to combat.

Several people told her that Colby O'Brien, a veteran gunner, actually had pics and vids of Captain Naero–real and digital–plastered all over his vidwalls like pinups, like some creepy shrine.

Stalk much?

She still had to see it for herself.

She contacted him, and he openly invited her into his small crew quarters to have a looksee.

The guy was in his fifties. Creepy.

Colby bragged about his obsession. He even started watching a new, top porn vid, with "Captain Naero" rewarding her bridge crew with a swinging orgy–right after a decisive naval victory.

Haisha, again. This was just too much!

Thank the Powers they did not bother to have the real faces and scans of her actual subordinates. And, good, they got the classified layout of her bridge totally wrong, as well. Not that anyone would care about or notice anything like that.

But still, how would she ever be able to set foot on her bridge again without seeing those vile images as it was?

She winced several times and then had to look away.

"How can you watch this crap?" she asked Colby.

The guy was nearly drooling, his eyes riveted on the holoscreen.

With the real thing standing right next to him, and the moron didn't even know, or care.

He shook his head. "Keep your opinions to yourself, kid. A goofy little inexperienced girlie like you could never compare to a smokin' hot dish like Captain Maeris. And her aunt and her mom are almost as hot as her. But she's the top. I can't get her out of my head. Lots of crew can't. That's why her page gets so many hits, and so much business. There's even a new one with her and Max Lii!"

Ick. "You're a sick, twisted freak, Colby. You realize that, right? This isn't real. People don't…they just don't do this kind of stuff."

Well...Saemar...maybe.

Colby grew a little irritated by her protests. "I said mind your own business, you little twit. You called me. You said wanted to see this–so take a good look. What the hell do you know? I bet she gets all the hot action she wants–every night–with anyone who'll give it to her hard and fast. *Haisha!* I wish I could get transferred to her flagship, just one night. Man, all the things I could do to her to make her moan and scream my name."

"I think you've lost it, buddy. Have a real relationship, with a real woman. Get some serious help."

This guy was never getting anywhere near her flagship. She'd see to that. Let him live in his sick, little fantasy world–all by his lonesome.

Colby chuckled, pweaking the controls. "You ain't seen nothin' yet. I paid extra for the special personalization package. Cost me a chunk of change, but damn–I can put a scan of myself directly in the action, right with my hot little love-bunny. I can make everyone of those guys look just like me. Just watch this."

No thanks, mister. This was getting waaay too creepy fast.

Jooli-Naero shot straight up to her feet.

"Okay. I've seen waaay too much. Time for me to go..." She turned to duck out the open panel of his small crew quarters.

He chortled and shouted after her, "What, afraid you might learn somethin', you little punk? Good riddance. Get the hell outta here, and don't come back. Who needs a chit like you...when I have my beautiful, little warrior goddess to dream about–every night and day?"

The panel slammed shut abruptly behind her.

Fortunately, that weirdo was the only one she met thus far who was actually obsessed with her. Naero rubbed her arms and felt like she needed about fifty mist showers.

The rest of the crew took some degree of fleeting interest, as a novelty, but more or less considered those porn sites little more than a glorified gag. Nobody else took them seriously.

Thank goodness.

Naero still blinked.

Then she raised both hands to her mouth.

Wait until she told Aunt Sleak. Her aunt would flip! There had to be something the Alliance could do to suppress such webnet pirate sites.

*

Naero met with Tarim at one of his ranges for a tek session, just the two of them. Neither of them needed anymore shooting practice.

Not being a Spacer or a tek, Tarim really didn't understand how starships actually worked. Naero quickly set the parameters on one of her portable training holocomps that she brought along, and called up the holos of two warships above them.

Tarim already raised one hand to question her.

Naero chuckled. "We're not in grade school, Tarim. Just ask if you have a question. But it might be better to wait until I'm done explaining a few basic concepts. Or, if I'm in the process of making a point."

"All right," he said. "I just want you to understand from the get-go that I'm not a tek or a scientist. I don't really have a clue about how starships or warships actually operate."

Naero held both of her hands palm out in front of her. "Right now, I just want you to watch and listen. Let's go over jump drive teknology. Without jump drives, starships would not be starships."

"N, I guess I roughly grasp the concept of jump tek from the vidgames with Ty, but I'll never be a tek like Tyber. Is there a simple way that you can tell me how jump tek works, and what are its advantages in warfare? I know that the higher the jump rating, the better it is. But I don't understand why."

Naero froze the holo ships above them.

"Jump drives allow starships to 'jump' from one star system to another, within range and reason. They do this by going into, or traveling through, and coming out of a Space-Time shortcut called 'jump space.' Some call it hyperspace."

Naero cleared her throat. "Using a jump drive to pass through the shortcut of jump space, starships can cover the vast distances of Space-Time much quicker, by folding Space-Time and traveling through the shortest space of the fold. So in essence, a jump drive is kinda like a time machine, too. It saves people time by covering great distances faster, and getting people to their destinations quicker. Speeding up travel, trade, and warfare between worlds."

The way Tarim's eyes moved and then stared, he still looked confused.

"So, what are jump ratings on jump drives for?"

142

"Jump drives currently have ratings between 1 and 8. Theoretically, those are the only levels of jump that are currently available and possible, with all of the knowledge, tek, and construction materials at hand. The higher the jump rating, the farther and faster a starship can travel through jump space with each jump. And it's always possible to compute a shorter, faster jump within the range of each rating."

Tarim rubbed his face. "So, what's the difference between all of the ratings?"

"Usually a difference in days, hours, or minutes. That's why speed of advance can be crucial during war time. A navy that can jump farther and faster than another has a distinct strategic and tactical advantage."

"I'll take your word for that. Why does a starship come out of jump space, and still have to proceed to a system, planet, or starbase and such? Why can't it just jump right to the destination and be there?"

Naero nodded and held up one hand. "Don't get too far ahead of me, Tarim. There's a good reason for that, and I'll get to it. But let's finish discussing jump drives. You started this. I want you to understand these concepts first. Higher rated jump drives are also more accurate and precise in their jump calculations, and can bring starships out of jump space, and back into regular, or standard Space-Time, closer to the target system, planet, or destination. Yet still within a safe distance."

"Is it true that most military vessels have higher jump ratings than private vessels?"

Naero nodded. "In general, yes. Most private and commercial starships are rated Jump-1 through Jump-5. Military vessels currently have ratings between Jump-4 and Jump-7."

"You said there was a Jump-8?"

"Most ships don't have Jump-8. That's still mainly experimental. But the theory and the raw tek is out there. Good teks and engineers modify and tinker with their own ships all of the time, attempting to gain whatever edge they can. But doing so can be perilous. A single malfunction during a jump–a *misjump*–can be extremely dangerous."

"How so? What is a misjump, and what happens to the ship and the crew? Can it dump them into a star, or smash the ship into a planet?"

Naero shook her head. "Not so much that. Although such calamities have happened, on super-rare occasions. The odds are simply very high against that sort of thing. But when a jump drive misjumps, it sends a starship into jump space out of control, and out of balance. While the ship bounces out of control for a random space of minutes or days, the physical stress forces on starships is intense, and can even tear ships apart. Next, the ship could be damaged severely and dumped out of space into the middle of nowhere. Dead space—where no one can hear or reach them in time before their systems fail, and all within perish."

"So, is that part of the reason why starships have to pull a safe distance away from a planet, or even other ships, before it is clear to jump?"

"Somewhat. But anything with sufficient mass in close proximity to the jumping starship can greatly interfere with the entry into jump space. And those calculations are made automatically. Jumping too soon or too close to another large mass can trigger anything from a misjump to the worst calamity—a gigablast."

"A what?"

"The ship and everything on it becomes a gigantic quanta-bomb. Protonic reversion reduces all the atoms into sudden, explosive energy. The starship blows up, obliterating itself and everything nearby it."

"That sounds incredibly bad."

"Exploding all of your atoms isn't usually good for anyone. But sometimes, as a last resort, a doomed ship will use this technique as a desperate, last resort in wartime. If a ship is going to be destroyed anyway, such a suicide run, plowing through enemies all around it, can do a lot of damage."

Tarim nodded. "I remember stuff like that early on in the Annexation War. Not so much now."

"No, thank goodness. Now things are pretty much conventional. One side simply trying to wear down the defenses of the other and crush them. I want to explain that, but first I want to make sure we're clear on jump drives and what they do."

"I guess so." His eyes still looked a little glassy.

Naero rolled her own eyes briefly. "Think of it this way. Two systems are separated by a stellar distance of say…ten parsecs, about thirty-three light years. A Jump-1 starship can reach that destination in about thirty days, or one standard month. Perhaps, even, by taking several smaller jumps along the way. That's the way the first jumpships traveled. But a Jump-2 starship can reach the same destination in about half the time, say, two weeks.

"Whereas a starship with a Jump-3 drive can reach it faster yet, in a few days. Jump-4, in a single day. Jump-5, a handful of hours. Jump-6, one or two hours. And a starship with Jump-7 can reach it in a matter of minutes—not even hours."

"Jump-8?"

"Like I said, Jump-8 is still experimental. I don't really know what it can do yet."

"Got it. I can see why a navy reaching a conflict zone within minutes would have a decisive advantage over ships that would take days or weeks to arrive. Can a ship be tracked or followed through jump space, to pursue it or see where it comes out?"

Out of the black, Naero thought of Baeven's unique vessel. Its capabilities seemed to defy all logic. She wished she knew what its specs were.

"Intel craft or some ships might possess experimental tek to do such things, but those capabilities do not exist on most ships. When a ship goes into jump, you normally can't tell where it is going to go or come out. You can plot and calculate all of the possible places that it *could* do so, but those variables are usually too many to attempt to track. And a ship could always come out of one jump, change course in any direction, and go right back into another jump. How would you know?"

"I see. Making a ship that gets away nearly impossible to track."

"Exactly," Naero said.

24

The Alliance spent almost two weeks containing, probing, and regrouping around both Helapine-3 and Kysarra-5. Yet that also gave Triax time to prepare and strengthen all of their defenses.

Oddly enough, the Alliance also busied itself with the pacification of several dozen Triaxian worlds, many with no apparent strategic value whatsoever.

Naero got called into one of the fleet labs one day.

Zhen was part of the medical research team working in conjunction with Intel.

They continued to study various Triaxian genocide devices, developing new ways to neutralize the various neurotoxins, nerve agents, and bio-weapons that Triax inflicted on its own civilian populations–and then blamed the Alliance.

Even Shalaen lent them a hand against all of that.

Intel had a plan to seed future Triaxian worlds with concealed or cloaked microfixers–well in advance of future pacification efforts. Sort of a genocide device inoculation that they could control.

The little nanomachines would actively seek out enemy genocide devices and stand ready to neutralize them as needed, on command or in coordination with Alliance efforts.

Naero communicated with Zhen through a bio-hazard screenlink and a shielded, sealed environment.

"What's up, Z?"

Zhen smiled through the clear bubble of her hazmat face shield. "Thanks for coming, N. I wanted you to be the first to inform Admiral Klyne and Admiral Sandusky. After months of research since Heaven-7, we've finally broken virtually all of the Triaxian cosmicide codes and formulae. A handful of them we cracked right here. Others have been decoded at other research facilities."

Naero clapped her hands together and grinned. "What about the newest generation of microfixers? Are they ready to go to work?"

Zhen nodded. "Almost. Ty said they'll be online in a few days, ready to mass produce in great numbers."

"That's great, Z. Excellent work. Then we can begin inoculating future liberated worlds against Triax's cosmicide devices. For once, we'll be one step ahead or our foes, instead of them being several steps ahead of us all the time."

Naero put in a direct call to Tyber's lab, in order to double-check.

His holo floated before them. "Ladies...what's up?"

"Hey, sweetie. Miss you!" Zhen called out.

Naero kept going. "Nothing but good news on this end, Ty. I hear you and your team are close to wrapping things up on the tek side of things with our new generations of microfixers?"

Tyber leaned eagerly on one of his counters, but he looked haggard and tired. Yet his excitement clearly overrode that.

"Better than we expected. The microfixers will be ready. And even more, the fixers will also be capable of detecting, tracking, and secretly deactivating and neutralizing the actual mechanics of the genocide devices, and rendering them completely inoperative."

"Good work, both of you and your teams. You've really made a difference. Intel can't implement this initiative quickly enough. And all of you have helped make this possible."

Zhen sighed. "We're about to save countless lives. Billions, perhaps trillions, who might have perished needlessly."

"We still need to be cautious and work in secret," Naero said. "We know Triax will figure out what's happening soon enough. Then they'll try to counter us."

Zhen nodded. "And we'll counter them, until their time runs out, and Triax falls into the abyss of history."

*

Naero helped prepare Strike Fleet Six for the next all-out assault on the two Triaxian stronghold worlds.

Despite the fact that the Alliance forces found themselves vastly outnumbered once again, they brazenly dared to attempt a two-pronged attack on both Triaxian bases. Strategically, their efforts looked insane to any military mind–even suicidal.

The Triaxian high command even hailed and mocked them, goading and daring them to attack.

Then, just before the lead elements engaged, something very strange occurred.

More than half of the massed Triaxian fleets and ships jumped out of the two systems–in the space of a few standard minutes.

Stunned, the remaining Triaxian forces made a feeble, confused attempt to pull back and regroup their scattered and broken elements.

Naero laughed and gave the command. "All forces, commence attack. Don't give the bastards any chance to reset their lines. Charge in and gut them!"

Now the odds against them were only three or four to one at best.

Acceptable odds for any Spacer.

The right wing of the entire Alliance forces thundered at Helapine-3 with twenty-three massed fleets. Eleven held back in strategic reserve at key points, depending on whether things went well or badly.

They faced seventy-four enemy fleets, with ten in reserve.

Yet almost all of those fleets had lost one third to one half of their complement of warships.

Admiral Sandusky, Spacer Intel, and the pacification fleets had done their jobs well in advance–and brilliantly.

Nebulae of fixers melted and dissolved the layered curtains of mines and death drones.

Admiral Maeris sent the massed Alliance fleets in in stacks of wedges, battleships and their biggest guns up front in three staggered lines.

The Hippolyta and fourteen of her amazon sisters held a reunion of half of their total number, anchoring the core of the Alliance assault. They roared their war cries in rage and fury.

Sixty 16-meter, rapid-fire quad guns were a blinding, terrifying force to behold indeed, especially when massed together. When all threescore of those gigantic 16-meter batteries blazed to life, they lit up the entire sector like a gigantic supernova.

Enemy ships vanished before them, completely obliterated.

The best Triax had to offer fled the field before them or got taken down in bright sheets of destroying light.

The Dromon Class planetoid dreadnaughts easily proved themselves to be the largest, toughest ships in the war. They had no equal. Battered and damaged repeatedly, they continued to fight on.

None of them had ever been destroyed or had known defeat.

Naero shot to her her feet from her command chair, shook both fists at the enemy, and cried out to *Hippolyta's* sisters over their links.

"That's it. Fight, you amazons! In for the Alliance. For *The Omaria* and all our dead!

"Hew them down and scatter their ashes in the flaming maelstrom of our wake!"

A great cheer split the links, as the crews of the Alliance roared in echoing response.

Aunt Sleak formed the various cruisers into diamond wedge wings on either side of the massed battleships. Then the destroyers next on the outer flanks, where their speed and great maneuverability would be key, in multiring formations on either side.

The Carriers brought up and protected the rear this time, their waves of starfighters ready to swarm, waiting for the fixers to do their work, and clear the attack vectors for them.

The Alliance fleets rode head-on into the fury of battle–straight into the teeth of waves of enemy fire, on wings of flame.

Haisha! By the Powers, it was a stirring sight.

The Alliance lost eight ships in the initial sortie, three destroyed outright.

Triax lost forty vessels–sixteen of them dust or reduced to burning wreckage.

Enemy vessels continued to flee in terror, whether they defected or merely voided the field.

Unfortunately, more than enough Triaxian zealots still remained to continue the bloody fight.

Triax attempted an envelopment strategy. They still had the raw numbers.

Admiral Sleak redirected the Alliance fleets on their secure link, including Strike Fleets Six and Fifteen.

"Captains Maeris and Wilde, Bravo-Hotel-2 helix assault formation. Ribbon-sweep through their port side on these vectors. Continue to concentrate all fire on their battleships and dreadnaughts. Take down their shields and maximize all damage. Leave their carriers to the smaller ships or let them retreat to the rear."

"When we come about, we'll be exposed, completely wide open to their many reserves," Naero noted. "You know they'll hit us hard."

"Planning on it. Our reserves and fighter elements will cut them off. Got your backsides, but I do need to use them as bait for a time, so make sure you wiggle. Next, figure-eight back through their starboard side. Same objective. Take down shields, eliminate as many primary warships as you can. Once you reduce their bigs enough, we can–"

"–split off and go on the hunt. So many of their ships are jumping. Do we know how many are actually defecting?"

"No clue," Aunt Sleak said. "We'll sort it out later. Just glad to see them go for now. Plenty of foes left to fight. Now ride!"

"N, watch our two-sixty, X-Y-Z!" Captain Rebecca Wilde called out.

"I see them, Becca. On it."

Five enemy fleets, clockwise galaxy tight formation. Designed to concentrate all of their firepower in a small, intense area.

"Okay, they're trying to break us, Becca. Not happening. *Mohawk. Panther. Swordbreaker. Strongheart.* Form your Alpha-Tango attack lines on splitting and punishment vectors.

"Take these heavy cruisers and destroyers, spin out and bring these fighter elements along with support to hold the attackers off. Bottle them up and delay them. Admiral Sleak is sending two fleets in to join you. Just hold them for a few minutes."

"Copy that, sir."

Two minutes could be a long time in a hot fight.

"I know things will get rugged. When we figure-eight and ribbon back, the amazons will link back up and take them on their right from above on their one-fifty-seven arc. Once we break them, you can form up with us once more, or retreat to the rear–if you need to do so."

"Don't worry about us, sir. We'll do our best. Give the girls their head. *Mohawk* out."

Naero trusted her people–even at the toughest times like these.

More than 100 warships from the two combined strike fleets spiraled off in precise, complex formations at full attack speed, screaming into the enemy, cutting off their advance.

Aunt Sleak sent in the two support fleets behind them.

Complications led to Naero and Becca taking almost twice as long to execute their actions, and to pause and help three other Alliance fleets that had gotten cut off and trapped.

They blasted their comrades free with raking fire.

By the time they got back to Naero's people, those battered units were still holding the enemy in place, but just barely.

Half of Naero's warships on either side were gone or in flames. Yet the remaining forces stayed steadfast, exchanging close-up duels and broadsides with the still larger enemy force.

"Sorry we're late, *Mohawk*. *Mohawk*?"

"This is *Swordbreaker*, sir. *Mohawk* is in flames and losing power. She's being towed to the fixer clouds. Glad to see you and the gals. We could use some help here."

"We're coming in white-hot and ready to fire. Have all your ships scatter out from your positions away from our incoming attack vectors. Coordinate on these marks."

Naero led her and Becca's sortie, looped down and unleashed their tsunami of firepower.

At the last instant, Naero's battered holding forces and the remains of the other supporting two fleets peeled away and out of the fight at top escape velocity.

Combined fire lashed the Triaxians, adjusted to the one-thirty-nine arc, like burning whips of destruction shooting out from twin, vengeful stars.

Then Naero and Becca executed a flawless, counterclockwise swing along the edge of the shattered enemy wheel.

Ships groaned. They pulled some heavy stress forces. A few smaller vessels lost power and fell back, or got damaged by sporadic fire.

But the majority of Strike Fleets Six and Fifteen kept their rapid firing big guns trained on the five enemy fleets.

Most of these foes had their shields negated by now.

Naero and Becca completed one full circle, and five entire enemy fleets burned and exploded.

"Break off and leave them to the sharks," Naero commanded. "All ships and crews, good work. Now let's tear the enemy right a new ass, just like the left. Follow me in and form up, mirror configuration. These vectors, on these marks. Let's burn right through them!"

Becca laughed openly. "Lots of them running every minute, N. We're close to breaking them."

"Close isn't good enough. Attack, Becca. Obliterate their entire starboard flank!"

"Wahoo! Light these fuckers up!"

The final battle for Helapine-3 lasted almost an hour longer.

Just when Naero thought they could stand down and assess their losses and damage, Admiral Joshua put in an emergency call from the battle for Kysarra-5, in the next system over.

The fight there had bogged down into a messy stalemate.

Even worse, many of the enemy ships that fled Helapine-3 had jumped in on the Alliance forces at Kysarra-5, tipping the scales in favor of Triax.

Seventy percent of the Alliance fleets there were now cut off and in danger of being completely wiped out.

"All available ships, this is an emergency," Admiral Maeris announced. "Proceed immediately to support our other fleets at Kysarra-5. They're outnumbered, trapped, and taking a pounding. Jump in on these vectors in multiple attack wings."

"All ships on our link," Naero relayed. "If you are sixty-percent combat ready or better, form up and jump with me. Any others, proceed through the fixer clouds and follow on, as able. Our brothers and sisters need us. We cannot let them down!"

25

Haisha! Two major battles in the course of a single, standard day.

Strike Fleet Fifteen was too beaten up and had to remain behind.

When Naero and her forces jumped in on the edge of the Kysarra-5 battle–several minutes later–at first look at the scans, things could not be much worse.

The fight had degenerated into the equivalent of a street brawl in a vast, muddy pit.

Triax had the Alliance forces almost fully contained and hemmed in close with sheer, superior numbers.

The Alliance forces could barely move and maneuver.

Ships rammed each other repeatedly, and fired directly into one another, negating most shields.

That was the basic, dire situation she jumped into.

Triax also had ships free of the mix and who still joined in fresh. They wheeled and spun around, sniping from above and below. Yet because of the nature of the enemy trap itself, the enemy strikers often hit their own ships as well when they tried to attack.

Either way, the Alliance forces were in a very bad way, bottled up as they were by an envelopment strategy that constricted tighter and tighter around them. The trap was similar to a long metal mesh rat trap, tapered at both ends and bulging in the center.

But the tightly packed enemy formations instantly told Naero what they needed to do.

"All ships, concentrate precise, destroying fire on the tapered end of the enemy rear positions. They won't be able to hold out for long against that. Once the breach is made, our trapped friends can escape to regroup. Ignore the other ships. Let our fighters keep them busy."

They maneuvered into position.

Nine of the amazons cut loose first, breaking up the packed group of ships and destroying many outright with their combined firepower.

The first Alliance ships saw daylight and shot through to escape the trap.

"Form concentric rings in convex pattern Charlie-Kilo-Romeo-8. We'll rake the rat trap rapidly along its full length. They'll have to break off and regroup–if they don't want to be destroyed."

Admiral Nathan Joshua cut in, just as the enemy trap began to break up, as planned. "Alliance forces. Do not allow the enemy to regroup. Repeat, stay on them as they scatter. Expand your rings and then hunt them down. Keep the pressure on. All reserves join in. Any ship that can still fight, let's break them, now!"

Despite being beaten up after hours of constant ship-to-ship combat, the battered Alliance captains did as they were commanded.

Even as the enemy tried to peel away and regroup, the Alliance fleets would not let them.

The plan worked for the most part, but there were still so many Triaxian ships remaining, that in the fighting and confusion, a good many of them were still getting clear enough to jump away.

Everyone on both sides seemed bloody and exhausted by then, but the fight did not let up. In fact, it grew even more confused. Triax ships were everywhere.

And the senseless losses for a senseless war only continued to mount.

But eventually, Triax would fall.

The enemy's days were roughly numbered, yet still numbered. They were finite.

The fact remained that the enemy continued to force the Alliance to pay a very high price for each victory along the way.

Once this battle ended, Kysarra-5 would await pacification.

A number of massive explosions suddenly rocked *The Hippolyta* to her core. She shuddered and shook.

"Rina, what's happening?"

"A dozen enemy ships just uncloaked and hit us point-blank with missiles."

"Shields are down, sir," Ensign Nick Alexander said.

"Second attack wave about to hit," Surina said calmly.

"*Haisha!* More missiles, Rina?"

"Alert the Marines," Tarim shouted. "Get everyone armed and ready to defend this ship!"

Surina turned and faced Naero, activating her shield and drawing her own blaster pistol and battle blade.

"Not missiles this time, sir. Enemy boarding craft–hundreds of them. They'll hit us in seconds–everywhere."

Naero readied her own weapons, just like everyone else.

"Spread out, everybody," Tarim said. "Stay sharp. Watch for entry points." He turned to Naero. "They mean to overwhelm us, sir. Just like they did *The Silver Devil.*"

"Like hell they will. All crew–everyone fights. Get our fighter waves back and have them attack the boarding craft up close. These killers are going to hit us from every direction. Defend our girl and each other. Let them come!"

Tarim shouted. "They're after our captain. Everyone defend her to the last breath! That is an order."

Hayden and a full rifle platoon of heavy Marines poured out of the lifts to reinforce the bridge.

Just as the enemy boarders blasted through the hull.

26

The enemy attackers penetrated the bridge blast shields alone, at sixteen key points.

The Triaxians swarmed on *The Hippolyta* and ripped their way in at seventy-four other key locations.

First the attackers tossed in explosives to disrupt shields, then smokers to obscure their entry points.

Spacer Marines and crew flipped up visor optics to target the attackers.

Scores of Triaxian elite Marines and Hevangian assassins poured in from all directions on grav wings.

There was no way to shoot them all fast enough.

They were sitting ducks with the enemy swarming above them.

"Cut the gravitics!" Naero shouted. "Split up and secure each of those access points. Let's take them on in zero-G!"

Spacers were superb fighters in null gravity.

But Naero and her people were already heavily outnumbered.

Hayden organized his Marines into sixteen, four-man fireteams, each with a shield pod in front of them.

"Naero!" he shouted. "You and your people back us up! We'll do the heavy lifting!"

"Right! Two-thirds of you–pair up with the Marines and assail each of the breaches. The rest of you, with me and Tarim. We're going to swirl around and tear the enemy to pieces at high speed. Blast and cut them as we go!"

The bridge was quickly enveloped in crisscrossing firefights.

The fireteams attacked the breaches, cutting down the attackers still trying to pour through.

Personal shields took hits and buckled.

Naero led eleven Spacers, rocketing up to clash with more than thirty foes.

Naero hurled microgrenades and exploding blades.

Some of the grenades were flashbombs, and stunned the foe.

Others blew the enemy up, just like her blades.

They gutted the enemy thirty and took out almost half of them.

More shot up at them from the sides and below.

Tarim dropped head down and spun, raking the packed enemy forces with his plasma machine pistols.

Foes withered before Tarim's blazing guns.

Naero saw Fenley Wilde, her co-pilot, shredded by an enemy mini-gun, a split second before he took it out with a pulse grenade.

Medical Specialist Xaevin Cheyenne knifed two foes with her battle blades, just before they were all three cut to pieces by heavy blaster cannon fire from below.

Naero saw the shock and surprise on Xaevin's face, just before her head and body exploded in pieces.

A split second later, precise fire from Leftenant Hayden and his microgrenade pistols took out the enemy blaster cannon.

A team of six Hevangian assassins cut loose on Naero herself with heavy stunners, driving her back and disrupting her shields.

The next barrage would take her down–they obviously wanted to take her alive.

"Captain, look out!" Surina yelled. She shot one assassin in the face and threw her battle blade into the throat of the next.

Then she flung herself directly in front of Naero and took the concentrated blasts of the stunners full on.

Direct hits drilled Surina into the wall, where she floated, bloody and helpless.

Two dozen assassins drew their poisoned shokkog blades and swept down at Naero, Tarim, and Enel.

Six of them broke away to to slaughter Surina.

Tarim slipped around to the side, giving Naero and Enel room to fight. Each rapid shot from his pistols ripped off a Hevangian head.

Enel tore into the six killers going after Surina like a demon unleashed.

He emptied his blaster pistol in the chest and torso of the first three attackers. Then he drew his own battle blades and sliced the hands and arms off two more–laying open one killer's throat with such speed and fury that he nearly decapitated him. The last assassin he smashed into the hull, held off the lethal shokkog, and crushed the assassin's skull repeatedly with his bare fist.

He secured a heavy blaster and gunned down any foe he could target.

Enel became a terrifying warrior in those brief instants.

Eleven assassins still came straight at Naero.

She smiled and accelerated to meet them, hurling blasting blades and microgrenades up into their bunching numbers.

That was just to knock them around and distract them.

Then she went on the attack with every ounce of her enhanced speed and might.

She drew her energy cutlass and went at them with it and her last battle blade.

Naero swept into them hard and fast, whirling, whipping kicks and flashing blades. She wheeled into them, spinning one way and back the next. She severed poisoned shokkog knives from their hands, crushed heads and torsos.

Like her mother before her, she transformed into The Invincible Cyclone. She crushed and slew her targets in a whirling dance of deadly kicks and stabbing, slicing energy blades.

In mere seconds, the elite enemy assassins floated and spun around her–crushed and butchered into bloody pieces, bubbling in zero-G.

Outside the ship, their fighters surgically blasted the enemy boarding craft off the flagship's hull–like removing parasites.

Hayden and his remaining Marines cut down the last foes trying to fight through the breaches.

Once the fighters blasted those last boarding craft away, the hull shields could seal, and the bridge was secured once more.

At a quick glance, twenty-three Marines floated lifeless, along with eight more of Naero's bridge crew, KIA.

Naero shuddered, trying not to think who else they had lost, but there wasn't time. She estimated more than four times that number of enemy dead.

Both she and Jeremiah checked the ship's systems.

Several battles still raged throughout the ship–including an intense fight around Medical.

Zhen. Their wounded in the infirmary.

Their people were still fighting for their lives.

"Half of you stay here with the wounded and see to our people. Defend the main bridge. Commander Jaylen is coordinating the other battles from the backup bridge. The other half who can still fight, come with me and Leftenant Jeremiah. We need to assist the rest of the crew."

"Lock and load, people," Hayden shouted. "Sergeant Steiner. See to our people here."

"Will do, sir."

The next nearest battle was a firefight still going on in the ship's galley down below, and the enemy did not have the codes for the lifts.

Fortunately, they had the enemy in that area trapped between decks. About sixty Triaxians against forty Spacers.

Hayden suddenly chuckled.

"What's so funny, Jeremiah?" Naero asked.

He grinned. "Help's coming. Check the readouts, sir."

Fifteen ships from Strike Fleet Six had already docked with *The Hippolyta*.

Hundreds of enraged Spacer Marines and Spacer crew flooded on board, armed to the teeth and fresh to the fight.

The fact that the enemy had attempted such a direct, brazen attempt on their fleet captain–and her flagship–sent them into a blazing fury.

Naero and Jeremiah reached the galley.

Once they took out the enemy shields with disruption grenades, numerous reinforcements poured in to cut the enemy down in short order.

Fresh Marines basically ignited squad shield pods, walked right in, and blasted the bastards to death at close range.

Only five Triaxians had time to surrender.

All of the Hevangians fought to the death. Some few even killed themselves with their own shokkog blades–rather than be captured and interrogated.

Naero did not mourn their loss in the least. All of these attackers meant to murder her and her entire crew.

She would never forget or forgive what their kind had done to her and her family–her people. Every chance she would get, Naero would make the Hevangians die.

There wasn't enough time to reach any of the other five remaining battles. Overwhelming reinforcements eradicated the enemy threat at each hotspot within minutes.

Naero addressed her courageous people over the com throughout their ship.

"All crew, good work. You held up and fought well against tough odds. The enemy came at us all to murder us, and you proved yourselves brave and true. You fought like lions–as I knew you would–for each other, and to defend our amazon's honor. I was beyond proud to stand and fight beside you all."

Naero paused and took a deep breath. "Help each other, now that this battle is over. We are family, and many of our sisters and brothers have fallen beside us, or are still hurt. Let's see to our people, and then put our brave girl back in order. Once again, well done, my brave and fearless crew!"

Naero did not look forward to the final casualty reports.

Zhen had been slightly wounded during the firefight that took place near the infirmary–just flesh wounds to her left leg and arm. She ignored her injures and helped manage the triage of the more severely wounded from the battle.

Admiral Klyne himself came over with an Intel investigation team, to study the enemy attack and interrogate the few enemy prisoners who survived.

Such enemy attacks were, in fact, on the rise, and new procedures had to be developed to help combat them.

Naero helped see to her bridge dead–personally. She owed them that much. She, Tarim, Zhen, and five other bridge crew members even helped the prep teams bathe and clean the bodies, and put them in their dress uniforms in preparation for burial.

So many fallen.

So much that needed to be done.

Their fallen friends had fought bravely, and deserved no less than the same care they would give family–for they were family.

Each loss was heartbreaking, and would radiate out from each tragedy, to hurt and cause pain to all who had known and loved them.

Then Naero, Tarim, and Zhen went to Leftenant Hayden, and joined the Marines as they honored their fallen in a similar fashion. 3rd Division personally prepared their own dead, and said their farewells to their battle brothers and battle sisters.

Naero witnessed one bright point in the midst of such loss.

When Leftenant Surina Marshall opened her radiant eyes in her medical bay medbed, Ensign Enel Maeris was waiting patiently, holding her hand. He had ignored his own minor wounds to remain by her side while she rested and recovered.

When he ducked out to get her some chow, other bridge crew promptly came over and informed Surina just how valiantly Enel had fought like a tiger to protect her–as she floated helpless in a sea of killers.

And when Enel returned with Surina's food, she took his hand back in hers, and looked into his eyes intently for a very long while, unable to speak any words.

27

Several days later–after the wakes for the fallen–Naero's Strike Fleet Six earned a week of well-deserved shore leave. They stood down while the battles to stabilize that area still continued back at the front.

In an attempt to help distract some of them from their recent losses, Chaela hurriedly finished organizing their WebBall team of fifty players.

They even had their first match that first night–and lost miserably to another team from *The Choturri,* who had been playing for months.

Actually playing a WebBall match turned out to be light years away from merely watching one.

Their opponents were definitely a better, more experienced team. Well-practiced, and used to playing in harmony with each other.

Saemar laughed afterwards. "Eighty-seven to twenty-three–not bad for our first try. Buck up, sweeties. We'll get better."

Only Chae seemed worried about the loss. She hated losing, and as their coach, she sulked more than anyone else.

Naero shrugged, opened a cooler around their grills, and handed around bottles of sweet Spacer poteen, ice cold.

"Hey, it's just a game, right?"

Actually, some of the tactics of WebBall stuck with Naero, giving her valuable insights into their next fleet battles with Triax. There were several things that she could translate into actual fleet tactics. New tricks to try.

Everything was a learning experience.

Two days later, they played another match, this time against a team of 3rd Division Marines. Naero recognized First Leftenant Jeremiah Hayden, one of the other team's captains.

They exchanged greetings and competed vigorously.

Hayden's Death Eyes beat them only by ten points.

Chaela still sulked afterwards.

At least they were improving, and against older teams with more experience. Naero liked playing forward, where her great speed, strength, and agility could make a difference. She wanted to be on the attack, but WebBall also taught one the value of a solid defense.

She determined that if they improved their defense, they would start wining matches.

She spoke to Chae and they came to the same conclusion, creating training and practice plans to help the team measure up more to their opponents.

The next day, Naero finally had time for another naval fleet battle sim with Tarim.

They met in secret, back on board *The Hippolyta*, while everyone else was still down on Vaenian-2 for the shore leave. Naero used one of their largest holographic training rooms, an immense sphere forty meters in diameter within the planetoid vessel. Every millimeter was covered in holoprojector arrays.

Naero waited patiently. Tarim was still learning all of the basic fleet formations.

Then she could teach him some of the more complex ones.

Spacers learned all this stuff from the time they were little kids, and played various vid and holo games involving these principles.

Tarim still had a lot of catching up to do.

And, admittedly, it was never his intent to become a fleet admiral himself one day.

All he wanted was to understand enough about how the fleets operated and fought so that he didn't feel so ignorant and helpless during their naval battles. And not feel left out of the heated debates Spacers sometimes had in the aftermath.

Naero held her standard fleet of fifty small blue holoships off to one side.

For the point of their sims, Tarim commanded the standard red fleet. "Standard line formation…"

His fifty ships stretched out in a long straight line, with his battleships at the center, flanked by his cruisers and destroyers, which balanced on either flank. Carriers behind his battleships, with his gunships and frigates protecting his rear.

"Arc, forward concave formation…rearward concave formation…forward convex formation…"

His line of holoships bent and flexed this way and that, pweaking to obey his voice commands. He wasn't that great with hand signals and the dexterous manipulation of the battle holo flows yet, either.

Naero didn't have the heart to tell Tarim yet that hand motions and signals from the tiny command sensors in his nanogloves could normally adjust formations much faster than voice commands. And they didn't announce your moves and telegraph your strategies as much to your opponents during most face-to-face sims, either.

By contrast, Naero could make subtle adjustments with custom pweaked signals, using just a flick of one finger. Master battle strategists often looked like concert musicians or orchestra conductors during a complex battle. Fingers and hands worked and flashed rapidly across the holodata fields and arrays.

Voice commands were merely used to supplement motions and rapid commands made by their hands, and to keep the bridge crew generally informed.

Tarim progressed through the standard patterns. "Plane formation…cube formation…tile formation, stack 4 X 4 X 4, Alpha-Charlie-1."

Most basic formations had a calculated response–a different formation that was designed to neutralize the tactical advantages of the other. Fleets shifted their attack and defense patterns constantly, in order to take advantage of these various options.

The key was to read the field, understand the big picture, and formulate a winning, overall response and fighting strategy–while constantly moving, adapting, and fighting.

"Wedge formation…double-wedge formation…diamond formation."

In a real battle as well as sims, damage stats and losses on both sides had to be taken into vital consideration during the constant flow of the battle.

"X-formation…star formation…spiral formation…and wave formation. Whew. I think that's all of the basic ones, N."

Naero shook her head. "Not quite, Tarim. You either forgot or skipped over the auxiliary formations of close, tight, dispersal, and wide dispersal formations–as well as spider, claw, and galaxy variations of the standard spiral formation."

Small motions from her hands caused her holoships to flash into images of each of the additional formations as she mentioned them.

"Show-off." Tarim blinked. "Just shoot me."

She smirked. "Shalaen would never forgive me." Naero stuck her tongue out at him. "Hey, you're the one who said you wanted to learn some of this stuff."

Tarim shook his head. "I know, I know. Will the instructor please proceed with the lesson?"

"What's got you so down?"

"What else… Shalaen. She's off on her own again. I know there's a war on, and both of us are always busy. But I really miss her. We haven't seen each other for weeks. I send her messages each day, but it's been three days without a response. It makes me worry."

Naero opened her eyes wide.

"We're all too busy. I'm sure there's an explanation for it, Tarim. And don't worry about her. If anyone can handle herself, it's Shalaen. Now pay attention. Say I shift my fleet into triple-ring, Charlie-Romeo-3 formation; how do you respond?"

In reaction to her hand motions, her blue fleet slowly shifted and approached his in that exact formation

She had the speed set way down, so that he could track every shift.

"Uh…sphere or cube formation–"

"Can't be both, Tarim–pick one."

"Sphere…Delta-Sierra-2 sphere formation, wide dispersal at first, envelope at the point of engagement, and then constrict."

Naero nodded, as Tarim's red fleet tightened around hers in slow motion.

"Very good. Sphere was the best choice, more efficient economy of force than cube."

They went through numerous variations and responses.

Tarim got about half of them right.

"Good, you're improving," Naero told him. "Now we need to talk about attack vectors and patterns more. Depending on your position and formation relative to your enemy, if you are in attack range, you want to maximize your firing profiles as you go in, utilizing the data from your battle computers, your scanners, and the constant flow of updated data streams coming to you from your bridge AIs. You also want to make your attack on the best optimal vector, using the most efficient arc of attack. Check your battle feeds."

Tarim adjusted on the fly. "This is why the main fleets engage first, and then the strike fleets arc in for their attacks after that."

"Correct. Basic naval strategy. Remember, you can attack from anywhere within 360 degrees. Straight on, to either flank, above, below, behind, or from any conceivable side or angle. But the idea is to concentrate destroying fire on your opponent's primary forces and degrade or defeat them as quickly as possible."

He launched his responses. "Shields, armor, direct damage to any and all vital systems. Disable or destroy as many primary warships as possible, in the shortest time possible."

"You need to plan your patterns and priorities of attack, and be ready to adjust them in an instant. Usually it is best to take out their big ships first. Battleships, carriers, cruisers, then destroyers—in that order. Yet there are times when it is wiser to take out their carriers first, or even as many of their lesser ships as possible.

"You can use a balanced attack of so many of your ships per enemy ship, an unbalanced approach, or even concentrate all fire onto one or a few major warships at a time in series, destroy or disable it, and then advance on to the next target. Just remember—"

"I know," Tarim said. "Your opponent is trying to do the same thing to you. Speed, efficiency, and effectiveness are key. The faster you can defeat, disable, or chase off more of your opponent's warships, the quicker you win the battle."

"If you want to confuse or soften up an enemy for another attack wave coming in at them from another direction, you go in fast, hit the foe anywhere and everywhere at random, and then zoom out as quickly as possible, timing things so that the next attack wave catches the foe at the moment of maximum confusion and chaos."

Naero walked Tarim through several classic engagement scenarios. She let him win each one, pausing several times and freezing the sim to give him tips and correct rookie mistakes.

Jumping on him and overwhelming him early on would only lead to him getting frustrated and discouraged, and giving up. She needed to challenge him slowly, while he continued to learn.

Advanced concepts, such as coordinating several strategies and attack plans all at the same time, or in waves or series, was still well beyond him at this point. That was more for the admirals anyway.

They kept at it for another forty-five minutes, before returning to their friends down on the surface.

28

That evening, Tyber came to Naero–barely able to contain his excitement–presenting another new fixer development.

To demonstrate the advances he and his team had helped Intel make, he and Zhen took Naero and a small cloud of newly modified fixers over to Tarim's mobile combat shooting range.

Tyber programmed his new fixers to defend and evade.

They scattered out over the practice range.

Ty turned to his friends and held up both arms invitingly.

"Go at them. Use any weapons you want here. Hit them with everything you've got."

They grabbed various weapon systems locked and loaded on the table, and blazed away.

They drew their own weapons.

Naero and Zhen tried some of Tyber's new throwing weapons.

The results were astonishing.

The new fixers and their microshields remained almost completely invulnerable to all but the heaviest, sustained, concentrated fire and ordnance.

They hit the fixers repeatedly, batting them around, but doing little overall damage.

Naero's most powerful microexplosive devices were about the only things that could routinely take them down.

Tarim was impressed, along with everyone else.

Naero had to ask. "What in the hell did you do to those fixers, Ty?"

Tyber shrugged. "Not much–just new phaze-shielding, flux-frequency nanogenerators and protocols. Similar to the ones we've been experimenting with on the fleet power cores. But my team and I have adjusted them to work on fixers–and personal shield devices, and unit and company-sized shield pods."

Naero had to ask. "Ty, this incredible. You've increased the shielding output and capabilities of this tek tenfold–and miniaturized it even further for a variety of tactical uses. Does Intel know about all of this?"

Zhen hugged him. "And honey, I hope you were smart enough to register the patents?"

Ty grinned. "Don't worry, I have, in part. Part of the process is in fact mine. But the other parts belong to Intel and Clan Maeris. Actually, I've helped make the shielding 847 percent more effective."

He opened a tek instrument case and handed out new personal shield device prototypes to them all. Then he closed the case and shoved it toward Naero.

"There's enough in there for you and all of your bridge crew, N. More will be distributed to all crew on board your flagship. Intel has approved the new devices to be distributed throughout your fleet, and then the entire Alliance. Power core shields will be updated on a regular basis with the latest updates. They won't be completely invulnerable, but they will survive much longer than before. And so will the rest of us, when things get up close and personal."

Naero shook his hand and congratulated him.

Then she and her friends took turns hugging him.

Zhen simply beamed with pride. Naero could tell how proud she was of her lifelong friend and lover.

This was a great moment for Ty. Naero would make sure that she put him up for promotion.

Shalaen arrived, even as they started to leave. She glowed blue in the night as she normally did, pretty and serene–unearthly.

Everyone was happy to see her–especially Tarim–and the friends all embraced each other.

But everyone could quickly tell that Shalaen had eyes only for Tarim, her beloved.

And he could not keep his eyes from hers.

Their duties kept them away from each other so often.

They had so little time together.

Tyber and Zhen grinned and flashed each other knowing looks as they excused themselves and said good night.

Naero did the same, and quickly left Tarim and Shalaen alone as well. She stopped and glanced back at them once.

Tarim took Shalaen's radiant face into both his hands, and looked into her eyes until his tears flowed freely down his young, handsome face.

"I don't deserve you," he told her.

Shalaen looked up at him as only she could and smiled. She placed her fingertips lightly over his heart. Tarim gasped.

"I know differently," she said.

29

The war with Triax never let up for very long.

Next, the Alliance forces moved into the dangerous Hevangian sectors, which included the Triaxian Capital Class World of Tarissa-1.

The Hevangians were well known for being beyond fanatical.

Beyond mere zealots.

To complicate matters for Naero and her ships, Strike Fleet Six received new replacement ships and a large number of raw recruits as replacements for the many killed and wounded they had endured over the past few weeks.

There had been weeks of intense heavy fighting, with many losses on both sides.

Naero did her best to have her veterans welcome the replacements, most of them either very young or much older. Efforts were made to make them feel at home with their new units, part of the team.

There was some cross-training between Spacers, miners, Matayans, and people from Joshua Tech. Everyone had something to contribute. But they didn't have a lot of extra time to sort out cultural and ability gaps between Spacers and various lander groups.

Not everyone was Tarim. Therefore, it was decided that each group should train individually.

Good ideas were shared with the others, just as with Intel. There was no contest. Spacers were clearly the best pilots–hands down. This caused them and their fleets to mostly lead and direct the war, with the other allies usually backing them up in support rolls or in reserve. They still saw plenty of fighting, and casualties of their own. Everyone did.

Strike Fleet Six tried to impress upon all of their recruits that they would require extensive further training at the front, in an effort to give them the greatest chances to survive their first few battles.

This became readily apparent early on. Both sides could easily spot the weak links during a battle–especially among replacement ships and starfighter pilots. Newbs who froze up or panicked could not function properly or do what needed to be done.

The highest rates of casualties were almost always among replacements, green ships, and inexperienced units.

As Naero had said before, the learning curve in war was very steep and unforgiving. Not a nice place for newbs and rookies.

That was why she trained the hell out of her replacements, pairing them one-on-one with veteran people in their positions when and where possible, for as long as possible.

Other matters complicated the constant flux of replacements.

Veterans had to constantly deal with the emotional and mental stress of arbitrarily losing family, friends, comrades, and acquaintances along the way.

There was no avoiding it. War was fickle and unlucky for many– without any rhyme or reason as to who lived or died, or got injured and maimed.

War by its very nature was an inherently dangerous business.

Two percent of all deaths and injuries alone came from accidents and mishaps–despite whatever safety regs and protocols were enforced. Sometimes things simply went wrong, whether from dumb luck, human failure, equipment failure, a cascade of errors, or the law of averages. Nothing was perfect, especially in the chaos and entropy during a war.

Survivor guilt became a major issue for military people in any war.
Why my buddy, and not me?
Why am I still alive?
She deserved to live more than I do.
It should have been me.

The suicide rate was less than one percent among Spacers, higher among the other Alliance forces. But such deaths were still devastating to the survivors who knew them.

Then there were those who simply kept fighting, and did not pull back until the enemy killed them off. This was more prevalent among fighter jocks and forward units.

Captain Hayden said that he had seen that same thing happen among a few of his people, who simply got fed up with the madness and decided to go out in a predictable blaze of glory. All they had to do was stand up and draw fire–then charge into it until they got cut down.

Officers and comrades in all units were instructed to be on the lookout for signs of traumatic stress in each other.

Some people were extremely good actors, and could hide their pain and inner damage very well. Spacers were known for being brave. For facing death without fear.

That was the standard expectation, of course, but sometimes that was all just crap. In war, everyone was afraid of something at some point, or all the time. Sometimes they feared multiple things, and with very good reasons.

But true warriors could manage the energy of their fear and make it work for them–not against them–or ignore it and do their duty anyway.

In the end, only the insane were truly without fear. They no longer gave a damn about anything–but that also included themselves. Anyone with half a brain wanted to survive the war and hopefully return to a life that would be better.

Naero and her officers walked a fine line of not wanting to coddle or baby their people, and yet give them the help they needed. No one had time for the former.

The trick was to try to spot emotional and mental problems early on, before they escalated, and get people the help they needed in a timely fashion.

Spacers were still human and still people. They were still imperfect, with failings and weaknesses unique to each person.

Death and loss, day in and day out, could wear down and break the strongest mind, the stoutest heart.

Naero wanted to help her people before it was too late. She couldn't afford to lose any of them. But it was better to send someone to the rear areas for the rest of the war than have them die uselessly.

As was her new wont when her fleet pulled back from the front, Naero created another alias to use to walk amongst her crew.

This time she chose to be a brunette, with curly waves of hair reaching halfway down her back. Heavy makeup again, but in a different style.

Daphni Romanov, replacement medtek in training. Quiet, reserved, intelligent and professional.

She patterned herself after Zhen, in many ways.

Naero normally took a few days to study her crews and how they were handling the war as individuals and small groups of mates. She liked hearing what they really thought, their unbridled opinions, good, bad, or in between.

She ate with them. She drank, gambled, and goofed around among them.

She could learn a lot as a medtek, and had a ready excuse to go around and talk to a lot of people about injuries, or how they were holding up under stress. Her primary function, after all, was to follow up on people's recoveries from various injuries and see how they were doing.

This gave her a chance to check records on how certain patients and their recoveries were proceeding in hospitals on pacified worlds.

Kelment, Mariisha, and several others whom she knew by name were doing just fine.

A month or two longer, and they would be fully restored to their old selves.

And hopefully, by then, the Annexation War would be over.

Most crew were ordered in to meet with Daphni-Naero, and in her role as a medtek, her job was to make a full report.

Others she had to track down among the fleet, if they were too busy to come see her on their own.

Many Spacers did in fact grow privately angry and bitter about the war over time. Most kept their frustrations to themselves. The many losses they all endured upset everyone–friends and family killed or horribly maimed. Wounds and injuries they themselves had struggled to recover from, and still be able to function and serve the war effort.

People needed someone to blame, so at times, naturally, they blamed the Alliance and fleet leadership. They cursed the command officers.

They even cursed her directly.

Fleet Captain Maeris and the rest of Alliance Command were cold-blooded death machines, merchants of death who simply played numbers games on battle computers with peoples' lives.

In a many ways, Naero accepted that as true.

But some people went overboard.

Their Fleet Commanders were robotic killers who drove their ships and crews into battle knowing full-well that a certain percentage wouldn't make it back. In every battle, someone was going to die. And all of their family and friends would suffer for it.

Some said that Captain Maeris and the others didn't give a damn about their dead and wounded.

Others sneered, saying she made a phony show of coming around and trying to help comfort those hurt. But it was all just an act. Something she thought she had to do as a duty.

Something the higher-ups had even ordered her to do, when she had been too busy to bother with it.

Other crew would try to defend her and the leadership. They all fought together in a just cause. Each warrior's fate was his or her own. They all took the same chances together.

Daphni-Naero heard it all, whether fair or unfair. Rage, rant, and reason.

Still, she strove never to take offense. She needed to hear what people truly thought. She chose to do this. Others should not be punished in any way for their personal opinions.

But whatever persona or job she chose for her forays, things always seemed to get unintentionally complex in regard to interpersonal matters and relationships.

Especially about sex.

Naero could play down, but not completely hide her looks. And being clearly attractive, others were repeatedly drawn to her.

Someone was always becoming enamored of her.

It even became tiresome.

She found herself continually forced to beg off several potential relationships, and continual, multiple offers of simple, "fun-in-the-sack."

The latter grew too numerous to track.

Spacers were as interested in "docking together" and linking up as much as any other species.

Perhaps more so, from what she observed. They were a pretty randy lot, it appeared. Spacers just kept their sex lives more or less private.

Yet with so much action going on, Naero started to wonder what was wrong with herself?

Why wasn't she constantly on the make for some action?

Was the world more like Saemar's view than she had originally believed?

Yet even she found herself very tempted here and there.

But no. She always knew for certain that it wouldn't be fair to use her aliases simply to fool around with some unsuspecting crew; her deceptions were borderline bad enough as they were.

Mason Elliott

The role she maintained as strike fleet captain was so different from her mundane personalities that she assumed no one ever suspected her, exposed her, or found her out.

Not yet, at least.

Although there ended up being numerous heartsick Romeos, and even a few yearning Juliets who kept asking about and looking around for her aliases, well after she had pulled her vanishing transfer acts.

If pressed on such matters, Naero merely instructed her officers to say that so-and-so was transferred to another duty, somewhere else, on a need-to-know basis.

30

    Long range scans picked up a massive explosion that suddenly took out an entire system in a remote area of space, far beyond the Hevangian systems, but still technically under Triaxian control.

    An ominous, incredible mystery unfolded.

    Spacer teks and scientists found that phenomena very strange and worrisome. The star in that sector had been very average, and showed no signs whatsoever of going nova, or collapsing, or reaching critical mass in any way.

    The quanta-blast explosion was so devastating that it did not seem to match even what the explosive output of such a star should have been. And it happened almost instantly, with no astronomical warning whatsoever.

    The fact that such a cataclysmic event escalated and occurred so rapidly had many stymied. It was completely unexplained and unnatural.

    Yet the weird event also took place in a far away, blank area of dead space, well beyond the Scutum-Crux Arm, in a lifeless, remote system of barren rocks and gas giants. No one could go there to check it out even if they had wanted to.

Very peculiar, but for the most part impossible to investigate, what with the prosecution of the war and all.

The Alliance already had its hands very full.

Every system in the Hevangian region posed a unique and separate problem and threat. The normal pacification strategies did not seem to apply at all.

Each world had its own planetary defense shield, and Triax had developed a way to keep Alliance stealth fixers from penetrating those shields.

Therefore, until the planet defense shield of each separate planet was taken down, there would be no way to neutralize any genocide devices seeded on those worlds.

Admiral Sandusky's shadow fleets and agents also had little influence on the majority of these fanatical worlds. And thus each Hevangian world turned into, more or less, a ready-made trap for Alliance forces to become mired in.

It became very clear to Naero and many others that they would need to rethink their strategies and come up with new solutions in a hurry.

Otherwise, they would quickly get bogged down for many months–if not years–dealing with all of those worlds and their petty problems.

First, the main war had to continue to be prosecuted to its fullest extent, without delay.

That reality continued on a daily basis, as the Alliance fought from world to world, and system to system, putting down the staunch, Triaxian Naval forces.

Already, sadly, three entire Hevangian systems had more or less committed cosmicide via mass genocide devices that either they or their leaders set off themselves. Some well in advance of the Alliance progress. The entire situation was insane.

It was Heaven-7 all over again, on an even wider scale, and there was nothing the Alliance could do about it.

The Gigacorps propaganda machine had a field day, blaming the alliance for every tragedy.

Hundreds of billions more dead–for no logical reason.

Naero spoke up one day at an officer's meeting with the Alliance admirals.

"I'm sorry to say this. It goes against everything I feel and believe. But I don't think we can sort out this Hevangian mess on every single world. There simply isn't enough time. And as we have seen, there is also little that we can do to keep Triax from scorching the earth in its wake as it retreats and de-populating entire systems through genocide. They have done so before we can even approach such worlds."

Nevano Kinmal shook his head sadly and looked down at his hands. "There must be something we can do. These people do not need to perish. It is the fault of their leaders perpetrating this madness. Can Spacer Intel or anyone get down on these worlds in advance and try to eliminate the leadership before they can trigger these terrible devices?"

Aunt Sleak sighed and shook her head. "Not with all of these worlds protected by planetary defense shields."

Admiral Klyne noted, "Our Intel presence on these worlds in the heart of Triax's most fanatical systems is limited or nonexistent."

"We're talking dozens and dozens of worlds," Admiral Joshua said. "Again, Naero is correct. We cannot reach them all in time, and even if we could, could we find a way to save them from themselves?"

Many others made protests.

Many others proposed similar strategies that had already failed.

Admiral Sandusky finally rose up. "These are still my people. I find it strange that many of you care more about them and what happens to them than Triax does. It is as if Triax wants to destroy them needlessly–in order to punish everyone–friend or foe. A sad state of affairs. But you only have one clear choice."

Even he hesitated to speak it, but Admiral Klyne and most of them knew that someone had to say the words. And it was better than Sandusky was the one to do so.

"Tell us, Admiral," Klyne said. "You and your shadow fleets have already saved trillions of lives. And I'll bet that you will save trillions more before all is done. But we need to hear this from you."

"Proceed with the war," Sandusky said. "Defeat Triax with all speed, and at all cost. Once Triax has fallen–once it is truly gone–then and only then will there be no further need for any of this destructive folly. Until then, we can only do what we can do. And no more. We will do what we can, but the war must proceed to its logical conclusion."

Naero and her captains proposed a plan, punching it up on the displays and everyone's pads.

"Blockade the worlds in this region and then push on, like the Admiral said, with all speed," Naero told them. "That is the only way. Sandusky's shadow fleets and rear-area forces will be spread thin, but they can handle the job, once we remove the main threats. Perhaps Spacer Intel can do a little more. But the cold hard truth of the matter is that there is only so much that we can do. We can't control everything on the ground on hundreds of new systems. We can't let that slow us down. That is exactly what Triax is hoping for: to prolong the war as long as possible and outlast us. To somehow find a way to survive and cling to their power."

Nevano Kinmal nodded. "Admiral Sandusky is correct. Once the war sweeps past these worlds, there will be less impetus for them to have any reason or pretense for scorching themselves. Any strategic value will be gone. They will have no fleets to use against us. And we can move on, especially if they are merely blockaded and not invaded."

"Under a blockade," Admiral Klyne said, "perhaps this will buy us time we need to find a way to get our pacification elements on these worlds, in order to change things for the better—more quietly."

Admiral Maeris pweaked the battle plan in several ways as they looked on.

"I agree, overall, that the main objective has to be to continue prosecuting the war, advancing as fast as possible. The Capital Class Homeworld of Tarissa-1 must fall. The Hevangians must be contained and bottled up, taking them out of the war as a factor. We can always come back to these systems and deal with them later, with the full power of the entire Alliance. And if they still insist on offing themselves, fighting to the last, or being burned out for no reason at all—we can fully oblige them."

"I think we are in general agreement, then, on Fleet Captain Maeris's basic strategy," Admiral Joshua noted. "Adjustments will need to be made along the way, of course. But concluding the war remains the ultimate, primary objective. Bypass, blockade, and neutralize the various Hevangian threats as best we can. That is the only viable solution for now."

Admiral Maeris rose up, hands flashing through the displays, shifting units and key supplies and resources. "The logistics look good. I say we proceed immediately. We'll need to bring up many more shadow fleet forces and secondary forces from the rear areas."

Kinmal and Sandusky spoke at once. "That should not be an issue."

Sleak continued. "Most of those systems are fully pacified already, any way."

Naero did see a potential danger of attacks in their thinly protected rear systems. But even that was unlikely with the Spacer Navy guarding their back door.

On their way back to their transports to rejoin their ships, Naero received an emergency call from an old friend of the family on her wristcom, via their secure channel.

Her outcast uncle, Baeven.

"Any word on Jan or Dan yet?" she asked.

"Negative. I promise you, Naero. I will inform you the instant that there is. But you and the Alliance have bigger worries at the moment."

"Wha–"

"Just listen, Naero. I don't have much time where I am. Two things: first, the Hevangians are going to go after your admirals and the Alliance leadership directly."

"Take out our command and control?"

"Exactly. And that also includes you, Naero. Strike Fleet Six has been a major thorn in their side since day one. Good for you. And don't forget, you still carry the KDM."

Naero shrugged. "Yeah, for all the good it's done me and Spacer Intel. I'm completely cut off from it, and Intel hasn't been able to make a dent in decoding or understanding any of it."

"Give them time. Triax doesn't know any of that, and still wants both you and it, desperately. They've made you a priority target, right up there with the admirals. And Shalaen, too, for some reason."

"Our security is the best, and Intel has agents guarding the admirals constantly. How do the Hevangians plan on pulling this off?"

"More new tek–a game changer called phaze armor. It's a new type of experimental cloaking that allows them to actually enter the astral plane, and take an astral form for a short time. In that form they are virtually undetectable and invulnerable. Plus, they can phaze right through walls, shields, bulkheads. Anything. Then unphaze, uncloak and go on the attack."

Naero thought about Kono's ship and resisted the urge to cover her mouth with one hand. That would explain what happened to *The Silver Devil.*

"*Haisha,*" Naero said. "Normal cloaking makes the user invisible–but not immaterial. How are they getting their hands on such advanced tek like this?"

"Unknown. But they have it now and intend to use it. Only problem is, it's still experimental–even for them. Utilizing this tek is a one-way ride. Anyone using it gets phaze-sickness. Within a week or two after exposure, the user begins to dissolve away. Their flesh melts off into the astral plane, leaving behind a very clean and very dead skeleton."

"Gross. That sounds…extremely unpleasant."

"And dangerous, N. Yet despite such high costs, the enemy can still use this tek to attack anyone, anywhere, without warning."

"The Hevangian assassins were once legendary for their suicide squads," Naero said. "I wonder why we haven't seen more of these phaze attacks, yet?"

"Plan on it. You can bet they'll be coming straight for you, and soon. Even in the midst of battles, possibly. So tell Sleak and the rest to be ready for them."

"Will do."

Naero suddenly heard alarms going off over Baeven's link.

Then weapons firing.

"Baeven?"

"*Haisha*–gotta fly," he said. Naero heard a large explosion.

The link broke off.

Be safe, Baeven.

Then other alarms began sounding, right in the hanger deck of the flagship *The Pearl Harbor*.

A voice sounded over the ship's com. "All hands, all ships. Battle stations and report. Arm yourselves and repel boarders. Strange infiltrators have appeared on several ships without warning, including *The Pearl Harbor*. We need to learn the extent of this attack. Protect the fleet leadership at all costs!"

Baeven said it would start soon. Naero didn't think it would be instantly. She paused a moment.

Most of the leadership could be on their way to their separate transports after the planning session, to get back to their ships, just like her.

Aunt Sleak and Zalvano might already be under attack on their bridge.

She snapped her head toward Tarim. "Get Leftenant Hayden and his Marines to help protect the transports, the leadership, and the decks in the vicinity. Let's proceed directly to the bridge."

She and her people raced back into the flagship, making calls on their wristcoms.

Several large explosions suddenly rocked the flagship. Power and life support flickered. Then backups brought them back online.

Naero continued feeding Klyne what her secret sources of Intel had uncovered.

Then she called Aunt Sleak.

That there was no reply filled her with concern.

She called Zalvano.

"Naero. Haisha, they came right through the hull. Hevangian assassins, the bloody sons of bitches!"

She heard the staccato sounds of blasters and other weapons blazing, grenades going off.

"Are you and Aunt Sleak all right?"

"Could be better. We're fighting on the bridge. Sleak got stunned after she shot a couple of them. Help's on the way. Get up here if you can."

"On my way," Naero said. She checked all of her weapons again.

These were the same murderous assholes who had attacked her mom's ship years before, killed many of their Clan, and ruined her brother Danner's life.

And that indirectly led to her parents' deaths.

They had also attacked Naero and her fleet, killing their people.

Time for a little payback.

31

The gravity on Aunt Sleak's flagship still worked when Naero and her small security team reached the shattered bridge blast doors.

A Spacer body lay just inside the entrance, crew shot dead as she had tried to charge in.

Blood trailed down the floor, out of the bridge.

They heard intense weapon fire, shouting, screaming, and explosions within.

The fight with the assassins continued to rage.

Naero moved her people back, sensing an ambush just within.

From cover and concealment, she sent in a few fixers first to spy things out.

That included two of the precious new Intel prototypes that could use stealth mode, and cloak themselves.

Most of the regular fixers got popped, showing brief views of a fire team of Hevangian sharpshooters blasting them.

The foe also covered the entrance with a pair of portable, crew-served chain guns. For good measure, the enemy also sent out a wave of float grenades and seeker mines against whoever sent the fixers in.

Explosions and stun blasts rocked the deck and pockmarked the corridor all around the bridge entrance.

Inside, the enemy waited for anyone foolish enough to charge the entrance. Several more dead Spacers and Spacer Marines inside attested to the enemy's lethal battle skill.

These were elite, professional assassins.

All of the Spacer bodies had been stripped of weapons and explosives.

Sounds of battle still rocked the flagship on other decks.

By all reports, suicide squads of Hevangians spread throughout the flagship, keeping others away from the bridge while the main assault unit pursued its objectives.

The admirals, and herself, most likely. Shalaen wasn't with them currently.

The smaller enemy teams were just distractions and decoys to buy the main units time. Yet they would still cause a great deal of damage as they sold their lives dearly.

If the foe could reach the power cores, Naero had no doubt that the enemy would attempt to sabotage, cripple, or destroy the flagship–if they were able.

But by now they were being swarmed on by Spacers and Spacer Marines.

Those foes would not last very long.

Naero, Tarim, and the rest of Naero's team took precious seconds to evaluate the battle data the remaining stealth fixers fed them.

Eight heavily armed attackers guarded the entrance.

Sixteen more, including one who appeared to be a leader, directed the assault on a secondary blast screen that had slammed down in front of the main bridge.

Within, seven Spacer bridge crew and one remaining Marine guard fired weapons and sent out smart explosives of their own to hold the enemy off.

The defenders appeared to be led by Fleet Captain Zalvano, and Admiral Sandusky. About twenty other crew and Marines lay stunned or wounded within the barrier, including Aunt Sleak, still clutching a smoking blaster rifle.

A dozen dead Hevangians lay scattered within also.

Every one of the assassins had been shot in the head or face to make certain of them.

Zalvano had the defenders set up back-to-back in a tight ring. Half of his people kept their weapons trained on the walls, constantly scanning and covering every angle.

Even the outside hull of the ship.

Naero spoke in a low voice. "The enemy must have used that phazing tek we've heard about. I bet some of them came right through the hull and the walls."

Tarim nodded. "The pattern of the fighting supports that. You can see where some of our people were caught by surprise and gunned down or knifed at their stations. Just like we saw before. My guess is, the enemy will use phaze tek again to get in there quick."

"I think that's a good guess," Naero said. "But they'll do so sparingly. That tek kills them a little more and a little faster each second they use it. Now follow me. I know of a secret escape passage that Aunt Sleak and Zalvano had put in when the life pods were doubled. We can get at the goons guarding the entrance through that."

Tarim smiled and readied his plasma machine pistols. "Sounds good. Everyone, keep a full spread of micro grenades ready."

They slipped down the hall and through a coded entrance into a small meeting room. From there they gained access to two other chambers adjacent to the bridge and some of the additional escape pods.

Naero coded the hidden panel to the escape passage.

"Activate gravwings. We'll open a panel slightly above and behind them. They might spot us, but there's nothing for it. We swoop in fast and take them out. Full-on attack, with everything we have."

Leftenant Hayden cut in on their secured link. "We've put down any attackers we could locate. Proceeding to the bridge. Other forces converging."

Naero turned to Tarim. "Warn Hayden and the others what they're walking into. Tell them to hold up until we begin our attack."

"Will do."

They swarmed into the escape tube like angry hornets, single file, moving fast. The kept their weapons trained out in front.

Naero coded open the hidden panel just inside the bridge itself.

She and her small team shot out and wheeled to attack, scattering a spray of microgrenades and bomblets below.

They fired down even as the enemy trained their weapons up at them.

The element of surprise worked both ways.

First the grenades knocked the Hevangians around and took out their shields.

The waiting micro-fixers quickly rendered the chain guns into non-firing scrap metal and plasteel.

Naero hit two of the enemy with glowing energy blades set to detonate.

The blasts blew off their head and arms even as precise small arms fire riddled their bodies.

The six remaining foes went down hard and fast, especially with Leftenant Hayden and his Marines charging in to lend their support behind a shield pod warping the air in front of them to deflect heavy fire.

Naero whirled just in time to see the main enemy strike force activate their phaze armor and walk through the barrier in bright flashes.

Naero pointed at the secondary blast barrier.

"Get everyone in there. Cut the foe down. I can snap the blast shields out of the way. Give me a sec."

She struggled on her wristcomp to input the override code as quickly as possible.

Vital seconds passed.

At last, the secondary blast shields popped back down into the floor and up into the ceiling.

She could only spot about half of the enemy strike team in a firefight with the dwindling bridge crew.

Where had the others gone? That was a new problem.

Even as they moved to engage, enemy agents appeared behind the defenders, as if by magic.

They lifted their ritual Hevangian shokkog, death blades steeped in lethal cocktails of poisons that dripped and ran off them and hissed on the duranadium floor. No known antidotes.

Two Spacers and the last Marine within died outright, screaming in agony as the assassin blades pierced their backs and throats from behind and hit them with those lethal poisons.

Naero fired four exploding needles in the face of the one trying to knife Zalvano. The head and helmet puffed away into red mist.

Tarim knelt and fired full bursts of automatic plasma bolts into the assassins crouching over Aunt Sleak.

The accurate plasma fire scorched gaping, charred holes through the assassins and flung them back against the chairs and consoles.

Tarim, Hayden, and the others kept up a steady hail of precise fire, moving in, cutting down any Hevangian and keeping fire on them until they were obviously dead.

Off to one side, Naero trained her weapons on five remaining Hevangians, including the leader—a tall young man with vicious scars crisscrossing his face.

They all held guns and weapons trained on a disarmed and battered Admiral Sandusky.

Sandusky snarled defiantly. "I'm good as dead. Kill these fucks!"

Two assassins stunned the admiral and slipped a rescue bag up around him, sealing him in it.

Naero barely spotted the shaped cutting charges packed on the outer hull behind them. She realized what they were going to do.

The male leader of the Hevangians sneered at her. "Clever little spack. Cut her down!"

Naero shouted aloud in warning. "They're going to blow the hull to escape!"

The enemy could have passed through walls—but they wanted Sandusky.

She sealed her combat armor and dove behind a bridge station all at once, just as the enemy fired and the shaped charges went off.

The hull instantly decompressed.

The assassins let themselves get sucked out into space.

Naero kicked off the console she hid behind and shot after them.

Leftenant Hayden and several of his Marines came on fast behind her.

Then the hull on the flagship auto-sealed behind them, throwing up shields to close off the breach.

In space, the Hevangians swept toward the wide-open loading hatch of a high-speed Alliance courier backing up toward them.

The other Hevangian agents on board the captured ship kicked and tossed the bodies of the courier's real crew and passengers out of the cargo hatch into the black.

Naero, Hayden, and the Marines hit their gravwings and raced after the enemy at top speed.

They swept in so fast, the enemy in the hold didn't even have a chance to shoot or get out of the way.

All of them smashed into each other and tumbled back into the courier's cargo bay. The loading hatch closed.

They wrestled and fought together amid the chaos within, as the small ship took heavy fire from all sides without. The Alliance fleets attempted to cut off the small armored ship and disable it.

The courier shot away, spinning and taking expert, evasive action.

The assassins had selected their escape vehicle with great care and cunning.

Naero grappled and kicked and stabbed at not one, but several Hevangian assassins, bouncing around in zero-G.

She shot one in the guts, both of them propelled in the opposite direction. Blood and entrails boiled out into the null gravity.

One of the assassins sliced at her with a dripping shokkog, and just missed cutting deep through the arm of her combat suit.

Naero flipped end-over-end and used the momentum to hurl a stun dagger into another foe. The shock charge went off and the assassin stiffened and floated.

A Marine cut loose with his assault rifle and cut the stunned female assassin into two bloody pieces.

Right before the shooter got knifed in the back from behind by another Hevangian who just phazed in.

The deadly shokkog point jutted out of the dying Marine corporal's broad chest.

The corporal blinked once at the poison blazing through him.

Then his face froze in death.

Naero, Hayden, and his remaining Marines found themselves outnumbered and fighting for their very lives in that tight hold.

She lost sight of Admiral Sandusky.

Then she felt the ship preparing to go into jump.

If they left that sector—and rendezvoused at some enemy staging area—all of them were good as dead.

Naero pushed off the hull again and muscled her way forward with raw strength. She kept spinning, kicking, and punching foes out of her way. She used elbows and knees to crush and shatter bones.

On her port side stood the compartment containing the small ship's power core.

On her starboard side stood the compartment containing the jump drive.

Naero's hands flashed.

Every explosive device she had left hit that damn jump drive.

She deflected off the ceiling and sped back out of the way as her devices cooked off.

She dragged two Marines back with her, one of them Hayden.

The stolen courier lurched into jump just as its jump drive exploded. The air all around them went blinding, white-hot, filled with burning fragments and plasma.

Not to mention the shock waves of the blast.

32

The jump drive blast killed or wounded everyone in the hold. No one escaped damage or injury, including Naero.

Shrapnel sprayed everywhere.

Naero winced in agony from several serious burn and shrapnel wounds distributed across her body.

Spacer smartblood and her nanosuit strained to stop the bleeding and close off the damage.

The hull of the courier struggled to seal itself against the many punctures and ruptures patterned out from the shattered jump drive.

The power core next to it was damaged also, but held together for the time being. Emergency shielding prevented the deadly radiation and energy core forces from cooking off completely.

At least for now.

Dead and wounded floated and bounced around everywhere within the hold.

Eyes stared, milked over pale in death. Some bodies had faces and entire heads ripped or burned off, along with other body parts.

Blood, entrails, and other bodily fluids and contents boiled around freely from the corpses and the seriously wounded.

Like her, any of the others who survived–whether friend or foe–struggled just to twitch or even move after the intense explosion.

Naero caught her breath, despite painful damage to her right chest and one lung. Her left leg felt numb.

Something else was wrong with the ship. She could tell. The superstructure groaned and screamed as if gigantic hands or claws were attempting to tear it apart like a loaf of bread.

Then she knew…as if things weren't bad enough.

The explosion right at the point of jump had caused a misjump–extremely dangerous.

The small courier careened out of control, spinning and smashing its way through jump space.

They could be tossed out anywhere, in any direction, within several parsecs.

They could come out on either side of the frontline of the war.

Or they could be torn apart and obliterated. Just random, scorched debris, spat out from jump into normal space.

They could emerge any second, anywhere at random in the nearby vicinity, or they could tumble through jump space for days, out of control, while the stress forces on their ship only increased.

She covered her mouth with both hands suddenly.

Admiral Sandusky floated right below her. Dead.

A severed Hevangian arm still clutched a bloody shokkog. The poison dagger had been plunged into the shredded rescue bag several times. The bag and everything nearby had also been shredded and torn apart by the explosion she had caused.

At least Sandusky had been stunned before he died.

It was a wonder any of them still lived.

Somehow, in her dazed state, Naero stumbled upon Leftenant Hayden by dumb luck.

He looked all right, overall. Nothing missing, no major wounds. Perhaps his shield had held up to the blast.

But his armored helmet was cracked and seriously deformed.

Through his splintered visor, Naero could see a head wound and possible concussion; blood had streamed down over his face. She hit him up with some advanced healing meds that worked well in conjunction with Spacer smartblood.

191

His flickering suit signs said that he was still alive and with strong vitals, just knocked out. Most likely from being slammed into the hull of the hold by the explosion.

Any Hevangian she came to got two in the chest and one in the head.

Just to be sure–Naero wasn't taking any chances.

Especially, not in her reduced condition.

She kept moving, staggering, bouncing around, trying to anchor herself, ignoring her own wounds and agony as she did so. She checked one floating body after the next.

She located five other surviving Marines, and did her best to stabilize and secure them beside their leader.

Who now groaned and tossed his head, blinking in pain.

The last Marine she worked on was in bad shape.

A very young Marine with short green hair and dark eyes. He smiled weakly at her and tried to make some smartass comment. Naero did her best to help him, but she was close to passing out by that time herself.

He took hold of her left hand and would not let go.

She finally had to pull her hand away to help him.

His wounds were simply too many and too severe.

Naero couldn't close them all off fast enough.

The poor guy bled to death in her very hands, while she struggled both to save him and stay conscious herself.

Haisha. Damn it!

Naero sobbed and drifted to one side, too dizzy to get back up.

She passed out for a bit–hard to tell for how long.

She wasn't sure.

When her eyes flickered open again, they did so to pain.

Leftenant Hayden yanked a big chunk of nasty-looking shrapnel out of her left thigh.

It hurt like blazes.

Her leg wound instantly bubbled and boiled with blood.

Hayden sealed it off and closed the wound quickly and expertly.

Naero was impressed, despite the pain that made her want to punch him.

Zhen couldn't have done a better job.

He fixed only one other wound on her upper right arm. He told her the rest had stopped bleeding, and should be all right, given time. He gave her a dose of the same meds she'd hit him up with.

Then he put two enemy machine pistols in her hands and propped her up adjacent to the far hatch.

The hatch that led to the courier's small bridge. Most likely one or two flight chairs, for either a single pilot, or a pilot and co-pilot.

Naero flopped her aching head to one side and stared at Hayden, lifting the pistols weakly.

She could hardly hold them up, let alone hit anything.

"What are these for?" she asked.

Hayden reached back over and activated her backup personal shield.

"Think about it." He jerked a thumb back. "Someone might be piloting this ship still. Keep an eye on that hatch. Blast the living shit out of anyone who comes through it. I have to check on the others, but it looks like you've stabilized them all just fine."

Naero swallowed hard. "I…I lost the kid…with the green hair."

"Private First Class Donovan? Yeah. I saw that, N. Not your fault."

She wiped her face. "Doesn't feel like not my fault. I caused the jump drive to go off."

"And a good thing you did. All of us would be captured and looking forward to Hevangian torture teams, or simply shot in the head by now. You did the right thing."

Naero smiled, sensing a little of her strength returning.

Hayden double-checked his people and their wounds.

A booted foot out of nowhere kicked him right in the face, stunning him.

The Hevangian leader phazed in right between them.

Naero tried to raise her pistols.

Too slow.

The leader booted her in the chest and smashed her against the hull.

She gasped for air and dropped both guns.

The Hevangian leader grinned, his face oozing with phaze disease over his skull bones. Terrible scars crisscrossing his face beneath that.

He snarled and gloated at the both of them. "You stinking, bloody spacks! You think yourselves so cunning and resourceful. Always messing things up. Always causing mayhem!"

He drew his shokkog, the poison streamed off the blade in rivulets.

"Now we have time to play. Poison for the good leftenant–my shokkog shoved through his eyes and into his brain. Death to your helpless wounded, that goes without saying. But you…I have not had a pretty spack whore like you to toy with, my dear. Not for a very long while."

He glared down at her with eager, unbridled lust. "I'm going to use your own blades on you, my dear. I'm going to enjoy slowly, slowly, slowly cutting…and slicing…and sawing you in half…lengthwise. From your gash all the way up to your pretty white throat. Now, how does that sound?"

"Screw that…and you," Naero told him.

Hayden tried to lunge forward.

The leader booted him to one side, leaned over him, and raised the poison dagger to stab forward.

With her last remaining strength, Naero plucked up her machine pistols where they fell and jammed them up into the leader's buttocks from behind and below.

She pulled both triggers, aiming the muzzles of both blasting guns up into the leader's jerking body cavity.

The exploding rounds caused the Hevangians torso to jiggle obscenely and then disintegrate. His head, neck, and part of one shoulder flopped, gory, to one side.

She completely gutted him with gunfire.

Naero fell back, completely spent.

Hayden staggered to his feet, grabbed a stray weapon, and went to secure the rest of the ship before they did anything else.

He returned shortly. "Good, the leader was the last of them."

Except for the cargo hold and an extremely small crew cabin, the courier did not have many amenities. It could carry passengers in the hold, but basically it was a one-or two-person ship at best.

They still had no way of knowing how long they would be stuck in jump space.

They rested, floating around with the wounded and the dead.

"Mist shower," Naero finally insisted, pulling herself up and forward. "We can't do much else until we come out of jump and see where we're at. We don't have gravitics, but all the other systems are holding steady. So I'm going to bathe. And I will kill anyone who tries to stop me."

Hayden raised both hands, and then brought them obviously to his aching skull. "Go right ahead. I'm going to float right here and pass out with my guys."

He proceeded to do so.

The ship kept shaking and jerking around without warning, battered within jump space.

Naero floated against and patted the hull. "Just hold together, baby. Just keep it together until we make it out."

Naero stripped down and slipped into the tiniest mist shower she had ever seen on any ship.

She was small, and even she had to slip in sideways and squeeze in.

Did they really recruit pygmies to be courier pilots and crew? It boggled the mind.

She collapsed on the floor and let the mist wash and wave over her in gentle, cleansing pulses.

So good. So relaxing.

She curled up in a tight ball and drifted off again on the mist shower floor.

She woke when the ship hit a patch of terrible jump space turbulence.

It knocked the ship around violently.

Naero smashed first into the ceiling of the mist shower, then back down into the floor.

She floated, gasped, and bled anew from fresh wounds and old wounds that re-opened, including the serious gash on her thigh.

She started to black out.

Naero feared she might bleed to death, naked on the mist shower floor, her lifeblood slowly seeping and running down the drain.

And she was too weak to stop it.

A voice murmured and call to her through a dizzy haze.

Strong hands pulled her out.

Someone weakly struggled to tend her wounds again.

Then she felt stout arms curl around her protectively.

Both of them passed out, floating above the floor but wedged under the tiny sleeping panel, holding one another.

*

Naero came to, warm and safe.

Her head still hurt and her body ached in several places, but as long as she didn't attempt to move or even blink her eyelashes, for the moment, she felt all right.

Then the ship lurched, groaned, and jerked around again in jump space, causing her eyes to pop open wide in fresh, sharp, stabbing pain.

She finally realized that she lay curled up in Leftenant Hayden's powerful arms, pulled close to his broad, bare chest.

When she turned her ear, she could easily hear his mighty heart thundering. He breathed at peace.

Apparently he had stripped down–to tend to several of his own shrapnel wounds on his torso, shoulders, and arms–while she was busy in the shower. He had clearly removed several bloody pieces of shrapnel from those various wounds. The shrapnel from the blast had penetrated even his combat armor.

Yet he had new wounds to his head, and the right side of his face was bruised and swollen. Blood had streamed down over his eyes again.

When the ship hit that patch of jump space turbulence, Hayden must have been tossed about and re-injured as well, just as she was.

When he'd called to her and she did not answer, he'd come and pulled her out, and closed her wounds off again. He must have barely finished doing so before they both passed out together.

Haisha, he was in fact a very handsome young man, barely three or four years older than herself. And a fine warrior, whom she greatly respected.

She could do much worse than wake up naked in his arms.

He had most likely saved her life–again–by not letting her bleed to death as she lay helpless, even though he was injured again himself.

She got up and found some stuff to clean the blood off him and check his wounds, although his breathing and heart rate all seemed fine.

Most Spacers simply needed time to rest and let their bodies heal, as rapidly as they did.

But maybe she should put some clothes back on before he woke up.

Yeah, that was probably a great idea.

But before she did so, she could not help leaning over him and caressing his chiseled face with the light touch of her fingertips.

She could not resist a sudden, wicked urge to press her lips against his.

Of course, at that exact moment, the ship jerked violently again, and Hayden's eyes flashed open in startled surprise. And then more surprise.

Naero pulled back slightly and smiled. She felt no shame.

Slight embarrassment, perhaps, but no shame.

Hayden seemed more embarrassed that she did.

"Uh…Naero? Are you all right? I hit my head and you got hurt in the shower. I stopped your bleeding again, before I blacked out."

Naero giggled and snuggled down with him again, rubbing her cheek and her long dark hair against his chest.

"You saved me, Jeremiah. You saved my life again, and we woke up, holding each other close. I like that…you holding me. It's very nice. I don't have a problem with it. In fact, I say let's do it some more."

She tried to pull his arms around her again.

But this time he resisted, and actually pulled away from her. "I'm sorry, Naero. You don't understand. I can't do that."

Naero grinned. "We haven't done anything…yet."

"And we're not going to."

Hayden backed away and held up his hands, looking very nervous. The cramped quarters of the miniscule cabin made it all super awkward.

In the end, Hayden backed down the hall like a crab.

Naero continued to smile and slowly came toward him, not unlike a female panther stalking her prey. "You know, a little snuggling might not be so bad?"

She saw Hayden swallow hard, considering all of it for a split instant.

Then he shook his head, violently in denial. "Naero...I'm sorry–I'm married. I have a wife. A little boy, and a baby girl on the way. I...can't."

Naero froze.

Dammit. Married. *Haisha!* Just her luck.

A great guy, and he was already taken.

Crap. Crap. Crap!

She sat back, clearly disappointed.

Naero crossed arms and legs in front of her, and let her long dark, shimmering hair cascade and cloak over herself.

"I'm sorry, too, Jeremiah. Honestly. I didn't know. Now I feel like a total idiot."

He sighed heavily and then nodded. "Don't. It's okay. It's not like it came up. We passed out and woke up together...at a very awkward time. Both of us were...hurt and vulnerable. We're both human."

He sighed heavily in relief once more, failing to notice that Naero was doing her best not to pout like a frustrated child.

He sighed with relief again, rubbing his face. "I'm just glad we stopped, and that you understand. Nothing against you, Naero. In fact, you are...extremely beautiful."

Yeah, for all the good that did her.

"But I love my wife and my kids, and I...I–"

Of course he did. Haisha. Please...please just shut up.

He was only making it all worse.

Naero smiled sadly and cut him off, doing her best to let him off the hook. "You're a good man. An honorable man. I understand honor, Jeremiah. Believe me, I understand it as much as any Spacer. Don't worry. I won't tempt you anymore, now that I know the score."

Hayden nodded and looked away, averting his eyes. "Thanks. Boy, that is such a huge relief. I'll just...go check on the guys. You should...maybe get dressed. Please get dressed."

He left pretty quickly and did not look back.

Yeah, bopping around naked with a bunch of Marines. Probably not the best idea.

Clothes. Most likely a good thing.

But Naero still cursed her rotten luck with good-looking guys she felt a spark for.

And even rarer–guys that she actually happened to like and respect.

It just wasn't fair.

She could not catch a break to save her life.

She didn't count Max Lii; that had been a unique case and remained so. How could she have possibly had an affair with such a high profile celeb–not to mention one of her junior officers–right out in the open for everyone to see? It was fortunate, in the end, that nothing had happened between them, either.

They fell out of jump ten minutes later.

Naero was dressed again by that time.

She checked their location in fear.

Thankfully, they came out in a rearward sector of the Alliance.

She immediately sent out coded Mayday calls for rescue.

The death of Admiral Sandusky and his loss to the Alliance quickly eclipsed any petty personal problems that Naero had.

The only good thing was that they had wiped out the assassin phaze squad, captured the dangerous phazing tek for Intel to study, and a few of the good guys even survived to tell the tale.

Just not certain embarrassing parts of the story, that no one needed to hear. Ever.

33

Naero recovered quickly. She and her people endured two more very intense engagements, and then her unit was forced to pull back. Strike Fleet Six was simply too beaten up once more, and had to come off the line.

Chaela had already entered their WebBall team into an open, single-elimination tournament that took place a day later.

Match-ups in the tourney would be chosen at random.

Saemar called in briefly and begged off from the match, saying she wasn't feeling well.

Just their luck, a key team member short and they drew a contest with one of the top semi-pro teams.

They all wore tight, two-piece, Nytex WebBall uniforms, patterned in neon blue, black, and silver for their team. Shorts down to their knees, and shirts from their ribs on up, exposing their midriffs; that was just the current style. WebBall shoes were like padded slippers, designed for pushing off in zero-G.

Each of them had a number on their front and back.

Naero wore number six, her lucky number.

Even in her skimpy little WebBall uniform, big, buff Chaela still looked like a Viking war goddess. Especially so with her two long golden braids.

She called the team together right before their match started.

"Guys, we're up against a tough one. We know this other team is far more experienced and just plain better than us. They're favored to win the whole tourney. We can play our usual game, or we can try one of our other strategies that we've been practicing."

"Scoring denial and cancellation," Naero guessed.

Chaela and several others nodded. "My exact thoughts as well, N. We don't have to win; we just try to not let them win by not letting them score, and by reversing as many of their goals as we can."

"Interesting," Enel said. "It sounds crazy enough. It just might work."

"What have we got to lose?" Naero said. "We know they'd beat us straight on."

All forty-nine of them spiraled up and slapped hands with each other in a spray of players, fanning out.

"Let's…go for it!"

They could only have two dozen players in the playing field at one time. Substitutes could switch in and out between serves, side outs, and time outs.

The denial strategy was simple. They formed up around the goals and did their best to track them when they shifted.

They tried to score as much as they could when they had the serve. But when the other team was up, they did everything they could to reverse scores and deny the other team any points.

They ended up with a fast-paced, low-scoring game, and only lost–in the end–17 to 13.

The other team captain even congratulated them. "Great denial strategy. But for you to win, you guys still have to get better at running up your own points."

"Thanks," Chaela said, shaking hands with the other team's coach and captain. "We'll get better. We haven't been playing for very long."

"You look like you have some great athletes. Is that little woman with the long black hair really Fleet Captain Naero Maeris?"

"It sure is."

"She looks very different than in her fleet vids in uniform."

Chae grinned and chuckled. "She's chameleon, all right."

They tried to call Saemar to tell her about the match and check on her, but she wasn't accepting any links.

Naero's battered strike fleet remained in the rear areas, scheduled for almost a complete refit.

People tried to rest and relax, but the war still raged at the front, and they would rush back to it soon enough. Technically, this wasn't a leave.

As usual, they prepared to hold wakes for their dead, continued to care for their fresh batch of wounded, and welcomed the inevitable new group of replacements.

Everyone kept busy.

Then Naero received private distress calls from Chae, Tyber, Tarim, and finally Zhen. One right after the other.

All of them begged her to come down immediately to one of the flagship launching bays–one already prepped for funeral services.

Something was seriously wrong with Saemar.

That's all they would tell her.

Naero raced down to that part of her flagship.

Tarim secured the door and would not let anyone else past that point but her.

She swept in. The lighting was subdued and down low.

She heard sounds of weeping and sobbing and went straight to them.

Her other friends stood gathered around the room, off to one side.

Ranks upon ranks of silver casketpods lay lined up in the darkened launching bay, ready for the funeral ceremony the next day, after the wakes that night.

Tyber stood up, his face wet with tears and red from crying himself.

Naero drew closer and found Chae and Z, sitting on the floor up against the hull.

They held Saemar between them. Their faces were red, too, and they also wept. But their arms were wrapped tightly around their poor friend.

Saemar seemed to have completely broken down and lost it. She was in her normal uniform, hugging her knees up close to her tight, trembling face buried in her knees.

She sobbed and shuddered uncontrollably, like one completely shattered.

Naero had only seen Saemar like this once before: back when Saemar's fiancé, Mitsubishi Hikaru, had perished in a fierce starfighter battle–just before Saemar came of age. Hikaru had died right before their wedding.

That had been a very bad time for Saemar.

She had never been the same since.

What could have happened to bring her that low again?

Naero got down on the floor and tried to help console her friend, checking her and trying to soothe her with gentle touches.

"Oh, Saemar... What is it...what happened?"

Her friend sobbed even louder, lunged forward suddenly, pulling away from Chae and Zhen. She nearly knocked Naero over onto her back.

Naero held her protectively, using her greater strength to remain upright.

Saemar curled up desperately in her arms like a very small, sobbing child. She shuddered and convulsed beyond control, still unable to speak.

All of them were at a loss.

Zhen and Chae closed in around them again, hugging them both between them. Naero stroked Saemar's curly auburn hair, soaked with tears and sweat.

Naero looked to her friends, like them, completely at a loss. She whispered to them softly. "How long has she been like this? Who found her? Does anyone know what happened?"

Everyone shook their heads. A guard had alerted Tarim when they found her down there like that, and the word spread.

They were all under a lot of stress, every day. Maybe Saemar had just cracked and given in to it. It could happen to anyone. Maybe she just needed to break down and have a good cry.

But this seemed much worse than that. Something had happened.

Like the time with Hikaru's death.

Naero looked around, rocking softly, and patted Saemar's back.

She saw all the casketpods from their latest losses once more.

Why had Saemar come down here?

Hundreds of shiny, mirror-finished caskets.

Who were these dead?

Were some of them from Saemar's unit?

Had someone died that Saemar cared about–much more than she had let on?

Naero held an index finger to her pursed lips, and then quietly called up a holoscreen above them with the latest KIA figures.

She scrolled down by unit designation.

Then starfighter pilots.

Saemar commanded a hundred fighter pilots in the 129th Tactical Starfighter Wave, with a total of five fighter squadrons of twenty, ten fighter wings of ten fighters each. She commanded the first wing personally.

Naero suddenly gasped slightly.

She saw the data flash across the holoscreen, scrolled back, highlighted it–and pointed it out to their friends.

Their mouths fell open, almost all at once.

Saemar had lost twenty-seven of her one hundred pilots during the last heavy engagement.

More than one quarter of her unit, KIA.

That included *all nine* of the other fighter pilots in her own fighter wing.

Everyone in her wing had been killed but her. Every single one of her closest comrades–wiped out.

And, knowing Saemar, most of the male pilots had been her lovers as well at some point.

Seven of those nine pilots were male, with two females.

Saemar didn't sleep with women.

Yet, when it came to her units, Saemar chose to fly directly with only the elite-of-the-elite.

Only the best pilots in her wave got to be in her direct wing, based strictly on merit, skill, and ability. Nothing else. Her wing had one of the top records in the Alliance.

And now, all of them had died in that last terrible battle.

All of them...except Saemar.

Their friend had lost her entire fighter wing and more than twenty-five percent of her entire unit, total.

All of them had been too busy to notice.

Naero swore at herself silently.

How could she have been too busy to notice something like that?

For Naero, it would have been the same as if thirteen or fourteen of her complement of fifty command warships were all completely destroyed–lost within the course of the same engagement all at once.

No wonder Saemar was a wreck.

She had known every one of these people...intimately. They had fought together, trained and lived together.

They were her closest family.

Saemar screamed and thrashed and tore herself out of their arms.

They released her.

She staggered toward the shining caskets in the subdued light of the silent hangar.

She stabbed absently at her wristcom.

Exactly twenty-seven of the caskets nearby lit up all around them, displaying their data screens and a holo image of the fallen Spacer pilot within.

Young, gallant pilots from all the Clans.

All gone now.

129th Tactical Starfighter Wave
  2nd Squadron
  1st Fighter Wing
1st Leftenant Teodor Donovan

129th Tactical Starfighter Wave
  2nd Squadron
  1st Fighter Wing
Commander Wendil Gordon

129th Tactical Starfighter Wave
  2nd Squadron
  1st Fighter Wing
Leftenant Commander Vaellani Lakota

Saemar went to each of the caskets for her people and stretched her arms across them, lying over them and placing her head down close. She sobbed and wept over each one. Then she whispered and muttered unintelligibly to each of them like a madwoman.

Her friends followed her from casket to casket, letting her vent, keeping their gentle hands on her. They tried to steady her.

When Saemar reach the last one—once she had said to them all whatever it was she mumbled to each of them—she collapsed to the floor like puppet with all its strings cut.

Naero dove and caught her, keeping her from smacking her head on the hard floor.

Saemar shrieked, struggled free, and scrabbled like a crab into a dark corner. She continued to sob and mourn. She curled up again, shaking violently, hugging her knees in tight.

Naero and her friends stayed right with her, trying to hold and touch her, to give her whatever solace and comfort they could. Tyber hovered over all of them protectively.

It was Zhen who finally tried to speak to her and bring her back.

"We love you, Saemar. Come back to us. Talk to us. We know you're hurting very badly. It's Zhen. Chae and N and Ty and Tarim are all here, too."

"We're here for you, Saemar," Chaela added.

Saemar kept her head down, but her hands shot out like claws in front of her, fingers twisting, clawing, and curling repeatedly at the air.

They rested their hands lightly on her forearms.

Naero tried to hold one of her hands.

At first, Saemar clawed at her and fought her off again, while continuing to sob and gasp, as if she couldn't draw in enough breath.

Then she reached out frantically and grabbed Naero's hand, and would not let go.

Saemar exploded into semi-incoherent babbling, strained and breathless.

"It's…they. They killed them all. The bastards killed everyone…"

She couldn't get any more words out for a long while. She was still having trouble breathing, gulping in air.

"Hikaru…just like Hikaru. Like losing him…all over again. Every one of my people. Over and over again. I watched them die. I listened to them all get killed."

Saemar clawed at the air desperately with her free hand, helplessly straining and reaching out in vain.

"Tried…I tried to help them…tried to reach them. Bastards… They cut us off. We all got cut off… So many foes. We fought, and fought, and fought. We fought for each other. We fought and died to help each other. To save as many of us as we could and break out…First Wing. My beloved First Wing…they saved us, Chae…saved us all…First Wing fought…they fought like champions…fearless…like angels of heaven in their fury. In the end…miracle…that any of us came back."

She kept gasping for air.

"I…led the rest of us back, N…we fought our way out of that hell…and we barely got out…Death trap. We lost so many…all of us…shot to pieces…Barely made it…back to our…our…"

Zhen pushed her way in.

"She's hyperventilating!" Zhen pulled out a plastic respirator bag out of her kit and placed it over Saemar's red, gasping face. She forced Saemar to breathe in and out of the expanding and contracting bag, calming her all the while.

After several tense moments, Saemar finally started to relax and breathe easier.

Naero still held her hand.

Zhen stroked her hair and spoke to her softly. "Saemar. I want to have Chae carry you to sickbay. I want you on a medbed. We'll all stay with you if you want. We'll stay with you all night if you want us to. Or if you'd rather get some sleep, I can give you something to help you with that. One of us will always be in the room with you. Don't worry. We aren't going to leave you."

Saemar nodded, still wincing and sobbing, shaking her head. "You don't get it. You just don't understand, none of you." She gasped again and put her head down.

They tried to be quiet and give her whatever time she needed to work through her pain and grief and get it all out.

She exploded again suddenly, blurting out a bunch of stuff. "We fought and died for each other! To save each other. First Wing gave their lives for the rest of us. So that the rest of us could get out. I had to pull the others together and lead the break out, and First Wing fell back without question. They held off the enemy, for barely a few seconds, while we broke out. Then...they got swept away. They sacrificed themselves. Without any hesitation. And we let them do it. I let them do it. We left them behind. I left them behind...to die...*for the rest us.*"

Naero finished reading the crew report summaries, flashing across the floating holoscreen before her eyes.

"Saemar, I know you're hurting bad," she said. "Believe me, I understand. Every battle, I lose people I know. Sometimes hundreds. Sometimes entire warships and their whole crews–all hands lost. Thousands, at times. But you have not read your reports from the survivors of your last engagement. Without exception–every pilot of the 129th that came back alive–all seventy-two of them insist, for the record, that First Wing fought with the highest valor to the very end."

Saemar bowed her head and slowly nodded. "They did. That they did."

"I'm not finished, Saemar. Not only that, but your pilots also concluded–unanimously–that only their commander, Wing Commander Saemar Maeris, could have kept the rest of them together and led them back to safety out of that nightmare. And she did so, they said, at great risk and at constant threat of losing her own life, heedless of any damage to her own craft and herself."

Naero put her hand on Saemar's head, bent down, and kissed the crown of her head.

"Can't you see, Saemar? All of you could have died in that deathtrap. Every one of you. You lost one quarter of your command. Your own wing sacrificed itself bravely for the rest of you. But you were the only one with the knowledge and experience capable of saving the rest. You saved three quarters of your people. They are all alive and thankful today because of you, and clearly state that fact. For the record, I want you to know that I'm putting you and everyone in First Wing up for commendations and citations for bravery, valor, and courage, well beyond the call of duty."

Saemar waved her hand at the caskets. "Give the honors to my beloved dead. I don't need them. I…I don't deserve them."

Naero shook her head. "No, Saemar. If you had died, everyone else in your wave would have perished with you. You all deserve these honors. They gave their lives so that you could have the chance to save all the others. They understood and accepted that fact instantly. You trained them to be capable of seeing what had to be done. And they did so, without question or hesitation. Only the elite of our elite could have done such a thing. It was a miracle of the highest honor and bravery. You need to trust their judgment, and accept that, in honor of them. I want you to see and admit that to yourself, when you reach a place where you can do so."

Saemar sniffed and wiped her red face, her nano makeup either rubbed off or smeared around in weird patches and patterns.

She kissed Naero's hand, and then rubbed it. She blinked and looked up at Naero, and then around at the rest of them, and smiled weakly.

"Thanks, everyone. You are all my good friends–my sweeties. I'm…I'm sorry I lost it. I can't really go nuts. You guys know. I'm pretty much already there." She laughed a little.

"Saemar," Zhen asked, "you can still come to sickbay and we can stay with you. Are you going to be okay?"

Saemar sighed heavily, getting serious. "No, none of us are going to be okay after this war, Z. We've all seen too much. We've all lost too much, and we're going to lose even more, before everything is done. But we'll find a way to salvage and save what we can, and make do. We'll all find a way to live and love and be all right. Because we don't have any choice in the matter. Because we're Spacers, and that's just what we do."

She got to her feet and stood up, wiping her face.

She glanced back at her lovers and friends lying dead in those caskets all around her.

She sighed and held out her hands. "I'm sorry, guys. Seeing my mates all in here in the dark, all alone. Knowing I would never see any of them again in this life. It just broke me down like you wouldn't believe. I thought I could take it. I had told myself that after losing Hikaru, nothing could ever hurt me like that again. I wouldn't let it. But I was wrong. If you love people, even for a short time, losing them is still incredibly hard."

"These kind of things are obviously hard on all of us," Chaela said. "And we should talk about them more often, amongst each other and our crews. We should get these feelings out in the open more, instead of letting them build up inside us until we can't take it any longer. To tell you all the truth, I've come close to have a similar breakdown like yours, Saemar. I just haven't had severe losses like this to tip me over the brink yet, thank goodness."

"You're right, Chae," Naero said. "If all of us are hurting like this, the rest of our people must be dealing with the same feelings and issues. All of us struggle to be brave and ignore what's going each day, until it turns toxic and festers inside of us, and builds to a breaking point. Eventually, something finally happens to set us off. We need to address these issues more and relieve some of this pressure, for everyone's sake, before it gets this bad."

Saemar leaned against the wall, shaking hear head wearily. "Thanks again, sweeties. Gotta go somewhere now and get some rest. I haven't slept well for days. I think I can pass out now for a while. Just stick me anywhere with a bunk."

Naero put her hands on her hips. "Saemar, you're coming directly to my quarters. That's an order. Anyone who wants to join us, I have plenty of room. I'll have some food and drinks sent up."

Tyber's face beamed. "Yay! Just like a sleepover when we were all kids and teens!"

Naero smiled. She herself forgot sometimes how young they all still were.

Chaela punched her wristcom. "I'm game. Just let me message Remy."

Zhen smirked and folded her arms in front of herself. "If Ty is going to spend the night with a bunch of pretty girls, I'd better be there to keep and eye on him."

"Awww, Mom..." Ty mock-whined.

Chaela snorted. "Yeah...you don't want him to come to, curled up with Saemar."

Most of them chuckled at that. Just not Zhen.

"No need to worry," Saemar assured them. "Ty and I settled that issue a long time ago, sweeties. He's just not my type, that's all."

Tyber looked hurt, confused, and indignant. "Settled what...when did we do what? I don't remember any of this."

And for some strange reason, Zhen got mad.

"Not your type? What do you mean, not your type? Anything with three legs is your type!"

Saemar looked at them indignantly. "I know you all think that, but in my own way, I'm actually very choosy and particular."

"How so?" Chaela asked. "What, they have to be male and still breathing?"

"And what's that supposed to mean?" Tyber asked again, even more offended now than before.

Naero chuckled and covered her face briefly with one hand. "Enough, you guys. Easy. We're all tired and not just a little rattled. Let's just cut each other some slack and watch over Saemar tonight. And one thing more: Ty and Z, you two can sleep and snuggle together all you want–but no fooling around. Seriously, I've wanted to say this since we were all teens, and I finally can, now. Even when you two *think* you're being quiet about it–trust us–we can still hear *exactly* what you two are doing. It's awkward and embarrassing–for everyone."

Zhen turned bright red, but did not say a word.

34

Tarissa-1 resisted all attempts to crack its complex weave of heavily layered defenses. Twelve Alliance fleets, including Naero's Strike Fleet Six, formed up in four equal groups to probe and assail the extensive enemy battle lines.

They sought out weaknesses. They tested strategies and tactics.

When nothing worked, they shifted from one attack formation to the next. They tried several optimal attack vectors.

Yet each time they wore the enemy down, the damaged enemy elements retreated behind their defensive screens of attack probes, drones, and AI seeker mines.

And thus the tables turned, and the Alliance fleets quickly found themselves being worn down.

Ensign Nick Alexander called out from his shields station. "Captain. *Hippolyta* shields down to forty-seven percent. Fleet shields reduced on average of twenty-nine percent–most by half. Eleven vessels below twenty percent."

"Send those eleven ships to the fixer clouds. My orders. No arguments." They kept fighting, but Naero began to see the futility of their current efforts.

Captain Mike Marshall called in from *The Condor*. "Looks like we're beating our heads against a duranadium hull, N. Are we going to keep doing so?"

"No...we've got enough of a headache. All ships, withdraw to the Beta line and regroup. Surina, advise Admiral Maeris of our situation and advise same for the other three attack groups. None of this is working. We should pull back before we lose someone for no good reason."

"On it, sir."

Naero sighed. "The enemy can keep this up all day long. At this rate, they can hold us off and bleed us dry—for weeks. We need to create or discover a better way."

They sent all of the data feeds to Intel. Perhaps Admiral Klyne and his people could figure something out.

She took a call from her aunt within that same hour. Naero saluted. "Admiral Maeris."

"At ease, Captain Maeris. Good work today. I wanted to pause for a moment and commend you."

Naero blinked and looked aside for a moment. "I'm...confused, sir. Our efforts today were completely futile. We accomplished nothing."

Her aunt smiled. "Of course the mission was a bust. What I'm referring to is you. You continue to progress and mature as a command officer."

Naero snorted a little. "How exactly did I do that? By failing miserably?"

"We could all see what was happening. That was no one's fault. Yet, I was curious as to how you would react."

Naero grinned. "And...apparently, I did well?"

"You did, in fact. You assessed the situation, and you retreated."

"Sir? I've never heard of anyone awarded a citation...for retreating."

"No, but you've seldom retreated on your own before, unless specifically ordered and forced to do so. Usually by then—in the past—you'd already lost a few ships and the rest of your fleet was all beat to hell."

"Thank you, sir...I think."

"Admit it, Captain. The old Naero would have beaten herself and her people bloody against defenses such as these, stubbornly trying to find or blast her way through at any price. You are a better, more balanced, and seasoned leader now. You're not making all of those new leader mistakes any more. I just wanted to commend you on that fact. I'm proud of you. Your parents would be also."

"Mom once told me: 'You can't always win, and sometimes even the cost of victory is too high.'"

"Exactly. You have grown both in experience and wisdom."

Naero smiled. "Thank you, sir. I understand now. I really appreciate that."

*

The Alliance fleets actually recovered quickly from several coordinated enemy counterattacks, and responded by making another serious feint toward Tarissa-1 to throw the enemy off.

After the Triaxians swept all of their forces that way to head them off, the Alliance changed course abruptly, and drove straight on to encircle and capture the rest of the unpredictable Hevangian Homeworlds.

Especially the Capital World of Valkeggoth-6.

It took the Alliance three days of heavy fighting to destroy or chase off the Triaxian fleets in that region, and to hold off the rest that tried to intervene.

Two more days allowed them to set up a blockade of those same worlds, complete with salvaged mines, defense drones, and refitted, robotic gunships from Triax itself.

The Alliance learned quickly from many harsh lessons. They knew better than to make any attempt to pacify any of the Hevangian worlds while in the middle of a war.

Isolating and containing them proved difficult enough.

The Alliance continued the process of constructing a complete blockade–and more–a containment sphere around Valkeggoth-6.

Without warning, the entire planet ruptured from within its core and exploded violently. The Alliance ships attempted to flee the destruction.

More than two dozen Alliance warships and their crews lost that race and perished, along with a population of nearly three billion Hevangians.

From all reports, Intel was baffled by whatever bizarre tek the enemy had used to destroy their entire planet. The enemy's insane methods and actions defied all logic and reason. There was simply no justification for such senseless death and destruction.

Many in the Alliance felt that if the Hevangians were crazy enough to slaughter themselves rather than be set free of Triax–then so be it–let them do so.

Any long-term answers to the Hevangian question would be decided well after the main war ended. Until then, the rest of their worlds were isolated by the blockade and given an even wider berth.

Naero's strike fleet and the Alliance could now return full time to the prosecution of the primary war against Triax.

Day by day, they blasted their way through the defenses swarming around Tarissa-1.

Many of the so-called Triaxian fleets and crews were still those from the other fourteen Gigacorps. They just changed their outer markings and insignia and their designations to those of Triaxian fleets, but their tek varied, and even their leadership and tactics were different.

They did not obey the Triaxians blindly. Nor did they allow themselves to be used a cannon fodder. But they remained competent foes, and resisted all efforts to get them to surrender or turn neutral.

When the fighting got too hot, only then did the mercs attempt to jump out. Naero and her people had captured enough of these ships after battles to know very well that their vessels and their mercenary crews were not Triaxian. It did not matter what they claimed.

And they gladly sued for mercy and surrender at the last need, while Triax maintained its policy of no prisoners. No mercy. No exceptions in the heat of battle for captured Alliance forces or vessels.

Naero had Tyber and his fixers pour over the captured merc ships, one after another, searching for solid evidence. But they were clean. That was the problem—they were always too clean.

No ship was that clean. No past histories or maintenance records? No ship's logs? No direct proof that the ships were anything but Triaxian vessels. Not even military records of where their crews came from. None of it made any logical sense.

Then Tyber and the teks discovered traces of a self-erasing aggressive virus in the computers of all of the captured enemy vessels.

This was, in fact, a virus that erased and destroyed any incriminating traces of information that could prove that these enemy ships were, in fact, illegal mercenaries—fighting for Triax. When they clearly originated directly from the other Corps navies. How very convenient for the Corps.

Together, Naero's teks worked with Spacer Intel to devise a counter-strategy. If they could expose the enemy ships and their true origins, Triax and the other Corps could be revealed to be caught in direct, flagrant, wholesale violations of the Fourth Spacer War Treaty.

The same exact treaty that the enemy hid behind, and held up constantly to keep the Alliance using only private military vessels and forces against them. While the most advanced Spacer Navy warships were effectively barred from the war.

Once Intel developed a strategy, they only had to wait for the proper opportunity to put it into action. That day would come.

Meanwhile, in honor of the fallen Admiral Sandusky, hundreds of liberated Triaxian worlds joined the Alliance wholesale.

And as such, thousands of captured enemy vessels were refitted by fixer clouds, updated with the latest weapons and tek, and joined the fight against their former tyrants.

Thus the Alliance increased its raw numbers by over a third.

And where their crew rosters could not be filled completely from the new Alliance worlds, there were finally plenty of new leaders and crews coming out of the extensive training programs that Joshua Tech had implemented from the very beginning.

The Alliance led another bold, concentrated assault on Tarissa-1.

At first, the Alliance forces nearly had Tarissa-1 encircled and enveloped.

Out of seemingly nowhere, enemy fleets flooded in from the final Triaxian stronghold Capital World of Najindo-9.

Far more enemy fleets than any Intel estimates could ever imagine.

The Alliance was forced to pull back and completely break off their attack on Tarissa-1. They fought a full-on, fighting retreat against overwhelming superior odds.

The Alliance used every delaying and punishment tactic that they knew to slow the enemy advance. Many of these were the same, very effective punishing tactics that Triax had used against the Alliance advance.

But now the tables were completely turned. Where had this sudden, massive influx of Triaxian fleets come from? And right when it appeared that Triax was on the ropes?

Reeling, the Alliance forces struggled to maintain good order. They fled back through several pacified systems in a vain attempt to spread out the charging tide of waxing Triaxian numbers.

But the enemy kept up their counterattack, bolstered by those same raw numbers of countless fresh fleets that only continued to grow. The enemy threatened to roll back the entire front line of the war.

The Alliance forces struggled to regroup, and conspired to make their stand around the critical forward starbase and Naval shipyards of DaVinci-5.

35

DaVinci-5 quickly deteriorated into another Triaxian death trap.

Naero and the other strike fleet captains charged in against the Triaxian hordes repeatedly, inflicting heavy losses in wide arcs of destroying fire.

But Triax merely absorbed those losses and kept advancing.

Relentlessly advancing.

The Alliance held for three hours of the heaviest fighting Naero had ever seen or endured, focused around the DaVinci-5 naval shipyards.

Finally, under withering, blistering sheets of direct enemy fire, the shipyard was evacuated, abandoned to the enemy, and quickly destroyed after the Alliance forces fled.

Once more, the battered Alliance fleets held the sphere of fire against all comers, vanquishing fleet after enemy fleet. They called in all of their nearby reserves.

They used all of their talent and skill–every trick they knew.

They held off Triax's overwhelming superior numbers for an entire day.

That supreme effort gave the terrified civilian population of DaVinci-5 time to be evacuated in huge miner ore carriers that rushed in.

Several million.

The brave miners and valiant pilots did the best they could, and then some.

Finally, the exhausted Alliance defenses began to crumble under the intense strain.

They were forced to retreat again, or be completely swept away and vanquished.

Admiral Sleak Maeris took charge of the rout and led a masterful fighting retreat once more. Calm. Efficient. Even punishing.

But in despair, the Alliance abandoned the last few thousands on DaVinci-5 that had not been able to escape, to their fate.

No choice remained.

Triax made an example out of such a "traitor-world."

The enemy pounded it with atomics and genocide devices, wiping out all remaining life on the planet surface.

And still the enemy charged forward, heedless of any losses.

Triax chased and fought the Alliance out of yet another previously pacified system.

The continuing retreat from DaVinci-5 remained staggering and bleak.

Naero and Strike Fleet Six helped the Alliance regroup around the next fall back line of defense prepared near Kholan-2.

Hundreds of ships passed quickly through the waiting fixer nebulae to refit and re-arm.

Then the massive enemy surge jumped in and came at them once again.

For the first time during the entire course of the war, Naero and her fleet found themselves cut off and nearly completely surrounded by a tightening sphere of enemy forces.

Superior numbers that had her and her people hemmed in tight.

In a choking noose–a kill zone.

Haisha. Dammit! Where had all of these extra fleets come from?

By their intel, Triax still could not have even possessed a third of these numbers in the entire twenty-sector area.

And now, suddenly the Alliance was being pushed back, swarmed on, and surrounded over and over again.

But now it was time again to hit the foe hard, slow them down, and make them pay the price–and just maybe–a little something extra.

"All ships. Follow me in on this attack vector," Naero ordered. "We're making a full sweep of the enemy formations to soften them up as they come online."

Priva Kothari, captain of *The Bulldog*, voiced her reservations. "Captain Maeris. The enemy fleets are clearly too many. We'll be the ones shredded…not them."

"Orders, Priva. The Alliance reserves will plow in right behind us in full support. Let the amazon make an opening. Everyone else form up and squirt through, all batteries blazing."

Hippolyta blasted several enemy ships straight in front of them, accelerating to attack speed and spinning wildly on its axis.

The planetoid smashed straight into several enemy vessels, shoving them out of the way. Sparks and flames erupted.

Her strike fleet roared in behind her, bristling with rapid-fire primary and secondary batteries.

They raked the enemy and the enemy raked back.

Shields buckled and ships caught fire.

The enemy made way for them, but kept up the heat all throughout the gauntlet.

By the time Naero's strike fleet finished its sweep, more than half of its ships were in tatters.

Against such numbers, they might as well have sprinkled the enemy with flowers.

They limped and formed back up with the Alliance forces, taking up a flank defensive position on Admiral Sleak's uttermost left, with fixers swarming all over them.

Triax and its seemingly numberless fleets regrouped in slow overconfidence.

They held the decisive advantage, and both sides knew it.

Then, as if that were not discouraging enough…

More Triaxian reserves continued to jump in.

Strangely enough, the Alliance forces should have executed another brilliant fighting retreat, and jumped out of such a hotly contested system.

And yet, this time–this time they held their ground.

They made a stand in the face of overwhelming superior odds.

The Triaxian High Command hailed them eagerly. "Alliance invaders. Prepare to be destroyed. Your defeat begins now. No quarter. No prisoners."

So what else was new?

Naero and the Alliance admirals awaited confirmation from Spacer Intel.

Finally the word came.

All stood ready.

"Admiral Maeris," Naero said. "Permission to engage exposure mode."

"Permission granted, Captain Maeris. Engage cloaked exposure microfixers."

Naero gave the command.

Tyber and the fleet teks controlling the hidden Intel devices triggered their protocols.

The spolymers on the outsides of the enemy fleet hulls blurred. Their scarlet, black, and gold Triaxian fleet markings and designations swirled and shifted.

A conversion wave swept over the enemy ships like a counter-virus, and reverted them to their former designations.

Still naval warships–but with varied colorful markings and insignia from all of the other fourteen Gigacorporations.

Admiral Joshua confirmed their success. "Good work, Captain Maeris. The micro-fixers your ships salted the enemy fleets with are working perfectly. Not only have they revealed where the illegal ships originally came from, but we now have all of their ships' logs, maintenance, and jump histories. We know where they were constructed, and where they have served, before being sent illegally to flood the Annexation War."

The Triaxian High Command mouthpiece laughed nervously.

He even yawned.

"More petty spack tricks? How un-amusing. No one cares what pitiful attempts you traitors and invaders perpetrate against us. No one cares, and no one will bother listening to your lying, spack ravings."

Naero did her best, ice-steel, Aunt-Sleak grin.

"Let's just put that to the test, shall we?"

36

Admiral Sleak addressed the massed Gigacorps forces aiding Triax.

"You and all of your illegal activities have been clearly and flagrantly exposed for all eyes to see. For the entire galaxy to bear witness to. The bulk of your forces present are not–in fact–Triaxian fleets. They are, in actuality, regular naval units from the other fourteen Gigacorporations, in clear violation of the Fourth Spacer War Treaty."

The Triaxian High Command did not even blink. "You have no definitive proof. And even if you do, who is going to listen or care about what a bunch of stinking rebels and invaders–who are about to die–have to say?"

Grand Admiral Micah Allen from the Spacer Naval High Command took that exact moment to cut in.

"We care, Triaxian filth. Your kind and your days are numbered, either way. But to the other fourteen Gigacorps, we give this warning: for months you have slapped both us and the Alliance in the face with a treaty that you clearly break at will on a daily basis. You insist that only private

Alliance forces can fight the Annexation War. While you pile in fleets from the other Gigacorps under false Triaxian or mercenary banners and designations to prop up these tyrants.

"We have all the proof we need that this is going on. But it ends now. All fleets that were not part of Triax Gigacorporation, prior to the start of the war, are hereby ordered to depart immediately, and leave the Annexation War under a signal flag of truce."

"And we know *exactly* now which ships they are," Aunt Sleak added.

The spokesperson for Triax fidgeted slightly. "Or what? And, for the sake of conjecture–not saying that any such ships do exist in our naval units, mind you–what are you prepared to do about it if they should not depart?"

Allen's face remain impassive. "Easy. Call your bluff. Triax already refuses to take prisoners under all the agreements of interstellar law. Any foreign ships caught in the Annexation War from this point on shall be shown no quarter. No mercy. No prisoners. We will actively seek to destroy them with extreme prejudice."

"This is outrageous, barbaric."

"Apparently it is not outrageous or barbaric when Triax does the same thing to the Alliance forces."

"But regular Spacer Naval forces interfering would bring about a Fifth Spacer War."

"Yes. It would. Then, by all means, let's do so. Let it begin now and here, without further lies and pretense. First, we shall destroy Triax. Then we shall systematically destroy every Gigacorps that has and continues to give Triax aid. You shall have five minutes to decide. I strongly suggest that you all choose swiftly."

The spokesperson stopped smiling and turned pale. "This is madness. There must be time to negotiate."

"No negotiating. Five minutes. Starting now."

"The other Corps will not stand for this. Their response will be swift and devastating, if you think they will stand by while one of their major allies and trade partners is destroyed! Who's bluffing now? What is your pitiful might against the combined forces of all fifteen Gigacorps and their populations?"

Grand Admiral Micah Allen knitted his hands calmly together. "We are ready to fight this war, you bloody-handed cowards. We will take you all on. Now. This instant. I have one hundred advanced Spacer Navy fleets at my command. They stand poised and at the ready to attack across all sectors. Five thousand unstoppable warships that are more advanced than anything the Corps have ever seen or can throw against us."

The Grand Admiral smiled calmly. "And that…is merely the vanguard of our forces. We have thousands more fleets ready to flood in and overwhelm whoever chooses to stand against us. Take all the time you need to consider these facts. As long as it is not longer than four minutes."

"Ridiculous! The Corps and their limitless fleets still outnumber the Alliance Navy by far. What do you expect them to do?"

"Simple. Abandon Triax. Immediately. The other fourteen Gigacorps do not need to suffer Triax's fate. Pull your fleets back and stay out of this fight, as we have. It is not in your best interests to prop up a sick and diseased animal such as Triax–which either way is going to be put down. No one can prevent that now. This is your final warning. Leave now or share their fate. Three minutes…and counting."

The spokesperson gasped and checked his links feeds, while he continued to bluster and haggle. He seemed to be at a loss.

"Two minutes."

Triax and its lackeys began to stammer and panic.

"One minute…to the start of the Fifth Spacer War."

Ships began to jump out of the Triaxian systems in droves. First in dozens, then in hundreds. Entire fleets fled back to their own Gigacorps. They did not have the stomach for another Spacer War; not now, at least.

Naero smiled eagerly, her strike fleet poised and refitted on the front lines.

Triax reeled in despair and chaos as its fickle allies betrayed and abandoned it to its fate, melting away like a mirage.

The remaining Triaxian forces struggled to regroup into some form of order.

"Hit them. Now!" Admiral Sleak ordered.

Naero merely waited for the word. Strike Fleet Six led the next heavy assault. Intel clearly had all of the illegal merc ships marked in the battle computers. If they found any, Naero made a point of destroying them first.

Shortly after that, even more ships fled the Triaxian lines and jumped out of harm's way. Fewer and fewer had any desire to sell their lives for Triax, very quickly becoming a lost cause.

Surina cut in suddenly. "I'm sorry, sir. Another enemy boarding attack."

"Who this time?"

"One of our destroyers. *The Warhorse.*"

"Ima's ship?" Naero grinned knowingly.

"Sir? Should we try to assist them?"

"Have we received any distress calls from *The Warhorse*, Rina?"

"No, but last reports said the enemy hit the bridge directly."

"Send *Duelist* and *Tarantula* to assist, but I'm guessing the action's already over by now. Go ahead and hail Captain Kalada. Let's make sure."

"Hailing." Surina sounded surprised by the rapid response.

"Captain Kalada responding, sir. On main screen."

Ima stood before her command chair calmly, wiping the bright red blood from her blades onto her sleeves to clean them off.

"Greetings, N," Ima said calmly. "Everything all right, my sister?"

Naero laughed. "Fine. We heard you might be having a little problem with enemy boarders?"

Ima smiled slightly, her dark eyes still flashing fire. "Not really. My crew and I have been waiting eagerly for one of these boarding attempts against *The Warhorse*. It wasn't any problem...not for us, at least. But we can't thank you enough for all of that new knife tek."

She voiced her war cry in an expression of sheer victory, and her crew responded in kind.

Off to one side, Naero glimpsed Ima's people and their Apache Marines piling up the enemy dead from the boarding assault in large numbers.

The Warhorse bridge seemed to have been painted in blood. Yet few of Ima's people appeared hurt at all. "See you at our next practice session, N?"

Naero nodded. "Wouldn't miss it, Ima. Take care, my sister."

"Always. *Warhorse* out."

Naero chuckled.

"Something amusing, sir?" Surina asked.

"Very. I wish I could have seen the looks on their faces."

"Who, sir?"

Naero laughed out loud. "Those morons on those enemy boarding parties. That's who–the dumb bastards."

"Sir?"

"Rina, if I were the enemy, the last ship I'd *ever* want to try and board would be one stuffed with knife-happy, Spacer Apaches. I bet Ima and her people went after the enemy straight on with their blades from the get go. They probably didn't even fire a shot. Shields don't stop blades."

Surina turned back around to her station. "I'll take your word for it, sir."

"Come to one of our training matches and you'll understand, Rina."

Naero continued to chuckle.

37

Naero checked in on Saemar to see how she was holding up.

After the incident, Saemar took only a couple of days' leave to work through her remaining grief and other feelings.

She insisted that was all that she needed.

Then she went to Zhen and got cleared to resume her duties.

Naero watched from the mobile flight command station module, a circular pod with clear viewscreens all around, including below, overlooking the entire launch hanger for 2nd Squadron.

The fighters could be launched from there, the bridge, or from a back up launching station in the hangar itself.

The 129th was currently attached to *The Condor,* under Strike Fleet Second, Captain Michael Marshall, one of two active, tactical fighter waves on that carrier.

Since returning to her unit, Saemar had thrown herself into training her new replacements.

Why did the newbs always look so young? Like a bunch of twelve- and thirteen-year-olds?

Yet a few of them were older than Naero herself, who still wasn't even twenty yet.

From experience, that all made it even more heartbreaking when they lost one of them.

Bright, eager, headstrong, hot to prove themselves.

Haisha...Naero still felt like that herself most of the time.

Naero smiled, watching spunky, vivacious Captain Saemar back to her old self. That was very good to see.

Saemar bounced around in her tight flight suit like she usually did. Her curly auburn hair framed her pretty face, and she was showing as much cleavage as she could get away with.

All frisky again.

Like some lander women on their worlds, Saemar would probably walk around topless if she could get past the fleet regs somehow. She had a young, voluptuous body with lots of curves to show off.

They got her all the notice she wanted.

And Saemar wanted a lot of notice, and more besides.

Word got around.

A lot of guys tried to get into her unit for that very reason. Yet most, especially the female pilots, were very well aware of Saemar's excellent flight history and service record, her many citations and awards.

She also had a rep for being one of the finest starfighter pilot trainers in the entire fleet. She did spend a lot of time with hands-on training with her people. Whatever one might think about her personal life, she pushed every one of her pilots to be the best, and expected them to work hard and learn right alongside her.

If she woke up next to a few of them at times, that was her private business. But Saemar never let her off-duty fun get in the way of her duty, and vice versa. She kept them separate, and demanded that others do the same.

With help from Wing Commanders Chaela and Saemar, Naero and her strike fleet had even developed a new tandem, tactical starfighter with boosted power and improved dual controls–the Ghost Dragon F59T.

Simulation could only teach so much.

For the first few battles, green pilots were no longer being thrown into the mix to live or die on their own.

They would go into their first several battles partnered with an experienced pilot and trainer who could help save them if they got into trouble, and vice versa.

The instructor could override at any moment to help the rookie out, and judge best, firsthand, when a pilot was ready to fight solo.

Under the new training program, within days, fighter pilot losses plummeted from thirty-four percent down to twelve percent–the lowest in the fleet–especially among replacements.

For all units, replacements getting killed needlessly only compounded the problems at work–and led only to the need for more replacements.

Once more, good ideas spread throughout the fleet as rapidly as possible. Fixers even produced several other popular tandem versions of current successful starfighter designs.

A good number of the Alliance units and even a few Spacer squadrons actually preferred to use the two-seaters full time, and very effectively. A team of two that worked and fought well together could be a formidable force, sometimes better than one pilot alone.

Survivability rates also increased. If one member of the flight team was injured or unconscious, the other could get them out. This went along with auto-protocols to jettison crew lifepods if a pilot blacked out or was seriously hurt.

Later advanced ship lifepods could even put injured pilots in stasis if they were badly injured, semi-freezing their condition until they could be retrieved and properly healed and restored.

Naero continued to monitor Saemar from the mobile flight command deck overlooking 2nd Squadron.

Saemar had her hands full with twenty-seven new replacement pilots. She and her remaining veterans struggled to check out each pilot on the new F59T Ghost Dragons, fresh out of the wrappers.

Naero went over the specs. These tandem fighters had excellent dual controls and a seat for the Trainer up behind the pilot, where the instructor could study everything the pilot did.

Saemar and her vets had finished the sim programs, and prepared to take the replacements out a few at a time, while the others waited their turns and studied the training sessions on the cockpit readouts and battle holos.

Naero listened in on Saemar's open audio feed.

"If you are going to make mistakes, make them here and now. Make all the mistakes you want and learn from them. Get past them now. Out in the mix, in a real battle–mistakes can mean death. And, sweeties, death is to be avoided. So listen and learn. When we tell you to do something, we do so for a reason. Do it. Even if you don't understand why right away. We'll explain it when it needs to be explained. We will always make time for Q&A."

One of Saemar's vets, 2nd Leftenant Maesara Taylor chimed in. "Sometimes we just want you to experience something first. Focus, study, and get the entire feel for each lesson. Save your questions for later."

She and Saemar nodded to each other; obviously there was great respect between them. Saemar had that with all of her people.

"All right," Saemar said. "Suit up and let's go out into the black."

Just as they were climbing in and the flight crews prepared for launch, Captain Chaela strode in, nineteen of her aces formed up in a wedge right behind her.

The two friends saluted, then embraced.

Chaela grinned. "Well, Captain. My people and I were off duty and had nothing to occupy our time. We thought we'd come over here and give you some help with your new recruits. Then we can all go out there and fly around together."

Saemar counted them. "Uh...that's great Chae. But we're still one short."

Chae shook her head. "No...we're not." She pointed up at the mobile flight command deck.

"Come down and join us, N. Mike's people told me you were up there. Get down here and give us a hand."

Naero rubbed her hands together and called down to them, "Sounds good. On my way."

When she reached the pilots, the recruits snapped to attention smartly and saluted her, although some of them also stared at her, mouths open.

Haisha, had *she* ever been that green?

Naero's friends, and the other veteran pilots who knew her, saluted casually.

One of the newbs actually stammered, "Fleet Captain M-M-Maeris...*Haisha!* It's...it's such an honor to have you train with us. Thank you, sir!"

Naero chuckled a bit at that. "At ease, ensigns."

Of course all of the newbs were ensigns. Crisp, shiny new flight togs and gear.

She turned to the speaker, a short tiny gal with pink and black short hair. "What's your name, Ensign...?"

The young woman turned scarlet and saluted again.

"Chang, sir. Tiali Wallace Chang."

Naero raised one eyebrow and smiled. "Got some Clan Wallace in you, huh?"

Tiali nodded. "And proud of it, sir!"

"I just happen to be Clan Wallace on my father's side. I guess that makes us distant cousins."

"Everyone knows that, sir. Both reasons why I'm proud of it, sir." Without any prompting, Tiali led all twenty-seven of the new recruits in a cheer that the others joined in with. Their raised fists pounded the air together.

"*Omaria! Omaria! Omaria!*"

"Huzzah! Huzzah! Huzzah!"

Naero stepped back, drew her blazing blue energy cutlass and saluted them quickly, sheathing her blade just as fast.

Tiali and several others cheered and actually had tears in their eyes.

Naero bowed her head to them. "Thank you. You honor me and my blood."

The recruits spoke in unison. "Your blood is our blood. The honor is ours."

Naero put her hands behind her narrow waist and spread her stance. "Very well. Pilots, suit up. Let's get out in the black in these tandems and learn a few things today."

Everyone secured their helmets and checked their gear.

"Ensign Tia…"

The ensign looked back, her mouth open slightly.

"You're with me. Take a breath. Relax."

"Thank you, sir. I am quite relaxed, sir."

Over her shoulder, Naero caught Tia turning to her friends and silently spazzing out, with her hands gesturing wildly, her face waggling, and her feet stamping in place with glee.

Some of them made faces and stuck their tongues out at her in clear envy.

They all climbed in, set their controls, fired up all systems, and prepared to launch.

Out in the black, Captain Chaela ran the practice exercise, and put them all through their paces using captured Triaxian stealth drones, seeker mines, and robotic gunships in training mode.

Training mode meant that all the ships scaled back the output of their weapon arrays so that they still scored hits that could be tracked and evaluated to determine simulated damage and kills, but of course they did no real harm.

And if a ship endured simulated damage, the ship systems would react or power down in kind, to allow the pilot to react to those situations as well.

If a clean kill was made, the warning systems would flash and blare in panic mode for several seconds and then go dead. The fighter would list in space for several more seconds before the systems powered back up or the instructor overrode the training protocols.

The new batch of recruits, including Tia, were rough around the edges, but they showed off many hot, agile, inventive skills.

Fighter pilots often trained from a very young age to become what they were–from the time they could float.

Naero understood that completely.

She had to admit, flying in tandem provided many opportunities for on-the-spot training and advice. These young pilots had the basics down cold.

But they still had not raised their skill sets to the level of an art yet. And that was basically what it took–a blend of experience and ability that combined honed instincts, finesse, and cunning in order to do many things automatically, without thought or hesitation.

Then they had to be able to read the battle and the continual stream of data that flooded at them. This included constantly shifting targeting profiles and combat orders. There remained much that could not be learned in mere simulation, but only in the crucible of actual combat.

With harsh realities and death all around.

The instructors gave them tips all along the way, showing them firsthand what to do, and how to both survive and fight effectively.

Together they could polish moves and tricks, or the instructor could even take over and let the recruits feel the magic in the controls as the vets executed them flawlessly. Then let the newbs try them repeatedly, until they had them down.

The trainers could slow techniques down and let the recruits practice them in slow motion at first, working out each element, before speeding them up once more.

Saemar called them together in scattershot formation. "Nice work, sweeties. For the rest of our time today, we're going to take turns jumping on single ships and small groups with larger sorties. This is also the way the enemy tries to peel us off and swarm on us in an attempt to overwhelm us. If we get the chance, we try to do the same thing to them."

Saemar took a deep breath. "You need to know how to resist and defend against these strategies and tactics, and how to get away when you are outnumbered and outmatched. Right now, I just want the recruits to focus solely on survival. Don't worry about doing damage to your opponents. Later on, we'll work on wave, squadron, and wing tactics to back each other up with, and to turn the tables on the bad guys. After that, we'll get into fleet defense modes, and attack strike methods to use against different types of enemy ships."

Naero joined in. "Excuse me, Captain Saemar. I just want to interject something here."

"Please do. Go right ahead, N."

"People, in your free time, I want all of you studying up and drilling each other on the various types of enemy ships you will be facing and their current strengths and weaknesses. You need to become experts on these matters and have the data in your heads. Help each other. You will be too busy flying and fighting in the mix to stop in the middle of a battle and read the latest intelligence dossier on, say, the Triaxian Centurion Class Heavy Cruiser, and where its shield patterning is weakest, due to a slight design flaw and the placement of its deflector shield projection hardpoints."

Tia spoke up. "Twenty-three meters directly forward of the front sublight engine nacelles, on both sides and below."

"Very good, Ensign. Can you or anyone else tell me why not to bother targeting the bridge until the shields are down on the same vessel?"

Another recruit jumped in. "Because the new Triaxian wave-flux shields lay down extra layers of protection over both the bridge and the cruiser's power core to improve both function and survivability."

"Excellent. So currently, what other design flaw on that warship allows the best opportunity to take the shields down, as quickly as possible?"

Silence.

"Uh, sir," Tiali noted, "there wasn't any info on that in the latest Intel dossier."

"Exactly. The Triaxian Centurion Class uses three very large Stellar Corps Quasar SJ303-K sublight engines, coupled with the jump drive and the power core, protected in the aft section of the warship. Yet concentrated fire or multiple hits on the aft shield node, especially when that type of ship is accelerating rapidly, will disrupt the wavering shields and take them down. It will also possibly damage the engines themselves, as well as other interlinked systems, leaving the ship even more vulnerable."

Silence again.

Tiali again. "Sir…that info isn't anywhere on record. How would we possibly know it?"

"Because I'm telling it to you now. It hasn't been officially confirmed yet, but I assure you, it works. Go with it. And if you stumble on something like that, report it immediately and spread the word."

Warnings suddenly sounded from the fleet.

Fifteen enemy carriers jumped in close, almost right on them in the rear areas, protected by two enemy strike fleets.

The overall command erupted from the fleet. "All ships, prepare for battle!"

Saemar gave the orders. "Shields up, full on. All training modes off. Fire up all weapon arrays and prepare to accelerate to attack speed. Form up into three wings of nine, led by myself and Captains Chaela Maeris and Naero Maeris. All three wings, tight three-talon support. Back everyone up.

"Battle computers online. Watch your optimal targeting protocols. Let's throck, sweeties! In on my mark. Enter the mix."

"We're with you, Saemar," Chae said.

"Copy that," Saemar said. "We need to buy our fleets time to form up and coordinate a counterattack. Delay and slow the enemy down. Containment cloud formation Tango-X-ray-4."

"They're launching now. Look at them swarm." Naero analyzed the enemy plan of attack.

Not good.

Everything favored Triax on this one.

"They've caught us napping back here," Naero said. "Our people are in a bad way. They'll try to overwhelm our defenses and take out all the helpless ships."

"More waves launching from our available carriers," Chae added. "Good thing we had some of them waiting in line back here."

"Time. We need time," Naero said. "Increase attack speed. Let's make some."

Fleet attack orders came down, trying to coordinate whatever Alliance ships were not disabled or stuck passing through the fixer cloud gauntlet. "All available warships and fighters, commence immediate attack on enemy formations. Expand into forward melting waves of the evolving Tango-X-ray-4. Re-enforcements are on the way."

"Here we go," Saemar told them. "We're up against mostly Triax Achilles 125D and E variants."

Twenty-seven Ghost Dragon tandems hit the advancing swarm with everything they had.

Four cruisers, eleven destroyers, and a handful of other smaller ships waiting nearby expanded the containment screen and joined them.

No battleships available yet. Naero knew for a fact that they were still locked in refit.

The Condor was the only carrier free and clear, out in the open.

It bravely advanced with the responders, right behind its launching fighter waves, secondary batteries already blazing.

The foremost, thin screen of defenders slammed into a vanguard of three hundred enemy fighters, or vice versa.

Having disgorged their lethal insects, the enemy carriers retreated behind the offensive waves of their two strike fleets without a scratch.

The two enemy strike fleets proceeded to swivel around on either flank to catch the Alliance ships stuck in the fixer clouds in a medium-range crossfire of big gun salvos.

The enemy attack stalled only long enough to attempt to absorb the few initial defenders.

Naero grinned.

The enemy commander leading the attack must be a complete dope.

Had he been bolder or smarter, he or she would have merely swept past the Alliance's thin, meager defensive screen—ignoring it entirely. Triax could have then concentrated all of their initial firepower on the helpless fleets stuck in refit.

They could have really done some damage.

Now, the defenders were in for a definite pounding, to be sure. But at least they could still maneuver and fight back.

Each precious second that ticked by, the odds of the battle would slowly swing over toward the Alliance's favor.

Anyone with any battle sense at all could see that.

This was the price commanders paid for being too cautious at times.

Yet, as expected, the withering enemy beat down quickly commenced.

Naero and Tia spun and fired and fought and got kicked around, along with everyone else.

"I'll fly and keep us alive, Tia. You focus on keeping our guns blazing and doing damage. Give anything around us sheer hell."

"On it, sir."

Naero bounced, bucked, stalled, flipped and spiraled, using every trick and every technique she could think of to keep them moving and make them harder to hit.

But they got pummeled anyway.

Tia calmly maintained a steady patter of blazing fire from their heavy blaster cannons. She fired micromissiles and discharged microbombs and mines right into the packed ranks of the foe to soften them up.

Shields reduced rapidly across the entire defensive screen under heavy, relentless, enemy fire from multiple attack trajectories.

One destroyer, a missile frigate, and two gunships got swarmed on and taken down in the heat of the initial engagement alone.

By then, the Alliance had fewer than five hundred fighters out in the mix against six times those numbers–or more.

Seventeen percent of those defending fighters were lost outright as well, in the course of the first pass.

Chaela's three wings remained intact momentarily, quickly joined by the rest of their wave forming up around them.

But three of their tandems were forced to pull away with heavy damage. Ghost Dragons were tough, but not indestructible.

Saemar kept the rest moving and fighting, coordinating with the other ships and Fleet Command.

"Inch the cloud back. Lima-Tango-4–tight loop, clockwise fighting retreat. Cycle back in on random vectors and keep firing–right in their teeth."

Naero performed the maneuvers in timed conjunction with the rest of the defenders. Tia kept acquiring and nailing targets according to the coordinated firing protocols.

Their few larger ships pulled back, many already heavily damaged. Their fighters did the same, but looped out of the way and then back again in crazy swoops and angles to blast the advancing tide of enemy fighters once again and keep them guessing.

This delaying tactic led to an effect where the defensive screen appeared to ripple, waver, and wobble, as the enemy attack continued to slam into it, bounce back, and then surge forward once more.

Only minutes into the battle, and the enemy punched gaping holes in the thin defense.

It nearly collapsed.

Then the foe would sweep them away.

Fleet orders saved them. "Retreat to tertiary defensive line. Form defensive sphere Delta-Victor-5 around *The Condor*."

Any of them that could still move pulled back and fell in around the battered fleet carrier. Loose formation, allowing them all to still maneuver and fight.

The deadly enemy pounding continued.

Then Naero noticed the enemy commander making a second fatal mistake.

Realizing his first error, he immediately divided his forces in half, sending one part to finally attack the gauntlet of refit nebulae ships close up. The trapped Alliance vessels attempted to break up, come about, and either join the mix or get clear and jump out.

The other half of the enemy kept up their assault on the beleaguered defenders, who were suddenly somewhat relieve to find that the odds against them were now halved.

The enemy leader should have stuck to doing one thing or the other from the outset, once they had committed themselves to an action.

Triax could have crushed the defenders within another few minutes at most.

Now it grew likely that the enemy would accomplish neither objective.

And in a few short moments, the tide should begin to turn against them–the price of indecision.

The defenders merely needed to do their best to stay alive until then.

Fleet orders gave them what they needed. "Scattershot retreat. Max out. Three-sixty dispersal. Form back up on coded signals."

The defenders suddenly broke away, poured on every ounce of speed, and fled in every direction possible.

The enemy tried to pursue them all, and only succeeded in confusing and jumbling its superior numbers up in all directions as well. This led to a further waste of valuable time, effort, and energy.

All the while, the Alliance fleets that we're able, began to form up and go on the attack out of the fixer clouds.

To make matters worse for Triax, a new Alliance fleet jumped in behind the enemy strike fleets, and also right behind the bunched-up enemy carriers.

The latter were sitting ducks, and came under instant heavy fire by the battered Joshua Tech Fleet just entering the system.

With multiple enemies at hand, Joshua Tech formed its fleet into a thin line and engaged the enemy from the direct rear. Yet its heaviest ships wisely pounded the carriers, who tried to disengage and move out to call back their fighter swarms and then jump away.

Anyone could see that Triax had squandered its initiative, and would very quickly suffer a horrendous defeat.

The rest of the battle went like something out of a text book over the next three minutes.

Triax did its best to retreat and jump away.

They still lost six of their fifteen carriers in the process, and the equivalent of one entire strike force–and by the end–nearly one half of their launched fighters.

By the time more Alliance reinforcements poured in, the clean-up phase was already underway.

Saemar focused on keeping all of them alive.

When the fires on board *The Condor* went out, they were cleared to land back in their damaged but still functioning hangar.

Their six friends from the three damaged fighters, forced to retreat, met them on deck. Naero and Tia's tandem fell over to one side and caught fire as soon as they zipped out of the cockpit on their gravwings.

Chaela and her trainee's fighter looked so shot full of holes, it was a wonder it could still function and fly.

Saemar and her pilot's Ghost Dragon came in too hot, lost power, and then flipped over, broken and smoking. The recovery team doused the damaged ship with foam fire retardant and the recovery team had to cut them out of the crushed cockpit.

Saemar and the handsome young recruit she flew with leaned on each other, staggering over to the medteks to get checked out.

Her ensign looked visibly shaken, about to go into shock.

Saemar leaned over him on his medbed, smiled, and whispered something into his ear while the medteks went over him.

His eyes got real big suddenly, and a weak grin spread across his pale face.

Naero and Tia ran up to them. Saemar took her cracked helmet off and turned to meet them.

Naero hugged her. "Great job, Saemar. You kept everyone together throughout that terrible mess. I think the readouts said everyone's more or less safe and sound. You sure your ensign is all right there?"

Saemar beamed, and then winked. "He's fine. Got a little banged up, but he even managed to save our butts once or twice out there."

She shook her curly head. The three of them began to walk toward the rest of their people.

"Don't worry about him," Saemar whispered. "I'll take extra-special good care of him tonight, sweetie. You can count on that."

Saemar also patted one of the tandems as she went by it. "I like these two-seaters, N. Did you notice how handy it was to have the pilot fly and the co-pilot focus on offense?"

"I did. I can see why people keep forming units of them. " Naero turned to Ensign Tia. "Great job–2*nd* *Leftenant* Tiali Wallace Chang. I counted twenty-six kills. That makes you an ace, many times over. Probably a few more in the battle computer that I missed. Excellent shooting."

Tia lit up like a pulsar, as Naero knelt and pweaked her new rank up on the young woman's flight suit, and authorized it in the fleet net via wristcom.

Tia nearly forgot to salute, but caught herself at the last instant. "Thank you, sir. But frankly, I couldn't have done any of that if I had to fly at the same time. I know very well that you kept us breathing out there. I'm not sure that I would have made it back from all that."

"You'll do well, Tia. Call me N, when we're not around any brass. We've flown and fought together now–and that makes us sisters, even though we were already cousins."

"Thanks, N. You honor me, so much."

Naero clapped arms with her. "The honor is mine, Tia."

Saemar stared at the ceiling of the hangar and spoke out loud. "Seriously, I'm going to ask my Strike Fleet Captain to help me form a full wave of these tandem fighters. Like others, I think they'll do well. A grand new option for my Alliance sweeties. I got a feeling some people will simply perform better in pairs."

That one was just far too easy–especially coming from Saemar.

Naero ignored her chance and clapped her friend on the back. "You know me, Saemar. I'm all for what works."

38

The cloaked microfixer clouds continued to reveal more illegal fleets from the other Corps along the entire front line of the war. They could no longer continue to prop up Triax. Under the threat of another full-scale Spacer war–which would quickly consume one quarter of the known galaxy–the other fourteen Corps turned tail and deserted. Wholesale.

The vast majority of the mercs jumped completely out of the war at an astonishing rate.

And they usually fled at what could only be inopportune times–for Triax. One or two fleets here and there at a time–at least several in almost every engagement at first, once they were exposed.

Triax even fired at some of their former allies as the other Corps ships abandoned them to their fate.

The Alliance and the Clans had called the Corps' bluff in a masterstroke.

And won big. This effort alone would shorten the war by months, re-assure eventual, total victory, and renew the Alliance's sure and steady advance.

Naero and Strike Fleet Six were held in reserve during the final assaults on Tarissa-1.

Prince Ellis of the Matayans and his fleets had pulled back, returning to their worlds to put down yet another inconvenient attempt by Triax to inflame yet another Matayan civil war.

Admirals Maeris, Joshua, and Kinmal fell upon the remaining enemy fleets in good order, dismantling them like a machine. They did their best to destroy or capture even the pieces.

More intense fighting still lay ahead. Triax made that clear each day. Yet the signs were posted for all to read.

Triax was going down in flames.

Nothing could prevent that now.

Further defections to former Admiral Sandusky's shadow fleets helped pave the way to victory, and much reduced loss of life on the growing list of liberated worlds.

Spacer Intel played a heavy hand in those factors as well.

Once Tarissa-1 fell, the Alliance forces spread out to the neighboring systems to consolidate their gains and scan for any further enemy attempts at counterattacks. They did all that they could to prevent any more use of Triaxian genocide devices or mass terrorism. Intel used their spy networks and cloaked microfixers to thwart whatever they could.

Because Tarissa-1 was so densely populated, special care had to be taken with it and other such Capital Class Worlds.

No one wanted a repeat of the terrible events on Heaven-7, or some of the other worlds, where entire large cities and their peoples were murdered wholesale.

Hevangian Homeworlds like Valkeggoth-6 that specifically chose to commit self-inflicted cosmicide en masse were, fortunately, rare and special cases.

Little could be done for an entire population that actively chose to kill itself. Reason always remained vulnerable to insanity.

Certain cities and regions on Tarissa-1 did not destroy themselves, but still made a show of defiance. Triaxian zealots and fanatics vowed to fight until the end. They threatened total mobilization and human wave, suicide tactics to punish and repel any invader.

Naero's Strike Fleet Six was assigned to help support the pacification efforts. Several heavy Marine Divisions were being combined for the upcoming ground campaigns.

Naero took a call from *Captain* Hayden, communicating through their holos to each other.

"Jeremiah, my friend. Congrats on another promotion. You deserve it…Captain."

"Thank you, sir."

Naero waved a hand. "Let's dispense with all that: we're more than friends. We've worked very well together on several occasions."

Hayden hesitated. "My rank equals that of a regular warship captain only, and you're still a strike fleet captain, sir."

"Well, unless the brass is watching or listening, let's be informal. That's how I am with my people, and that's an order."

Jeremiah smiled "Very well, N."

"So, what's up?"

"Admiral Maeris has ordered my unit down to the surface with 3rd Division. Your security people will have to fill in for us on our ships while we're gone."

"Of course. My Security officer, Tarim, is already on it. You and your people don't need to worry about us. Just stay safe down there. Good luck, and be careful. Return to Six, as able."

"Thanks, N. Will do."

"What's the current plan? I haven't had time to read my orders fully yet, but my people are supposed to support you guys with whatever help you might need. I have several of my cruisers and destroyers refitting for close assault and ground support mode. Numerous fighter wings stand ready to swoop in, also."

"Frankly, we're hoping to avoid direct combat and fighting in built-up areas like the gigacities. Intel will most likely have you refit a good number of your ships with our improved version of the enemy's mass stunners."

Naero nodded and crossed her arms. "I've seen them at work, firsthand. Our version is much better?"

Hayden nodded. "Covers an even wider area, and when those stunned wake up, after a few hours, the actual neural damage and pain are much less. Like that of a migraine or a very slight concussion."

Naero crossed her arms. "But if it is used on large populations, there will still be indirect casualties. Hospitals. Vehicles crashing. People falling down. Fires or explosions ignored or neglected."

Hayden nodded. "There is no perfect way to do this, Naero."

"I know; I wish there was. That many people. I can't help doing the cold math."

"It's still better than slugging it out against partisans and terrorists, fighting our way through the streets. That could take months, and the casualties would be staggering. Such a bloodbath would go beyond what stunning the cities by sections would cause."

Captain Hayden sighed. "Hopefully, the civilians will see very quickly that they cannot prevail, and that such resistance is unnecessary in any case. We're not here to conquer them. We don't want to fight them. Their world remains their own–just without Triax's dominion or influence–and that is to their gain, not their loss. Once they realize how little they actually need the Corps–then they will accept being liberated from their tyrants, just as all the other worlds have."

Naero laughed at him. "You don't have to sell me on the facts on the ground, Jeremiah. Just let us know where we can assist."

She watched the situation develop over the next several hours.

Heavy elements from six separate Spacer Marine Divisions surrounded and made contact with the six largest gigacities that still resisted. Hundreds of billions of lives remained at stake.

Thankfully, three of those gigacities chose to surrender, and accept the pacification forces and their simple demands–a new freedom from Corps rule, which cost the landers nothing.

Two still played for time, trying to delay the inevitable by playing useless politics.

One last gigacity–and, unfortunately, the largest–threatened not only to fight to the last, but to set off several genocide devices if they were attacked.

Including a dozen large atomic devices.

Yet such devices were now easy to scan and go after. And from all that Intel could deduce, most of that threat was pure bluster.

Even when Intel searched and scanned hard for them, there were no such devices to be found.

Intel took the time to double-check, but they finally gave the word that any such devices had already been fully neutralized.

The Spacer Marines promptly stunned the outer ring of the city. They walked right through its first line of defense and used fixer clouds to rapidly dismantle them without firing a shot.

This was a very clear demonstration and a warning.

Again, the Alliance informed the population well in advance as to what was going to happen, and why further inconvenience and indirect injury and loss need not be multiplied.

Once more, the city leaders made a show of defiance, and fired many weapons throughout the remaining districts into the sky.

The Alliance negotiators kept the holdouts blustering and fuming–until nightfall.

Then the Marines made their move, under the cover of darkness.

"Very well," the chief Alliance negotiator finally announced. "You leave us no choice. Before we are forced to stun the rest of the city, we're sending in the Spacer Marines of Bravo Command. They'll focus on killing all of your leaders, anyone in charge–your complete command and control–including all of you. In a matter of hours, all of you will be dead. Then the people can pick new leaders and make better choices…once you are all permanently out of the way."

The city leaders paled, even through their holos.

Many of them shaking with outright fear and terror.

The head of the City Defense Force even exclaimed. "Not those bloody-handed devil dogs! We heard what they did to the High Command on Semaka-6."

"Good. Then you know exactly what to expect, and that you have little time left. They will fall upon you shortly. Good luck to you, and farewell. We will speak with your replacements after you are gone."

The Alliance Chief Negotiator broke off the link.

In seconds, the Triaxians scrambled in panic to get the links back up and call the Alliance back.

The Alliance people let the Triaxians sweat things out for a few more long minutes.

While Bravo Command–already in place like the ghosts they were rumored to be–merely broke some windows and popped in stun and flash bombs and tear gas throughout the city–in key locations.

Just enough to terrify the city leaders and let them know what could quickly follow.

Finally the Alliance negotiators opened the links again.

The Triaxians fell all over themselves to give up.

"Please, please call off your bloody Marines. We surrender! There's no need for any further loss of life."

"We give up. Our cities are yours."

"We'll pay you not to kill us–please, please–just let us live!"

Naero laughed out loud in her command chair and nearly fell out of it.

So much for fighting until the last drop of blood.

The Marines of Bravo Command were in fact legendary throughout the known systems. So much so, that they had an air of the supernatural around them. Which, of course, Bravo played up all the more, for the benefit of their enemies.

The best-of-the-best among the elite ground attack forces, Bravo Command were the absolute masters of night fighting. No one beat them in the black. They were said to be phantoms, wraiths who slipped in more silent than a whisper–and left only death and destruction behind.

Just the mere rumor of Bravo Command being sent in to take out all the city leadership had broken the enemy's spirit and will to resist.

Naero loved great showmanship when she witnessed it.

Yet she had no doubt that Bravo Command could have more than lived up to its legend.

Legends had to be backed up with force and results, if need be.

Everyone on both sides fully understood the truth of the matter.

If Triax had not surrendered–Bravo Command wasn't bluffing.

Not a single one of those gigacity leaders would have made it through the night alive.

39

Naero slipped into her dress uniform and thought about what it meant to command people in battle. To lead a ship, an entire fleet, during wartime.

One of the highest honors she had ever experienced.

Their duty was to fight, and fight they did, any time, anywhere.

But the admirals had been right. There was so much more involved in command than simply fighting on the front lines. So many greater and lesser issues, and much more in between. Maintaining a fighting force took a great deal more to keep their people ready to fight. To keep them well-trained, well-informed, well-supplied, and fit for service–physically, mentally, and emotionally.

In effect, a good leader was not only a good planner, but also a good steward. You took care of your people and primed and groomed them for battle.

Naero pweaked up a mirror wall on the nanosurface of her quarters.

Everything in place, just the way she liked it. She looked fine; pretty good, even.

So why, in the midst of all of this chaos did she still sleep alone at night? Perhaps Saemar had it right after all.

As usual, it was all Naero's own fault, really.

She purposely kept herself too busy with the war to take up matters of the heart. And that was just her own excuse. More than anyone else in her private fantasies, she thought about Prince Ellis quite a lot from time to time.

If only things had been different…but they weren't.

She left her quarters for the ceremony, and her Marine escort of four slipped effortlessly around her, one pair in front of her, one pair in back. Two female Marines, two males.

They guarded and protected Naero in rotating shifts, but she knew all of their names. Naero was on a friendly basis with all of her guard shifts. They were in full, shining battle dress tonight–as if for a parade.

They all proceeded quickly to the assembly hall, and Naero entered into a sea of crew and representatives from every ship in Strike Fleet Six. Thousands cheered when they saw her enter and approach the podium.

Admiral Sleak Maeris and many officers had waited for her and others to arrive. More officers from the entire Alliance continued to pour in and queue up in their appointed places.

Name after name was read, and Spacers from all Forty-Nine Clans came forward to receive the promotions they had earned thus far, during the course of the war.

Naero clapped and cheered until her hands were sore and her voice grew hoarse and cracked.

She shot to her feet when her people came through, and programmed their new ranks in on a special pad given to her for that exact purpose. Then she embraced them, and thanked and honored them for their valor– for their camaraderie, service, and sacrifice.

Four of them blazed especially bright in her heart:

"Tyber Maeris, hereby promoted to the rank of Tek Leftenant Commander."

Naero felt like a crybaby sometimes, when it came to her closest mates. She struggled not to let any tears show.

Ty grinned. They hugged each other for a long moment.

"Doctor Zhentisa Maeris, hereby promoted to the rank of Medical Service Commander."

Naero could not help tearing up a little when they embraced. "You work so hard, Z. All of your research, your work with Intel, our wounded. You really deserve this. Congratulations, my dearest sister."

Zhen wept openly and almost sobbed. "I love you so much, N. And did you see my Ty? He looks so handsome. I'm so proud of all of us."

Then from her bridge crew:

"Enel Maeris, hereby promoted to the rank of 2nd Leftenant, strike fleet flagship pilot and helmsman."

Naero embraced yet another comrade who had become a good friend, like so many. "Great work, Enel. I am always proud and honored to have you at my helm. Fight well, *abani.*"

Enel pulled away, grinned, and winked at her. "Thank you, sir. N, I'm just glad I haven't given you any further reasons to shoot me in the goddam head!"

They shared a good laugh together and embraced once more.

Enel had also been wounded three times on their bridge.

Each time he came back to her within a week.

"Surina Marshall, hereby promoted to the rank of Leftenant Commander, Flagship Communications Specialist."

Naero had come to trust and rely on Surina and her knowledge and expertise. Rina was also an excellent pilot and leader in her own right, who read people well and always had Naero's back.

"Surina, you're going to make a formidable captain yourself, one day."

They hugged each other. "I'm honored to serve at your discretion, my captain. N, you are the finest, bravest leader–and the most astonishing battle tactician–that I have ever had the pleasure to witness in action. You need to know just how much your people love you, respect you, and are willing to follow you into combat."

"Thanks, Rina. Coming from a go-getter like you, that means more to me than I can ever put into words. I hope I never let you down."

For the first time ever since they had known one another, Surina's eyes reddened and swelled up with tears.

Rina smiled and shook her head slightly. "Not possible, sir."

Once the ceremony ended, and they were all back on board their various ships and off duty, Naero ordered rousing parties to commence for all of her people throughout Six, in honor of all of those who had earned promotions.

And anyone who wanted to celebrate that.

A day later, Naero slipped over to the heavy cruiser, *The Minstrel* as general tek Pharrah Barrett. She used nanofilm, programmable contacts to change her violet eyes to blue, and set her nanowig to a short black bob, curled in on the sides and edges. She saw a new makeup style with painted eyes in some vids on one of the webnets that seemed popular, and gave them a whirl.

She made Pharrah-Naero Barrett somewhat shy and introverted. Quiet and aloof–someone who read a lot on her pad, stayed in her quarters, and kept to herself. She didn't attract a lot of attention.

Which made some others take note of her.

Pharrah quietly performed her assigned duties. She sulked when she had to go to PT and combat training in the mornings. Naero even made her alias rather clumsy and awkward, and not very good at fighting.

The other teks attempted to take her under their wing and did their best to try to help her.

A male tek from another deck–ten or twelve years older than her, in fact–took a shine to her alias and pressured her to go out with him.

The guy just wouldn't let up. He even started to get abrasive about it–as if he could force her to spend time with him.

Several of the other female teks banded together and finally stepped in. They asked Pharrah-Naero, in public, if she was at all interested in the guy or not–right in front of him.

Pharrah blushed blood-red and quietly squeaked, "No," with her head down.

Her mates strongly proceeded to advise the pushy, older guy to hunt elsewhere if he was lonely.

Taking their not-so-subtle hint as the threat it was, the pushy jerk stopped coming around. The guy was clearly too old for Pharrah-Naero anyway–older than thirty. Very creepy.

Her friends took her out with them, trying to get her to loosen up a bit and come out of her shell.

Tawny Maeris, a tall, brunette tek with brown eyes tried to counsel her. "Honey, you need to understand. That pouty, helpless-little-kitten routine you put out is like a magnet to every predator and control freak out there–male or female. People who like to bully or dominate someone quieter and weaker than them will just home in on you like a seeker missile."

Pharrah-Naero pursed her lips together in angry frustration, with a hint of humiliation. "I'm not helpless, and I'm of age. I do my work. I do my duty and everything expected of me. I know what I like and what I don't like. I don't…care for a lot of people. And usually, I just want to be left alone. Why is that so hard for some people to accept?"

Tawny looked at her friend, tek Yasha Keller, a short curvy blond with amber eyes.

Both of them rolled their eyes at the young newb.

"Pharrah, you don't want to hear this, but Tawny's right. You need to cowgirl up a little–if nothing else, to protect yourself. *Haisha*, kid–have you even slept with someone yet? Do you even understand what these type of people want from you?"

Pharrah-Naero blushed again, and looked down.

Yasha sighed. "I'll take that as a no."

"I'm not a baby. I know what sex is…even if I haven't done it yet. I've seen some vids; like anyone, I was curious. And honestly, it looks…" she made a face "…really gross."

Tawny and Yasha shook their heads and waved their hands adamantly.

"You can't go by porn," Tawny said. "All porn is stupid fantasy. That's never real."

"Sweetie," Yasha added, "when you are ready for it, love and sex can be really great–especially with someone you really care about, and who cares about you. Spectacular, even."

Pharrah-Naero wrung her hands in frustration. "But I'm not looking for sex. I–I'm not looking for anything right now. Honestly, guys. I'm happy alone. I just want to be by myself."

Tawny put her hand on her arm. "Pharrah, that's perfectly fine. Forget sex. You want to be by yourself? Be by yourself. But Yasha and I are just trying to warn you about how some other people might see you. Be a little stronger and more forceful. Believe in yourself. Show a little Spacer pride and confidence."

"T is right, honey. You got 'victim' written all over you. Some people see that, and its like puttin' blood in the water to attract sharks. There are always jerks who want someone weaker than them to push around. And you got a big holographic flashing blurt board hanging over you that says

Quiet and meek. Ready to be bullied and taken advantage of.

"By the Powers, Pharrah–we're at war," Tawny said. "You need to toughen up a little. Take a look at our fleet captain, Captain Maeris. Now that's tough!"

"Yeah," Yasha added, "she's smaller than you, and she's tigress, a fighter if there ever was one. So one day, this huge, loudmouth mook comes over from one of the other fleets, shootin' his yap off. Saying how her dead parents were a bunch of phonies–the fight circuit was rigged and all fake–bragging how he was tougher than her and her whole family put together."

"Well…he was three times her size," Tawny added.

Pharrah-Naero blinked and let her mouth fall open a little, lifting her fingers to her teeth. "*Haisha*…what did she do?"

Tawny's eyes glistened. "You shoulda seen it, kid. I'll tell you exactly what she did. She challenged that gigantic mook to a sparring match, right then and there, for the honor of her parents, her Clan, and herself."

Yasha jumped in. "She took that mook down like a falling rock. Kicks flashing, her spinning and whirling around–just like her mom, The Invincible Cyclone. Same exact fighting style. We all saw it happen.

"It was a thing of beauty. But the point is, she stood up for herself, and didn't take a lot of crap. You need to back yourself up a little more…kinda like that."

Pharrah-Naero rubbed her arms. "I…I don't know, guys. I'm not much of a fighter."

"Yeah," Tawny said. "Yeah, we've noticed that, too."

Yasha leaned in slightly. "Along with everyone else. That's our point. You're very cute, honey. If you didn't paint your eyes like some punk teen…"

"Yasha's right. That look's just too young for people of age…"

"…you could even be pretty–when the time comes, and you're ready for some real romance."

Tawny crossed her arms in front of herself. "Until then, you need to grow up and look out for yourself a little more."

"Stick with us," Tawny added. "We can help you work a few things out, and see what your options are. We've seen newbs like you come along and get taken advantage of, time and time again."

"And it is too painful to watch," Yasha said.

"There are some pretty tough lessons to learn out there in the adult world–especially during wartime. A little more backbone would do you some good, kiddo."

Pharrah-Naero smiled. "Thanks, guys. I hear what you're saying. I'll try to do better. I really appreciate you two looking out for me and trying to help me out."

"Hey, that's what your mates are for."

"Yeah, we watch each others' backs and take care of one another."

"And we also buy each other drinks and chow," Tawny told her. "Like you're going to buy us a round, right now, to celebrate growing a pair."

"But…I don't drink."

Her new friends grinned at her and spoke in unison.

Mason Elliott

"Start."

40

Like Naero, Tarim lost half of his blue forces in their latest sim.

But he succeeded in destroying her last big, and gained the upper hand.

"I think…" he said cautiously. "I think I have you."

Naero grinned. "Not yet, you don't. Evasive retreat in Foxtrot-Zulu-4."

"Cut off remaining blue elements in Echo-Victor-3 envelopment patterns."

She lost three cruisers, seven destroyers, and two carriers.

"Surrender," Tarim said.

Naero grinned. "Never. My crews fight to the last."

They battled back and forth.

In the end, Tarim had nine red ships left. Two carriers, one battleship, three cruisers, two frigates, and two gunships.

"Congratulations, Tarim. You've won again. I think you're really getting the hang of this."

Tarim laughed. "I know you're only letting me win, N–still trying to build up my confidence. I'm almost there–where I want to be. You don't have to keep taking it easy on me anymore. In fact, I wish you wouldn't. Punish me when I make stupid mistakes. Make our matches more challenging. It doesn't matter if I win or lose–as long as I keep learning."

Naero nodded. "Very well. I can do that."

"I know you can. You're the best, N. One of the best, at least. Everyone says so."

"Shall we have another go, then, Tarim? Or are you tired, yet?"

"One more. Really come at me this time."

She smiled slyly. "If you insist–be careful what you ask for, my friend."

Naero overwhelmed him in precisely thirty-seven seconds.

*

The fleets from the other Gigacorps still massed on the borders near the Annexation War, keeping close watch, poised to protect the rights to their own territory, and to make sure that the regular Spacer Naval forces still kept their distance and did not interfere directly in the war's final outcome.

As they themselves had been clearly exposed to be doing, illegally, all along.

Yet the systems surrounding the final Capital Class World of Najindo-9 were now much closer together, and did not need as many fleets to defend them.

Triax had purchased plenty of time to layer its final defenses in dense spheres and waves of robot death ships, remotely piloted killer drones, cloaked and uncloaked smartmines–as well as its remaining, formidable mass of conventional fleets.

All of the zealots who were still defiant and insane to the last.

Everyone understood that these Triaxian fanatics were never going to surrender.

The Alliance made its plans for the next phase of the campaign. What everyone hoped would be the final phase.

Every Alliance warship, every vessel and fighter, was checked over, refitted, and upgraded with the latest tek.

Crew and replacements went through further training and preparation.

Leaves were planned in rotations, for as long as they could be sustained. Every member of the Alliance strove to ready themselves for the final push.

The initial engagements had already started.

Then out of the black, Chaela came to Naero in private.

"Hey, Chae. Happy to see you, *abani*."

"N, I want you to marry me and Remy. Today, if possible."

Naero raised her eyebrows. "I'd be honored, Chae. May I ask–what's the sudden rush?

Chaela shrugged, her long blond braid swinging slightly as she did so down her broad, athletic back. Her large blue eyes softened.

"So many have died, N. Any of us could buy it, each day. Any day. Saemar and I are out in the mix with our fighter wings just like everyone else. We know what can happen. What does happen. I just…I want to mean something to someone before it does. If and when it does."

Naero took Chae's hands in hers. "Whatever happens to all of us, we will always mean something to each other. We bleed and die and fight together for something better. That makes all of us more than mates. It makes us family; but you and I reached that point long ago, my sister."

Chae smiled and hugged her. "I already know all that, N. It's Remy. I'm just crazy about my guy, that's all. And he feels the same double for me, the poor sap. We just, you know, want everything to be straight between us…just in case. You know."

Naero nodded and smiled sadly. "Yeah. Sure thing, Chae. You two just let me know when and where. It doesn't have to take long at all."

Spacer weddings could be as elaborate as the couple could wish, but the standard ceremony was usually relatively simple and short, normally performed by a starship captain or sometimes a Clan elder.

Wartime forced Naero to perform the rite on many occasions in her role as captain. Often they were done in haste.

Many on the eve before a big important battle.

She never refused a request. Sometimes it was the last joy two people had in this life, before one or both of them went on to the next journey. And Naero would not deny anyone that.

Anyone who faced death each day understood the power and value of love.

Everyone deserved, in whatever time they had, to be the people they wanted to be, with the people they wanted to be with.

The most people she ever married at one time were forty-three couples, on a flight deck on the fleet carrier *The Bulldog*. Most of the couples were male-female, with a few male-male or female-female. That did not matter. People loved who they loved.

There might not be time later, when all faced death on a second-by-second basis throughout the course of the war.

Time and love became incredibly precious.

The call came up, and Naero's Strike Fleet raced forward to enter the mix.

Their new mission gave them little time.

Naero performed the ceremony over the comlink, while Chae prepped her Ghost Dragon F59F to lead her fighter wing out into the black.

Remy stood ready at his gunnery turret, a secondary battery on board *The Hippolyta*. That was his battle station, when he wasn't crunching numbers for fleet accounting and payroll.

"Chaela Maeris of Clan Maeris, and Remy La Fontaine Valmont of Clan Valmont. As your captain in charge of this ceremony, it is my honor and privilege to preside over your union."

Naero had to check her updating scans for a moment, and pweak the fleet's attack vectors and formations.

"Marriage is a sacred commitment of honor and respect that should not be entered into or taken lightly. Marriage takes two people devoted to one another, and joins and binds them into a single partnership of love and support, so that they may face all of the challenges of life together, and build a future of respect and mutual agreement and affection.

"Together, they are stronger that they were on their own. They compliment each other, building upon their strengths, and shoring up one another's weaknesses. They lay the foundation for a secure life and family, and the continuing future of our people. This is a foundation built on love, trust, respect, and honor. The two of you honor us all today, and we in turn honor both of you."

Chae broke in. "Sorry, N. Gonna have to speed it up. A few minutes more and I gotta launch."

"Very well, then. Let me be brief. Chaela Maeris and Remy La Fontaine Valmont. Do the both of you agree to be married to one another? If this is so, please say, 'I do.'"

"I do."

"I do."

"Do you agree to enter into this partnership, bound by love, honor, respect, and trust? To forsake all others and to assist, support, and serve each other, for as long as you both shall live? If this is so, then together, please say, 'We do.'"

"We do," Chae and Remy said in unison over their links.

"Then by the authority of the Free Spacer Clans given to me by my rank as captain, I now pronounce the two of you married–husband and wife, wife and husband. Let your life together be long, and filled with joy. Remy, you'll have to kiss her when she gets back. Fortune favor you both!"

"Who's kissing who?" Chae shouted with a laugh, right as she launched.

"Wahoo!"

The links broke off. Naero turned in her command chair, studying her scans and setting her forces for the battles ahead.

41

Rats always fled from an impending disaster. Such was widely known.

The same phenomena seemed to be occurring, directly connected with the impending fall of Triax Gigacorp.

Naero and the rest of the Alliance fleets were quickly becoming caught up and distracted with heavy interdiction duties.

At times, the prosecution of the actual hot war even ground to a standstill.

Basically, they spent more and more time pursuing and intercepting a tide of countless private Triaxian vessels laden with stolen wealth from a decadent, fallen empire. Strings of transports loaded with loot, and even slaves. Vessels of every shape and size, fleeing in all directions, simply adding to the chaos and uncertainty.

Triax even took advantage of the situation to scatter their agents and terrorists into rear areas, using the fleeing hordes as camouflage to hide their numbers. To use an old metaphor, they hid and lost themselves by becoming fish among numberless shoals of other, panic-stricken, fleeing fish.

The Alliance fleets soon found themselves overwhelmed.

Joshua Tech, the Matayans, the Miners, and the newly liberated worlds offered a partial solution when consulted.

Secondary fleets of other private ships, non-warships, and vessels basically unsuited for combat on the front lines assumed responsibility for inspection and interdiction duties. They were guarded by older military vessels that served best by patrolling the rear areas.

This shift of forces freed up elite and frontline elements from getting bogged down checking cargos, manifests, and IDs.

Smugglers, military, and paramilitary personnel attempting to flee off the grid without surrendering were still captured, and held for inspection and trial as needed.

By now, the new Alliance worlds had their own military courts and tribunals up and running. These were fully capable of prosecuting individuals, or entire system bureaucracies. Contraband was captured and converted into anything that might help the war effort or help the local systems improve their conditions.

Many other factors had to be considered on liberated worlds. Conditions on many Triax worlds were found to be quite deplorable, as some might readily expect. The miners were never surprised by such facts.

Therefore, teams of fixers were controlled by Spacer tek handlers to improve water, food systems, and living conditions everywhere they went–under the protection of the Alliance Defense Forces. They leapfrogged from world to world, from system to system, as possible and as needed.

As more and more worlds became liberated each day, Triaxian fanatics and terrorists continued their attempts to sow chaos and destruction among them. But they did so against the sweeping tide of change and freedom. And free peoples craved and demanded order, fairness, justice, stability, and peace.

Local forces on many liberated worlds found their hands full seeking out and neutralizing the lethal mix of atomic, chemical, biological, and conventional threats and agents used by the Triaxian terrorists. Intel stepped in the assist.

Such terrorists found themselves falling increasingly out of favor, and the locals on each liberated world hunted them down and slew them without mercy.

Yet only the total defeat of Triax would bring a definitive end to the unpredictable, sporadic murder of billions of civilians. Until that time, efforts could only continue to prevent and limit such terrible occurrences. Not stop them completely. The war must conclude.

*

Spacer Topeka-Naero Nelson transferred in on board the destroyer *The Star Witch* to work in logistics, as a supply loader on transports. She had a long, bright green ponytail and hazel eyes.

She was brash and loud. She exchanged rude jokes and gestures with her mates, and routinely invited anyone who had any kind of a problem with her to chomp on her lily-white butt and chew with gusto. She gambled and won and lost; she brawled when brawling was required.

The work was hard for glifter teams, and the hours long, especially on the rim of battle with ships always in need of resupply.

She slept when and where she could.

And though some thought her young and innocent at first, anyone who mistakenly tried to snuggle up to her or cop a feel without her permission got a swift boot in the crotch and a stout whack upside the head.

Topeka-Naero didn't take any crap–not from nobody.

She earned the respect of many in just a few short days.

But loaders were always full of poop, bragging about who they could trounce, and who they could bounce–as they put it.

They remained the top bullshit artists of all the Spacer ranks and jobbers.

And Topeka-Naero slung it thick and fast with the best of them.

Not an hour went by that someone didn't start talking trash about either fighting, sex, or some combination of the two.

"She's not so tough. I could beat that slank down with one hand secured behind me and my ankles strapped together."

"Why, an hour with me, and I'd drain all the juice right out of that lucky bloke. He'd black out with a smile, dry up, and blow away like dust and flakes on the wind–after I was done with him, he would."

Topeka-Naero chimed in. "I'd like to spar with this uppity fleet captain of ours, I would. She acts all tough and all that, but one punch from me and I'd lay her out, but good."

Every one suddenly paused and just stared at her.

Then they fell over themselves laughing.

Topeka-Naero blushed and snapped at them. "Go on, now. You scum can't laugh me down. I stand by my words. I can take her!"

Even more laughter.

"You stupid little twit," another loader said. "What kind of drug-induced smoke are you puffing out of your orifices? You, a gangly chit like yourself, take the mighty fleet captain herself down?"

Her new mates all piled in.

"*Haisha!* Not in a gazillion years," one loader said.

"Are you illegitimate? Can't ya read, ya moron?" another asked.

"Belay that. Why gal, don't you know who her parents were?"

"Did someone slip wild-cherry-flavored blast inta yer mother's tit-milk somehow? Why…your brain is cooked. You must be daft, gal."

"I still say I can take her," Topeka-Naero insisted. "Make the challenge. Get me a match with her. She comes around the ships to practice. Send word that I want to scrap."

"Calm yourself. Save your sand for the Tri-asses and pound it up them."

"Tri-asses?" Topeka-Naero said, scratching her head. "Why in the heck do you call 'em that?"

"It's just a play on Triax, gal."

"Because, as everyone knows, anyone who's a three-holer is filled to the very brim with thrice as much crap! That's our enemies for you; damn and blast them all!"

Everyone had a good laugh at that, even Topeka-Naero.

One of the older loaders pointed his finger at her and cocked a brow over his bleary eyes. "So, lass. You be a sweet little gal, and don't be challenging the good fleet captain none, or bothering her or any of the officers. They've got better things to do than finding time to stove your fool head in."

"Yeah, ya silly git."

Topeka-Naero pouted and muttered and fumed to herself for hours after they put her in her place.

42

When the time came for Strike Fleet Six to back off the line, Naero was more than ready for shore leave this time.

And so were many of her people. Everyone knew this could be it, coming up.

The last few weeks had been extremely rugged, but the next few promised to be the worst they had ever seen.

As for Naero, she chose to get away to an isolated mountain retreat on some backwater world–all by herself this time.

She gave others–even her closest friends–plenty of warning not to bother her.

This time, she wanted to be completely alone with her thoughts and feelings.

Naero lived like a hermit for two glorious weeks. She turned off all com devices and channels except the ones to Baeven and Spacer Intel, and the one for her callback link. The latter, duty required that she leave it open.

Then she slept, cried, took long walks and hikes, and stayed up at night slugging down Jett and Spacer poteen. She gorged herself on sweet blue, mystery-meat Spum and junk food. She went a few days without washing, until she couldn't handle her own stink any longer.

Then she bathed naked in a beautiful, freezing mountain waterfall.

There, where no one could see her, she broke down and cried again within that cleansing, icy-cold water. She wept for all of the senseless loss she had witnessed thus far.

And all that was yet to come.

That was the real truth and paradox about even a just war.

It was all both necessary and senseless–all at the same time.

Naero stayed up at night sometimes, thinking and musing, scribbling poetry. She thought about her life thus far.

She stayed out on the roof one night and watched the stars wheel overhead, of course caused by the planet's own rotation. She always found that phenomena so weird. No wonder landers were so messed up and thought everything revolved around them.

And for the first time in her life, she got so drunk one night that she actually threw up. First time for everything.

She put on her battle gear and unleashed her fury on a dense, dark-green bamboo forest that blotted out the sky and sun. Swords. Knives. Guns. Bombs.

She cut down, kicked, and blasted bamboo to bits until she lay spent and breathless among a wide swath of wreckage.

On the fourteenth night–her last–Naero went up to a high mountain top in the keen, thin wind under the stars, and meditated in one of the deep modes she had learned from her parents.

She did so in order to cleanse her thoughts and emotions–to prepare herself. She practiced with her twin katanas in ritual, meditation sword forms her father had taught her.

When the recall summons sounded on her comunit, Naero felt more than willing to return to duty.

Now, she was ready.

In for the final push.

43

Naero took one more run at going among her crew.

Telline–Telli Barrett worked on the battleship *The Athena* as a galley server, dishwasher, swab, and whatever else was needed. She had gray eyes and a long, pink French braid of hair.

Spacer galley food was always top notch, so nobody ever dared call it slop unless they wanted to start a fight. But Telli-Naero served meals regularly on the line for a handful of days.

Telli-Naero was an outright, unabashed flirt and winked at and grinned and pouted, breaking hearts every chance she got. When guys or gals got fresh or wanted to bunk up, she got a dreamy look in her eyes, sighed, and let them know they didn't stand a chance. Telli was saving herself for her guy–a handsome fighter jock with the 77th Starfighter Wave.

Naero learned a lot from working in a galley. Everyone had to eat, so she met almost everyone on the ship three times a day or more. 385 Spacers from every walk of life.

From stunning Captain Vanna Fae and her perfect mane of white-gold hair and mirific azure eyes, down to the other dishwashers and swabs.

Everyone ate and gabbed. Everyone fretted and worried about the final phases of the war, trying to survive and muster out to get back to their lives, families, and friends.

That seemed to be the general consensus.

All of Naero's people–and, most likely, everyone in the Alliance– were utterly tired of the war by now, and cursed everything that went with it.

But they had also come this far together, and every one of them was completely determined to see things through.

Triax must be destroyed.

If chatter did pass over or touch upon the Alliance leadership or Fleet Captain Maeris, it was usually positive.

Except for the whispered gags and laughter about those whacko digital porn vids, still making the rounds out there. They were a rude joke.

And they still riled and embarrassed Naero completely, but she didn't let it show whenever mention of them was made.

Then one day, someone commented that it must have been nice to grow up rich and pampered, like Captain Maeris must have been. What with her wealthy celebrity parents and their fame and all.

Another crew got upset and set them right. "You got that all wrong, mate. I know it for a fact. I know Naero Maeris. I worked with N–"

"Who the hell is 'N?" another crew cut in.

"Her mates call her that. It's a nickname; short for Naero. Now if you please let me finish what I was trying to say originally, without so many interruptions…I worked on board one of the Maeris merchant fleet ships under her aunt for nearly three years. I can tell you whatever you want to know about them both."

"Oof!" someone exclaimed. "I wouldn't want that duty. Working for the steel dragon herself? Everyone's heard what it's like to serve under Admiral Sleak Maeris, the captain's lady aunt. She looks like a vid model, but she breaks backs, balls, and necks as easy as breathing! Little wonder that her niece is a hard driver as well."

"Why, you've got bugs in your skull. Yes, they're both hard drivers, a plain fact to be sure. Everyone knows that. But I'll tell you what. I never made better pay and profit shares than under the admiral. And they're both fine officers, as well as being easy on the eyes. I worked for the captain and her aunt when Naero was a two- and three-striper, right after she did her two years of tactical training with the Spacer Marines–right around up to the time her folks got themselves killed out there, exploring the Unknown Regions.

"And when you say Captain Naero grew up pampered and rich, then those bugs in your noggin' must have gobbled up all your brains. She's our gal. She's a Spacer–through and through–just like the rest of us, by the Powers! Born and bred. She's one of us, I tell you! Her parents were gone most of the time, and spent all their money on their exploration fleet that got wiped out. Naero and her younger brother–Jan, that tail chaser–why they practically grew up working for their hard-nosed aunt. And she was tougher on them than anyone else the whole time.

"Captain Naero worked hard through the ranks, and earned her stripes well. She did everything, and never blinked or complained. And she never had credits to throw around. I never saw her do so, anyway."

The man sighed deep suddenly. "My friends, I wish you could have been at that wake they held for her parents. Look it up in the Clan Maeris archives, if you want a real eye-opener. The good captain loved her parents dearly; that much was very clear. We all loved them, for the people they were, the way they made us feel. The people they made us all want to be. But when Naero spoke at their wake–I tell you true–it was like poetry. She stood there in the light, all beautiful like her mother, and when she wept– why, we all fell to our knees and wept with her. And when the time came to cheer, we damn near blasted a hole through the hull."

The man rose up proudly. "That's the kind of person our Fleet Captain is. And I'll strike down anyone who says otherwise. She's one of us. She's our blood–through and through–and she always will be. By the Powers! Do you know what she calls us? Do you know what we are to her? The other officers tell us that she calls every one of us her lions–her swords of light. That tells you what she thinks of us. And that's why every one of us would follow her, straight into perdition's hottest flames, whenever the need arises."

Telli-Naero sniffed and wiped her red eyes.

"Why, Telli, I didn't mean to upset you, dear girl."

"No, it's all right. I have seen that vid–the vid of that wake they held for her parents–just like you said. I remembered watching it. It does make you want to both cry and cheer."

He patted her on the back. "You just bet it does. Now enough of such foolish talk about the captain being spoiled and pampered and all that. Has anyone heard how soon we're going back into the mix?"

Telli-Naero took her dustvac back into the kitchen.

She saw a young cook sitting alone, Eugene Blooding. Dark curly hair and moustache, fit, stocky medium build.

He had a loaf of warm shuma bread, sitting in front of a tub of butter with a knife. He'd tear off a hunk of bread, butter it, and then dip it into a bowl of what looked to be a strange black gravy.

Then he'd pop it in his mouth and chew in what looked like ecstasy.

Yet he still manage to look rather melancholy. All of the other kitchen staff ignored them both.

"Hey, Eugene. Whatcha got there?"

"Aww, nothing much. I was feeling a little homesick and sorry for myself, so I made a mess of my family's secret black gravy. If we was to get ourselves killed in one of the final battles, I wouldn't want to go on the next journey without tasting some of it again. It is mighty fine indeed."

"Can I try some?"

"Sure. Pull up a chair and join me, Tell."

He looked at her again, with sudden concern as she did so.

"You all right, Tell?"

"I'm just fine."

"You're eyes are red. You look like you've been–"

"I'm fine, I tell you. Someone just told me a sad story, that's all. It got to me."

Eugene sighed sadly himself. "Plenty of those to go around."

Telli-Naero knew very well, as everyone in the kitchens did, that Eugene was still mourning the loss of his own gal, a pretty medtek on a cruiser that got destroyed, not three months before. Only a few others on that lost ship got away.

She stared at his fixins. "How do I do this?" she asked.

"Easy. Do like me. Butter a hunk of bread, and just dip in it. Good stuff."

Naero followed suit.

So good!

Haisha. The taste was…incredible…fabulous even.

She had never made love to anyone yet, but from descriptions from her friends–especially Saemar–eating this yummy black gravy had to be the next closest thing. Akin to experiencing a taste-bud-numbing orgy of flavors in her mouth.

The gravy was that good.

She couldn't even speak for a long while.

All she could do was stuff her face.

Finally the bowl was empty, and her face and hands a complete mess–as if she'd been an infant who'd been finger-painting with gravy.

Eugene laughed. "Dang, girl. I know it's good, but you went plum wild. You got it all over you."

She wiped the residue off on more bread and devoured that as well. "Eugene...I don't know how to thank you. This was so fantastically delicious! As you would say, thank you kindly."

"You're most kindly welcome, Tell."

"Eugene, that black gravy of yours is some of the best stuff I have ever tasted. I might even like it better than Spum, and I love Spum more than life itself. Thank you again, so much. You've really brightened my day. Why...I could kiss you!"

Eugene's eyes went wide and then they sparkled a little.

"I'd be right pleased as punch if you would, Tell. A pretty little thing like you? Haisha, I don't mind telling you. Shoot, I could use a kiss or two, before we go into these final battles. It'd be nice to get some kind of love before we–"

Telli-Naero tackled Eugene, right in front of everyone, bore him to the floor, and wrapped herself around him like a python.

She gave him a long, deep kiss that left him gasping and blinking on the ground.

She stood up and smiled over him, hands on her hips while he caught his breath.

"You and I are going to stay in touch, mister. One day, I'm going to have my own ship. And you are going to come and cook for me, and make that stuff every day."

Eugene struggled to rise up. "I'd sure be right proud and h-happy to d-d-do that," he stammered.

The entire kitchen burst out laughing.

Everyone thought she was joking, but Naero meant every word she said.

44

Naero held a last planning session with her officers, including Captain Hayden. They spoke mostly about the final phases of the war and how everything was winding down.

It was certain that there were still plenty of deadly fighting and challenges ahead of them, though.

After the actual planning session ended, Naero had dinner and drinks brought up for them all. The bells sounded, and the watches of the night grew rather late.

Naero made her rounds and lifted a glass to her *abani*, Jeremiah. They sat down for a bit as things broke up.

"So, now that we finally have some time, tell me about your family, *abani*–my brother."

He smiled, and proudly showed her some pics and vids of his son. "This is my little boy, Jason. He's a great kid. I can't love him enough. I see him every chance I get, but you know how that is."

"I don't yet, but I can imagine. He has your brown eyes. I bet he has a lot of fun with his daddy."

Naero poignantly thought of her own father.

Jeremiah smiled and nodded wistfully. "We have such a great time. We goof around and laugh and laugh. He loves to laugh and giggle, the funny little bugger. He makes Ronnie and I laugh until we're all fit to bust. He's going to be a great big brother to his little sister Lydia, when she comes around. And that won't be long now. With any luck, this war will get over with and I'll be there this time."

"You call your wife Ronnie?"

"Short for Veronica." He smiled sadly and got a far away look in his eyes. "She has the prettiest hands and feet. Sometimes at night when things are quiet, she lets me put lotion on her hands and feet and massage them. She has flat feet, so her arches can hurt her sometimes. That's kinda of how we met. I took her boots off when she was exhausted and gave her a great foot rub. Well, one thing led to another…"

Naero smirked at him. "I can think of worse hands to end up in. That actually sounds pretty sweet and romantic, Jeremiah. She's a Marine, too?"

"Yeah, that's pretty standard. Both of our families are. She's a 1st Leftenant, also with 3rd Division. She's a mek trainer. But she's on maternity leave right now. She hates it some days, but frankly I'm glad one of us is sitting this war out."

"So, you're going to name your new little girl Lydia? Where does that come from?"

"My mother's name. She was a Marine Colonel. She died in action on Vaetarra-5."

Naero snapped her head up at the mention of a very famous Spacer Marine battle. "Vaetarra-5? The Clans and The Death Eyes lost a lot of good people during the course of that action."

Jeremiah nodded. "That they did, and my mom was one of them that went down fighting to the last. I was seventeen at the time. When they told me she was gone, I was already well on my way to becoming a Marine myself, just like her and the rest of my kin."

Naero rested a hand on his powerful forearm. "I lost my mom, too. I can relate. Don't worry, they'd both be proud of us and what we're doing. Never forget that."

Hayden nodded. "I know that. I've tried to live up to the examples she set for me."

Naero sat back and looked him in the eye. "You're an excellent leader, Jeremiah. A fine warrior, and one of the bravest I have ever had the pleasure of fighting beside. I never have any doubts or worries with you and your Marines backing us up."

Being with Hayden was like being with her lost, best friend Gallan.

Hayden lifted his glass to her. "N, I could say much the same for you, my friend. I'm proud to know you. Your people love and respect you, and with good reason."

Naero lifted her glass, and they clinked them together before draining them.

*

Tarim challenged Naero to a final, all out simbattle between their two practice fleets, while they still had time to do so.

Naero hesitated somewhat.

She wanted her friend to be sure he knew what he was asking for.

"Tarim, you've been progressing very well, but let me warn you. You're still pretty much an amateur at space fleet combat. Are you sure you really want to challenge me full-on…in a real match?"

Tarim nodded vehemently. "From the beginning, it was never my goal to equal or surpass a master such as yourself, N."

"But you've seen first hand what I'm capable of…repeatedly. In actual combat?"

"Again, I don't intend to win. That is not my goal. I know you are going to trounce me. But at least once, I want to feel what it is like to experience the command of a space fleet battle in real time, with no limits. To make it as real as possible. This is the only way. And if I am to face defeat, why not have it be at the hands of the best opponent I can possibly find?"

Naero nodded. "You honor me, but don't think because we are friends that I'm going to take it easy on you. If you want me to come at you full-on, that is exactly what you are going to get."

Tarim put his hands behind his back and bowed his head slightly. "Then bring it. I would never expect anything less. I know very well how formidable an opponent you are. In fact, I am counting on just that. I will do my best as well."

"Very well then. We'll make use of the isolated bridge simulators that the junior officers utilize. A real contest is not like the vid games we've been using for our various sims, Tarim. We won't be in the same room; we won't be able to hear each other call out orders to give each other clues or hints about our strategies. We'll react to everything as it unfolds, in real time."

Tarim looked eager. "Yes, I understand. It will be much more like a real fight. I will be on my bridge, commanding my ships against you and yours. And we will need to respond to each other with all our instinct, skill, and cunning, in real time. Even if it is only once, that is the exact experience I seek."

Naero smiled and shook his hand. "Good luck to you then, my friend. May fortune favor the bold."

Tarim sighed slightly and grinned. "Indeed. It always does."

Once they were in place and the AIs set up, everything was ready.

The signal went up, and the sim commenced.

Naero's standard blue fleet of fifty ships drew the lot at random to be the defending force.

"Defensive formation India-Whiskey-6."

Scanners picked up Tarim's red fleet jumping in and approaching from the exact opposite direction, forcing her to take the time to reposition her ships around the planet they were defending.

A pretty simple Delta-Mike-3 formation for Tarim.

Something strange, however, about the scanner readings on his carriers and fighter waves.

What was the clever little bugger up to? A mirage strategy, perhaps? Where could he have learned that? She never taught it to him. No, it couldn't be.

She positioned her fighter screens. Tarim, his.

They prepared to engage.

Battleships fired at extreme range. No reason not to. Minimal results.

If he was going to pull something...

Ahhh, here it was.

Risky.

Tarim divided his fleet into two forces. The superior half–in Foxtrot-Yankee-2 formation–acting as a head-on holding force. The other inferior half–with only two bigs–moved in as a small strike fleet in Delta-Sierra-5, carriers naturally hanging back.

Naero countered effortlessly.

"Delta-Delta-2, forward cones on the flanks. Cruisers and destroyers, concentrate consecutive fire with all battleships on the lead forward enemy elements. Fighter waves 2, 4, 5, 7, 9 and 10–hit all five bigs hard. Get those shields down!"

Naero plotted the course of the battle and its variations thirty moves ahead–in a matter of instants.

Even Tarim couldn't make it this easy for her.

Seconds later, red battleship-1 was in flames. Red battleship-3 withdrew.

The beginning of the end for Tarim's red fleet, even with his strikers sweeping in and doing moderate damage.

All just a matter of time and various responses now.

Then five more red carriers jumped in, as close as they could.

Too close, in fact. One red carrier came in too hot–too close to the blue starboard outward elements.

The resulting explosion took out red carrier-5, blue destroyer-19, blue missile frigate-4, and blue gunship-1.

But the other additional four red carriers deployed additional fighter waves that quickly enveloped her entire starboard flank.

"Spiral back in Kilo-Tango-9, raking fire on the remaining bigs. Fighter waves, reduce those enemy squadrons. All ships, concentrate all secondary batteries on repulsing enemy fighters."

How in the hell?

Tarim could overload and increase his starfighter contingent to these levels, but how could he possibly double the number of his fricking carriers? The sim wouldn't allow that, unless he hacked it.

She checked. He hadn't.

Five scanner deception drones collapsed when fired upon.

Tarim's five phantom carriers–the ones holding back–simply vanished.

That sneak! He *had* managed to pull off a mirage attack.

It made things a little tougher and more interesting, but she was already countering nicely.

Naero stuck to her strategy and her guns. First, his other three bigs.

Then his cruisers, and finally those damn carriers. The real ones.

Tarim conceded–43 seconds later.

They rejoined each other outside the simchambers.

He thanked and hugged her. "That's it; I'm satisfied, N. I've accomplished and learned all that I've wanted to know and experience. I won't feel so ignorant and left out now among our people when they discuss such things."

"*Our* people, Tarim. Nice to hear you say it. Our people."

"It still does not make me a Spacer. Nothing ever will."

Naero put one hand on his, and the other on his handsome face. "That doesn't matter. I say you are one of us, Tarim. You are. My personal bodyguard. My friend. My brother. You will always be one of us, *abani*. And I will take it extremely personally if anyone ever treats you or says otherwise."

Tarim bent down and kissed her hand. "Thank you, N. I can never thank you or…our people enough, for all that you have done for me."

"And is that why you stay around? To protect me? You know, of course, that Shalaen and I are sisters. When all is done, I want you to be with her, even if it takes you away from the rest of us."

Tarim nodded. "I will go willingly, N, when she allows it. For the time being, my beloved insists that you are in more danger than she. Until she says otherwise–she has commanded me to protect you."

Naero blinked. Another eye-opener.

Interesting.

45

In the rapidly shifting haze of war, it became truly difficult at times to tell friend from foe. And thus great care had to be taken, especially in the very heat and ferocity of battle, to avoid tragic friendly-fire incidents.

That remained just one of the many hazards of complex ship-to-ship space battles.

Despite all the risks of war, one by one, the enemy systems leading up to the final Capital Class World of Najindo-9 continued to fall to the Alliance.

Alliance fleets converged like sharks, smelling Triaxian blood in the dark waters of space.

Everyone on the Alliance side was weary and fed up with Triax's brutal tricks, games, and delays that only further held off what was deemed by now to be the inevitable.

Triax Gigacorporation was going down in flaming defeat. One of the worst defeats in any interstellar naval history. And yet in their utter hubris and their twisted madness, they would never admit to the folly of further combat and senseless resistance. Unbelievably–even at the very end–the insane sons of bitches still clung to the last tatters and shreds of their vile powers and absolute tyranny.

Their last pockets of fanatics and zealots seemed more than willing than ever to lay waste to and destroy further life–heedless in all directions– out of nothing more than what appeared to be pure maniacal hatred and spiteful denial.

And it became very clear that it would still cost many more lives to drag and burn the mad wretches out of their last shitholes.

Triax as a sick, diseased monolith never even entertained the possibility of surrender.

They meant fully to go down in utter flames and despair to the very last, and drag as many others into death, destruction, and sheer hell along with them. They remained entirely devoid of any honor or semblance of sanity.

Against such a mad and determined foe, the duty of the Alliance remained clear:

To put an end to Triax's multitude of evils, for all time to come. To fall upon them with all fury and final vengeance, and see the task finished.

To blast Triax straight to hell.

This was the beginning of the end at last.

Naero and the other strike fleets now went into battle with entire fixer clouds developed to neutralize mines, drones, and entire enemy ships. They performed all of these functions, as well as doing their best to minimize damage and keep Alliance ships from being destroyed, or first captured and then destroyed.

Many Triaxian ships did try to surrender, especially mercenary ships and naval vessels and crews that simply wanted out of the war.

But it remained tricky dealing with surrender ships.

By now, the enemy admirals had suicide devices attached to the power cores of all the remaining Triaxian vessels under their direct command. Enemy ship captains who wanted to give up had to pretend to keep fighting, while Intel agents and or fixers slipped on board to disarm such devices, and prevent the Triaxian High Command from remotely blasting any defectors to atoms.

This became a deadly cat-and-mouse game.

Even then, defectors could still be attacked directly and taken out before they could retreat to the rear zones of battles, boarded, and pacified. The same thing with enemy fighters who wanted to surrender.

Sometimes battles were so heated that any defectors were simply ordered to jump into a neighboring surrender system, where they could give up away from the front. Some captains simply fled the war zone entirely, going rogue, and fled into the other Corps areas to start a new life, and never looked back.

Either way, every ship that refused to keep fighting helped the Alliance greatly.

They riddled the dwindling Triaxian lines with fear and doubt.

But then the enemy also tried to use the defector situation against the Alliance.

Some Triaxian ships only pretended to surrender, and then started fighting again once they were in a better position to cause much more damage.

Pretenders were usually shown no mercy because of the destruction they could cause, especially in rear areas. They were routinely destroyed, and all further attempts at surrender ignored.

Word quickly spread.

At first Naero sent escorts to deal with any pretenders if they tried anything.

When that became unfeasible, and enemy ships began defecting in entire waves, Naero instituted a frontline policy that all enemy vessels had to agree to shut down their power cores, have them secured, and get towed until they reached a safe staging area. Some suspect enemy ships were even told to dump their cores outright.

Such practices caught on with the entire Alliance and continued to be modified on the fly.

With each new system pacified, the crumbling chains of Triaxian tyranny and subjugation dissolved and fell away.

After the fierce fighting, secondary elements, older and lesser warships continued to be stationed in the rear areas to further the transition process.

As they had learned from past efforts and mistakes, many of the Triaxian populations had been heavily brainwashed to expect subjugation, genocide, and mass destruction of their worlds at the hands of hated spack invaders and their rapacious brigand allies.

Intel broadcast teams took over the communication systems of each liberated world as quickly as possible. They flooded the information webnets with counter broadcasts.

First, the Alliance strove to calm everyone and keep populations from committing mass acts of suicide.

Mothers–STOP–don't give your children that poisoned candy!

Next, they needed help locating and neutralizing any genocide devices that Triax might have left behind, usually found in heavily populated areas.

Once the natives on each system realized that the invaders were not going to commit mass rape and pillaging of their cites, it started to dawn on them that they were–now–in fact, finally free of Triaxian oppression at last.

Once a planet was fully pacified, the celebrating could truly begin, and the planning for new and better futures. Within hours or days, these peoples quickly realized that they could govern themselves and get along just fine without Corps domination and theft of anything that had value. Even better, in fact.

All this, while the war swept past them and left these worlds behind to stand on their own and fend for themselves.

Even Triax could not be everywhere at once, as their power faded. If no immediate threats presented themselves, many liberated worlds were simply bypassed while the war sped into its final phase.

More would be done, once the fighting concluded.

Naero and her people geared up for the fight in the next system, Noraga-8. This system was a key area with a vital enemy naval shipyard and weapons research bases scattered all throughout that system.

At first, it appeared that the Alliance fleets took on the usual Triaxian spread for that type of system.

Then Naero's long range scans picked up something very weird.

Her long lost phantoms.

The huge enemy flagship, protected by twenty enemy fleets, immediately broke away from the battle in what seemed to be a great hurry once again. Almost a panic, as soon as they were detected.

Again, what were they so worried about? Intel plainly had no idea the enemy kept so many forces concentrated in the one system. It didn't make any sense.

The Alliance had only ten fleets in the Noraga system currently.

Twenty enemy fleets, on top of the fifteen already involved directly in battle, could have easily pounced on the Alliance forces and overwhelmed them in short order–before any help could arrive.

Why, instead, were they running away from a chance to deal the Alliance such a major defeat? Again?

First, Naero called in more forces to support them, in case the enemy changed its mind.

Then she attempted to analyze and track the odd movements and actions of their phantoms.

Now the big flagship docked at the distant naval shipyard and research facility at Moon Noraga-3.

A desolate rock where Triax tested weapons.

Long range scans revealed that the enemy loaded something onto the enemy flagship. They did so in an enormous hurry.

Their secret cargo? Missiles and warheads, apparently. And not just regular ordnance, but some kind of new tek by the looks of things.

Scans divulged that this new enemy ordnance gave off strange energy signatures, which didn't match anything Triax had ever used against them in the past.

As more Alliance fleets poured into the system, Naero and her forces went straight after the still-mysterious flagship.

If they could get in close enough, perhaps they could disable or delay that flagship before it got away. Her sense of warning went nuts.

Every fiber of her being warned her to stop that ship.

Aunt Sleak called out to her. "Hold off, Naero. Wait for the reserves to arrive and back you up."

"We can't. The enemy commander is completely focused on something new and important. Just like before, they clearly don't care about this battle. They have their own separate agenda. We have to try to catch them before they jump."

"It's suicide, Naero. Our forces already have their hands full. Those twenty fleets are not going to ignore you if you try to get in there. They'll tear you apart."

"Admiral…trust me on this. Please. We're going to pursue. Send as much help as you can in after us. My gut says we'll need it."

"I'll do what I can, Captain. You realize, of course, that we are still fully engaged here? Don't get you and your people killed."

"Copy that." Naero cut the link. "All ships," she commanded. "Full attack on the large enemy flagship at that distant shipyard. Concentrate all long range fire as we go in. Ignore the rest. Help is on the way."

They raced in, sniping at the enemy from afar, but with little real chance of doing much damage.

At twenty to one odds or worse.

Amazingly enough–the enemy held true, formed up, and immediately began to jump out, in good order.

They didn't even bother to shoot back.

The large enemy flagship vanished into jump right along with them, once it pulled free of the shipyard.

Intel must have gained more updated information.

Naero finally got its designation from the system AIs.

The large phantom ship was *The Kronos*. It's commander was, in fact, High Admiral Maximillian Jaxxon Dreth, last surviving supreme commander of all remaining Triaxian fleets and forces.

Their phantom might finally have a name, but Naero was already too late, once again.

She sent fixer waves sweeping into the enemy research base to search for any data files or intel left behind.

Even as the remaining Triaxian zealots blew up the shipyard, the research facility, and themselves.

Naero lost most of the fixers she sent in.

Tyber and Surina scanned the few fixers that made it back, skimming for anything useful.

Ty called to her in great concern. "Captain, we've been forced to isolate one of the fixers. It picked up some kind of heavily encrypted Triax research files, but they are protected by attack viruses unlike anything Surina and I have ever seen before."

Surina cut in. "Captain, this is beyond us. This is beyond anything Spacer Intel possesses or has ever encountered. Where could Triax come across something as menacing and as virulent as this stuff?"

"Just tell me if you can crack it."

"Not in time to be of any use to us," Tyber added. "I don't think anyone can."

Naero might know someone who could.

She got on one of her secure channels to Baeven and his strange ship.

This time, fortunately, the outcast answered right away. "How's the war winding down, Naero?"

"Horrific. Need a huge favor. Came across some secured files on some kind of new Triaxian super weapon. But we can't get past the security measures; they're unlike anything we've seen before. And we have no time."

"Do a shadow-level-13 Intel duplication and send me the raw data files, complete with those defenses. I'll see what Jia can do with them."

The mysterious Jia. Another one of Baeven's weird, unseen crew?

Ty and Surina prepared and sent the files. Naero already made ready to jump after the fleeing enemy fleets.

Baeven came back a few minutes later. "What the hell did you send me? It's even giving Jia fits. But from what we can tell, it does not look good at all. This must be alien tek. Whatever the enemy is planning with it, it's going to be big. From what we can tell at the outset, we think they're trying to unleash something that will destroy an entire system and everything in it."

Not good.

"We'll know more in a little bit, if we can crack the rest of the defenses. They are very tough. To be safe, tell Sleak and the other Alliance leaders they'd better focus on stopping those enemy nutjobs at all costs."

Naero broke off instantly and opened her link to Aunt Sleak once more.

"Admiral. Contact all the other admirals in the Alliance. Get every fleet and ship that you can to Najindo-9. Anything that can float and fight. We have intel that the enemy is planning the biggest surprise for us yet. We need to hit them before they can unleash it, and take them down once and for all."

"What's this new threat, Naero?"

"An advanced weapon that can destroy all life in an entire system. Deets when we have them, sir. What's the population of the Najindo system?"

"Among the heaviest in all of Triax. Trillions–multiple billions each on several worlds. The most heavily populated of all of the Capital Class Systems. The crown jewel of their bloated empire."

"Then we'd better get in there and stop them. I feel certain that the Triaxian Supreme Commander means to take everyone down with him, if he can manage such a grand slam."

Naero didn't wait for further orders. Minutes to the nearby, neighboring system at maximum jump.

Everyone knew where the enemy was heading.

There wasn't any place left for the bastards to go.

She again called for reinforcements, seized the initiative, and sent her fleet into jump, prepped and ready for battle.

46

The combined firepower of the main guns of six Alliance fleets tore a breach through the dense Triaxian defenses surrounding the last Capital Class System.

More fleets rushed in now that the way was clear, pounding and decimating key enemy elements.

Najindo-9 remained the key to capturing the entire system, and a battle royal in its own right had just begun.

More fleets from both sides jumped in, engaged, and locked together in deadly combat.

Naero and Strike Fleet Six raced after the secret Triaxian armada, led by *The Kronos*, Admiral Maximillian Dreth's huge flagship.

The same ship that barely escaped from the Triaxian Naval Shipyards.

The same enemy shipyards that had been blown up and completely destroyed on Moon Noraga-3 in an effort to hide the enemy's most vital secrets.

Five entire enemy fleets came about, fanning out in various formations to intercept Strike Fleet Six.

Two hundred and fifty warships against fifty; five to one odds.

While Admiral Dreth's fleet pulled farther away, at top speed, with his remaining fifteen fleets still held in reserve.

The lopsided battle ensued.

Aunt Sleak and the rest of the Alliance sent in three reserve fleets to assist at the last possible moment.

Naero's hands flew across her holoscreens to instantly redirect her fleet.

"All ships, follow my lead, Romeo-Sierra-1. Let the reserves hit them and bust them up. Screen out and sweep over the top of these foes. Keep up the attack. Rake them with all batteries as we soar over them, but continue to advance and overshoot them. Do not stop. Keep going at full attack speed, no matter what. Drive on!"

Mike Marshall called out to them. "Naero, we'll never catch them at this rate. Both forces are at maximum acceleration."

There had to be a way.

Varcas Adams called out from scanning. "Several new fleets jumping in, interposing themselves between the enemy and the sun, cutting them off. One of those fleets is extremely odd–multiple planetoid vessels of all sizes, sir."

Naero put both hands to her mouth.

Klyne told her in secret that those new ships were in production.

These had to be them.

The Titans.

An entire fleet–comprised of all planetoid vessels–leading several other Alliance fleets in to back them up.

They cut the enemy flagship off and engaged all the other ships as they piled in. They stopped the enemy advance in its tracks and stomped on them.

The enemy fought fiercely, doing their best–even sacrificing entire ships–in an effort to allow Admiral Dreth's flagship to break away. That was clearly their objective.

"All ships, concentrate all fire on the enemy flagship," Naero said. "Destroy or disable it at all costs!"

Naero and her fleet did what they did best, racing in to hit the enemy hard from optimal vectors.

Yet even as they did so, every enemy fleet and ship broke off from the other ongoing battle and attempted to reach this new one.

Such madness only added to the intense confusion.

Worse still, enemy warships activated their jump drives close in, committing flaming suicide, gouging burning ruts of destruction through both friend and foe.

Multiple ships on both sides burned, broke up, and exploded.

Naero's fingers flashed in fury. "Triple-stack, Sierra-Victor-3 formation. Wheel above the battle in an inverted cone. Pour all fire on the enemy. Disrupt their shields; I want their shields down in their exact center within one pass."

Several more enemy warships prepared to go into jump, in order to obliterate the Alliance formations and gut them.

The Titans spiraled out and did their best to sweep forward and intercept the looming jumpers, sending sheets of destroying fire against them.

They unleashed the fastest rates of fire Naero had ever seen from any major warships.

The sheer volume of it obliterated entire swaths of enemy ships.

Only one in seven of those suicidal foes flashed into jump.

The Titans blasted the other six straight to oblivion.

If the enemy wanted death, The Titans would give them all they could stomach.

Naero's fleet succeeded in collapsing most of the enemy shields at the core of their formations.

For an instant, shields collapsed on *The Kronos.*

Then backup shields came on, before it could take much damage.

Without warning, the enemy counterattacked, swarming over *The Hippolyta* and her ships in an attempt to take them out.

The envelopers became the enveloped, and Naero and her people struggled to stay alive and break free.

Admiral Dreth revealed himself to be an exceptionally clever bastard.

Once actually forced to fight, he proved to be a more than capable opponent.

Shields reduced rapidly on all of Naero's ships, as the enemy used her own tactics against her and her people.

Collapse shields, then destroy them all with overwhelming fire.

The Titans had their own problems, stretched to their breaking point and outnumbered. They focused on fending off other enemy jumpers trying to plow through the mix. With their own hands more than full, they were incapable of coming to anyone's aid.

Naero and everyone else simply had to fight it out on their own, against superior odds.

The Hippolyta and the other bigs were hemmed in, fighting for their very lives.

Only her cruisers, destroyers, and such could still maneuver.

"*Mohawk, Panther, Swordbreaker–y*ou are our only hope. Lead all equal and smaller vessels on close-wheel, Charlie-Whiskey-6 attacks, right on top of the packed enemy ships hemming us in. Hit them in every vital spot with everything you've got, and I mean everything. Drop your garbage on them and set it on fire if you must, but bust us out. Our only chance is for you to blast us free!"

"Copy that, sir. Engaging in close assault formation…maximum fire underway. Unleashing all possible ordnance."

So much heavy firepower hit Triax in such a tightly confined space that it was difficult to sort out what actually went down.

Two things happened.

First, *The Kronos* slowly pulled away from the general quagmire of the confused battle.

The Hippolyta broke and blasted its way free not an instant later.

"Continue to pursue that flagship." Naero commanded. "Smash into anything blocking our way. Knock them aside! Any ships available, try to get out in front of them!"

The two huge warships took poundings from relentless assaults directed at them from both sides.

Both vessels sustained heavy damage, but kept up their chase, still punching at each other like well-bloodied prize fighters.

Once she had time to think straight, Naero recalled that she still waited impatiently to hear back on her secured link from Baeven–urgently concerning the strange, heavily encrypted Triaxian tek files they captured from that enemy research base.

Only her outlaw uncle and his strange, miraculous ship possessed the ability to decode those files in any time frame to be useful.

Naero trusted her instincts fully now. A final endgame masterstroke was about to unfold. Of that she felt certain.

By the thin facts alone, the enemy admiral had destroyed his own naval base for some desperate reason, and the fixers deduced that some major enemy research project had indeed just been finalized there, only scant minutes before everything went all to hell.

What, precisely, did the enemy load up and whisk away from that top secret base in such a hurry?

What was the new enemy objective? What was this new super weapon they now prepared to unleash against them all?

Admiral Dreth seemed charmed and strangely fortunate. He had barely escaped thus far, and now he and his damaged flagship made every effort to abandon even the last chaotic battles around Najindo-9.

The enemy commander did so at all hazards–setting an evasive course directly toward the system's star, for some bizarre, unfathomable reason.

Naero did all within her power to keep after them.

Baeven's link on her com finally flashed and sounded in warning.

She took the message immediately.

Transmitted holo readouts and schematics passed rapidly before her eyes.

A pity she could no longer teknomance.

"Stop that enemy fleet at all costs!" Baeven warned her.

She had never heard such fear in his normally calm demeanor.

"Triax has developed a way to cause a chain reaction in their sun and force it to explode like a massive gigabomb–a quanta bomb of tremendous destruction. They will most likely attempt to do so with specialized, advanced missiles by the looks of the intel we just decoded for you." Baeven paused and caught his breath.

"Naero, this new super weapon will kill everyone currently in that entire sector, and on all of its worlds."

Naero covered her mouth with one hand, staggered by the scope of the approaching atrocity–flagrant cosmicide.

Triax would murder trillions, in spite of its own defeat.

How typical.

The Alliance really should have expected something exactly like this.

She knew now that there had been good reason to follow her gut instincts and pursue that fleet and flagship to the death and take it out.

Every fiber of her being just told her so.

Naero shot the details to Tyber, Captain Hayden, and the rest of the Alliance forces–instant priority one.

Yet most of the warships on both side remained locked in the deadly, final struggles focused around Najindo-9.

More enemy ships attempted to converge, doing all that they could to cut *The Hippolyta* off.

Naero's flagship emerged as the only chance that anyone had to stop the Triaxian High Commander, once and for all.

They were the last hope to prevent the enemy from murdering…everyone.

47

The Hippolyta burned on several levels and shot forward drunkenly. Naero had no choice. She ignored direct fire from several enemy ships still attempting to block their way.

She rammed two of the enemy ships and spun them off to either side, all vessels taking even further damage.

The rest of Strike Fleet Six would need to help finish off the remaining Triaxian warships.

Only *The Hippolyta* had the toughness and moxie to bully its way through the mix and stop Admiral Dreth.

They either caught the flagship and stopped its mad mission, or they all died.

It became that brutally simple.

Once clear of the battle, Admiral Dreth would struggle to regain enough power to launch his new stellar disruption missiles into Najindo-9's sun. Doing so would cause a hyper-critical, quanta-chain reaction, effectively annihilating everyone in the entire system within the space of approximately one standard hour.

Naero and her crew squeezed every drop of speed from their battered amazon, trying to cut the burning enemy flagship off.

Naero prepared to ram and board the enemy vessel–to put an end to the final Triaxian madness and the very war.

Her sense of warning suddenly spiked again.

Instincts told her what was coming.

"Everyone–draw weapons. Repel boarders–another assassin attack!"

Not now, of all times.

A final, full suicide platoon of Hevangian killers phazed through the blast shields and hull, swarming right onto the bridge within seconds. They emerged out of cloaked phaze, heedless of the lethal effects of their tek.

An insane foe, already bent on certain death for any and all. So what if the phaze armor process killed all of the users horribly in a matter of hours after utilizing it? Phazing sickness–a horrible way to die.

If only it were quicker. Naero fully intended to take the assassins down much faster.

Hevangian High General Garrok Shul Dreth himself led this assault himself, his body already suffering from phaze-rot, which was slowly devouring his face and other flesh.

Thanks to Naero's warning, the Spacers on the bridge were ready for the attackers this time.

Fire erupted from both sides almost instantaneously.

But the Spacers fired first.

Tarim waited for them to completely phaze in, and then fired his pistols rapidly.

His explosive plasma rounds splattered bursting heads and torsos off a dozen enemies in a matter of seconds.

Captain Hayden and a squad of Marines emerged from the lift and cut loose with heavy squad support cannons.

Two Marines fell.

Naero saw two of her crew drop.

Tarim himself took a shot in the chest and went down.

But her people stood up to the intense Hevangian assault and chewed them to bits.

Garrok Shul drew two black glowing energy blades and launched himself straight at Naero.

He was obviously doped up on speed enhancers, moving in a blur with his gravwing.

Bent solely on killing her, if nothing else.

Naero hit him with several exploding knives to take down his shields.

Then she drew her energized battle blades off her shoulders and set them to delayed detonate.

She sprang into the air and met his attack with her own gravwing.

They dueled rapidly for several crucial seconds.

Blades flashing and sparking.

Naero took several painful cuts, including a deep gash to her right thigh.

Her suit and her smartblood immediately sealed the wounds up.

A painful jab to one hand where Garrok tried to disarm her.

The bastard was good with blades. He didn't use a shokkog, because he knew her energized blades would cut right through them.

But no one bested her in a straight-up knife fight.

No one.

She butchered him in midair.

Slicing tendons. Cutting muscle groups.

She severed his right arm at the elbow, letting it drop.

Naero slammed Garrok into the upper hull hard with both knees smashing into his chest.

His ribs crunched, crushed, and snapped.

She rammed both blades up deep into Garrok's guts, triggered the detonation sequence, and spun him around. She smashed him into the hull again and pinned him there, between her secondary personal shield and the ship.

He took the blasts full on.

Her blades exploded, eviscerating the Hevangian assassin leader.

His legs dangled only by shreds of scorched flesh and bloody cartilage.

But Garrok Shul still managed to laugh.

Naero leaned in and whispered to him, her voice hissing, "That's for Clan Maeris and what your kind have done to my family, you vile, murdering fucks. You find something funny about that?"

Garrok laughed as he hissed his last breath. "I knew just how to take you down…you stupid…spack cunt."

Naero dropped him and whirled.

Too late.

She already knew.

Two elite Hevangian killers had held back, just waiting for this exact moment.

They uncloaked and phazed in, right on top of her.

Ritual, poisoned shokkog blades in each hand, descending.

Naero could almost feel them piercing her flesh already.

Captain Hayden swept in next to her on his gravwing at top speed.

He knocked her painfully aside, yet shielding her with his own body.

He shot the two killers right between the eyes at point-blank range.

Right before they could stab him through his shields.

The short delay rounds from his microgrenade pistols blasted the Hevangians' heads and torsos off, right down to their bloody hip bones.

Naero caught her breath, recovered, and flipped back off the blast screens. She placed her hand on Hayden's right arm as he sheathed his pistols. Both of them quickly noted–this fight was over.

"Thanks. I definitely owe you more than one now, Jeremiah."

Hayden nodded, guiding them back down toward her bridge command chair.

Naero smirked and then sighed. "You sure you don't have a younger brother somewhere that I could meet?" *Haisha*, he was a great guy.

That wife of his better be something else; she was a lucky gal.

They dropped down to check on Tarim.

Their friend had turned pale from a lung shot–pretty bad.

Tarim didn't have smart blood to save him.

Naero and Jeremiah quickly stabilized him the best they could. Medteks came by quickly to carry him away.

Tarim grabbed Hayden's arm. "I can't be with Naero. Whatever happens, promise me you'll protect her."

Hayden nodded, clasping arms with him up to the elbow. "With my life, brother."

Tarim fell back, pale, onto his medbed and blacked out.

Hayden checked his gear and returned to the nearest lift below, his eyes still flashing fire from the heat of battle.

"Going to ready my boarding teams, N. Get us on that flagship to finish the job."

"Copy that," Naero called back to him.

She dropped down to her command station and pulled up her flickering holo displays, vectoring in on *The Kronos* once more.

The delay had cost them precious minutes.

Most of her own battered fleet lay crippled and floating behind her, but the rest of the enemy ships were also out of the fight or destroyed completely.

Several smaller Alliance vessels and numerous fighters somehow raced ahead to cut off and delay the enemy flagship.

"All ships, my brave lions, indeed. Great job," Naero declared. "In for the final assault. Let's put a stop to this madness!"

48

The Hippolyta used up most of its remaining power attempting to cut off and ram into the badly damaged and listing Triaxian flagship.

But the assassin attack did its work holding them off.

Even as they closed in, *Kronos* jerked free and regained enough power to launch a desperate barrage of stellar disruptor missiles toward the sun.

"No!"

Naero screamed and gave the panic order. "Stop those missiles, people. None of them can get through!"

Fleet fighters and warships blocked the missiles' paths, taking out the lethal devices with concentrated waves of fire from main guns and secondary batteries.

Three enemy missiles nearly broke loose.

When all else failed, three brave fighter pilots smashed into one missile in order to destroy it.

The destroyer *The Kit Carson* arced in at high speed, directly into harm's way to intercept the last two.

The destroyer took them broadside.

All three rocking blasts annihilated any smaller ships in the nearest vicinity, mostly other fighters and one frigate that were attempting the same suicide maneuvers.

Rings of cutting energy and destructive force sliced out into space before the blinding, looming, gargantuan sun.

The Kit Carson broke into three main sections an instant before it was completely vaporized.

A large section of *The Hippolyta's* northeastern outer layer was sheered clean off, along with the entire nose section of *The Kronos*.

The final handful of Strike Fleet Six warships took major damage, and burned or listed, losing power and dropping back.

A swarm of avenging fighters plugged up *The Kronos's* launch tubes with bombs and missiles—fired straight in.

The enemy wasn't going to launch anything else.

Kronos shuddered and took heavy damage again, several areas now completely engulfed in flames.

Strangely enough, not a single Triaxian crew had hit the lifepods yet.

Did they all intend to go down with their mad commander and his flagship?

Naero guessed they had a more sinister intent.

Admiral Dreth surrounded himself with Triaxian zealots.

A call came in from Captain Hayden and his fierce Marines, all prepped and ready to command the boarding teams. Life support and power to most sections of *The Hippolyta* flickered and went down.

Naero's brave amazon had fought well and would only die slowly, fighting and resisting to the last.

Hayden called out. "My people and I are ready to go in and get the job done, Naero. Punch us in!"

"You're going to have company, Jeremiah. My crew and I are coming with you. Everyone fights! We'll see this job through together."

Hayden grinned. "Join us for the fun. I'm sure those Triaxian fanatics will give us a warm welcome, N. My Marines and I don't like to admit it, but we could use the help on this one, especially after taking down those bloody assassins."

"Make no mistake, Jeremiah. This is for all the creds. Admiral Dreth is completely insane. I'm sure he fully intends to drive his ship straight into the sun and set off those stellar disruptor devices firsthand. We have to get on board and have our teks and fixers neutralize those bombs. Then Dreth can take his sun bath all he wants."

"Affirmative, sir. That's the plan, then. The rest of our fleets can't stop them?"

"Not in time, or they already would have. Even *The Hippolyta's* a battered wreck. Everybody else is pretty beaten up as well from taking out the last enemy threats. We don't have enough firepower to bust up *Kronos* before it reaches the star's gravity well.

"Jeremiah—if *Kronos* sets off those devices, in less than an hour, the Cosmic chain reaction will turn this star into the biggest quantabomb the galaxy has ever seen. Everyone racing this way to help and all of the inner systems and their entire populations will be slaughtered."

Captain Hayden grinned. "Then it looks like we're it, and we can't let that happen. We insert and cut down anything that moves. See you and your people in the boarding tubes."

Hayden broke their link.

Naero rose up out of her command chair and called to Surina and Enel. "Take command, Surina. Enel, get us in close. Get us in there."

Her pilot sounded worried, struggling and constantly trying to reset the impulse and navigation controls. "Captain, we're losing power by the second. She's barely responding."

"I'm trusting both of you with our ship and with all our lives. I know you both. You'll find a way. Link with Rendar in engineering and anyone else. I know we're in a bad way, but he'll give you everything he can."

Surina took the vacated command chair and immediately started working to help direct the crippled ship, her hands a blur among the displays. "Good luck, sir."

Naero turned in the lift, jammed with other crew.

They donned their armor or pweaked their helmets up on their sealed flight togs, readying various weapons for the assault.

No one hesitated.

Everyone moved with purpose and direction.

Naero smiled, extremely proud of her people.

"Fortune favors the bold!" she shouted aloud.

On the way, they passed through one of the ship's armories.

Naero and everyone else loaded up. They went in heavy.

She tracked the chase on her wristcom.

They had one last shot.

The Hippolyta would ram into *The Kronos* again from below, several decks beneath the main bridge and behind the ruined missile launch tubes. On contact, Hayden and Naero would insert their boarding parties, and proceed to their objectives with all haste.

According to the assault plan Captain Hayden transmitted, the Marines had analyzed the enemy flagship's layout. Once inside, they would split their forces.

One team would race to neutralize the disruptor warheads and jettison vital parts of them away from the flagship.

The other team would attack the bridge to take control of the vessel and kill or capture Admiral Dreth and his entire command.

Right now, Naero was leaning heavily toward *kill*.

Somehow she felt that maniac would more than oblige them.

They had less than an hour before *The Kronos* would begin to be pulled in by the star itself.

And not much longer after that before they passed the point of no return.

Naero and her people prepared to slide or jet down the boarding tubes using gravwings, immediately after impact with the enemy flagship. Magnetic grapples and tow cables would take hold, and staggered series of charges would blast a way through the hull on contact, open the tubes, and inject their boarding forces into the enormous flagship like a virus into a host.

Captain Hayden gave the warning. "Prepare for impact and insertion. Going green. Mark. Eight seconds!"

The boarding forces all tried to relax in zero-G. Bracing oneself never worked any way.

At seven seconds, both ships collided, groaned, and buckled together. The sounds of grinding and shearing metal screamed like warring demons.

The boarding charges went off, boring through the enemy hull. Robotic plasma cutters darted in as needed.

The insertion lights went green.

"Go, go, go!"

Naero dove into her tube head first, heavy blaster pistols extended right out in front of her. Sweeping forward with her gravwing.

Weapon fire erupted back and forth dead ahead.

Like a dummy, she had forgotten to activate her personal shields.

Naero did so quickly, right as she spilled out into the fighting.

Two Triaxian heavy Marines flew up right before her, lifting plasma rifles.

Naero shot them point blank through their face shields, tearing their heads apart and flinging them back. She kicked off their bodies and flipped around, twisting and soaring the other way.

Enemy blasts just missed her feet and legs.

They were in a hangar, empty of starfighters. Duranadium beams and structure up top, about forty meters above the deck.

About a hundred Triaxians were spread out below, behind a heavily fortified position at one end of the hangar, guarding the way to the upper decks and the main bridge.

They were in the process of bringing in autoguns and squad support cannons, hurrying to get them set up.

Naero redirected off a beam.

Again, heavy blaster, particle beam, and plasma fire tore up the section of supports right where she had been.

Keep moving.

Change position and direction every two seconds.

Evasive flying.

The enemy gunners kept missing her by centimeters.

She finally zipped down and took cover behind a pile of heavy machine parts and equipment.

Hayden and his Marines were down, already formed up and leaping forward in teams. They covered each other expertly, finding cover, returning accurate, sustained fire on the enemy position.

They closed in.

They attempted to punch through the warping and coruscating waves of the enemy squad shields.

Naero's people busied themselves dueling with the foes up in the air and the superstructure, shooting down at them all from above.

Dead and wounded dropped or floated everywhere within seconds.

Marine meks squirted in, rose up, and charged forward, guns and cannons blazing.

"Hayden," Naero warned, "be advised, the enemy's setting up heavy squad cannons and autoguns behind their position. It looked like they're preparing to fire."

"We have to get those shields down. Then we can soften them up and get in before they can cut loose!"

An intense barrage of micromissiles and negation pulse bombs swarmed at the enemy and detonated with a flash. Multiple loud, rocking bangs, pops, and explosions went off to further stun and startle the enemy.

Right as the enemy shields collapsed.

But two enemy autoguns came online, just as it looked like the Marines would overrun the enemy position.

The rapid-fire enemy guns disintegrated two Marine meks up close, and cut down a score of other attackers.

Naero sent in a wave of fixers.

They swept in and penetrated the enemy defenses.

The Triaxians couldn't shoot them all down. The devices were simply too small and too many.

Once at the big guns, the fixers quickly dismantled and reduced them to non-functioning components.

With the top sections clear, Naero sent her forces down at the enemy from above.

Hayden and the Marines regrouped and came at the foe from below.

Caught in a terrible crossfire, threescore remaining foes went down under a hail of heavy penetration fire, rockets, and grenades.

Naero and Hayden called in the remainder of their assault forces, almost at the same time.

"Get the rest of our people down here," Naero said.

"Send in the Marines," Hayden ordered.

She glared at him and cocked her head. "Seriously, Jeremiah?"

He laughed. "I always wanted to say it–finally got the chance."

"Do you think taking every deck is going to be like this? We don't have enough time for that."

More troops from the second assault wave poured in through the tubes, including Leftenant Tycho Decker and a full squad of assault meks.

"We'll find out," Hayden said at last. "We don't have to take down the entire ship–just the main bridge and those missile tubes."

"Copy that."

The Kronos lurched forward suddenly.

Explosive robotic charges on the outside of the vessel suddenly ripped the boarding tubes away.

The Kronos broke free from *The Hippolyta* and flung itself off.

Dozens perished right before their eyes.

The outer portions of the hangar transformed into a ragged, gaping wound in the enemy flagship.

Their gravwings struggled to keep all of them from getting sucked out into the vortex of space.

"Everybody inside!" Naero commanded. "That's the only way forward now. Remember our objectives. We'll divide our forces up accordingly."

"You heard the lady," Hayden said. "All in."

They made their way into the interior of the ship. They cut and blasted through sealed bulkheads and hatches as needed.

Naero asked Hayden his professional opinion as they checked their complement readouts. "Do we have enough troops to complete both missions, still?"

He nodded. "I think so, but it's slim now. Sorry, N. Either way, this looks like a one way ride. Pretty sure we can complete both missions, but I'm thinking we'll still get a super tan in the end."

Naero took his hand briefly. "Forward it is then," she said. "I've transmitted our situation to the fleet. If they can send help, they will. Let's get our part done, and trust to our mates. Leftenant Commander Tyber, proceed with Gunny Kowalski and his Marines with the other half of our fighters to the missile bays. Blast your way in if you have to. Wreck those devices. They cannot go off in the sun, at all costs, whatever happens to anyone. Got me?"

Ty smiled. He actually saluted. "You know we will, sir. We're on it."

Zhen would be proud, but angry at Naero if they all died in the process.

Naero and her team went with Captain Hayden and the heavy Marine assault unit.

Strangely enough, they faced very light opposition on their way up toward the main bridge.

A few attackers with small arms and grenades, taking shots at them here and there. Easily dealt with and put down or bypassed.

Too easy. What was waiting for them?

Nothing to do but find out.

"Proceeding to the main bridge," Hayden announced. "Just through that open deck and beyond those blast doors, and to the next wide open deck around the curve. Perhaps this won't be so difficult after all."

Naero studied the schematics.

And her sense of warning went wild.

"I don't know, Hayden. This is the only approach from this entire side of the ship. It's wide open, but it also looks like a perfectly designed kill zone to me. Let me send in some fixers to check it out and scan our approach."

"Fine by me. Send those goomers up ahead for a look see."

Naero did so.

As soon as they emerged from around the curve, into the open…

A heavy, blinding wave of solid interlocking fire shredded them to pieces and heavily pockmarked the thick opposite blast wall.

49

The main bridge to the Triaxian Flagship lay dead ahead, according to the brief scans the destroyed fixers sent back.

Protected by heavy, defensive blast shields, bristling with rows of auto-guns set in the very walls, and vault-like bulkheads completely blocking their way.

The heavy weapons set within those blast shields stood poised and ready to mow down any troops that dared to attempt any kind of assault.

But this was it. Their tough nut to crack, and they had no choice.

They had to get past those guns somehow and take out the bridge, before they all died, the flagship went into the sun, and everyone in half a parsec got killed when the star went nova.

Naero tried sending in larger waves of fixers first.

"They can dismantle those guns and chew through the walls, breaking them down into raw components."

She sent in hundreds.

No dice.

She sent in a cloud of thousands.

No good.

Those that the autoguns did not take out directly were dropped by electron pulse waves and disrupted before they even made contact with the guns or walls.

Tyber and the teks sent over a beam cannon, cannibalized out of one of the enemy secondary defensive batteries.

The enemy shielding even held up against that.

Several blasts couldn't even make a scratch, before the Spacer-rigged weapon completely burned out.

Captain Hayden and his Spacer Marines did not look any more eager than Naero and her crew to take those guns on up close and personal.

"That's an intense amount of firepower," Naero said. "How can we beat them, let alone breach those blast walls?"

"I'll send in a mek unit with overloaded shield pods. It's our only chance. They might get close enough to set some bunker busting fusion charges."

Hayden lifted his hand, giving the order to Leftenant Tycho's valiant meks.

Everyone else hugged the walls.

The meks shot forward, glowing shield pods blazing and warping the air in waves directly in front of them.

As soon as they got into the open, the auto-guns flared, blinding the entire area with their intense, withering fire.

The six meks formed a wedge of interlocking shields that shrieked and screamed against the intense assault trying to chew through them.

They leaned into the barrage and struggled to push forward with all of their enhanced power.

The meks tried to launch volleys of micro-grenades and rockets to take out some of the guns.

The enemy rate of fire was such that any ordnance that left the mek shields was instantly vaporized and repulsed.

The meks would need to reach the walls and set the bunker-busters manually.

One auto-gun jammed and stopped firing.

The mek wedge instantly made for the weak point.

The other auto-guns kept blazing.

Hayden watched his readouts. "Leftenant, pull back. You only have minutes left on your shield pods at best. They're overloading too fast!"

Tycho ignored him, always glacier-cool under fire. "Almost there, Cap. About to set the first charge."

"Tycho, get your people out of there. That's an order, damn it!"

The mek on the far left took out one of the autoguns up close.

Then her shield pod went down.

She ignited her rockets and tried to shoot forward.

She overloaded her power core and activated her bunker buster.

But the autoguns chewed through her backup shields and her mek in a heartbeat.

Corporal Flannery was instantly vaporized.

Her fusion charge cooked off and damaged two more autoguns and scarred the bulkhead.

Light damage at best.

"People, only seconds left on our pods," Tycho noted. "Set your charges and your suits to critical like Helen did and in with me. Let's punch this fucking hole! Ooh, Rah!"

"Ooh, Rah!" four Marine voices yelled, in fearless unison.

Naero and Hayden read the blast projections at the same time.

"Retreat to the last bulkhead!" Naero screamed.

"Get back!" Hayden ordered.

They made it halfway to the other bulkhead when a tremendous, partially shielded explosion rocked the enemy flagship, tore through the defenses, and ripped another gaping, ragged wound in the hull of the ship.

The explosive decompression sucked out a mek and several Spacers and Marines.

Naero and Hayden led their remaining forces forward.

A glowing rupture yawned amid smoke and flame.

Most of the autoguns were down, but not all.

Hayden sent in his last two meks to clear a path for their combined strike force.

The meks and their shield pods stepped into the teeth of the remaining autoguns, giving the strike force a clear path straight in.

Spacers and Spacer Marines set their shields and gravwings and swept through the breach.

Naero led the sortie to port.

Hayden took starboard.

Within, the bridge was partially filled with smoke and all of the lights, gravity, and power seemed to be down.

The flagship listed, powerless, but still propelled toward the sun by its own rapid forward momentum.

At some point very soon, the gravity of the star itself would latch hold and suck them all in even faster.

Grenades and weapon fire from enemy positions rocked their shields, knocked people around, killing two troops outright.

The Spacers propelled themselves off every angle and commenced their attack. Enemy fire revealed their positions behind a barricade of blast shields and consoles.

The enemy took fire from almost every possible direction.

Spacer grenades and charges gnawed at their shields and disrupted their defenses.

Then, at the right moment, Naero sent her fixers sweeping in to activate a negation pulse, similar to the enemy disruption blast.

Every Spacer and Marine instantly got a coded command: Take cover. Power down all shields!

Their people pulled back just as the pulse hit.

It thrummed through the shattered bridge in waves, knocking out all the enemy shields.

As it passed, the countersign was given: Shields back up.

Resume the attack!

Now their weapons punched straight into the enemy and cut them down.

Half of the enemy number perished in a few instants.

High Admiral Maximillian Jaxxon Dreth activated a reserve shield pod around himself and started laughing.

Why was the bastard laughing?

A full score of enemy meks popped right out of the walls where they had been held in check. Enormous Sterodan warriors in combat armor emerged out of the floor, walls, and ceiling, backed up by squads of Ejjai shock troops in full battle suits.

At the point of victory, the Spacers found themselves cut off and outnumbered–seven to one.

And the enemy troops kept pouring out of every hidden shaft and hole.

Nothing to do but fight.

Chaos and death erupted within the dark, smoky orb of the shattered enemy bridge as the helpless flagship spun further and further out of control.

Only the matchless Spacer expertise for fighting in zero-G environments kept them from being swept away and killed at the outset.

But against fresh forces, and hi-tek numbers, they would not survive for long.

Like everyone else, Naero spun, kicked, and cut loose with her weapons in the tumult.

297

She shot Sterodans in the face and head as the enormous brutes fired at her and tried to drag her down.

If they got hold of her, they'd tear off her arms and legs.

As she saw them do to others.

Her assault rifle empty, she drew blaster pistols and blazed away rapid fire into the snarling teeth of the Ejjai shock troops. She whirled, spun, and kicked, snapping necks and shattering bones.

Bubbles and blobs of blood bobbled and boiled everywhere from the dead and wounded.

A com came in from Tyber. "Good news, N. "

"A little busy, Ty."

She shot the legs off an Ejjai alpha at the hips.

The bitch still tried to blast her, spinning away and bleeding to death.

"We've reached the solar disruption warheads. Our fixers are disarming them as quickly as we can. Where did Triax get tek like this? It's way beyond anything I've ever seen before!"

A wounded Sterodan body-blocked her from behind, nearly winding her her.

Naero flipped and flung three exploding energy knives into his head and shoulders.

The explosions decapitated the muscle-amped freak, just before he grappled for her slender legs with his huge meaty paws.

Naero sliced off his fingers at the same time.

"Naero, you still with me?"

"Just barely, Ty. We're getting murdered up here on the bridge. Outnumbered. Finish up there and get what help you can to us, ASAP!"

"On the way. Leave the fixers behind, everyone. Get to the bridge any way you can!"

Below, on her six, Naero wheeled and spotted Captain Hayden and a big knot of Marines.

They just finished blasting their way through the last enemy meks.

Now they charged Admiral Dreth's position in a direct, all out assault.

Both elements concentrated heavy fire directly at the other.

Personal shields warped and winked out on both sides.

This was the kind of up-close, heavy punching match that the Marines excelled at.

But they were still outnumbered.

And the enemy closed in on them from every angle.

Naero had her own problems.

Only three surviving friendlies nearby–all fighting for their lives.

A sphere of enemies closed in on her directly to take her down.

Flashing, spinning, zero-G kicks knocked several enemies back as she played off them with her gravwing.

Naero whirled in flight, flinging grenades, bomblets, and energized throwing knives and blades in a full spread.

Then she curled up in a protective knot.

All of her ordnance went off the next second, at close range.

The intensity of the blasted negated her shields and bounced her around.

But she took out scores of enemies attempting to close in on her.

She looked through her cracked visor on her combat armor and tried to get the damaged suit to heal itself and re-seal.

It wouldn't respond.

Fire erupted on her three. Ty and the others poured in, trying to assist.

She drew her battle blades and energized them. Not to explode, but to slice through nearly anything they touched.

Naero raced at top speed, becoming a blur, slicing and cutting their foes as she she raced and circled past at top speed. She became a blur of death.

Other Spacers noted her attacks and quickly imitated her.

Soon the enemy numbers found themselves caught in a slashing hurricane of energized blades.

When her blades cut out, Naero sank one into a Sterodan face. The next into an Ejjai belly.

At last, it looked like they had a chance to win.

Then the flagship groaned and buckled, suddenly accelerating forward.

Oh, no.

Haisha! The star's gravity had them.

Even if they won the fight, now there wouldn't be any time to escape.

No more time to think about that.

Just keep fighting.

Down below, she caught sight of Captain Hayden dueling straight up with Admiral Dreth.

Both of them circled the other, firing pistols at each other. Shields went down. Shots penetrated both their armors.

Neither combatant let up.

Guns empty, they drew energy swords.

But something went weird with the enemy admiral.

Even as Naero tried to fight her way down to help Hayden, she watched as the Marine captain ran the admiral through the chest and abdomen four times in as many instants with his glowing blade.

How was Dreth still standing? Still alive after such terrible wounds?

Naero drew her own energy cutlass and sliced an Ejjai in half.

Then what looked like either steam or ichor of some kind roiled off of the admiral, and he literally began glowing from within, as if there were a power core inside of him.

His veins seemed to pulse and glow with weird, coruscating energies. His very flesh radiated like hot orange and greenish-yellow coals, translucent and glowing. The energies burned right through his ragged combat armor.

Captain Hayden ran the admiral through the throat, but Dreth only laughed and backhanded him–sending him flying twenty meters to smash against the wall.

Dreth yanked the energy sword out of his throat as it were an annoying insect. He broke the sword over his knee and cast aside the pieces.

All of his terrible wounds seemed to seal back up.

Two more Marines stepped in and fired their heavy blaster cannons right into Dreth.

Whatever kind of monster or thing Dreth had become, he strode forward, impervious, crushed the armored helmets of the two Marines with his fists, and incinerated them in their powered armor where they stood.

Naero heard them scream.

Captain Hayden swept back in, nailing Dreth with microgrenades.

They did little damage to the admiral-thing, but they did knock him back a bit.

The flagship rocked and shuddered again.

Naero saw the blast shields of the bridge dome shatter and buckle in.

Somehow Enel and Surina on board *The Hippolyta* had gotten the planetoid dreadnaught moving again.

They rammed it right back into the flagship.

One of the ship's big quad guns yawned its immense, 16-meter maw down at them like a huge glowing eye of death.

Naero flashed down and sliced at the admiral-thing with her energized cutlass.

He chortled at her as the deep wounds she inflicted re-sealed right before her eyes, like some kind of energized gel.

"You filthy, arrogant spacks can't kill me now. None of you can. But I'm dragging you all straight with me into hell. You can't stop me from destroying our sun–and everyone in this entire system!"

More Spacers and Marines poured in through the breach, battling with and cutting down the remaining foes.

"You're wrong," Naero said. "You've already lost, Admiral. We've disarmed the stellar disruption devices."

She flipped and sank her sword through his shoulder and hewed nearly down to his thigh, almost cutting him in twain.

Dreth kept laughing, and wrenched the cutlass from her.

He melted it into slag with his bare hands as she watched.

His horrifying wound resealed again.

Dreth seemed to be made of raw, gelatinous energy within.

Invulnerable. Unstoppable.

He lifted both hands and came at Naero, still laughing. "Doesn't matter, spacks. Fuck everyone. Even if the devices are deactivated and dismantled, the raw components in them will still ignite once they hit the sun. You can't stop this ship. You can't prevent the cataclysm."

Dreth continued to laugh. "Now I'm going to roast those pretty violet eyes of yours, you little spack whore. Right in that beautiful face of yours, so like your mother's."

Naero stepped back and drew two battle blades, setting them to explode. She steeled herself. "Come and try!"

"Die, monster!" Captain Hayden rushed the thing unseen from behind, thrusting an activated bunker buster into its torso with his left hand.

Hayden screamed.

He lost his hand, melted down to his forearm.

Dreth backhanded him as before, sending him flying.

Naero got her flickering shields back up and kicked Dreth in the face twice to keep him distracted.

She pressed her attacks in spinning fury.

Whirling, battering him with rapid, wheeling kicks.

Then she shot around Dreth, grabbed Hayden where he lay dazed, and tried to zip free of the blast zone.

The fusion device Hayden implanted detonated. The raw force of it smashed Naero and Hayden into the wall again.

Dreth swelled up like a toad on fire from deep inside, ballooning and about to burst.

Glowing energy shot out of his mouth and eyes and several rents.

Yet unbelievably–he still did not die.

He stalked and staggered toward them where they lay. The thing he had become wobbled, struggling to reform itself.

Naero strained to catch her breath, to rise up and fight this vile thing somehow.

It stalked toward her and Hayden, silhouetted before the gigantic glowing bore of *The Hippolyta's* main cannon number one.

Naero called to her ship.

"Enel, Surina–anyone. Fire main cannon number one. Immediately!"

"Captain?" Enel's voice asked.

The Dreth-thing was almost on them.

"Fire, damn you!"

Naero grabbed Hayden and tried to zip away.

Her battered gravwing failed.

The bore of cannon number one whined and heated up white-hot.

The Dreth-thing's fingers stretched out to tear her life from her.

Somehow, Hayden rose back up to his feet right beside her.

Both of them punched and kicked the Dreth-thing side by side trying keep it distracted and hold it off.

Naero staggered and tried to launch herself at the monster again.

Jeremiah stepped in directly in front of her, emptying a pistol in Dreth's face.

The monster smashed a large fist down on Hayden's head and shoulders with a terrible crushing blow.

At the last instant, Naero lunged back in, sinking both of her last battle blades set to explode. But the blasts only delayed the monster.

She leaped away with all of her bunched strength, dragging the stricken Hayden with her as he crumpled.

Naero rolled them back, barely out of *Hippolyta's* line of fire.

The world went blinding white, and then strangely black.

A vast hissing SHHHZZZTTT blazed and sizzled through the flagship.

When the air cleared, the horror that had once been Admiral Dreth was gone. The massive beam annihilated all matter and energy within its path.

A 16-meter-wide, yawning, glowing tunnel had been bored straight through the length of the flagship.

Naero felt like cheering.

"We got him!" she couldn't help shouting.

Then she stopped, staring down into the cold dead eyes of her battle brother, Captain Hayden.

His neck and shoulders looked scorched and crushed badly, right through his ruined armor.

That last blow from the admiral must have mashed and snapped his neck and shoulders.

A blow he had withstood for her.

It was like losing Gallan all over again. As if she lost Jan–as if her brother lay dead in her hands.

Her mighty *abani* was already gone, his great spirit fled.

An immense sorrow overtook Naero–an agony far worse than any physical wound.

She and Jeremiah had fought side by side throughout the conflict.

They were mates.

Naero kissed Hayden's cold lips. What did it matter now? Then his forehead.

Naero sobbed, smoothing his hair.

They had lost a brave Marine, a great leader, and a good man and friend.

"Sorry, Jeremiah," she whispered through her tears. "Sorry I won't be able to send you home…to your family."

She would never be able to thank him for his valor, for his mighty sacrifice. He had saved them all. A heavy debt that she could never repay.

Ty staggered up to her, bloody and covered with medpaks. Yet all of his concern was for her.

"N, what happened?"

"The good captain's dead," she said plainly. "He died well, fighting valiantly to the last against a mighty foe. His death is a great loss."

"Well, N–if we don't find a way to stop from falling into the sun, we're all going to join him very shortly. If we die, Zhen's going to be royally pissed at us both!"

The two tangled vessels lurched to a halt again, and started drawing back the other way. Naero could feel it.

Both ships moved away from the sun.

Naero called out over her wristcom. "Surina? Enel? Did Rendar get the drives working again?"

"Not enough to pull us back from the brink, Captain."

Then…how?

Another familiar voice cut in over their link.

"This is Admiral Nevano Kinmal, Naero. My daughter Shalaen is close to passing out, but we aren't about to let you and your people get incinerated today. Prepare for rescue."

Naero picked Captain Hayden's body up and looked around. The fighting was over. The rest of their enemies lay dead and defeated. Her fierce people made sure of that.

Ty and she leaned on each other.

The Alliance had won, at immense costs.

Yet victory still remained theirs.

Her own words sank in deep.

Triax–the worst of the worst–was gone.

No more.

The Beast no longer existed to plague or torment anyone.

Triax Gigacorporation joined the rotting garbage heap of history.

The Annexation War–was finally over.

50

Alliance fleets surrounded the living star of the last Triaxian Capital Class Homeworld to fall.

Triax, most decadent and brutal of all the Gigacorps…no longer existed to murder or poison humanity, Spacers, landers, or any of the other known sentient races.

Its former slaves knew freedom now that had not existed for centuries.

With the Annexation War finally concluded, the Alliance forces gathered together at the appointed time and place to honor and pay tribute to their fallen, and to each other.

While Naero waited in her dress blacks for the ceremonies to begin, she was greatly pleased to be introduced to Jeremiah's widow, Veronica Hayden–a very pretty, very pregnant redhead with gray eyes. She was also a Spacer Marine, and proud of her son, Jason, a fair-haired boy of three who had his father's beautiful brown eyes.

Naero could tell at a glance how much this woman had loved Jeremiah, and part of her felt glad that at least the two lovers had known that much joy together.

Veronica looked to be every bit as brave as her husband. She and Naero made small talk and got to know each other a bit, before they were called to take their places.

When the time came, Strike Captain Naero Amashin Maeris stood at attention on the launch deck of the massive Joshua Tech Fleet Carrier *The Undaunted.* She stood beside all the surviving captains of Strike Fleet Six, and the proud Marines of Captain Jeremiah Hayden's 3rd Division command, assembled in his high honor.

All of her friends stood nearby. Zhen and Tyber. Chaela. Saemar. Tarim and the radiant angel, Shalaen.

So many others–all her family now.

She smiled sadly.

Zhen had been so glad that Tyber survived that she cried and slept beside him in his medbed for the first full day thereafter.

Naero scanned the tens of thousands assembled.

Each of them a hero to her mind–many times over.

All resplendent in their dress uniforms. Each of them majestic in their valor.

Beautiful beyond all song, poetry, or mere words.

They stood with their heads held high, among the very best that the courageous blood of the free Forty-Nine Spacer Clans and their allies had to offer.

They had fought long and hard, against terrible foes and odds.

And never knew defeat.

First their admirals spoke.

They praised them all with great praise.

Then the captains who wished to speak said their piece.

When Naero's turn finally came, she stepped up with her battle smile fixed upon her face.

And every eye fixed upon her.

"My beloved brothers, my beloved sisters, my mighty Clans and our valiant allies–whom I honor and cherish more than the breath of life itself. Nothing…no words or treasure can ever match the blood we have shed together, for the sake of Freedom and Liberty.

"All of you know how I see you. My fiercest lions. How you fought– for me–for each other–for Liberty itself. How you fought for trillions in enslaved chains whom you do not even know–whom you will never know– yet still you gave the last full measure, without question, in order that all may know and live in freedom."

She looked down. "Our losses are beyond all tears and sorrow."

Naero choked up and drew her cutlass. She saluted the honored dead gathered together with them in rank after rank of shining casketpods.

She knelt down, and the gathered thousands knelt with her.

She kissed her blade and offered it to the fallen, in highest token of their mighty sacrifice.

Many present followed her lead and did the same as she.

She bowed down low, placed her sword before her, and touched her forehead to the floor. She gasped and watered the deck with tears that rained down from her eyes.

She finally rose up, saluted again with a flourish, and sheathed her blade. Then she found her voice once more.

"My swords of light. May you shine bright in the honor and glory that is forever yours. None can ever take it from you. But we the living are gathered here today to pay honor to our victorious fallen. Those whose valor and sacrifice are beyond question. Their precious lights have been extinguished in this life. Their fierce, shining blades have been shattered and broken, along with our hearts. Their loss among us can never be equaled or replaced.

"We return them to the light that burns forever, just as their memory shall always shine and live on forever in our hearts."

She paused and placed her hands behind the small of her back.

"So many deserve special note. The fearless crew of *The Kit Carson*– three brave starfighter pilots who stopped a missile at the cost of their very lives. Yet, if we read all of their hallowed names, it would take more time than is possible.

"We must, therefore, go on and live our lives in their names, in their honor. As they would want us to. Our joy shall be their joy. Our love shall be their love. Our children shall be their children. For they can no longer do so for themselves.

"Yet I will pause to speak one name for the sake of all, and praise my good friend, Major Jeremiah Hayden. The bravest warrior that I have ever known, and the embodiment of what it means to be a both a Spacer and, foremost, a Spacer Marine. My brother in battle, who fought bravely until the very end, and gave his life for me, and for the sake of us all. You must all know and remember this fact for all time: without his great sacrifice, the enemy would have slain me, all of our people, and murdered our fleets, and all the trillions that now live in freedom within this very sector. All of us would be dead. Therefore, let the highest of all Spacer honors be bestowed upon Major Jeremiah Allen Hayden, and upon his Clan, in his mighty name."

Admiral Sleak Maeris stepped forward, holding aloft the gleaming Spacer Medal of Valor, set in a priceless frame.

The crowd gasped in wonder and wept when Admiral Maeris gave it over into the hands of Jeremiah's proud widow, Marine 1st Leftenant Veronica Cherokee Hayden, holding their sleepy, fair-haired son Jason close to her heaving breast.

Veronica smiled sadly, tears streaming down her red, stricken face.

Aunt Sleak embraced her.

Veronica remained heavy with their second child, the girl they had chosen to name Lydia, after Jeremiah's deceased Marine Colonel mother.

Yet he had surpassed even the latter. Not even his valorous mother had won such fame.

In all the history of the Spacer Clans and their legacy of courage–the bravest of the brave–fewer than a hundred such apex awards had ever been bestowed. Only three upon those who had still lived.

One of those was Lincoln Maeris, during the Second Spacer War, Naero's mighty kin of old.

At her own command, Aunt Sleak went forward and placed another such medal respectfully and gently into the opening casket that held Jeremiah's body.

She kissed her fingertips and touch the casket as it re-sealed.

Then the admiral stepped back and nodded to Naero.

The time had come.

Strike Fleet Captain Naero Amashin Maeris stepped forward and launched brave Major Hayden's casketpod out toward the star herself. She saluted and knelt again and wept for the loss of his blood, and that of so many other brave warriors and *abani* among their allies taking the next journey.

Haisha, such a stirring sight it was to behold.

Naero rose up to stand at attention and salute the brave fallen a third time. The casketpods for *The Kit Carson* and the three pilots shot past her.

They all saluted as waves of shining, silver, mirror-finished caskets, filled with either the remains or the memories of their valiant dead, followed Major Hayden into the star.

So many others.

They returned Spacers and landers, Matayans and miners, and all else who fought on their side, back to the stars from whence they came.

The living sang songs in honor of the dead and the living.

They wept, openly and proudly. Tears blazed on their proud, uplifted faces. The faces of warriors forged into shining steel in the crucible of courage.

The drummers thundered, the pipers piped, and waves of Ghost Dragons and other fighter waves roared over in formation and back around again.

They filled the heavens in all that sector with blazing, shining light, enough to rival the star itself.

Thiolins broke out in rich, sweet, swelling Spacer music.

None less than the four masters of their age: Mitsubishi Yuzuki, Grandon Kowalski, Rhiannon Fae, and Seamus Flynn, stepped forward to honor them all, and play for the brave Alliance, before the stars.

They played two songs, and the crowd cheered in awe at each one.

Then the four masters bowed low, and stepped down in homage.

For the grand tribute was not yet complete.

An elder Spacer in long, black, flowing robes, a long, shining white beard, and platinum white hair stretching down his back, took the primary stage, and all others gave way before his magnetic presence.

In honor of the fallen, Grand Master Thiolinist Ezekiel Luna Alexander too his place before them all. He began to play, silhouetted against the stars at the prow of *The Undaunted.*

The Maestro played three heart-stopping tunes flawlessly with his aching, nearly crippled hands.

Three melodies, each one sadder, and sweeter, and more beautiful and radiant than the one before.

For they spoke to the heart and soul, and pierced to the very core of the Clans in deepest, reverent memory.

Every heart was moved, and no eye remained dry.

And though the tunes all had lyrics that each Spacer knew well from birth...

...the same beloved words caught in every throat, and could not be voiced by any breast or heart pounding within.

Even by an entire multitude of assembled heroes.

And thus the sweet tunes of the lone thiolinist sang out across the Void and across all ships and worlds, and spoke for all.

The grand master gave voice to the heart and soul of the vast multitudes and hosts arrayed, silent and thoughtful, beneath all the Powers and the lights of heaven, and all the glories and mysteries of the known universe.

With his mighty gift, the Maestro thundered what could not be put into words, and expressed in music all that their bursting hearts and souls could not utter.

When he finished, Zeke shattered his priceless thiolin and his bow over one knee, and cast the glittering fragments out beyond the launching screen shields and into the black.

Toward the bright star.

The Maestro never played again.

Less that a day later, he slipped away peacefully in his slumber, and his spirit joined the Alliance fallen, on to the next journey, in highest honor.

51

Naero spent six heart-wrenching days going on board each remaining vessel that had served under her authority with Strike Fleet Six. She personally saw to the disbanding and mustering out of their volunteer crews.

None left their ship without clasping hands with her or embracing at some point along the way. She would not allow it.

With the war over, the private ships themselves would be returned forthwith to their Clans, who had only lent them to the Alliance for the war's duration.

As their commander, their great captain, Naero thanked them repeatedly. She bestowed any last awards upon them, and made personal note of the many citations for bravery and valor that their unit, and ship, and so many of them had rightfully earned.

These were now her family, and they hugged, embraced, and kissed cheeks as they said their bittersweet farewells and departed.

Naero wished them all every happiness and success.

Had it been in her power, she would have sent them all back to their families and friends in triumph, laden down with the heavy hoarded wealth of crushed enemy despots and tyrants.

Such was their valor and their worth in her mind.

But much like her, they laid down their arms, eager now only to go back to their little lives and take up their own private obligations and ambitions once more during peace time. Just as it should be.

Yet Naero had made many friends. There would be an explosion of trade and exploration among the entire Alliance and the many hundreds of liberated worlds. And Naero vowed to meet with them again and work out trade ventures for them all among the stars. In the future at some point, once her own path became clear.

She surprised Captain Max Lii and his jealous entourage with a long, deep, luxurious parting kiss which left both of them breathless and yearning for more.

Finally, after the others were all gone, Naero went to the fixer clouds, where the battered *Hippolyta* again was being repaired and made fit once more for service somewhere.

Many found planetoid vessels ugly, unlovely, and unstreamlined.

But to Naero, the amazon was fierce, functional, and beautiful. *The Hippolyta*–like her namesake–remained tough, formidable, and enduring. Let the Thirty Amazon Sisters fight on.

Time and time again, Naero's amazon had proven herself. No foe had ever triumphed against her and her four huge guns. Battered and stricken she may have been, but she still remained indomitable and unvanquished to the last.

Naero went on board, rode the lifts and movers, and walked the bridge and all of *Hippolyta's* empty decks, alone with her many thoughts and sorrows. And the soft, quiet tread of her own small feet.

She had never felt such a lack, such loss. Not since the deaths of her parents and Gallan, Jan's abduction, and Jeremiah's loss.

The weight of it all threatened to crush even her fierce and mighty spirit.

That was when and where Aunt Sleak and Zalvano found her at last.

Each of them embraced her.

Zalvano spoke softly, straightforward. "Naero–you missed your own citation ceremony, and the bestowal of all of the many awards and commendations that you've so rightly earned."

Naero shrugged, then sighed. "I don't care about all of that so much. Are they not going to give them to me or something?"

Aunt Sleak shook her head. "No, once an honor has been awarded, it remains part of your service record and your Clan's honor. Forever."

"Then what's the big deal? Like everyone else, I'm just plain sick of this war–all of the senseless death and loss."

Surprisingly, it was Zalvano who grew angry and gave her a talking to. "Not all of it was senseless, Naero. Do not speak so. We were all part of a great and noble effort. A terrible evil has been vanquished and destroyed. Trillions of people are now free. We took down and destroyed one of our greatest enemies of all time. That, spacechild, is something to be roundly celebrated."

Aunt Sleak smiled with great pride and held her head high.

She gently put her hand on Naero's face and lifted her chin up as well.

"I had the great pleasure–nay–the great privilege, to watch my beloved sister's only daughter go forth with vast courage and the highest honor, and acquit herself to the respect and admiration of our finest warriors and leaders. To see her counted great and equal among them–as I knew she would."

Aunt Sleak kissed her on both cheeks and then released her.

Zalvano smiled, stepped forward, and took Naero's hands in his.

"These are high honors for one so young, Naero. And the blood of your mighty mother and father sings with joy and triumph in your veins. They would be so very proud of you, were they here. For you have made a name for yourself next to theirs, to stand beside them in proven honor for all time. You have done these things, by yourself, on your own."

Naero embraced and kissed them both.

"You are my blood. This is the blood I come from," she said softly. Then she quickly shook her head. "Nay, I did nothing alone. My family and my friends and my brave people have always been with me and by my side. So many helped me, and paid the price I have not. I could not have done any of this without the least of them."

She thought again of poor Jeremiah and his family.

So many that died deserved to live.

Aunt Sleak chuckled a bit. "Perhaps it was well that you bypassed the ceremony, Naero. You're so short. All of those citations would have filled your jacket. They would have had to run them down your pants."

"My legs are short, too," Naero said, glancing down.

All of them laughed again at that.

Zalvano asked her, "So, what's the great war hero going to do now?"

Naero shrugged again, then clenched her fists and opened them. "Dunno. The same as everybody else–go back to being a Spacer. But truthfully? I feel like...like I'm going crazy inside. *Haisha!* Like I could burst. So much has happened…and Jan's still missing. I've never taken any time to process it all. All I did was keep fighting and keep going forward to the next task at hand. Like running away, in a sense. Now it's all crashing back down on me. And I don't think I can handle it. I need to…get away somewhere for a while."

Aunt Sleak patted her on the shoulder.

"More than understandable. You're still so young. Go ahead. Take a few days. Get your head on straight. Just don't go too far. You still have the KDM within you. And what if those bizarre powers of yours return at some point?"

Naero shook her head. "Fat chance of that. It's been months so far, without even a tingle. Even my old headaches are gone. For better or for worse, I think that part of my life is over."

She had even nearly forgotten about Om, the Kexxian AI lost within her mind.

"Whatever," Aunt Sleak said, with her own grim smile. "Just prepare to get to work for me the minute you get back. And plan to work hard. Remember, you owe me a lot of credits."

Naero's mouth dropped open. "How much do you think I owe you?"

"Let's just say…a lot."

"How much? I need to know."

Zalvano smiled. "No, you don't. Trust me."

"I'm serious. Give me a number."

Aunt Sleak whispered an amount in her ear.

Naero's eyes popped open wide like iris valves. "*Haisha!*" she shrieked. "Holy shit!"

Her knees felt weak.

She needed to sit down.

Naero started to panic.

She'd be in debt to Aunt Sleak for years to come.

Now she *really* had to get away.

Far away.

Maybe even change her name and start over.

She knew how to do that.

Suddenly…it came to her.

Naero had a very good idea about exactly where she needed to go to get away from all of her troubles and hide out for a while.

And with whom.

She even managed a brief, sly, eager grin.

The time was more than right. She'd put it all off too long as it was.

Naero knew precisely what she had to do.

Too bad if her aunt and Klyne and Spacer Intel wouldn't approve. Too bad if they all didn't like it one bit.

Her life was her own. She was tired of taking orders, for a while at least.

She'd work it all out with them, after the fact.

After she got back, let them be angry.

Now, to make her getaway.

THE END

Please Post a Book Review Right Now

Please post a review of this book if you enjoyed it. Twenty little words are all that is required. Twenty words that say what you liked about this book while it is still fresh in your heart, mind, and soul. Please do so now before something else makes you forget.

Here is the link for The Annexation War, if you purchased it on Amazon:

http://amzn.to/1gmxGQk

Please click on the link and post your review now.

Done? The author would personally like to thank you very much.

In this busy world, everyone is pressed for time. Our time is so important, no doubt. It has reached the point now where authors of nearly every stripe compete not only for sales, but to garner reviews from their readers. Some authors even stoop to "purchasing" reviews in social media that some services now offer in bulk.

In the publish or perish work of competitive fiction, book reviews from readers are golden, they have now become a commodity even.

Many in the business even consider book reviews as important, or even more important than book sales in some ways. As crazy as that sounds.

So therefore, trust us in this. If you have authors whom you adore, and you want to read more of their books in the future, please post as many reviews for them as you can in all of the forms of social media that you use.

Doing so will help your favorite authors in numerous ways that you cannot even possibly imagine. Never forget that fact. Book reviews matter a great deal.

And if by chance, if you find that there is something about this book that you don't like, and you really do want to help authors, before you slam them with bad reviews, try briefly contacting them instead with your concerns through their contact info that is always readily provided, or through their publisher. Most authors, especially new ones, are usually happy to get constructive criticism that will make their books better. Only hating, online trolls slam authors with bad reviews without giving them a chance. Real pros and fen contact authors directly with any valid concerns. That is the current, accepted etiquette. Please don't be a troll.

Amazon Kindle Review Link for The Annexation War:

http://amzn.to/1gmxGQk

Barnes & Noble Review Link for Naero's Fury:

http://bit.ly/1fe4CqQ

Smashwords Review Link for Naero's Run:

http://bit.ly/M9nrEn

<u>Other Review Sites</u>

Good Reads

Google

Pinterest

Reddit

Please post one or more reviews for Mason for each of his books, everywhere that you can.

Thank you once again.

Cheers,

Mason Elliott

Please Join my New Releases Mailing List

Please use either of these two links:

http://bit.ly/1L2QpUL

or,

http://eepurl.com/FgQzv

Be first to learn about my new releases. I promise that I will not share your info or spam you. I will use the list only to inform you about my publishing projects.

About the Author

Mason Elliott grew up loving Science Fiction and Fantasy in all of their myriad forms. That love has transferred into his dedicated writing. Like most writers, he lives a spartan lifestyle and yearns to devote his life even more to his writing, and someday retire on the Pacific coast. So be a fan, buy his stuff, and enjoy!

Mason's Amazon Author Page:

http://amzn.to/1tXR7XK

Friend Mason on FB at this link:

http://on.fb.me/1qnBfJd

Like Mason on his FB fan site where he does most of his blogging:

http://on.fb.me/1ogFGcT

Follow Mason on Twitter at:

http://bit.ly/1nsqOSs

Visit Mason Elliott's website at

http://masonelliott.authorcontacts.com

ACKNOWLEDGEMENTS

First I would like to dedicate this book to my daughters. And as always, to the readers who have supported and believed in me for so long and on into the future. As I have said before, I will do my best to provide you with more great stories, for as long as I draw the breath of life.

Once more, none of this could be possible without the tireless efforts of my fabulous editor, Jennifer Cummings, the publishing board, and publicist Josh Marten. Special thanks again to all of my Beta readers, especially Lois, Paul, Doyle, Katherine, and many others. And eternal, constant thanks to my online writing group, my fellow toilers in the salt mines. I know we will always back each other up.

Please enjoy the following teaser from the first Spacer Clans Adventure, Book One:

NAERO'S RUN

NAERO'S RUN

by Mason Elliott

"We've got more than enough to consider here," Aunt Sleak said. "We'll post our final decisions on the Spacer ClanNet. All crew, take a breather. We're out of jump in less that two standard hours. Everyone on duty needs to be at their ready stations. Dismissed."

Naero went back to her quarters to do some laundry and a little more reading before they emerged. With regular effort, her quarters were less of a disaster than usual. She'd kept her bunk and her floor more or less cleared off, and slept in her bunk regularly now, instead of on the floor or in zero-G or a float bag.

And definitely not in her flex chair, as she had for years because she either couldn't get her bunk panel out or it was too piled up with crap.

Being small had its advantages. She could curl up like a cat and get comfortable almost anywhere for a snooze.

But keeping her quarters in better shape was a promise she made and kept–to herself–and her parents.

They emerged from jump with the customary shuddering of the ship. The fleet spread out into is standard formation, emerging back into real SpaceTime.

Naero punched up their positions on one of her screens, even though she didn't have bridge duty for several hours.

The Shinai flanked *The Dromon* on the port side, with *The Slipper* posted starboard. Their two smaller ships, *The Nevada* and *The Ardala*, brought up the rear this time.

A red hot scarlet particle beam, 60mm in diameter, lanced through Naero's walls like they were paper, disrupting her wallscreens.

A direct hit from a big gun.

At the very least, from a heavy destroyer.

Warning lights flashed immediately.

The rupture in the hull led to an immediate explosive decompression.

Naero held on tight to her bunk and went flat on the floor as the hull sealed itself.

All ships were vulnerable coming out of jump. They couldn't activate their shields until right after they emerged.

Someone had been waiting for them.

The Dromon continued getting rocked by multiple hits from what felt like several spinal guns and secondary batteries.

But the big planetoid could take it and give back plenty, her quad main guns humming and whining to life, coming online.

Naero hit her wristcom. All her screens down.

"Bridge. Status?"

"We stepped into it. They were waiting for us. We're under heavy fire. Multiple bogeys."

The general alert sounded.

"Battle Stations. Battle Stations."

Aunt Sleak cut over the com. "All hands. All hands, to your stations. Prepare for battle. All ships, all batteries, return fire. Launch all fighters."

Naero suited up and raced to the drop bay of her fighter. She met Jan along the way.

More intense fire. *Dromon* reeled and fired back.

She and Jan almost got rocked off their feet again.

A security team intercepted them at the launching bays.

Their fighters had already dropped with their backup pilots.

"The fleet captain wants you two at your secondary defense stations, not out in the mix."

Jan started to protest.

"Orders are orders. Get to your stations."

They ran to their remote gunnery stations, small secured cubicles with a chair and a console, operating triple pulse turrets on the hardpoints above them.

Naero brought up her autotargeting displays, weapons already powered up and humming.

The secondary battery gunnery stations operated independently and were well-protected. They were also fully automated, but they still functioned more effectively with a human interface.

Coordinated targeting profiles came online as she watched.

Jan operated a torp turret nearby.

Directly ahead of the fleet. Twelve elite Matayan destroyers, each with a dozen escort fighters.

Half of their number pursued and attacked a convoy of two dozen independent mining freighters.

Aunt Sleak's fleet scrambled, launched, and deployed a total of threescore fighters in a standard Alpha-Charlie-1 defensive screen.

They were outnumbered two to one.

"All batteries make ready. Incoming torps," the bridge com sounded.

Countermeasures took out half of the blips heading their way.

Spacer fighters and the forward defensive batteries blasted the rest.

"That attack's a diversion," Naero muttered.

Shinai's fire control and com computers fixed on and monitored all channels–including those between the hapless freighters and the corsairs.

"Mayday, mayday, we are under intense corsair attack. All ships. Assistance, assistance. Heavy damage and casualties."

"What do you want?" another panic-stricken voice cried out. "We'll surrender. You can board us. We have no goods and few supplies. Please, stop firing. Our ships are full of workers–full of people. You're killing civilians. We're on fire!"

Scanners displayed an awful, one-sided battle among the transports.

Most of the old bulk freighters didn't even have weapons.

Each of the heavily armed Matayan destroyers was more than a match for them or most of the ships in Aunt Sleak's fleet.

Except for the 6m quad spinal guns of *The Dromon*.

One crippled freighter broke apart and exploded under concentrated fire from three destroyers. It didn't have any shields, and only minimal armor. Its two turrets either didn't work or had been taken out already.

Static and Matayan battle language rang out in triumph.

Dromon's four primary guns cut loose, lighting up the entire sector. Its blue-white blasts ripped into the lead corsair flagship and its wingships, disrupting their shields.

The starboard wingship took two hits and listed to one side. Its aft section exploded.

"This is Captain Sleak Maeris of Clan Maeris. Enemy vessels, be advised: Cease hostilities and vacate this system or be destroyed."

Matayan curses and laughter her only reply.

"Clan Maeris," one of the freighter captains cut in. "This is Captain Philsen of *The Botaru*. Help us! Our situation is desperate. The corsairs are trying to destroy us. We don't know why."

"Acknowledged. We're coming in. Disperse if you can. You're still too bunched up. Scatter and concentrate on defensive actions. Jump if you're able. We'll try to draw them off. We're boosting your distress call."

Three more corsairs turned on the fleet, with all twelve dozen fighters full front on intercept.

The other trio of Matayan attackers kept after the freighters.

Naero heard the pleading and the screams on the open channel, just before another freighter got blasted to oblivion.

Naero realized she had tears on her face.

Was that how her parents went? Blasted to death by Matayan guns?

The rage she felt nearly overwhelmed her reason.

She checked her systems, gripped the controls of her gunnery station, and forced her emotions to go cold.

Against superior numbers, Naero and her Clan Fleet closed for battle.

Amazon Link to Naero's Run: *http://amzn.to/1eRKCOb*

Please enjoy the following teaser...an excerpt, from the next Spacer Clans Adventure, Book 2:

NAERO'S
GAMBIT

NAERO'S GAMBIT

Naero's Gambit Amazon Link: *http://amzn.to/1lx5Tyy*

by Mason Elliott

Klyne set the huge Mystic testing room on board *The Kathmandu* to muted gray. Smartwalls, floor, and ceiling, Naero saw no equipment, no padding.

The lights were set low.

From experience, Naero knew that in a training room, just about anything could pop up out of anywhere.

She wore nothing but her black Nytex flight togs.

To her surprise, Klyne and his two adepts wore dark gray Nytex togs also, but with hoods and masks pulled up over their heads. Only their keen eyes showed.

All three of the Mystics appeared to be in top physical condition, including Klyne.

One of the adepts was female, with huge green eyes and light freckles across her nose. The other was male, with the black slanted eyes of the Lii-Kim Clans.

If black was the color of Spacers, the Mystics traditionally wore gray.

They all sat with their legs crossed in lotus fashion, focusing their abilities through meditation, and mental discipline. They formed a triangle, each side about three meters apart, with them at the points.

"Follow our instructions," Klyne said. "Take your place among us. Sit in the center; sit as we do. Face the instructor."

A circle of white light appeared at the center of the triangle. Naero walked over and sat down in it, facing Klyne. Her skin barely began to tingle.

A wider ring of similar light appeared, including the instructor and his two adepts.

Every hair on Naero's body went stiff with electric force.

"You have chosen to come before the circle of Spacer Mystics to be tested for Mystic training. Speak your name."

"Naero Amashin Maeris."

"You agree to be tested?"

"I do."

"I am Klyne, the instructor. My assistants are Adept Iselle, and Adept Makita. We shall refer to you as Adept Candidate Naero. Follow our instructions. Respond only if asked to respond. If you require any medical attention, it will be administered at the end of the testing. Until then, you are expected to endure and continue to do your best. If you understand, say yes."

"Yes."

"The training will begin. Defend yourself."

Without warning, Makita's attack smashed into her.

She blocked one or two out every four or five blows.

A snapwheel kick sent her flying twenty meters, nearly winding her.

The only things that saved her at all, once again, were the experience and knowledge she gained from her training sessions with Baeven.

Makita proved stronger and faster than her, but he still paled in comparison to the outcast's terrifying prowess.

Makita charged her.

Naero met him part way.

She took several punishing strikes, but flipped him hard to the ground.

He swept her legs.

They tangled on the ground, wrestling, slipping out of holds, twisting like snakes. They pummeled each other all the while.

They broke, crouched low, and launched themselves at each other again, like Telurian fighting blue cranes.

Naero landed a whipkick on the side of Makita's head.

He clipped her under the chin, grabbed her leg and ankle and swung her hard into the floor, stunning her.

She struggled to get up.

For a few dizzy moments, she couldn't.

She rose up and staggered back into her fighting stance.

She half-smiled.

"Come on."

Makita bowed his head, just slightly, and drew back.

"Defend yourself, "Klyne said again.

Naero whirled to face Iselle.

Too late.

An invisible force slammed into her arms and torso, flinging her back.

She rolled with the strike and came back up into her stance.

Iselle fought her from a distance, punching and striking with her hands in rapid combinations.

Naero struggled to advance, to close the distance between them, while heavy, unseen blows rained down on her from every direction, knocking her one way, and then the other.

"Telekinetic combat," Klyne called out. "Try to sense and block the blows. You cannot see them. Reach out with your battle senses, with your mind. Feel them coming. Counter and deflect them. True masters can fight thus, without even moving, simply by concentrating."

At least Iselle still had to physically move in order to project her attacks. That was some help.

Closer. Get closer.

Iselle thrust both hands forward violently.

A wall of force drove Naero slowly back. She pushed against it, slowing it even more.

"Resist. Focus on the energy before you," Klyne told her, "before it smashes you into the far wall. Fight back. Defeat it."

She rolled to one side and then the other. The barrier felt solid.

Naero leaped up four meters, felt the top, and flipped herself over it.

Iselle withdrew a step, cupping both hands loosely on the sides of her face.

Spinning orbs of pure telekinetic force shot out, rapid-fire.

Naero barely perceived them where they warped through the air; they made explosive popping sounds.

She tried to dodge them. One whirred past her head like an invisible ball at high speed.

The next clipped her left shoulder, spinning her aside.

Another knocked one leg out from under her.

She kept her feet and ducked, weaving to either side in turns.

Iselle directed her attack at Naero's feet.

Naero lost her footing, slipping and sliding on what felt like a bunch of invisible ball bearings cast beneath her.

She tried to roll back to her feet, but panes of force battered her from all sides, keeping her off balance.

It felt like being a rubber ball, bouncing around in a box that someone shook.

The sides of the box rapidly closed in.

They tightened all around her, threatening to crush her.

She couldn't breathe.

Iselle released her without warning.

Naero sprawled, gasping, face down on the floor.

"I'm somewhat surprised," Klyne noted. "Preliminary tests demonstrate no psyonic aptitude or innate talent to my trained senses whatsoever. That in itself is very rare. After your battle with the former

Danner entity, we simply assumed that you would exhibit some kind of psyonic ability."

"I burned myself out dealing with the entity. I burned both of us out. I'm a nud once more." She admitted it openly. "None of my former abilities have returned."

So she wasn't psyonic anymore. Not even a teknomancer. Disappointing, but not the end of the universe.

"Yet I sense something incredibly strange within you," Klyne said. "What could it be?"

Was it Om? He was still inside her somewhere. He had not emerged again either.

"Take your place at the center of us once more. Face me again."

Naero did so, resisting an urge to massage several bruises.

Klyne positioned himself directly in front of her, sitting lotus fashion just like her and the others.

"I'm going to attempt to merge directly with your mind telepathically, one of my gifts. I'm also an Auralcognitor. Once I link with your mind, I can sense any type of psyonic energy field you might have, active, passive, or latent. I might even be able to trigger or bring them out to the surface. There might be some discomfort. Shall we proceed?"

"Sure."

"Do as I do. I will show you how to place your hands to effect the mind merge."

Klyne cupped his left hand firmly behind the base of her skull.

Naero followed his lead.

He placed the fingers of his right hand on precise spots on her face.

Thumb on her forehead, directly between her eyes.

Index finger on her left temple.

The next two fingers curled slightly in front of her left ear. His smallest finger hooked at the point of her ear and jaw.

As soon as Naero placed her right hand the same way, she gasped slightly.

Thin hairs of what felt like burning hot energy threaded their way slowly through the layers of her awareness.

She could feel Klyne connecting with her thoughts, joining their two minds.

The dull ache continued to grow.

"You should be feeling the initial discomfort. Hold still. Keep focusing. Almost there. Almost..."

A spike of pure agony exploded within her skull.

Naero screamed, transfixed as if by lightning.

Through the torment, a voice awoke in her mind full-force.

Protocols unlocked and engaged. We...are.

Interface...partial.

Om awoke, reacting instinctively with fear and vast power.

Threat detected...Protect all access.

Neural net...INTRUSION. UNWARRANTED.

LEVEL 1.359 DEFENSIVE RESPONSE.

An intense blast wave of white-hot psyonic energy fanned out rapidly from the epicenter of her immolated mind.

Naero continued to scream.

As if far away in the distance, Klyne and his two adepts also shrieked.

Naero blinked, her eyes and mouth frozen open.

She lay with her head to one side, in a puddle of her own mixed blood and spittle.

More pain struck her when she attempted to move.

Blood continued to stream from her eyes, ears, nose, and mouth–a bloody mess.

It felt as if a fusion grenade had blown her head open.

She reached up with her hands, to make sure her skull was still intact.

Some kind of noise.

Warning alarms sounded.

A ship. Yes, they were on a ship. The Spacer Intel Ship *The Kathmandu*. She was...being tested, for the Mystics.

Something had gone terribly wrong.

Naero focused, getting to her hands and knees.

She heard other voices, groaning and whimpering.

Makita lay sprawled in a broken tangle, blasted across the room. His gray clothing had been shredded and scorched into tatters. He choked and coughed.

To the other side, Iselle fared little better. She lay convulsing, blasted, scorched, a yellow-white bone of her forearm sticking out of her wrenched flesh. One side of her face was blistered, her red hair burned, some of it still smoking. She trembled and shuddered in pain and terror.

Naero looked around for Klyne, and found the instructor in a burned, bloody heap, lying beneath a dark red smear on the far wall. His hands were charred black, and he was missing fingers.

Naero could not walk. She couldn't even stand. She crawled to Klyne as quickly as she could.

He still lived, just barely.

Then she noticed the intense effects of the blast, all around the room, less than a meter up.

A massive expanding ring of Cosmic force had sliced into the duranadium hull of the smartwalls, punching a deep crease right through them where they buckled, all along its full diameter.

The force of the strike disrupted all systems. The entire training room was compacted, crushed, and heavily damaged.

Rescuers struggled to force their way through the various ruined doors and access panels.

Mergeworld

Book One

Mergeworld 1 Amazon Link: http://amzn.to/1uboBDC

by Mason Elliott & Garan R. R. Faraday

David Pritchard woke up gasping from one nightmare and went straight into another. A terrible agony tore through him as if the universe twisted him inside out.

Then he snapped back again.

What in damnation had just happened? Something…was very wrong.

Startled, groggy, it only took an instant for his bleary mind to figure it out.

Flames engulfed the front of his college apartment building. The stench of smoke, and the sounds of screams and breaking glass outside, only confirmed it.

He felt dazed, and blinked his scratchy eyes. The first thing he instinctively reached out for was the framed picture of his dead parents.

That was the last picture he had of them, taken a few years back, right after he started college in South Bend.

They hugged and smiled at each other in medieval garb at the Bristol Renaissance Faire up in Wisconsin. The picture froze both of them happily in time, retired in their forties. Unlike many parents that age, they weren't divorced and they still loved one another. One of their Ren-Faire pals had taken that picture for them on their digital camera.

The same camera retrieved from the car accident on the Illinois highway on their way back home from Bristol. A tractor-trailer jackknifed in the heavy rain and took them away.

The same weekend David begged off going with them.

He had blown that picture up in Photoshop, printed out an 8 x 10, and bought a nice oak frame for it. He kept it with him wherever he went. He'd die before he'd part with it, fire or no.

All that history and pain flashed through David as he clutched their picture close to him in the dark. He didn't even have to see it, just cling to it in his hands. That picture always sat prominently behind his small alarm clock on his night stand with his smart phone and wallet while he slept. That was how he found it, even in the semi-dark. He also grabbed his phone and wallet.

His clock normally flashed bright green. Power outage, probably from the fire. And the backup battery must have gone dead. Light switches? Nothing, of course, due to the fire.

The growing reek of smoke triggered his desire for self-preservation. Once he got out, he could call his friend Mason Tyler, who lived in a duplex over on Allen Street. His buddy Mace would help him.

Somewhat more awake now, David struggled not to panic. He staggered out of his room like a robot. His lanky, five-eleven frame stumbled down the hall toward his front door. He stubbed his little toe hard in the darkness. A second later, he grunted and cursed the sudden blinding spread of pain, but kept moving.

Oh, hell. No way out the front.

Dangerous ribbons of smoke curled violently through the metal front door frame and snaked up across the ceiling like an upside-down waterfall. The paint of the metal fire door already bubbled and blistered. David choked and swallowed hard.

If that door had been wood, his entire apartment might have already been completely engulfed. He might not have even come to. He saw no sense in touching the steaming door knob.

The apartment building stairs acted like a natural chimney, funneling the fire and heat straight up.

A window—climb out a window. He was only on the second floor.

His three richer roomies were already off on spring break for the next week, to the Bahamas or some such. Their parents could afford such junkets. David could not.

He suddenly realized two very important things. First, the fire hadn't spread to the back part of the apartment building yet.

Next, he was only wearing navy boxers and a gray T-shirt over his shaking frame.

Early April in South Bend, Indiana, could be any weather from sun and sixties to a flippin' blizzard.

Clothes. Only seconds to throw some on. Even in the dim, flickering orange light spilling out of the thick curtains, he spotted his laundry basket on the couch.

The smoke in the living room grew thicker. He put his precious picture, smartphone, and wallet down for only a few moments.

Jeans. On. Socks. On. He snatched up his thick blue, gold, and green hoodie from the back of the old couch where he usually left it, and pulled into its soft, warm comfort. Stocking cap. Popped on his head. Wool scarf. Around the neck. He sat down and jammed on his old gray Nike running shoes, feeling a pair of thin gloves and keys in his hoodie pockets still when he bent over.

Ready to ride, or, at least, climb out the back window to escape burning to death.

He stuffed his folks' picture, wallet, and smartphone into his dark green Jansport backpack with his pad, gel pens, and a few books. He zipped it all up.

To the back window. He pulled the curtains aside and yanked the big panel open.

He jumped slightly at the sight of some guy who had already climbed down the back of the building from the third floor. Their eyes locked, only a window screen between them in the dim, pre-dawn light and the cold morning air.

The guy looked utterly terrified.

"Watch out!" he warned, trying to keep his voice low. "Those things are killing people. They're everywhere!"

"What things?" What was this guy freaking out about?

The guy jolted, wide-eyed, and then choked.

A bloody iron arrowhead jutted out the front of his throat. In the time it took them both to blink, another arrow punched through the front of his chest, out of his T-shirt. The poor guy's mouth gaped and worked. Then his eyes rolled up white. He fell backwards, head down.

David grabbed for him but missed, his hands blocked by the barrier of the screen. He tore it away and stuck his head out the window.

He spotted strange movement down in the darkness.

Two dark, twisted, hunched-over figures loped in on bandy legs and clawed feet wrapped in fur and rags. They were smaller than humans, about four to five feet tall, and very skinny and wiry.

Whatever they were, they were definitely not human.

One of them slit the dead guy's throat from ear to ear with a long, wicked-looking rusty knife.

Blood spurted bright black in the night.

The other creature sniffed the air and snarled up at David with a greenish-black, twisted, inhuman face. Long pointed ears stuck out of holes in its ragged hood. It had a big warty nose, and gleaming green eyes. It gave full draw to the same kind of short, black bow of jagged horn that the other one carried.

The creature took dead aim at David.

And fired.

Mergeworld 1 Amazon Link: http://amzn.to/1uboBDC

Mergeworld

Book Two

Amazon Link for *Mergeworld: Book Two*: http://amzn.to/1neuq0x

by Mason Elliott and Garan R. R Faraday

"Several of the enemy mage prisoners have escaped," a runner came to warn them. The young trooper looked terrified.

Mason drew his Spillers. They would have to be enough. After the bath, he didn't have all of his other guns. And there wasn't time to go after them.

It also worried him that he still felt–off his game, somehow. Something was still very wrong with him, but he couldn't figure out what. Perhaps that was merely what sorrow and depression felt like.

Blondie shook the terrified runner. "Calm down. Tell me what you know. Which prisoners? How many of them?"

"S-six, six, I think. They tried to free the rest, but the guards on the scene shot two down. Then the enemy mages fled this way, and started killing everyone they could find with magic."

Troops screamed, and close by to the west, magic blasts went off, and the sounds of battle and further bursts of magical rapidly sped their way.

The runner continued to stammer, "The tall n-n-necromancer is leading them. Five others. I don't know their names. As soon as they broke out, the duty officer sent me after you two and the Thul woman."

Blondie let the runner go. "Try to find the Thul. Go. Keep spreading the alarm."

"Yes, s-sir!" The young runner looked only too happy to keep running.

"They're coming for us, aren't they, Blondie?" Mason asked, hefting his Spillers.

Blondie clenched both fists, and violet magefire flared up to his elbows. "Yep. Just like I said they would. How do you want to do this, Mace?"

"Hmmm…too many to hit them head on. Let's go at them from the flanks. I'll hit them on the left."

His blond friend nodded. "Then I'll take them on the right. The necromancer's going to be the toughest of the lot. Let's peel off the other five, if we can, and then take him on together."

"Sounds good, Blondie. Let's ride."

They skirted around to either side, trying to stick to cover and stay out of sight. Mason quickly lost sight of his friend.

It did briefly occur to him that this would be an excellent time for Blondie to turn on them all, and help the mages make good their escape. But at this point, Mason had no choice but to keep trusting his good friend.

Blondie said that his abilities were returning.

He could tell them anything he wanted. How would they know if it was the truth or not?

From the sounds of things, the militia troops were putting up a pretty good fight and delaying the enemy at least somewhat. Each precious second they could hold them back, more troops would pour in.

Yet even as Mason got into position to attack, the enemy mages continued to push through, causing death and destruction all around them, and leaving many casualties in their wake.

Startled troops could slow the enemy down, but they would be hard pressed to stop six enemy mages bent on a rampage of devastation.

They were lucky that it wasn't all thirteen of the mage captives on the loose.

At Blondie's urging, Major Bill had spread several of the captive mages out to other nearby, secret locations–beyond the limited range of their prisoners' telepathy.

Mason spotted the enemy. The necromancer strode out in front with another sorcerer. A pair of enemy wizards marched slightly behind them on either side, guarding their flanks and watching the rear.

Blondie stepped up and raked the enemy left and the middle with violet lightning that knocked four of the six off their feet, and stunned the two flankers.

The first flanker on the other side turned to attack Blondie. The second one raised his hands and his eyes got big when he saw the Pistolero step out and aim both of his pistols.

Click! Click!

Nothing. Mason's guns wouldn't fire. He cocked and pulled the triggers again.

Nothing.

By then the one mage was charging Blondie, exploding anything that was made of wood around him. He sent the shards and splinters and whirling debris at Blondie, while the necromancer and the other sorcerer still looked dazed and tried to regain their feet. And the mage facing Mason shot greenish-yellow flames out of his hands at all before him.

Mason dove out of the way, tucked and rolled out of sight, and then crouched and ran. The enemy wizard would be on him in seconds.

Finally he came to a building and ducked inside. He scrambled out of sight into an adjoining back storage room and ducked down. He tried his guns again. Still nothing. Why was this happening,? Now of all times?

Blondie needed him out there.

Maybe if he reloaded. Yeah, that would do it.

Slowing his breathing, doing his best to stay calm, he broke out his spare cylinders for his guns and swapped them out. He was fast at it, but every second counted.

He went back out into the fight. As he expected, the fighting quickly turned Blondie's way, and blasts of magic nearby showed where the foes were pursuing Blondie hard and blasting everything around him. Blondie fought back as best he could, but from what Mason could tell, his friend was outnumbered four to one.

He raced that way, not even trying to stay under cover this time. He had to catch up quickly, and take them from behind, if possible.

Mason sped around a building and almost slammed into the same enemy mage as before. This one seemed to be holding back and protecting the rear of the other three while they stalked Blondie.

Mason had intended to shoot them on sight, but he clobbered the mage from behind now that he was right on top of him. The mage grunted and dropped, unconscious.

Pistol-whipping worked better in this instance. Mason dragged the mage back out of sight and quickly gagged him, and bound his hands and ankles behind him.

At this distance, Mason would not have any trouble taking out the other three with one or two shots, once he spotted them again. And their spells gave them away when they fired. Hopefully, Blondie was staying ahead of them.

Mason rushed forward once more, spotted several troops closing in with bows and crossbows, and motioned for them to go around and close in from one side or the other.

Finally he spotted the necromancer and the one wizard, crouched down and making plans of some kind.

Mason took aim at them with both barrels.

Click. Click.

Crap, not again. What the hell was going on?

Even worse, the necromancer turned and locked eyes with him.

"There's the other one. Let's get him!" All of their hands glowed with magefire.

Mason turned and ran for it. Dark lightning and exploding ice covered the area he had just been in.

His foes were right after him. Archers tried to fire upon the mages, but they swept the troops away from their positions with blasts of power.

A stone or outcropping of brick caught the toe of Mason's boot. He hurtled down upon his face, and tried to roll back up to his feet.

The third enemy mage stepped out right in front of Mason.

Now, the three of them had him fairly trapped.

"Kill him!" the necromancer roared.

The wizard still hesitated an instant. Then he prepared a spell, his hands beginning to glow brighter and brighter.

They were only a dozen or so feet away. Mason hurled his useless pistols at the wizard.

One missed as the fellow dodged to one side.

The other smacked him squarely in the face and dazed and bloodied him.

Mason expected to be cut down from behind by the other two enemies any second.

He glanced back just as the two stood ready to unleash their spells.

Amazon Link for *Mergeworld: Book Two*: http://amzn.to/1neuq0x

Please enjoy the following teaser from The Citation Series, Book 1, *Naero's War:*
The Annexation War

THE
ANNEXATION
WAR

Annexation War Amazon Link: *http://amzn.to/1gmxGQk*

by Mason Elliott

Naero's flagship, *The Hippolyta,* was one of the latest, Dromon Class dreadnaughts. These warships were fashioned out of dense, iron-nickel planetoids, not less than half a kilometer in diameter. Incredibly tough and rugged on their own.

It took the most powerful mining plasma-borers–working in precise conjunction with construction fixers and an army of teks–months to hollow out armored crew quarters, lift and transport tubes, launching and loading bays. Next came space for power cores, sublight engines, jump drives, backups, gravitics, life support, sensor arrays, communications, navigation, weapons, main bridge and backup bridge.

Set in the exact heart of *The Hippolyta* were its signature big guns. A quad of the largest production guns ever constructed on any ship of war: Four, *16 meter*, rapid-fire, particle beam cannons.

Cannons any larger than that exploded, melted, or otherwise were not feasible within the limits of current tek and materials. Thirty-six secondary batteries, assorted specialized weapons and gun emplacements, and forty-five advanced fighters.

Seven hundred and forty able crew, including a full Rifle Company of two hundred and forty Spacer Marines, and all of their equipment, vehicles, and gear for ship's security and rapid response deployment. Strike Fleet Six's Marines came from the 3rd Spacer Marine Division–known as *The Death Eyes*–because of their superb snipers and their overall, excellent marksmanship ratings. Marines made up a third of the warship's complement.

Their motto: *If We Can See It...We Can Kill It!*

The main bridge was a massive armored dome constructed on top of the dreadnaught's big metal, rough-hewn orb, protected by heavy blast doors, and the latest, most advanced shielding in the fleet. Within, the circular bridge was laid out in four levels under the huge dome, a dome sixty meters high.

Each bridge tier was separated by the height of a few steps from one to the next. The inner three levels could rotate in any direction, independent of the others.

The fleet captain's command nanochair and station occupied the highest tier. Each bridge station had its own secondary shielding, in case enemy fire penetrated the shields, the blast screens, and the hull.

In combat, bridges were routinely targeted, for obvious reasons.

From that primary vantage point, the strike fleet captain could direct battles in three hundred and sixty degrees, through an advanced, battleholo display surrounding her, full zoom data-feeds, constantly updated by battle AIs. Naero could manipulate the displays by nanosensors programmed into the fingertips of her nanosuit gloves.

The battle display system also recognized her voice pattern, and would respond to voice commands, or commands punched in manually through pads on her command chair, or via other backups.

The next bridge level down from hers held the secondary bridge stations: Helm, Weapons, Communications, Navigation, and Scanning, spaced out equally along their ring.

The third ring held all of the twelve tertiary bridge stations, that monitored, controlled, and coordinated all of the ship's other important functions:

Engineering
Gravitics
Life Support
Power Supply
Security
Shields
Medical
Jump and Sub-light Drives
Damage Control
Alliance Fleet and Intel Communications
Main Computer
Launching Bays

The fourth ring went to the two powerlifts, leading from the bridge to the other movers, decks, and levels of the ship. All lift and access points throughout the ship were constantly guarded by two battle-ready Marines, stationed on either side.

If a warship was boarded by enemy assault craft during a battle, invaders could be cut off and eliminated between decks, before they could reach a vital area.

Today, Strike Fleet Six had a mission–a simple one.

Captain Naero Maeris and her fifty warships proceeded to probe the next system on the outer, port arcwall of the Alliance advance at Beleron-4.

A routine run. Current intel assured them to expect little or no Triaxian presence or resistance.

By any stretch of the imagination, Beleron-4 was a nothing world, in the middle of nowhere, with zero, nacha–absolutely no strategic or tactical value whatsoever.

Checking it off the list on the pacified worlds of the Alliance system-hopping schedule was more-or-less just a formality.

But it still had to be done. And Naero and her lot drew the duty at random.

So why did Naero's sense of warning go bonkers?

After they jumped in, simple three-stack, Delta-India-3 formation, the reasons for alarm grew perfectly clear.

They came in right on top of twenty Triaxian fleets of the enemy's latest warships.

And a gigantic new flagship–as huge as *The Hippolyta*–the advanced design of which did not even register as existing.

It had never been seen before.

Naero shot to her feet, kicked her command nanochair back out the way and sent it down into the nanofloor of her top-tier bridge control station.

She instantly called her battle display holos up in spinning, horizontal glowing ribbons and rings all around her.

Data relays went wild. Her fingers flashed among the highlighted screen arcs, taking control of them and their parameters.

Multiple warnings sounded, and with excellent reason.

Nothing about this was good in any way.

Haisha! Twenty enemy fleets could chop them into confetti–well before any other Alliance forces could even jump in to help.

No strategy, no formation could possibly save them against superior numbers such as these.

"All ships, full withdraw. Emergency retreat on this vector, in Charlie-Romeo-7, cone-ring formation. Shields and all weapons full front and hot. Maximize all targeting profiles on the lead attacking enemy elements–they'll be on us in seconds. Whatever happens–we fight until our carriers and some of our ships can break free and jump out behind us. Get the carriers out first!"

For a split second, everyone braced for the sheets of flame that would quickly overtake and overwhelm them.

The Annexation War Amazon Link: *http://amzn.to/1gmxGQk*

Please enjoy the following teaser from the next book in The Citation Series, Book Two:
The High Crusade

The Citation Series, Book Two
NAERO'S WAR:

THE
HIGH
CRUSADE

Amazon Link to *The High Crusade*: http://amzn.to/1DbFD5F

by Mason Elliott

General Walker's Marines from Bravo Command maneuvered into position under the cover of darkness using their stealth gear.

Naero agreed to slip in ahead and bait the trap, in her battlefield role as Shettana–*The Dark Angel of Death.*

Get ready, Om. The show's about to start.

I will need some time to prepare, concentrate, and focus enough of our energies in reserve, before you deplete them all.

Just get ready and keep us ready. I'm going to set our game plan in motion.

I will do all that I can to assist. Call upon me when you require me. Good hunting, Naero.

Thanks, Om.

The invaders would do anything to have a chance to destroy or capture her.

She was–in fact–the actual, literal bait, and the trap was being set for an entire invasion force of Ejjai elite, ravaging the Corps border world of Tholos-4.

No local planetary army, military, or militia had been able to stand before the horrific onslaught of the alien invaders.

The Ejjai hammered the local landers into submission with advanced artillery, orbital bombardment from Ejjai fleets, and close assault gunships and gravtanks.

Then the terrifying collection process began, and all the living, wounded, and dead were hurled into the shrieking, whining processing blades of the robotic meatships.

The horrible sounds of the meatships warred with the screams of their countless victims.

Given time, Ejjai mass cloning factories and robotic ship and weapon-building factories would also be established onworld.

The murdering bastards had already wiped three major cities and their mixed populations off the surface of the hapless planet, before Naero and the Marines could even deploy on world.

The enemy left those lost cities little more than red, blackened, burning scars and stains that could be viewed from orbit.

Nothing left alive.

Ejjai hyaenanoids loved carrion.

Every man, woman, and child of any kind, species, or age that the enemy captured was routinely tortured, killed, and processed into rotting ration blocks in the horrific, robotic meatships of the invading aliens. That included any sentients, pets, livestock—anything and everything that was meat.

The meatblock rations were only frozen to keep them from breaking down, and decaying completely.

Hatred was too gentle a word for what most humans felt for the Ejjai invaders and their extreme methods. Spacers, landers, and each of the other known races that encountered the Ejjai quickly learned to feel the same way.

This vile, uplifted, intrusive and opportunistic species needed to be completely exterminated, wherever it was encountered.

The invaders proved that they were incapable of co-existing with any other living things.

The Ejjai could only dominate, torture, and destroy all life that they encountered, anything they could sink their teeth and claws into. Uplifting them, and giving them advanced weapons and starships had only turned them into a galactic abomination, an interstellar menace, a virulent plague.

An utter nightmare.

One that needed to end for the poor people of Tholos-4.

Naero and her Marine allies were here to see to that.

It was amusing that the Ejjai always saw themselves as invincible, the supreme warriors.

Shettana and Bravo Command quickly intended to disavow the foe of such jaded notions, time and time again.

The Marines of Bravo Commander were the textbook picture of professional warriors. A legend among all the known systems.

Naero loved serving with the elite of the elite. Together they made a fantastic team.

Even the Ejjai had learned grudgingly to fear them from their initial engagements, and the proof was there.

Every invader force that came up against Bravo Command had been completely wiped out–in record time. And then Bravo quietly packed up and headed on to the next world, ready to do it all over again.

The enemy struggled to halt the Spacer advance and throw it back.

They tried everything they could think of.

Increased enemy numbers.

Different tactics.

New weapons–traps and tricks of many different kinds.

The Ejjai generals turned themselves inside out trying to find a solution–way to achieve victory against the Spacer advance.

Bravo Command slipped in and ruined the invaders' sick, twisted party, every single time.

And Shettana, The Dark Angel of Death, used all of her amazing, Mystic powers and abilities to help the Marines keep up the pressure, and drive the enemy to terror, madness, and distraction.

General Walker worked closely with Spacer Intel, always making sure his leathernecks had the latest high-tek toys, weapons, and armor that came online.

As a result, they landed an entire Marine Division on Tholos-4 and slipped into position, without the enemy even knowing they were there yet.

By the time the Spacer Fleets swept in to destroy the enemy naval forces–Bravo Command would already be implementing their plan to put the foe down hard and fast on the ground.

Three Marine infantry regiments, one artillery regiment, plus specialized units of meks, armor, and air-to-ground support.

The ghosts of Bravo Command spread the impending Shadow of Vengeance and Death over their foes like an unseen net, without any knowledge or awareness among the invaders themselves.

Bravo and Shettana prepared for another stunning series of lightning attacks.

All became poised and ready, while the heedless enemy celebrated their vile victories and atrocities.

Naero struggled to remain silent as she slipped in among the foe. Death and damnation to any invader who thought they could invade the human sectors with impunity, death, and Cosmicide.

On every world, the invader needed to be taught that bloody lesson.

Naero strode right into the belly of the beast.

Alone.

Defiant.

Confident in her skills and abilities and all of her comrades depending on her and backing her up.

Her cloaked combat armor made her virtually invisible. The Ejjai could not even smell her.

She used her gravwing to slip into the most heavily guarded command and control bunker the enemy possessed. With her skill and her tek, she could crawl upside down on the ceilings like an unseen insect.

Her miniature vidcams and audio collectors fed data to Intel in real time, covering everything she saw.

Naero's small contingent of cloaked Intel fixers and microdrones stayed close, ready to disrupt key enemy systems and communications when ready, planting microbombs and detonation devices as they went.

The Invader High Command celebrated their latest triumph with what one might expect from them–a huge, decadent, disgusting feast–held within a shielded bunker.

They set up their victory celebration within a huge underground arena, probably used by the Tholosians for some kind of urban or regional sporting event.

Ejjai got drunk on stinking, fermented grog made from human blood. They shipped it in from the meatships by the tankerful.

Under the bright lights of the hi-tek arena, tens of thousands of Ejjai feasted and celebrated their latest victories. The enemy generals praised their troops and used the huge arena vidscreens to plot out their next attacks on the three nearest Tolosian cities.

On the center of the playing field, Ejjai transports and appropriated trucks had also hauled in and dumped huge piles of human corpses from the local population for their undefeated troops to feed on.

Piles of fresh and not so fresh meat, diverted from the enemy meatships to help sate the troops in large numbers.

One of the piles was all dead children and infants.

Even worse, to Naero's horror, some of the bodies in the various meat piles were somehow still alive. They twitched or cried out in pain and terror. Some weakly attempted to crawl away, despite broken or missing limbs.

The Ejjai quickly seized them and began tormenting them even further, laughing hysterically at the sport. They stabbed, cut, and skinned them alive—or otherwise got creative.

As Ejjai were wont to do.

Ejjai were among the vilest, most disgusting creatures Naero had even encountered.

She resisted the very strong impulse to cut loose on them right then and there.

But she couldn't—not yet.

These monsters needed to die. Every single one of them.

And very soon, she would have a direct hand in launching the attack that would accomplish just that.

The timing had to be just right, so she steeled herself.

The generals. Reach the generals and stay ready.

Six Ejjai generals held court like warlords at huge tables overflowing with comconsoles, sensor stations, map screens, and piles of loot. And the bloody remains of horrific, eviscerated meals.

All Ejjai clone troops were female. Smaller male Ejjai concubines were kept around on leashes for fun, for the leaders. They even dressed them in human clothing and poorly fitting human lingerie.

As an oddity, one of the generals even had a human male dressed up as a concubine. But the poor guy apparently had to be kept in a heavily guarded pen off to one side—to keep all of the other Ejjai from devouring and murdering him, most likely in that order.

Naero circled around the generals and studied the arena, trying to devise the best way to take them all down.

She listened intently to the plans the enemy generals were making, feeding it all to Intel.

"So, are all of the atomics and genocide devices in place yet?"

Another general pulled up a mapscreen displaying all of their installation of such devices planet wide.

Naero instantly transmitted all of that data directly to Spacer Intel as well—priority alert.

Intel and Bravo Command were most likely already neutralizing the most vital elements of the enemy plot. These genocide devices could be scanned and located from orbit. But it was always good to be sure, and to know their exact locations.

The Ejjai generals scoffed. "We will be ready for anything the enemy can throw at us in less than a day," one of the other Ejjai generals boasted.

"They won't know what's going to hit them until it's too late."

"Good, very good. Speed things up if you can. Get it all up and ready."

"Don't worry, sir. We will be more than ready to deal with their so-called Bravo Command—and their spack witch."

All of the Ejjai generals had a good laugh and congratulated each other.

The lead general stepped up to a waiting podium and addressed the crowd.

"Great news, sisters! We have it on good authority that the spacks are sending their precious Bravo Command and their spack witch Shettana against us."

Lots of cursing and booing about that roared up.

Their lead general continued. "This time, we are more than ready for them!"

Huge rounds of applause to that.

"Let me just say that we have some heavy duty surprises of our own ready and waiting and in store for our enemies. We can't wait for them to get here—and have them all for dinner!"

That brought an even bigger round of cheering, cursing, and applause.

"We will engage the spacks in a matter of days, and with our increased numbers and new weapons—I say we're going to kick their asses and stomp them bloody. We will gut them! I want all my girls out there to feast on spack Marine flesh until you puke!"

Further rounds of cheering and vile responses.

"We will ferment their blood in our huge vats and get drunk on it!"

More horrendous rounds of cheering and applause.

"And once we have captured their filthy spack witch, all of you will watch as I personally cut her up and rape her with red-hot knives, and torture her to death over the course of an entire week. She'll sing to all of us with her screams. Then I myself will feast upon her guts, and eat her heart while the light in her eyes fades. I'll crack her skull open and eat her brains!"

The Ejjai went crazy.

"Wait until we post *that* on the webnets for the spacks and the skinners to watch! I promise you victory. We cannot be defeated. And we will sweep the human skinners and all the other inferior races into our meatships and out of all existence. They are our prey! Yet another galaxy that shall fall to us and our mighty masters!"

More about their mysterious masters. Interesting.

Furious cheering continued in waves.

"So my warriors. Feast on meat until you vomit, and then feast some more. Then prepare for battle as we crush our foes and ravage the rest of this world. We shall drown it all in blood and swim in it! Prepare for our ultimate victory! Our time has come. None can stand against us!"

They erupted in an orgy of celebration and vile gluttony.

Fights broke out among the meat piles, and the Ejjai fought with and murdered each other in their frenzy.

The lead general returned to the others, rubbing her claws together eagerly in the midst of the chaos.

"My sisters, I have a special treat that I've saved just for us, at this exact moment. Please, enjoy my precious gifts to you all." She motioned to a large knot of troops off to one side among some gravtanks.

A full squad of Ejjai in heavy battle armor led out six terrified human women, all of them naked, and extremely pregnant.

None of them had a mark on them. Yet.

But from the looks on their pale faces, they all knew very well what the enemy generals intended to do with them. Each of them was heavy with child in the later stages of pregnancy.

That they had remained unspoiled and unharmed up until now would quickly change for the worse–the worst fate imaginable.

Although they were unbound, there was no chance for any of these captives to break free or escape on their own against so many foes.

The generals each glared at them and gloated. The Ejjai generals slavered and drooled, snapping jaws and smacking lips.

Each general had a set of rusty, bloodstained butchering tools that they began to place out in front of them in heady, eager anticipation of their coming feast.

Then the squad of Ejjai troops guarding the six women suddenly staggered a few feet away as if drunk.

Some melted into slag where they stood.

Other Ejjai troops exploded.

The six human captives looked around in confusion.

The next instant, they all vanished.

The six Ejjai generals shot to their feet in stunned surprise.

They couldn't even speak, but a few flung cleavers and knives at the spot where the captives had stood.

Their weapons fell harmlessly to the ground.

All of this was captured and displayed on the big arena screens, and slowly attracted the attention of the astonished crowds.

Then Shettana appeared as if by magic, right before the lead Ejjai general, resplendent in her full Angel of Death mode. She was all dressed in black, shining black hair flowing in the wind, violet eyes burning above her mask.

Twin blood-red katanas crackled and hissed in the damp air, at the ready in either hand.

Every eye fixed on her–while the mini-gravpods from her fixers whisked the six cloaked, female captives away to safety.

Naero only had to buy few more seconds for them to make it out. Fierce Marines waited nearby to take charge of them and keep them safe.

With the six captives out of the way, at last Shettana could go to work.

"I have come for you, filthy Ejjai cowards. I am Shettana!" she cried.

She rammed both of her swords through the lead general's eyes and out the back of the Ejjai's scorched skull.

Two of the generals tried to run.

The other three tried to attack her.

It did not matter.

Bolts of scarlet lighting tore forth from both her blades, ripping and blasting the other five into charred pieces of meat and bone.

Naero cloaked and shot away, as the area around the tables was engulfed in torrents of enemy weapon fire the very next instant.

Then the gravtanks, gunships, transports and other vehicles lined up nearby began to explode.

Naero projected multiple holos of herself all over the arena and in the in the air, drawing fire in all directions.

She used *the voice*, her words booming and echoing from several directions.

"EJJAI FILTH. PREPARE TO MEET DEATH. FOR SHETTANA IS THE DARK ANGEL OF DEATH, AND HAS NO FEAR OF MURDERING COWARDS."

The Ejjai fired in panic from so many angles that they cut down each other by the hundreds–just as Naero planned.

Fear began to infect them.

Gouts of red lightning lashed into the arena stands from several directions like gigantic whips of destruction. The devastation flung dead and dying Ejjai everywhere in a cyclone of slaughter, adding to the total chaos and confusion.

"NO MERCY, EJJAI SCUM. NO ESCAPE. FEAR IS MY MOTHER, DEATH MY SIRE, AND I THEIR DAUGHTER! YOU CANNOT HARM ME. THERE IS NO ESCAPE FOR YOU!"

Just as the enemy started to figure out they were shooting at holos and murdering each other wholesale, Naero merged with one in her mirror images in the midst of hundreds of Ejjai in the arena stands.

Multiple thin rods of red Chaos energy shot out from her, fanning in a diameter of thirty meters.

First she impaled hundreds of the shocked invaders.

When she spun, the red blades chopped them all into smaller gory chunks and pieces.

Torrents of unleashed Ejjai blood suddenly gathered and swept down the arena, carrying others away in a sudden red rushing tide of gore.

Naero cloaked and flashed away again.

More enemy fire stormed and tore at her former position.

She took the place of another holo, and sent forth a sweeping hurricane of of Chaos bubbles and orbs of every shape and size into another section of the stands.

The explosions collapsed that entire section. Wreckage toppled inward.

Next she appeared on the field before the horrendous meat piles, in the midst of hundreds of more frantic enemies.

Half of them flung their weapons away and ran in terror before her as she raced toward them. So much for the valiant Ejjai.

"STAND AND FIGHT, SCUM!"

Naero surged and fought with the mob of foes, sweeping one way and then the other, cutting them down by dozens, by scores.

She moved among them so fast they could not focus their attacks.

Then she would abruptly change direction and sweep another way before they could hem her in.

She unleashed more scarlet lightening strikes.

She sent random Chaos blasts into packed pockets of foes.

At times she just whirled and passed through them with her swords fully extended, mowing them down in lines and bunches.

Once she had shattered them completely, she merely turned her back on them and began walking away quickly and with determination, toward the nearest exit.

Naero set her shield pod full on.

Three enemy tanks roared at her, cannons blazing.

Naero dodged and deflected their blasts into the stands.

Two gravtanks she exploded with Chaos bombs.

The last she sliced the last in half with her swords and kept walking calmly, straight through the burning wreckage as the gravtank exploded directly behind her to either side.

She ignored all enemy fire directed at her, kept walking, and cut down anything stupid enough to attempt to stand before her.

She crackled with destroying red lightning as she passed into one of the exit tunnels, laying waste to anything before her.

The enemy regrouped and poured into the tunnel in hot pursuit.

Just as Naero hoped they would.

Another kill zone. How convenient of them to all bunch up for her.

She turned at bay, just before exiting, and focused all of her energies in an intense Chaos blast cone.

The massive detonation tore the tunnel apart and blasted shredded pieces of the packed invaders out the other end, right before a massive fireball that followed hard thereafter.

Naero cloaked, and called out over her secure link.

"You guys ready? I've got them primed, but I'm also almost out of juice."

"We're in place and ready to join the show, Shettana. You okay? Do you need us to extract you?"

"Negative. I can finish my part. It just takes a lot of energy to sustain attacks at this level. You guys know that. Did Intel take care of those genocide devices?"

"Almost all accounted for."

"All right, I'm setting up for my final show. They'll take the bait, all right. You guys hit them hard when they do."

"Hard as we can, Shettana. You know us."

"I sure do, and I can't wait to watch it all go down–right from the front row. Copy that. Make the legends proud, Bravo."

She took up her position in the center of the fallen city nearby, just outside of the shattered arena.

She formed a Chaos construct around her that duplicated her and her every move.

Her construct became a scarlet, giant version of herself, semi-transparent and fifteen meters tall, red and glowing with huge blazing swords.

She stomped on a meat ship and slashed at it until it exploded.

Then she attacked the clone ship factory next to it.

"FACE ME, COWARDS. SHETTANA SHOWS YOU HER MIGHT. SHOW ME YOURS. FACE ME AND PERISH!"

Yet in actuality, her energies waned with each passing second.

It wasn't like being back on Janosha where there was limitless Cosmic energy to tap into. Away from the Mystic Homeworlds, Naero's energy levels and her abilities were not infinite or limitless. She made a good show of it, but even she could not sustain these levels of attacks for very long.

The entire enemy invasion roared to life , and locked on, bunching and sweeping her way, to engage her from all directions.

The Ejjai went insane with fury.

Up in the skies above and beyond Tholos-4, the Spacer navy sent the invader fleets spinning down in flames.

Thousands of Spacer Marines suddenly materialized out of the black at key points and positions.

Phantoms who owned the night.

The black was their domain, their element, and they surrendered it to no one.

Bravo Command unleashed a torrent of concentrated, interlocking fire against the bunched up invaders. Veils of destroying fire, artillery, and ordnance–a deluge of precisely timed destruction that no living thing could possibly survive.

Within a matter of minutes, a quarter of a million Ejjai invaders flashed and flared into a sweeping typhoon of white-hot death that overtook them.

Naero had done her job.

Completely drained of all her mystic energies for the moment, she could barely stand.

Even as she staggered away, a full platoon of gigantic Sterodans in phaze armor appeared all around her.

They piled on and overwhelmed her with their greater mass, and several shock charges that hit and rippled through both them and her. The shock charges rattled Naero's teeth in her skull.

The Ejjai and their mysterious masters still wanted her and the KDM alive and intact, apparently.

Naero grinned.

Yet another trap, and she had stumbled right into it.

This time, the enemy thought they had her at last.

Yet Naero knew something they did not, and called out into her own mind.

Om–you're up. They've got me.

Take these bastards down hard and fast!

Amazon Link for *The High Crusade*: http://amzn.to/1DbFD5F

Please enjoy the following teaser from the next Spacer Clans Adventure, Book 3:

NAERO'S FURY

NAERO'S FURY

Naero's Fury Amazon Link: http://amzn.to/1hLrPpO

by Mason Elliott

Naero still hadn't done it much, but going into a direct trance to enter the Astral Plane shouldn't be all that difficult. Master Vane had shown her how once. And she had gone there lots of times in her sleep, in her mind, to speak with Khai, using their astral crystals.

Before her friend Khai had vanished without a trace.

Yet she had never been completely trained in astral travel, and didn't know that much about exploring or moving around. Master Vane had taken her there once, just to teach her the basics and give her his marker. Many other times later to spar with her.

If nothing else, she could probably focus on his marker and locate him.

Zhen had roused Naero and reminded her it was time. And that she and Shalaen would monitor her while she was in the astral trance.

Naero focused her mind and abilities, controlling her breathing. Remembering the little she had recently learned.

Within several minutes of focused meditation, she open her eyes and found herself floating in the Astral Miasma, the nebulae of energy. She hugged her knees to her chest in her astral form.

Om spoke to her, even more easily here than in her own mind before.

I have accessed some of the Kexxian Matrix's data files on The Astral Plane. Like everything else, they explored it quite extensively.

Om, I'm naked here. I'm not complaining–but just tell me–how do I put astral clothing on again?

You control everything here by imagination, and force of will. Concentrate on your favorite clothing and they'll appear.

That's easy.

She looked down and saw her favorite Nytex flight togs, programmed just the way she liked them.

Naero blinked, spinning and twirling in one spot, turning upside down.

Why can't I move more than a meter at a time in front of us?

You're not used to this reality. So it's not clear to you.

The air around her looked opaque. Not mist. Not smoke or vapor. And it glowed slightly with its own bluish-gray light.

In the twilight she glowed softly blue-white with her own light. From within.

"I once heard rumors that the Mystics could travel and send messages this way, but I thought it was all just a myth."

Since the other planes are entire universes within themselves, it is said, they are all nearly infinite. Thus, it is difficult to pin point any kind of location or person unless you already know them.

Naero instinctively tried to stand up, but there was nothing to stand on.

Then she recalled Master Vane's Marker, and it appeared right before her. Where she found him, she would find the other High Masters.

At least she deserved a chance to be heard by them all. To try to explain herself and her actions. What happened with the obelisk was clearly not her fault.

But they would still blame her for it–especially Mater Vane, who seemed to blame her for everything since Hashiko's death.

Naero could not simply stand by and let the High Masters decide her fate without herself being present at her trial, in some way at least.

She focused on the crimson and black star more and swept forward, seemingly at great speed.

She came to an abrupt halt, like a starship coming out of jump at its destination.

The opacity around her partially melted away. She proceeded forward, opening her visual field far wider. She made out the area around her as the miasma peeled back.

Slightly below her, she saw spheres within glowing spheres, all spinning within greater spheres.

Her own sphere, glowing white-blue, suddenly surrounded her like a glittering soap bubble.

Yet it did not pop when she poked at it.

One sphere in particular, the largest, glowed and pulsed blood red, containing a withered old man with a long beard, pacing impatiently.

Burning eyes vanished and re-appeared at random all over his bald head. The red sphere absorbed Master Vane's marker.

Was this his true form? What he really looked like?

His scarlet sphere was also flanked by two smaller spheres with figures inside them.

Om made a calculated guess.

His current guardian adepts, no doubt. The ones you rescued from the enemy Darkforce generators on Janosha.

I think so, Om.

At most times, every High Master had at least two champion adepts protecting him or her, each of them very close to mastery themselves. Just as Hashiko had been.

Naero studied Vane's new guardians for the very first time, and tried to see into their spheres.

Something about each of them did seem strangely familiar.

One of Vane's adepts, the male, appeared to be so deep dark black, he could be a singularity. This adept's sphere was flat black on the surface and barely transparent.

If Naero had been able to breathe, she would have gasped.

Instead she simply raised her hand to her mouth.

She recalled that she had seen many of these adepts long before.

In her dreams, nightmares, and crazed visions. Perhaps even on the Astral Plane somehow.

Vane's other adept was the white female, the exact opposite of the other. So brilliant and blindingly radiant, she could be a pulsar. Her orb was like a high intensity bulb, blinding and almost completely crystal clear.

It occurred to Naero that during her initial testing, Klyne had male and female assistants as well.

She couldn't guess what the significance of that pattern was all about. Perhaps just some weird Mystic, egalitarian tradition.

Then why weren't any of the High Masters female?

Everyone seemed to ignore her where she floated.

The next larger sphere, farther away, glowed silver-blue.

If she focused intently on it, she discovered she could zoom in with her third eye–her mind's eye.

Within that silver-blue sphere, a silver man sat serenely, neither young nor old. Master Tree, in his purest form of order.

Two smaller guardian spheres flanked him.

Master Tree's female adept glowed with intense blue energy in a deep blue sphere.

The male likewise glowed with vibrant green force within a green sphere, a shining sword sheathed down his broad, athletic back. He seemed very familiar somehow.

Naero did a double-take. Long blond hair. Green skin. Big glowing sword.

Yep. In the flesh–or–astral form at least.

It was Khai! She was sure of it. He was alive.

Had he actually succeeded in his great task of forging his mystic sword in the heart of a gigantic pulsar? Was that it on his back?

Naero gasped again. Now that she knew what he looked like, Khai was also the dreamy green hunk from many past, pent up nightmares. The one who kept sticking his astral sword through her head.

What did it all mean? She wasn't nuts enough yet?

Now she knew for certain she needed serious help.

And to do some serious dating at some point, once-and-for-all.

If the Mystics continued to let her live.

Khai must have sensed her inner turmoil, or thoughts, or maybe just her concentration on him.

Mr. Green-god even glanced her way for a second, looking just as confused and puzzled by her sudden appearance.

Neither of them had ever met the other in person.

Naero covered her face with one hand and looked aside, withdrawing her sphere suddenly further away.

How fricking embarrassing.

She crept forward again. Slowly.

The third and final sphere glowed golden, and contained an equally golden child within, energetic and bristling with lightning. He bounced back and forth inside like a gigantic electron.

Master Jo of course.

Two flanking spheres.

One of his adepts had no clear form, eyes gleaming within a shifting, flickering miasma like the Astral Plane itself. His female counterpart shifted shape from one fantastic creature to another.

When she suddenly made out their voices, she could sense that an intense debate had been doing on. One that still continued.

"We cannot be certain in this matter," the golden child insisted. "We do not dare act in any rash way."

"Agreed, High Master Jo," the serene silver man added. "She might yet be another Trickster from what I can tell."

"Yes. Quite possible, High Master Tree."

The old man in the blood red sphere blustered impatiently. "Fools! Always conspiring against me. Taking positions opposite of mine for no reason but to anger me. I've been telling you all along, this child is clearly the Great Destroyer–long foretold. Our duty is clear. She is a threat to all existence. To multiple dimensions. She must be eliminated, at once, before she can grow even more powerful."

"High Master Vane," Tree said. "None of us can be sure of that fact. Including you."

"I am."

"You are always certain when it comes to destroying someone," Jo added. "Your pure Chaos answer to everything. Destruction or Creation."

"It works."

"No. It doesn't. It only delays and worsens the inevitable," Tree said. "The Universe shall have its way. We all know this. You were mistaken with the last savant when he appeared, and now he remains at large—a renegade beyond even our control."

Baeven? We're they referring to her uncle?

Vane rolled his eyes. "Idiots! The Renegade is the Trickster, I say. This child must in fact be the Great Destroyer. Just look at the powers roiling within her. They will surely corrupt and overwhelm her entirely and drive her mad in the end. She will go berserk on a scale that makes her recent outbursts feeble and puny by comparison. She must perish now, while we have a chance to put an end to her. While the only crimes she has committed include destroying an entire planet, and another of the vital obelisks!"

"We still don't understand the purpose of the ancient obelisks. And we've studied the mysterious disappearance of Janosha, and we still cannot be certain in any conclusive way, that she had anything to do with it."

"Really? Who else could it be then? Planets like Janosha aren't in the habit of just obliterating themselves suddenly for no reason at all. Everywhere she goes, destruction follows!"

I cannot allow this.

Quiet, Om. Don't do anything. I'm trying to listen.

Naero…they're discussing our destruction. The Chaos Master means to destroy us.

Master Jo continued to protest. "You can't just kill off every entity that manifests Cosmic Abilities such as these. Our universe is peppered with them. We must continue to locate and guide them—not find excuses to execute them. Like the Others have told us, Tricksters often appear to oppose Great Destroyers. Without the former, final victory is never possible. "

"High Masters," Tree said. "This young woman also possesses the Kexxian Data Matrix. We cannot destroy her without destroying it. Intel and The Spacer Council of Elders value our wisdom, but even they would not agree to such action."

"Regrettable," Vane said. "Yet I cannot take the risk. I have decided this matter on my own."

"You have no such authority on your own," Tree insisted.

"Idiots! I cannot stand by and allow our galaxy—perhaps our entire universe to be destroyed—just to satisfy your foolish, philosophical, and theoretical whims."

Master Vane turned to his adepts. "My finest students, obey me. Delay these fools. Keep them occupied whilst I act for the good of all existence."

More rapid than thought, the male dark ensnared the blue sphere and its satellites in coils and tendrils of darkness. While the bright female enveloped the golden sphere and its companions in waves of of pure light.

Naero tried to pull away, but in her panic she did not know where to go.

High Master Vane sped straight at her with impossible speed.

I must act, Naero.

No, Om. Please, this is already bad enough. Don't do anything.

I cannot comply. I must defend us!

Naero went down on her hands and knees before Master Vane. She called out, using *the voice* to project her words.

"Please, Master Vane. Do not attack me. I only wish to be trained to control my abilities. I have struggled hard to do so. I still don't understand what happened with the obelisk."

Vane bore down on her, arcs of pure scarlet energy bristling around him.

"Far too late for that, monster. Nothing is ever your fault, is it? Now, you must perish for the good of all. I told you this hour would come."

Instinctively, Naero drew back again, trying to evade his attack. She rose within her receding sphere.

Vane closed in once more, gathering his powers.

"Don't do this," Naero begged. "Please. Help me. I know I can't fully control all of my abilities yet. I'm trying as hard as I can. I can't be responsible for what will happen if you attack me. I can't control myself."

"Yes, and look at the results? Countless lives crushed and eradicated. Janosha vaporized—an entire planet. You must never be allowed to reach your full potential. Now—monster—hold still and embrace your fate."

Naero put her hands out before her, holding her palms out defensively. Pleading.

"No. Don't. I can't—"

"I know, Maeris. You can't help yourself. That is why you are *an abomination!*"

Vane smashed into her, piercing all of her defenses as if they were shattering glass.

In the distance, she sensed that Master Jo and Master Tree finally broke free.

Too late.

Master Vane attacked, trying to overwhelm her with raw power.

He pummeled her with impossible blows.

In the end, he beat her up badly, but only succeeded in knocking her around once more.

Om roared in their mind.

Kexxian defense protocols unlocked and on line.

An energized, glowing armor of some advanced origin formed around Naero like a hi-tek battle suit.

Naero saw out of her third eye as it awoke and burst into radiance like a blue-white star.

Master Vane came at her once more, all of his powers focused through his primary scarlet, burning eye, centered in his forehead.

All of his other flaming eyes closed as he concentrated, his skull wreathed in weird cosmic flames like a mane of cosmic fire.

"See how powerful you have already become? No adept could have withstood those lethal attacks. We must finish this now, before the others can interfere."

"Please, Master Vane. Please–I'm begging you–please, don't do this."

"Maeris, just as I foretold–you shall fall before the greatest of all Cosmic attack techniques. And I am one of the few who have ever learned to master it: The Eye of Annihilation!"

The same Chaos technique that had destroyed Hashiko–even she couldn't control it properly.

A massive blood red beam of destroying Cosmic force shot straight at her.

It all happened so fast. Naero heard Om screaming.

Reflection defense. Analyze incoming cosmic assault. Duplicate and reflect attack tenfold!

Just before the incoming blast vaporized her, a blue-white beam shot out of her own third eye to war against Master Vane's powers.

The Cosmic flows flared intensely.

Naero screamed as if her body and soul were being sucked through the eye of a black hole's needle.

The wide blue beam quickly drove the red beam back to its source.

At the last instant, High Master Vane cried out in terror.

"Impossible! There can be no such–"

The destroying energy ignited on contact.

A massive detonation on the Astral Plane blinded the area within a few light years.

High Masters Jo and Tree barely managed to withdraw and shield the others. All of their spheres shattered.

Pure cosmic energy punched into High Master Vane right before Naero's eyes.

It drove him back like a white-hot comet.

He struggled against it with all his might.

To no avail.

The reflected attack obliterated High Master Vane to glowing ash and dust, screaming in the wake of his own annihilation.

Vane's dying force of will echoed off into the universe.

Naero would have caught her breath if she had any.

The outcome left her completely stunned for a shuddering instant.

Om...what did we just do?

We had no choice, Naero. My sole purpose is to defend our current form.

Naero stared down at her hands in terror. Tendrils of Cosmic energy rippled and still curled off of her body and her sphere like smoke.

Om...*Haisha!* We just killed a High Master of the Spacer Mystics!

Naero's Fury Amazon Link: http://amzn.to/1hLrPpO

Please enjoy this teaser for The Citation Series, Book 3:

Naero's Trial Amazon Link : http://amzn.to/1oaMNE3

NAERO'S WAR:

NAERO'S TRIAL

Naero's Trial Amazon Link: http://amzn.to/1oaMNE3

by Mason Elliott

On the third day of Naero's trial, the Prosecution and the Defense made their final, closing statements.

Master Jo spoke first, for the Defense.

"In the final analysis, I would both conclude and insist that Naero Amashin Maeris has proven herself time and time again to be an honorable Spacer, and that her word is without question. She is also vital to the survival of her people in many important ways. Naero Amashin Maeris is a noble, invaluable warrior and a proven leader who has served the Clans and the Alliance well, in both peacetime and war. A Mystic Champion who is now part of the great and mysterious Cosmic Prophecy, long foretold. There is still so little that we do not know about those prophecies; who can say what her role will be in the end?"

Master Jo paced a bit. "And on a very basic level, she is a Spacer. As such, she has the right of all Spacers and all sentients to defend herself, to the death, against anyone who attempts to kill her. Reluctantly, she only resorted to lethal force when High Master Vane attacked her with the intent to destroy her, and take her life. Even after she had tried to get away from him, and begged him repeatedly not to attack her.

"She cannot not be convicted of murder for defending her own life against someone trying to kill her. Those are all many good reasons why you must see fit to exonerate her of these erroneous charges. We cannot take the life of this hero."

The Defense finally rested.

Master Tree was given the final word in the trial for the prosecution.

"Hero? First, let me also revisit the reckless side of this renegade, outlaw Spacer, who fled from justice and had to be brought back by force to face her crimes in shackles, in order to keep her from getting away once again. On several occasions, Naero Amashin Maeris has proven herself to be dangerous, unpredictable, and out of control. By her own words, she has more than once declared that if she ever lost control and became a threat to any of her people, that she herself agreed that she should be put down–and destroyed.

"The cold blooded murder of a High Mystic Master has not demonstrated this fact readily enough? Beyond all doubt? If she can slay a High Master of the Mystics so easily, how much more is she a danger to all? And she even admits that she cannot control her abilities. Her very existence has become such a clear and present threat that it cannot be ignored and must be dealt with. I repeat, she has admitted on several occasions that her powers can go out of control and be very dangerous.

"Next, she also clearly admits that she killed Master Vane. Now, of her own accord, she claims that she killed him in self defense. But she has thus far presented no single shred of proof of that. She claims that Master Vane attacked her, attempted to kill her, and that she killed him, as she now conveniently claims–in so-called self defense. And I remind everyone in this court, once again. It does not matter who she is, what she is, or whatever else she has done. No one is above Spacer Law.

"Not even the infamous, Naero Amashin Maeris."

Tree took in a breath and clasped his hands behind his back. "What are the facts, therefore? A High Mystic Master lies dead, murdered by his own student, who openly stated that she could not stand him. Who openly admitted that she killed him. Nothing else can be proven, beyond those facts. Nothing else exists as fact. And this case must only be decided, based solely upon the facts. Nothing else.

"A Spacer on trial for her life could readily claim and say anything. Merely stating something does not make it true. That does not prove it to be fact. According to the facts of what is known, Naero Amashin Maeris is clearly guilty of murder, and will undoubtedly say and do anything possible in order to get away with her crime. As anyone logically would, in order to escape punishment, justice, and execution."

Naero fumed. Haisha! What the hell did they expect her to say? Yes, I offed the asshole, I loved it, and I'm a fricking monster. Go ahead and kill me?

I wish that weren't so painfully funny, Naero.

Me too, Om.

Master Tree went on to demand that the jury uphold one of the key tenets of Spacer Law and Spacer society:

"Spacers do not murder other Spacers and take their lives! Naero Amashin Maeris is not above that law. Naero Amashin Maeris broke that solemn law. And like it or not, the law demands justice. There is no way around that law and no way to escape it. That law demands that she face the ultimate punishment for her being guilty of committing the ultimate crime!"

Tree emphasized his final point with a single, upraised index finger. "That punishment is immediate Death, by execution. To be carried out by beheading, at the hands and the blade of the Mystic Enforcer!"

The Prosecution rested its case.

Admiral Klyne looked slightly pale as he instructed the jury of Mystic Elders to decide the case and announce their decision after their period of deliberation.

Naero went back to her cell in silence feeling sick, unable to meet Khai's utterly heartbroken glance. She felt stunned and numb. She didn't know what to think. All that she could do was await the jury's decision, along with everyone else.

Yet it was her fate alone that was being decided.

But when she thought about it further it wasn't just her fate.

Everyone waited for eight long hours.

Naero could neither rest nor sleep.

Then everyone was summoned back to the court room.

A decision had been made. The jury had arrived at a verdict in her case.

Admiral Klyne announced, "All rise for the verdict to be read."

They did so.

The jury leader stood up and read their decision.

"According to Spacer Law, and based upon all of the facts and evidence presented, we the jury find the defendant, Naero Amashin Maeris, of Clan Maeris...guilty of murder in the death of another Spacer."

Naero gasped, nailed to the bedrock of the planet itself in almost complete shock.

Guilty meant...

Master Tree rose up. "This Mystic trial has ended; it is over. A verdict has been reached. Without question, this grim crime is punishable among our people by death. Under the circumstances, the sentence is to be carried out immediately and without delay."

Naero, I can–

Shut up, Om.

Naero gasped and covered her mouth with both hands as she sobbed and went down on one knee.

Then she dropped her hands to her abdomen and her eyes met Khai's in explosive waves of desperate horror and regret.

Their child from their love within that distant star barely grew within her. Now, no time remained to tell Khai all that she needed to before he performed his duty as the Mystic Enforcer.

Before he took her head…ended her life, and the lives of his own family.

Naero Amashin Maeris clenched her fists, and rose up with her head held high to meet her fate with her eyes clear and wide open, if that was what must be.

Amazon Link for Naero's Trial: http://amzn.to/1oaMNE3

Edition Notes

If you do not see this edition note here in this spot on the copyright page and on the very last page of your ebook or print version of this title, then you are not getting the final, polished version of this novel that the publisher, editors, and author intended for you to receive. Please contact either the publisher or the author via their emails or websites if you do not see the following update code:

High Mark Publishing Update Code K2428E